CW01497539

Broken Compass

Robbie Daniels

SRL PUBLISHING

SRL Publishing Ltd
London

www.srlpublishing.co.uk

First published worldwide by SRL Publishing in 2025

SRL PUBLISHING
THINKING DIFFERENTLY, DELIVERING CHANGE

ISBN: 978-1915073-45-7

1 3 5 7 9 10 8 6 4 2

A CIP catalogue record for this book is available from the British Library

SRL Publishing is a climate positive publisher offsetting more carbon
emissions than it emits.

Prologue

Him

He watched her from his hidden position at the end of the street. Her and the little dog. Sooty. He spat the name out. *Sooty*. He'd called it Sooty. Sooty for its jet-black fur. *Very original*, he'd thought at the time. Now, she called it by a different name. She pulled on the lead gently and he noted how the dog hesitated before it trotted to her heel, the pair now strolling side by side up the curving pavement of the close. Sweat began to drip down his forehead, stinging at his eyes. It was hot, the sun already beating down on him in his grey hoodie, but he paid no attention to the perspiration pooling under his arms, his heart beating, his mouth dry, body clenched. He didn't dare take his eyes off her. Not after all this time.

The light of the morning caught her red hair, colouring it temporarily into a flame, entrancing him into a stupor. Piled into a messy bun, those few tendrils loose, framing that freckled face he couldn't see from this distance, but he didn't need to. He'd studied her face so intently he would know exactly how the small freckles would pepper her skin. The fire upon her head danced dangerously in the summer breeze as it escaped its hold from the clip at her crown, swinging down her back, the sun's rays entangled in each strand, threatening to burn him alive. He allowed it to captivate him, enjoying the sick pleasure of its show, its owner clueless to a hidden audience. He closed his eyes, remembering the first time he'd seen her. Those jade eyes sparkling mischievously. Those same copper flames cascading over her small, narrow shoulders. Her red-bitten lips with the deep cupid's bow, just the perfect shade of crimson and the scattering of brown freckles across her button nose. He knew her pale skin would be developing more little tan flecks by the day in the summer, dotted over her nose, her cheeks, down her chest, encouraged by the sun. He shuddered, suddenly cold in the stifling heat. Bumps flayed his skin as he pulled himself from the memory of her, from all those years before. Opening his eyes, he resumed his watch of their path from his safe distance.

A couple out on their own afternoon stroll approached her from the opposite direction, hand in hand. He smirked at the bloke who was desperately trying not to stare at her as they passed, how he overcompensated for his transgression by planting a kiss on the forehead of his oblivious partner. He sneered. He'd seen the way others looked at her before. It used to rile him. But there was no doubt about it, however angry he got, no matter how he hated it. She was striking. It was all part of her attraction.

They were walking away from him now, up the road. Her and Sooty. He felt the flicker of panic stirring as he watched her move away, threatening to conceal herself from his line of sight. He had to get closer. He couldn't risk losing her again. He stole across the green, away from the hedge of number

2

five, keeping his distance from the pavement that curled around the border. Bowed in his body, hood up, he caught glimpses of them flash between the threshold of the bungalows that framed the small, grassed area as he stalked quietly.

Sooty seemed reluctant to walk to her heel, he could see her impatience as she pulled on his leash again, more vigorously than before. He couldn't blame the little dog. He wouldn't like to be tied to her either. The road bent around in front of them as he came to a halt behind a picket fence of number fifteen. She faced him now, although she didn't know it. He took her in, the picture of innocence with her little nose up in the air, her easy gait, the casual swing in her shoulders. There was a hint of a smile on her face, he imagined her breathing deeply. Inhaling the fresh breeze around her. Relishing her freedom. The liberty she stole. He gritted his teeth. Not for much longer.

Sooty bounded down a drive to his right, he could hear her irritated cry as the dog darted away. He kept hidden, observing how she followed him down past the small car in the driveway of the bungalow across the road, her back to him once more. The dog settled himself on the doorstep. To his delight, he watched as she pulled the keys out of her back pocket, the sound of metal upon metal music to his ears. Heart quickening, he felt the moisture leave his mouth, anticipating the confirmation that finally, *finally*, this was it. The final piece of the plan was slotting into place.

She reached for the door before hesitating, her sudden halt stemming his excitement. Maybe he had got it wrong, this wasn't hers after all. Instead of inserting the key into the lock, she pulled something out of her back pocket. He strained his neck to see, he could now hear his heart thumping into his chest. It was her phone. She was studying it hard, apparently glued to the screen.

Sooty was scrapping at the door now. The scratching noise of his claws violently ripped through the quiet cul-de-sac. She was too busy doing something on her phone to notice. Sooty was becoming more ferocious in his desperation to be acknowledged. It was like nails on chalkboard. It would usually irk him, set his teeth on edge, but not today. Today it made him smile. This wasn't the flighty, hypervigilant, cool and collected woman he remembered. She was distracted. It made her easy to get to. Easier to follow. It was better when she was not alert.

She raised her key to unlock the door, finally confirming this was her new home. He licked his lips, suddenly aware of the dryness of his mouth, as she put her phone back in her pocket. He watched as she put her key in the lock and turned it, glancing over her shoulder as the door swung open. He ducked quickly behind the bush of the front garden to his left. The thorns bit through his thin hooded top, stealing his breath but he didn't flinch. He waited a beat, before peeking back over the hedge. Just to watch. He was content just to watch her. For now.

Little Sooty bounded through the door gladly as her auburn hair caught the sun, burning against her scalp again. Sending sheets of flame into the air. Oh, that hair. That beautiful head of hair. It was how he knew. How he'd known since the first time he saw her again, after all these years. It was her. She was the one. He watched, bent and concealed, as

4

she gave the close a sweep behind her before following Sooty over the threshold. The door slammed shut behind them and he rose from his hiding place with a smirk.

Finally. It had taken everything he had, but he had finally done it.

He'd found her.

1

Madeline

Madeline sighed and straightened her back. Pains shot through from her shoulder blades, slicing down her spine. Her little Scottie dog, Timmy, watched her sleepily from the corner of the room. She smiled as she looked into his dark eyes that had been intently following her as she moved. He'd made himself comfortable in the pile of coats she'd abandoned earlier, paws tucked under his coiled frame. Tilting his head, clocking her gaze expectantly, he lifted his head from his resting place. The furry black tail peeking from under his curled body began to thump against the puffer jacket he'd made into his bed. She pulled out her phone and checked the time. 17:33. Boxes and clothes still littered the living room floor. Her muscles spasmed again and she winced. The rhythm of the tail quickened and she sighed. It would be a good time to take a break.

'Come on, then.' Three words were all it needed. Timmy leapt from his temporary bed, the ferocity of his tail powering his flight. Madeline searched around the room for the box labelled *Timmy's stuff* as the dark ball of fluff collided with her. She flinched, claws dug into her shins, tearing at her skin as he jumped up at her legs excitedly. She pushed him down, shooing him away as she spotted the box she was looking for. Dog still dancing around her feet, she tripped across the room ungracefully. Tutting as she caught herself, she bent and dug through the contents of the box, producing the new harness triumphantly. 'A-ha!'

The sight of the harness was enough to send Timmy into overdrive. Overcome with delight, he had abandoned his destruction of her legs and was now chasing his tail around in a circle. Madeline chuckled, before sighing as the little black tornado wreaked havoc on the boxes and once-neat piles of clothes. They played the game, him expertly darting out of her reach, teasing her as she scrambled to get his harness secured. He played. She battled.

Eventually, his excitement wore off and he tired just enough for Madeline to get his harness clipped on over his shoulders. Dog fastened in, she strolled down the hallway, phone and lead in hand. Readying his lead in her left hand she swooped and hooked it through as he chased past. Her Converse waiting at the front door, she slipped them on, forgoing any jacket. It was a warm evening and she was perspiring slightly from the combat even now the heat of the day had passed. Timmy gained his second wind, pawing and crying at the door desperately, willing her to hurry up. She rolled her eyes and tutted. Anyone would have thought he'd never been for a walk in his life. She finally released him from his prison and he darted out of the open door on his lead, nearly wrenching her shoulder out of its socket. Another battle ensued, will versus will as Madeline struggled to reach around to lock the door behind her. Timmy wouldn't relent.

Pulling on his restraints, eager to get going. Finally, Madeline felt the key slot into the lock and turned it. The satisfying *click* told her the bungalow was locked up and she slipped the keys into her pocket. She glanced at her phone for a quick time check before sliding it into her back pocket and followed her impatient dog down the drive and out onto the pavement.

Happy to be out, Timmy took the lead with his confident little strut and they eased into a comfortable pace together. The sun hazed lazily down from its evening position in the sky. It had been an unseasonably hot May so far. Madeline smiled to herself, feeling the relief of the warm breeze around her t-shirt, cooling the sweat that prickled her skin. The gentle gusts blew through her long, light auburn hair, chilling her scalp and the nape of her neck. She closed her eyes, enjoying the pleasant sensation. Timmy's nails tapped the pavement at her feet, content to be by her side now he was out. The evening sang with a lazy hum of insects and indigent tunes of birds. She felt her shoulders droop and her back straighten simultaneously, the warmth from the pavement underfoot melting away any unease her body had held. Treating herself to another deep breath, she emptied her lungs of all tension. It had been a long time since she had been this relaxed.

The neighbours were out in their gardens, pottering, weeding, and watering their lawns. Spray from their hoses drifted across her path, the mist settling across her cheeks. Silver-haired heads in every direction indicated the average age of the resident in this close at about seventy years old. Age was just a number here. There was no hint of frailty or decay in the upkeep of their homes. The gardens were bursting full of colour and scent, driveways were meticulously swept and there was the subtle whiff of drying paint from the fresh fences. Timmy stopped occasionally to sniff a lamppost or a rogue weed creeping through the tarmac, before bouncing back away. Madeline greeted a few pensioners as they passed. It was the polite thing to do. They returned the gestures in turn, breaking from tending their small gardens, able to work now the sun of the day was no longer boring down on them. She pulled her phone out of her back pocket and flicked on her Maps. Reaching the end of the close, she noted the sign. Robin Close. Added a quick flag to the location. Checked the time. 18:08. Seven minutes.

They turned left out of the cul-de-sac, Timmy still ahead and leading them into the heart of the village. Little Molton was not a large village, but it seemed to have enough. On moving day Madeline remembered passing a post office, a farm shop, and a local pub in the car, the main road somewhere out to her North. All picturesque, countryside construction, flint and stone walls, clay tiles and single-glazed windows. She took in the quaint limestone cottages around her. An array of cottage plants; hydrangeas and roses snaked their way up the old brickwork and around the picket fences. Small Cotswold-stoned driveways. Roses and peonies along the edging. Clematis climbing up the trellis'. She paused, noting the delicate white petals. Fingering her phone out of her pocket, she squinted and glanced up at the position of the sun lazily in the sky. Studying the orientation against the compass on her map, she smiled to herself. South facing. This particular genus likes a south-facing sun, she checked yesterday. It was good to be aware of one's surroundings at all times. Carrying on her way, she nodded and waved courteously at more of the elderly residents. Timmy was still out in front, his chin stuck proudly in the air as she followed his lead.

They continued up the path, venturing further into the village. Madeline marked another flag in her maps. 18:11. Ten minutes total so far. Nine yesterday. The pavement began to dip in its kerb, narrowing and finishing their concrete journey, continuing for pedestrians on the opposite side of the road. Madeline did her checks, head turning slowly each way down the road. Always look left and right. Check once, and check again. She pulled gently on the lead, Timmy needing little encouragement to scurry behind her for the safe crossing. He pattered across the tarmac, making straight for a small patch of grass and cocked his leg. Madeline waited patiently for him to finish, glancing around under her brows. The initial concern subsided quickly. It was okay. The grass wasn't attached to any garden, driveway, or residence that she could see. It would be incredibly rude to allow him to relieve himself on someone's lawn. Madeline was conscientious, respectful of others, unlike many she had crossed paths with before. The thought brought with it old memories, crashing over her with a powerful shudder as his leering face flashed before her eyes. Squeezing her lids tightly shut, she shook her head, discarding them from her mind quickly. Timmy finished his business, and with a wipe of his paws on the grass they resumed their route.

They were walking out of the cottage area now and into a new-build housing complex. Madeline gazed at the juxtaposition of the new housing, with its bright red-bricked walls and thin black tiled roofs, copy and pasted over and

10

over in rows. The houses looked so out of place out here in the countryside, nestled amongst the lush greenery and pastel walls of the charming cottages. She felt her lips curling. She'd never liked these new builds. Here, the driveways were all paved, possibly swept but they weren't neat. There was no foliage growing against these fences. Brickwork was sloppy and uneven, each driveway space catering only for one small car at best. Houses were cramped together, the front gardens no more than a metre-squared per residence, the turf lumpy, clearly bogged in the ground underneath. The windows were tall, indicating three storeys. Family homes. Madeline snorted. These days, families had a minimum of two vehicles, children needed space to play and explore without being overlooked from every angle. It was as though no thought went into the construction of these homes. Squeeze in as many houses as possible. More houses more money, she supposed. She clicked her tongue. Everything was about money these days, never about doing the right thing. Most of the cars that couldn't fit on their drives were parked in line down the side of the road as far as she could see. She pursed her lips as they squeezed themselves around an inconsiderate Volvo obstructing their way. Its left wheels were parked too far onto the pavement, driven up the kerb. At least the other drivers had the decency to leave the pavement free for pedestrians.

Ambling past the new builds, Madeline spotted the green footpath sign ahead. It was small, directing them down a dingy walkway between two of the poorly constructed houses. Despite her need to explore, Madeline felt her chest reactively clench as they approached the cut-through, but soon saw it was wider than it looked at first glance. Their

11

footsteps echoed on the newly-paved brickwork, reverberating on the cold walls, shadows enveloping them and bringing in a new chill. Timmy lifted his nose, sniffing at the air. Suddenly perking up, he quickened his pace, pulling on Madeline in his haste to reach the end. She allowed herself to be led with caution and widened her eyes in astonishment as she understood his urgency.

The brickwork gave way to a dusty dirt track, ceasing without warning, leaving the hurried builds behind. Beyond, the landscape developed into thick, rolling fields as far as she could see. Even Timmy, raised as a city dog, seemed to be momentarily stunned by the drastic change in scenery. He halted, pointed ears alert and little ebony tail at attention. Madeline came to a dazed stop next to him, taking in the view. For miles around there were nothing but fields, broken by collections of forestry and greenery. So much green. Evergreens, ferns, olives, and sea greens. Even the browns were spectacular; shades of gold, bronze, light and dusty. The footpath guided them left and right, around the pastures of the beautiful countryside. Tearing her eyes from the scene in front of her, Madeline removed her phone from her back pocket. Pulled up her maps, marked another flag and another time stamp. 18: 15. Fourteen minutes. She debated a moment, tapping an idle fingertip to the side of the screen before taking the left, following the dirt trail out and away from the concrete jungle.

The land dipped and rose for miles, stretching endlessly under the clear blue sky. The village must sit at one of the highest points, she noted the gentle sloping around her. Dust from the dried mud kicked up at her heels. The breeze still tickling at her back, she took a deep breath of the clean, fresh air into her lungs feeling her tightened muscles of the past year untangle. Timmy sprinted across the track, left and right, in front of her, following his nose. She smiled warmly. He was enjoying his little adventure. And with another deep inhale, she realised, she was too.

They walked for a while, Madeline periodically checking her phone against the map and making more time stamps. Eventually, the sun began to dip in the sky and a slight chill developed in the breeze, setting goosebumps on her skin. She took it as her cue to turn back.

Timmy had started to flag now, walking behind her heel. They strolled back over the country paths and found the cut-through back to the garish housing estate. The sun was starting to set, casting shadows across the ground. Adrenaline coursed. Animal movement out of the corner of her eyes demanded her attention, the outlines of the low sun playing tricks on her. But she gripped Timmy's lead a little tighter and quickened her step. Not enough to garner attention, but enough to get her home quicker. The shapes made her feel uncomfortable. Without warning, a loud bang rang violently around the quiet and soulless ground. She jumped, a fast shape snatching her consciousness from her left and she froze, clenching her muscles and gripping onto Timmy's lead, ready for the assault.

Heart in her mouth and sweat beading on her lip, she watched the young man leap chaotically away from the door he just slammed, down the driveway of one of the new houses. He paid her no heed at all, apparently oblivious to the turmoil his rowdy exploits caused her as he raced away in

13

front of her path with a deep worried expression on his face. Madeline felt her lungs loosen and her shoulder blades droop, reassessing the threat as benign. Limbs flapped aimlessly as he battled between a pile of papers and a briefcase that were threatening to spill out of his gangly arms. She felt a small, warm body leaning against her feet as she watched, mildly amused by her body's initial reaction to his excursions. He fumbled at his key fob, jabbing it rapidly as Timmy sat on her feet. The offending Volvo from earlier clicked, flashing lights indicating its owner had unlocked it the first time despite his repeated prodding. Her heart began to slow, her mind catching up to her body. She loosened her grip on Timmy's lead, taking a deep gulp of air. Relaxing her posture, she watched, still as stone, as he tried to prise his driver side door open in his haste, ignorant to anyone around him. The blue lanyard around his neck swung ferociously as he juggled his paperwork, briefcase, and keys. She heard a horrible clang as the driver's door swung open, bouncing on its hinges and the lanyard got caught in the crossfire. The motion took him off guard, trying to regain balance on his long, spindly legs and nearly dropping his briefcase in the process. Keys jangled loudly as they smashed against the car's bodywork. She winced as the noise rattled in her ears. Amongst the chaos, he suddenly turned still. Too late to look away, she watched with alarm as he sharply looked up and met her eye. His brow furrowed. Unblinking, he stared at her. One, two, three seconds. Holding his glare.

Her smile disappeared.

He knows.

Amusement gone, caught by the unexpected direct look

straight at her, she felt her face redden. Unprepared for him to notice her presence with such vigour, the familiar panic began to rise. His eyes seemed to bore through her, seeing her, reading her mind, she stood rooted to the spot. Sweat began to perspire across her brow, anticipating her next move.

Run.

He knows.

No. She didn't know him, she was sure. How could he know?

A stray piece of paper broke free from his arms and drifted in the breeze, unnoticed by its careless owner. Just as she was contemplating her options, fuelled by the adrenaline running her system his gaze softened. The corners of his lips curled and... a faint smile? He was smiling at her. She knew she needed to respond. Act normal. She tried to meet it with one of her own, but found her mouth wouldn't curve like she needed it to. Still stood awkwardly, she tried to break the uncomfortable standoff by giving him a small wave instead.

Please. Please let it work.

He narrowed his eyes, just for a flash, before opening his mouth. Baring his teeth. She felt her heart leap, her mind take control. Preparing for the attack. Wait. No. He was grinning. Beaming at her. His eyes crinkled and sparkled, his demeanour softened, all havoc and worry gone from his body as he smiled warmly at her across the paved expanse. Relaxed, suddenly tall but approachable, like a loveable bear, the abrupt transformation took her aback as he showed her every one of his pearly whites. She felt her face burn again as she found her own to return, bashfully. The uncomfortable feeling of horror diffused away, replaced by a gentle heat that spread to her fingers and she felt her own smile widen, prickling at her cheeks. It was a nice feeling. One she wasn't accustomed to, so different to the usual fear that raced her heart and kept her on her toes, so she let it be. They held each other's gaze like this, before he finally broke it, clambering into the driver's side of the Volvo. Releasing every inch of tension with a large exhale, the hundreds of thoughts and plans in her mind ebbed away, no longer needed. She let new ones come.

I am safe.

It isn't the same as last time.

Timmy, relieved for the break in the walk, was still sat patiently at her heel. The Volvo pulled away, taking the chaotic driver to his destination and leaving the pavement clear for them to walk safely. She gave a small tug on the lead, encouraging him back on their journey, letting her feelings from the aftermath of the strange exchange wane away as they turned into Robin Close. Timmy fell back in stride beside her, each step serving to process the false alarm as just that. She inwardly laughed at herself for her overreaction. Of course it wasn't the same.

*

Madeline barely made it through the door and removed her shoes before Timmy was harassing her for his dinner. She dug through his cardboard box again and fixed him a bowl of kibble. He gobbled it down quicker than she could blink, it barely touched the sides. Finally satisfied, he promptly curled back up in the pile of coats on the floor with a little huff and closed his eyes. Dog fed and walked, Madeline sank into the floor next to him tiredly. She gazed around her, sat surrounded by boxes on the plush pink carpet, her legs outstretched.

The bungalow was quiet. She had no radio or TV set up yet, she could hear the gentle sound of Timmy's deep breathing beside her. A lawnmower lazily thrummed somewhere in the evening outside. Inhaling deeply, she took stock of the room.

The walls were painted in a gaudy light blue, and Ivy's decorative plates still adorned the walls haphazardly. The carpet, while thick, was a sickening shade of bubble-gum with a brown oriental rug in the centre of the room, never a fashionable choice no matter what decade you were born. She wrinkled her nose at the décor before breathing it away. Ivy had questionable taste but Madeline swiftly felt her disgust replaced a wave of sadness at her memory.

Madeline would never have been able to afford a two-bedroom detached bungalow in the middle of the Cotswolds like this without Ivy's help. It was a small silver lining in the pain of her passing. Madeline had loved her grandmother. And although she knew it would come someday, it had been before Ivy's time and really broken her heart when she passed. Guilt rippled through her body. She hadn't been there for her final moments. As a nurse, she knew the importance of providing comfort in people's final moments. Memories tried to resurface of that night, a cocktail of darkness, strangers faces, worry. Fear. She quickly batted them away. There was nothing she could do about it now. But she should have been there to hold her hand.

Ivy only had one child, Madeline's mother, Penny. Penny's conception was a miracle and Ivy was not blessed with any more children. Her husband, Madeline's grandfather, had passed when Madeline was five years old but Ivy had doted on her only grandchild like she were her own. Madeline was a happy accident, the result of one of Penny's dalliances as a young woman exploring the throes of her sudden sexual maturity. Penny had been too busy for any more children as Madeline grew, but she had no need for Ivy's assets. With two successful divorces under her belt, and the next marriage in the pipework, she had her own money. As a single, twenty-eight-year-old nurse about to begin work on a stroke unit in the NHS, Madeline did not. Penny had been more than happy to sign everything over to her only daughter when Ivy passed, before flitting back off to the three-storey townhouse in London with her latest aged fiancé.

Madeline had never had the closest relationship with Penny. She knew she had been young having Madeline and although Penny never said the words, she had always got the impression that the child was never wanted. From a young age, Penny had insisted the child address her by her first name, moaning that "Mum" made her sound too old. The little girl didn't know any different and applied the same logic to Ivy. She had never called her "Grandmother", despite Ivy's gentle encouragement. Ivy had suggested alternatives, Nan or Nanna. Grandma, maybe. Madeline had been firm. Ivy had smiled sadly at the child's insistence, never arguing with her. She remained Ivy.

Madeline had met her first serious boyfriend when she was sixteen. She had moved straight out of Penny's house and in with him within three weeks. Rather than be concerned her daughter had moved in with a stranger and his family, Penny seemed to be glad she had flown the nest. She had immediately sold up their two-bedroom house on the outskirts and moved into a luxurious one bed flat in the city, the success of divorce number one under her belt. Since then, Madeline had very little contact with Penny over the years, they kept the interaction to a minimum. Penny was selfish. Far more interested in going out and conning her way into the lives of older, wealthy men who supplied her with the most expensive bubbles and purest white powder money could buy. If she couldn't snort her sins she would drink them. Madeline had stayed with that boyfriend until she went to university and they finally split. She had moved around a fair bit since then, but never lived with Penny again. Mother and daughter were both happy that way. They had scheduled contact on birthday's and at Christmas, but their relationship never developed. It bothered Madeline when she was little. But as an adult, she always said she didn't care. She was better off without her mother in her life.

She thought back to her first boyfriend. He was her first. Her first time. They say the first time should be special and he was. She smiled, recalling the sweet memory. They had lain together afterwards, she curled up on his chest, his body warm against her face, the blood pooling between her legs. It was warm, sticky, but she didn't care. She had wanted to savour the precious moment, knowing she would take it with her forever. He was such a sweet boy once. It was a shame how they ended, but hindsight is a wonderful thing. She knew it was for the best in the end.

Madeline gazed at the box in front of her, attempting to muster up the will to attend to it. She was tired and her back still ached, not helped by her position on the floor. Instead, she laid herself out on the carpet, placing her delicate hands across her chest. Her long copper waves fanned around her as she settled her skull into the pile. Staring up at the ceiling. Studying the plastered swirls and rings, patterned above. It was the old Artex that was all the rage at one time. She could see a few yellowing rings in one corner, indications of a leak from years before. Being in a bungalow, she surmised the water tank was up there in the loft. Timmy was still snoring gently from somewhere in the coats. She sighed, finally feeling the weight of everything crash over her. It had been a stressful year. More memories tried to resurface, torturing her mind. She closed her eyes, breathing in a waft of lavender from the room and saw Ivy's face. What would she think if she could see where her granddaughter ended up?

No. No, you mustn't think that way.

I am Madeline Hamilton. I am a good person.

She wasn't running away, not really. This was a chance at a new start. A new life. Everyone made mistakes didn't they, didn't everyone deserve a chance to right their wrongs? Madeline certainly believed so. She always gave people a chance. It was part of what made her a good person. Mary tried to barge her way into her mind. She shook her away. Mary was her past. Her past was firmly in the past. It could not get to her out here.

Timmy groaned next to her and stretched his body out. She tilted her head to the right and saw a little black paw emerging from the heap next to her. She was grateful for his company. He would love to come on her planned adventures around the area. It had been a great idea to get him. He'd already settled in. And no one would question a single woman with a little dog. They would just think she'd broken up from a boyfriend, escaped an abusive relationship, something like that. Normal. Just what she wanted.

With a huff, she sat up and examined the boxes and piles of clothes around her dejectedly. It was too hot in the living room. It would take her forever to unpack all of these, and the humidity of the day was still hanging around. The trouble with the seventies builds was they retained heat too well. With a groan of her own, she decided to sack off the rest of her unboxing in favour of a cold shower and an early night.

Hello, my dear old friend. Or lover? What would you call us? It doesn't matter in the end. I've missed you so much, I thought about you every day. The only one that ever said no to me, the only one that ever got away from me. Did you ever think about me?

You've no idea how good it is to see you. How good it feels to be back doing what I love. I crept in, quick as you like, did you even hear me? Of course you didn't. You are far too trusting, far too naive. Too wrapped up in your own little world to see the wood through the trees. I stepped past the little dog, he didn't even make a sound. He just gave me a look and trotted away. He won't come near me now, though. Maybe he knows better than you. He knows better than to trust.

Are you as quiet as me when you sneak around? I imagine you try to be. You sleep so soundly, you know, your breathing is so deep I even detected a little snore before. Did you know you snore? Well, you do. And you twitch your nose in your sleep. It's cute. Like a little bunny. Sometimes I just like to watch you sleep. You mumble in your sleep and turn over a lot but I don't need to move. I know this is your pattern now. You won't wake until your alarm goes off at six thirty in the morning. I know these things about you. How is that, you ask? Like I said, I like to watch. This isn't my first time after all, I like to watch them all sleep.

It's so good to be here, to be with you, just near you. I had that feeling when I was watching you earlier today. Tonight is the night, *I said.*

My blood was coursing to the surface before I came here, bubbling and boiling away under my skin. I was irate, I'll be honest with you. It doesn't do to get angry. But there's something about watching you, even just being near you calms me down. Your presence. It relaxes me.

You are different. So very different to the others. You are special. You've captivated me for a long time. But, in the end of it all, even those that sparkle lose their charm. Your time will come too, my love. Just like the rest of them.

2

Madeline

Madeline rose wearily. Her muscles still throbbed painfully from the day before and the dull aches had not been helped by the unsettled night she'd had. Ivy's bed was in the master bedroom but she hadn't fancied sleeping in her old, sullied sheets, choosing the small bed in the spare room instead. No one had stayed in it for at least a year. Probably longer judging by the smell. The bedding was musty and mothy, the mattress lumpy and the air in the room stale. She'd tried to tolerate it but ended up stripping off the sheets and cracking the windows in the middle of the night. The sun that was heating the Earth by day had been taken over by the cool English May nights and she had shivered uncontrollably in the lack of cover. She had her own bedding, but it was neatly packaged somewhere and she didn't fancy digging through the boxes at two in the morning. Instead, she had stumbled into the living room to find something to wrap herself in. Timmy was content finally sleeping in his own bed, leaving the piles of coats blessedly free. He barely raised his head to look at her as she wrapped the puffer around her body and settled back in the small room on the old single mattress.

She'd slept fitfully, seeing Ivy's face in her dreams, jumping her awake.

Rubbing her eyes, she sat herself up on the uneven mattress, feeling grateful she had had the sense to delay her start date by a week for the move. Moving was tiring in ways she had never experienced before. Aside from the movers Penny had paid, she'd had no help. Penny's solution to any problem was to throw money at it, but they were only paid to move the boxes from one end to the other. The boxes had arrived from Penny's on the day she moved in, items carelessly shoved into any box they could fit. In contrast, Madeline had meticulously labelled the belongings she had with her, every item within filed and piled neatly in their cardboard restraints. But even with her thorough organisation, she knew it would take all week just to reorganise and work out where to put it all.

She unwrapped herself from the puffer, beads of sweat across her brow as the rising sun warmed the room. The night, whilst cold and clear, had done nothing to remove the festering smell, which was now being heated again in the morning rays. Screwing up her nose and stretching out her limbs she dragged herself out and into the living area. Timmy's head shot up as she entered, ears alert eyes bright and little tail wagging expectantly under his curled body. Timmy usually took a while to wake up in the morning, but today he leapt straight up and ran to greet her. Madeline giggled, fussing him before putting him outside and sorting his kibble into the steel bowl. He cocked his leg for the quickest relief against the roses and raced back in through the back door, jumping at her legs again, spinning in circles and chasing his tail. Madeline watched him curiously for a moment, before slowly putting down his breakfast. Timmy didn't hesitate, wolfing it down whole. Fascinated, she observed how the kibble was quickly demolished before her eyes. She was concerned about the risk of choking, but he finished with a smack of his little mouth, airways clear and belly satisfied. Content, he stretched out his front legs and promptly curled himself back into his bed, back to ignoring her completely. But today, he'd ran to greet her. He had been excited to see her, not the food. It was progress. She smiled to herself, turning away to attend to her needs.

There was no food for her own consumption in the bungalow, so Madeline reluctantly settled for an instant coffee. The bitter steam hit her nostrils, and screwing her face up she made a mental note to find and unpack her state-of-the-art, bean to cup coffee machine as a priority. Sipping her disappointing brown liquid she stood in the kitchen, looking through the open plan into the living room, boxes scattered across the floor still waiting to be unpacked into their new homes. The endless piles daunted her a little. Wondering where to start, she cast her mind back over the past twenty-four hours. She decided it would be useful to begin with the boxes labelled as 'bedding' and 'kitchen'.

She'd always been an organised person. She made to-do lists, lists of lists, and squeezed the most out of her time and schedule. It only took her three minutes to use the toilet to urinate, start to finish. Seven minutes for a body shower, fourteen if she was washing her hair. Another ten to dry it. An average of six minutes to eat breakfast—usually porridge. Occasionally Weetabix as a little treat. Lists kept her disciplined. Efficient. They helped her to think, cleared the anarchy of her mind when she was overwhelmed. Timings kept her safe. Contained. She knew exactly what she needed to do, when and how long it would take. Being organised and controlled prevented panic, fear. The disorder and danger of the unknown and uncertain. It protected her.

Her organisation had paid her dividends over the years, and again today. Thankful for her forward planning when packing, she quickly found the bedding and made up the bed in Ivy's room with her fresh sheets. Her treasured coffee machine winked at her as she unwrapped it from its bubble wrapping, her fingers tenderly brushing its surface as she set it on the worktop. She loved this machine. She hadn't bought it herself, but if she had, this would have been exactly what she picked, down to the colour, settings, and attachments. She huffed at the thought. No, she hadn't bought it, but she had certainly paid for it.

Madeline swiftly moved onto unpacking the kitchen crockery and utensils sent by Penny. Ivy had plenty of cupboard space. Big change from the tiny kitchenettes she had been used to before. But unlike many of her generation, it seemed Ivy had only made use of a third of them, and the rest of the shelves were caked in years of disuse and grime. Madeline set about finding her rubber gloves and got to work on cleaning them out.

As she worked, her mind wandered. She was keen to get out and explore more of the area later. Little Molton was nestled in the heart of the countryside, very different to the urban environments she was used to. There was a town somewhere nearby, but from her research she knew it didn't house a large population and she was looking forward to small village life. The air was even different out here. Clean. Fresh. Remote, easy. No one in a rush all the time, no one breathing down her neck, no one that would have ever heard of her or any hint of the past she was leaving behind. Out here, those vile lies written would never have been heard of, never been read by the eyes of Little Molton. Those papers would never have had the chance to be chip paper here, words that taunted and teased her over again as she hurried through the street in her disguises. Here, she was free. Free to reinvent herself. Madeline craved normality, the anonymity that a regular life would bring. When Ivy passed and the bungalow came to her, it was a chance at a new life she jumped at taking. A village would be her chance at normality. To lay low. Living in London had taught her that hiding gets you noticed. Popping to the shop, taking the dog for a walk, working full time, having a commute. Idle chatter with the neighbours, being polite, a good citizen. That's what people ignore. Hiding away, being secretive, being mysterious attracts gossips, stares. A village was a good place to hide. Hide in plain sight.

Wiping down the cupboard door with her damp cloth, she peered up at the sun out of the kitchen window, wiping her brow. It was a large pane, affording a fantastic view of Ivy's garden. It was stunning. Very aesthetically pleasing. Ivy had had it expertly landscaped and maintained by gardeners who had visited weekly when she slowed down and her arthritis kicked up, gnarling at her joints and withering her muscles from the bone. Madeline had never had much of a green finger, but she was keen to learn. The lush, green grass was surrounded by shrubs of all colour and scents; evergreens, hydrangeas, lavenders, roses, everything she would expect in a countryside cottage garden. There was a little bench underneath a crab-apple tree at the far end, positioned to face the small bird feeder. Madeline had been looking forward to taking her morning coffee out there tomorrow. But that wasn't what made her look out there now.

The sun was low in the sky, and it was still early in the day, throwing long shadows from the birds that flew in and out. Something had caught her eye from the fence at the back. She felt the bile begin to rise in her throat and swallowed it back down, eyes searching the garden with urgency. Nothing else moved, and her worry began to recede.

Fear makes you do stupid things.

Remembering her past had made her nervous, she decided. She shouldn't be thinking about it. This was a new start. Just as the thought began to settle her, a shape, a shadow, something passed quickly in her periphery, along the evergreen bushes that ran alongside the east fence. She froze, eyes trained on the source of movement. The sun continued to shine down upon the garden, the shadows stretched. The rays illuminated the array of colours, warming the ground but Madeline felt her body fill with ice. Her heart rate quickened, wondering for a moment whether her eyes were playing a trick on her when, unmistakeably, the hedge rattled again.

Without hesitation this time, she ripped out a kitchen knife from the new block on the work surface, her heart in her mouth. She pushed it down, back to her chest. Righting her mind. It wouldn't do to panic now. The shake in her hand betrayed her as she turned the key in the back door. With care and caution, she pulled the door open slowly, stepping out in the back garden and around the corner to face the hedge.

Visibly trembling now, adrenaline taking over, she gripped the knife. The sun was warm but the grass was cool. Dewy drops were still present in the shade. She didn't step too far into the garden. Two steps away from the threshold to the door. Key stored safely in her pocket, out of reach from any intruders that could lock her in, or out. Right hand gripping the knife, blade upwards. The hedge, across from her now, she waited. She knew it wasn't her imagination, she had seen it twice.

'Who... who's there?' Her voice was pitiful, it cracked and betrayed her fear. By means of a response, the hedge vibrated ferociously. Flinging herself around, she gripped the handle, raising the knife across her body. She was only five foot five, nine stone dripping wet, but she knew better than anyone the damage that could be done with such a weapon. A black shadow leapt out of the bush and she cried out, lifting the knife, ready to slice at the attacker. The shape hissed and snarled as it dashed in front of her, streaking across the garden. Soft fur brushed between her legs as Timmy raced from the open door behind her, chasing after it, barking incessantly. Yapping, he pursued the cat down the garden, jumping up at the fence where it had made its escape.

Madeline laughed as the relief flooded her body, watching Timmy spring on his little back legs up at the boundary. The cat was long gone by now, but Timmy would not give up on his pursuit. She breathed easy and lowered the knife. She was too jumpy, she knew. But she couldn't be too careful. Shoulders relaxed and terror abated, she called Timmy in. It took a few tries. Timmy was insistent on guarding the area of the fence in case the feline had the audacity to return. Eventually, after much coaxing and bribery, he heeded her call and strutted back to her proudly. She followed him through the door, throwing one last look out in the garden before re-locking it behind them and placing the key back into her pocket. Sliding the gleaming knife back into its block she picked up her rubber gloves and resumed her cleaning. Confident his garden was safe, Timmy had taken himself back to bed. Curled up like nothing happened.

*

It was late before Madeline stopped. She had been unpacking all day. She hated to admit it, but she had thrown herself into the task trying to distract herself from her fright earlier. She tried to ignore the racing thoughts, but they crashed back in.

What if it's happening again?

She stuck to her coping mechanisms, her lists, ticking things off periodically as she accomplished tasks and made new to-do's. The thoughts gradually weakened their intensity over her, her itch subsiding. Stress and worry didn't sit well with her. She didn't like to feel anxious. Timmy had stayed out of the way for the most part, dozing the day away. But now as he started to follow her around, she realised the rays were long across the living room floor once more. With a pang, she realised the time.

'Sorry, boy!' Madeline pulled up her phone and tapped on Maps. She hastily grabbed Timmy's harness and lead from their new home on the hallway pegs. Timmy's tail swung like a little rudder. Clever boy. He knew what it meant. She struggled to put his harness on again, his tail propelling his entire body like an unruly motorboat. After another excitable scuffle, she got him clipped in and hastily slipped her Converse on her feet. She checked the time and slipped her phone in her pocket. 19:14. She unlocked the front door and Timmy darted out into the front garden.

Guilt struck as Timmy raced in front of her to the hydrangeas that lined the drive and cocked his leg. She had been so caught up in her own head that she forgotten to let him out at all since that morning. She punished herself inwardly.

Timmy forgave her quickly, finishing his business and happily trotted down the path. He looked back occasionally, checking she was there. They fell into their now familiar step with each other. Timmy, nose in the air proudly, happily sniffing the range of summer scents whilst Madeline followed a pace behind, enjoying the breeze and the rhythm of the march. She took her phone out of her back pocket, noting the time again. 19:15.

They walked at a gentle pace down the street, slower than yesterday. Madeline was curious to see the difference. Timmy didn't pull, he was content to walk with her today, matching her speed. The elderly of the neighbouring bungalows were out tending their front gardens again. They exchanged more courteous greetings as she passed.

Reaching the crossroads at the end of the close, she checked again. 19:21. Perfect. She could rest safe in the assumption it would be a leisurely seven-minute walk from the end of her road to the front door. Potentially six if she walked in a hurry.

Madeline and Timmy turned left and crossed the road, up past the quaint cottages. More elderly neighbours, more pleasant exchanges. She looked around, studying the paths closer this time, for sign of any further footpaths or cut-throughs. There was a small inlet between two of the cottages on her left. She made a mental note to explore that tomorrow.

Another check. 19:24.

They walked into the new housing estate, meeting another walker on the journey. Timmy and the spaniel gave each other a sniff before carrying on their paths. The spaniels owner barely acknowledged Madeline. Nose stuck in her phone, not paying attention to where she was going or who she was passing, Madeline stopped, the path not wide enough to avoid an inevitable collision. Her shoulder smarted as the woman carelessly walked into her, the impact enough to knock her off course. The consequences of her ignorance were still not enough to drag her attention away from her phone however, as she muttered a curt 'sorry' under her breath and barked at the spaniel to follow her. Madeline watched the woman swan away behind her in disbelief, as she did the same to an elderly gentleman out on his evening stroll who had not noticed her. The man tripped, catching his feet but the woman's head did not lift. The spaniel was bouncing around her feet, clearly vying for his owner's affection but finding none.

Madeline raised her eyebrows derisively as she made eye contact with the elderly ambler. He shook his head and gestured at the walker disdainfully. She smiled. Wordlessly, they exchanged the same sentiment.

Rude. Ignorant. Get off your phone.

The man tutted, rolled his eyes at Madeline and crossed the road. Their silent exchange over, she turned and followed Timmy.

Her heart rate quickened as they approached the Volvo again. It was just as recklessly abandoned as the day before. Today, three wheels were on the pavement, one teetering off onto the road. Madeline studied the car in awe. It was mildly impressive how the owner had achieved that feat. She found herself looking towards the red door of the house that she had seen him emerge from the day before. Wondering why it was always left in this way. As if it were hastily parked. Like he was in a rush. She could see how that happened once, but twice? That's just bad parking.

Or he's been running, too.

She shook the thought from her head. A local bus pootled down the road in front of her, a stream of cars trailing behind it. Realising they would have to stop where they were. The only way to squeeze past the car on the path would mean she would snag her t-shirt on the spikey bush bordering the pavement. She didn't fancy that. But they could not step out into the road and make it past the Volvo and the line of cars at the roadside whilst the bus was coming the other way. Timmy was less happy about waiting at her feet today, but after gentle commands he beckoned at her side with a huff.

Madeline didn't like waiting. It set her on edge. Best to keep moving, keep going. Never stay in the same place for too long. She felt uneasy from her worry earlier in the day. Her shoulder still throbbed from the encounter with the woman, she could feel her heart pulsating through the veins, tormenting her. The wait was agonising, the bus was in no hurry as it trundled down the narrow village road. The bends meant it needed to take extra care. Madeline breathed deeply, attempting to stem the nerves beginning to stir.

Please.

Hurry up.

She tapped Timmy's lead against her leg impatiently, feeling the palpable anticipation. She glanced around at her surroundings, keeping an eye on who was about. No one was appearing to take any notice, but she knew appearances were deceiving. Someone could always be watching her.

The bus finally passed, blowing up warm air into her face from its engine, the cars behind following closely. Just as she was allowing herself to breathe, she felt the force on her chest. Her heart leapt, racing now with panic, trying to work out what just happened. She was standing, hands to her chest, feeling across her stomach, her arms, her head. Cars continued to stream past noisily. She heard a strange scuffling at her feet, trying to right her senses. She looked down. Timmy was scrapping at an empty paper food wrapper, licking and gnawing at it ferociously as if he had never been fed. Yanking him away, she saw more takeaway containers, littered over the road, blowing in the breeze. The last of the cars pulled away behind her and leaving her stood in her daze.

Her mind put the pieces together. She'd been hit by takeaway containers. Someone. A driver must have thrown them out of the window. Looking back down the road in shock, a hand emerged from the Range Rover, flinging out something. Bright orange. It bounced on the road, sparks on the tarmac before burning out. A cigarette.

35

Quelling her heart, she tried to breathe calmly. She knew it didn't help that she was already on edge. The shake tried to surface on her skin, the itch insatiable. She counted. Repeated the process, bringing herself under control. Why would someone do this? Were they aiming for her? She tried to shake the paranoia from her mind.

No, can't think that way. I am a good person.

The Range Rover indicated left, veering violently off the road into the drive of one of the cottages. She could hear the gravel flying from where she stood, the ferocity of the sudden braking, bouncing off the door panels. A young woman, blonde and loud, exited the car. Her obnoxious voice carried on the air as she ran down the drive and banged rudely on the cottage door. Madeline watched on, mouth agape and heart thundering in her ears. The door opened by one of the elderly's she had seen the day before, the woman delightedly embracing them, not giving a second thought to the rubbish she had discarded over another human only moments before.

It wasn't anything personal, that she could now be sure of. The woman was invited into the cottage, she felt the tremor as the door was slammed to. No confrontation, no indication she was even aware of her presence. Perhaps the woman hadn't known she would hit her. But it still unsettled her. Suddenly she felt exposed. It was too much, in too quick succession, both people, their careless actions directly impacting another. The itch was threatening to take over, crawling over her mind. She took out her phone. 19:34. Timmy had a good walk anyway, they didn't need to go further today. Tugging urgently on Timmy's lead, she guided him back down the road and across up to their close. But she walked quickly, just in case. Back to where she knew she could be safe.

Him

He watched her in the window. She seemed to be unpacking something, kitchen utensils of some sort. He had stolen his way into the small back garden earlier that day. The fence to hers was tall but the bungalows here backed onto fields. No one could see him unless they were in the field. That didn't matter, he would be able to see them first. He took his time shimmying over the boundary.

As he watched her, he seethed. How dare she think she could just carry on her life. He wanted nothing more than to present himself to her. Reveal himself. But she would panic, she would race away from him again and he couldn't have that. He'd almost lost her once before and he wouldn't make that mistake again. This time, everything needed to be done properly.

Through the wide kitchen window he watched as she unpacked her coffee machine, setting it up on the worktop. It's chrome piping gleamed in the morning sun. That coffee machine, he thought bitterly. He had bought that coffee machine. He'd researched endlessly, poring over the different brands. Different settings. Types. Pods, bean to ground, barista. It had been expensive, but worth it. He'd saved hard. A little away each month. All of that, just to see her with it now, no thought whatsoever to where it came from and how.

He clenched his fist. Feeling the anger beginning to boil under his skin.

Injustice. She would pay.

The window was large, but the sun had moved in the sky. It was obstructing his view, its golden rays reflecting off the glass. He needed to get closer. His anger, frustration mixed with curiosity, longing and disbelief. He had searched for her so long, he couldn't believe she was finally here, in the flesh, in front of him. He wanted to count every freckle on her face, watch every strand of blazing hair lick around her shoulders. She was alluring, it was part of her charm and she had sucked him in with her devilish ways. It was against his better judgement, he knew, but he had to see her up close again. He was drawn to her. A moth to her flame.

He began to rise from his hiding place behind the bush, untangling his legs from underneath him. Making to steal closer, perhaps underneath the window, just a bit closer. He made to stand, and to his horror he saw her turn through the window.

He ducked quickly, his heart racing. Peering through the small gap in the hedge and saw her face searching out of the pane. *Shit.* The glance was quick, he couldn't be sure. Did she see him? He remained crouched, hidden, still. Straining his ears for any sound.

A rustle from the bush to his left startled him, directing his attention away from the window. A black cat stalked out from the shrubs. Hackles raised, it hissed at him menacingly. His mouth turned dry, he was panicking now. Never liked cats. And now the fucker was threatening to ruin everything. Expose him. It arched its back, the high-pitched snarl setting his skin on edge and baring its sharp teeth. Awkwardly, balanced on the balls of his feet he tried shooing it away with his foot from his bent position. Freezing, he heard the sound of a key turning in a lock, and a small click. The back door being unlocked. Shit. She had seen him.

He was trapped behind this stupid bloody bush. He knew he was taking a risk, but he couldn't resist the urge to just be nearer to her. Now it would be his undoing, she knew who he was, of course. She would recognise him instantly. It would be game over.

'Who... Who's there?'

He heard her call pathetically out into the garden. Despite the intensity of the fear of being found, he rolled his eyes. Of course she would plead like this, so innocent. He scoffed unintentionally. The noise upset the hissing cat. It launched itself at him, whipping its nasty little claws across his body. He felt the skin break underneath his hoodie as its vicious little talons sliced across his arms. In its frenzied attack it bolted out of the hedge, squealing loudly for the world to hear.

He held his breath as he heard the dog, barking madly, somewhere nearby. Its shrill yapping ringing through his head. Getting closer. And stopping. He risked a peek through the gap in the evergreen.

She was there. All five foot nothing of her, peering out across the garden. His eyes widened at the knife clutched in her pale fingers. Her hair gleamed in the sun, the most beautiful shade of auburn he had ever seen. It changed colour in the light as she slowly turned her head, surveying the scene. Her face, freckled to the perfect degree giving her the appearance of a summer glow. He held his breath, taking her in. She was outrageous, he had to admit. He watched as she visibly relaxed her shoulders, having watched the cat race across the lawn. She was calling the dog to her. He crossed his fingers. The dog sat stubbornly. Just staring at her. It didn't move and he prayed it wouldn't give away his hiding place. *Please go in. Don't come any closer.*

His legs were beginning to numb under his weight. His back burning from its stress position. His lungs stabbing, protesting at the hold of his breath. Just as he felt his body give in, with blessed mercy, the little dog beckoned to her. Peeking through the shrubbery, he saw how she backed into the bungalow, closing the door gently. He heard the key turn and the click.

A lawnmower started up from next door. Finally, he slumped in his hiding place, releasing the air gripping his chest.

This was too close. Too close. He had been stupid. But it all hadn't been in vain. He knew she was nervous. Jittery. Isolated. Coming out with a knife, she was still suspicious. Scared. But she never suspected he was there. He had the upper hand.

Now he knew he could get in and out unseen and undetected. The hedge concealed his hiding place and the fence was easy to scale. He would be coming back. And he wouldn't be so careless next time.

Tick tock, Little Red.

3

Madeline

After the experiences with the two women and the rogue cat in the garden that morning, Madeline felt jittery. She pulled up her lists on her phone, made annotations to an old one and created some new. She liked lists. Lists kept things ordered. Laid out plans. Lists rationalised her racing thoughts and calmed her disordered mind. The itch she had to be careful to scratch quietened, bringing her back down and under control. It was a trick she had learned as a child, a way of managing and keeping herself composed in the face of danger, uncertainty; her red cloak defence against the wolf's teeth baring down on her. Little Red, that was the name she adopted then, as a thirteen-year-old girl sitting in her school psychologist's office.

Being there was not her choice. It was insulting, degrading. No one would understand, let alone the wrinkly old bag who insisted she tell her about how she was feeling through her wheezy breaths. She had glared, pouted, refused to speak. The woman was infuriatingly patient with her, many early sessions sat in silence together. The therapist theorised she was mute, a product of an unknown trauma she had suffered, in need of love and attention. These words were never uttered in their sessions, the aged cliché of a therapist would never be that unprofessional. Through ajar doors, hiding in the shadows, she had overheard every debrief between the psychologist and the headmaster of the school. It was imperative teachers supported her in lessons, apparently.

"She needs time to trust, to trust her teachers, to trust me..."

"...Very characteristic of children who have suffered traumatic incidents or abuse..."

"...No contact with any guardian, or parental figure..."

Listening intently, she gritted her teeth as her silent shadow stalked the halls of the school after hours. They didn't know the half of it. And they never would.

The psychologist desperately changed tact week after week. She cycled through gentle questioning, visual imagination of thoughts and feelings, encouragement of arts and crafts and the introduction to strange-sounding music, all to no avail. She remained stubbornly mute. Finally, she was presented with an array of toys and books, placed deliberately and slowly in front of her, one by one.

Can you relate to these stories?

She sat in the uncomfortable chair, legs poised and arms folded, studying each item from a safe distance. In perfect control of her body and her mind. She wasn't stupid, she knew exactly what this task was designed to do. A form of toy-therapy. Tease her out, build her trust enough to spill every little secret she held. She remained tight-lipped. Until the therapist presented her with the Grimm's fairy stories. The image, burned into her mind forever from the opened book, placed on the splintered coffee table between them. The illustration of the young girl, baring up against the big bad wolf towering over her, her little red cloak and long red hair flowing heroically as she took down the beast. Enchanted for the first time, in spite of herself she broke her vow of silence. The stories of good versus evil, doing the right thing, never being greedy, the good guys always win; they were a comfort to her, solidifying her strength in the path she was on. She saw herself in the characters. Overcoming atrocities and great peril, innocent and undeserving of the pain they'd endured yet surviving. To her surprise, she found herself opening up a little. Then a little more. And for a while, she insisted on being known as Little Red.

You are a good person. Just like Little Red.

It wasn't your fault.

The woman's words rang in her head, providing her comfort. She'd always known she was unlike others, even as a child. She had a strong sense of right and wrong, standing up for what was good even when others seemed to cower from it. Fear and anxiety that crippled other children around her only made her stronger, her sense of duty guiding the way. But hearing it from another, an adult, a professional. Reminding her she was a good person, she didn't deserve what she had been through. She was Little Red, up against the wolves that hid everywhere, in sheep's clothing, threatening to blow, blow her house down, eat the little piggies or her grandmother, pretending to be good until that brief moment where their façade slipped...

The psychologist suggested she made a list, verifying the ways in which she was like those very characters. The task cemented what she knew. Doing what was right didn't always come with accolades or praise, it wasn't always understood by everyone. Even the best people make mistakes. Mistakes are lessons to be learned, lessons that make one stronger.

Madeline made full use of those now honed techniques from her childhood, compiling her latest lists, methodically laying out her plans for the future and filing her memories away neatly. She managed to get a decent sleep. Ivy's face filled her dreams, memories of that night trying to resurface, but by the time Madeline had woken the next day she had forgotten all about it. She was still in the spare room, but when she rose and looked around at everything yet to be unpacked she groaned, the feeling growing again. It was unlike her not to get her affairs into order but she knew she needed a release. Lists helped, plans were essential. But they were nothing on the effect she could get from scratching that itch. It would gnaw at her, biting, eating, burning at her brain. She gave in, found her phone, unplugged it from its charger in the living room wall and pulled up her Maps.

Little Molton was a small village, but it wasn't isolated. Other small, equally as beautiful villages surrounded it, and many were in walking distance. Madeline liked to walk. She would walk for hours, clearing her head, making plans. She had been a runner in her youth, but as she got older, she found a brisk walk could do the same for her fitness now her joints were more delicate. But her encounters yesterday had given her a feeling of uncertainty. She couldn't put her finger on why. Perhaps it was she had not expected to be assaulted by dirty takeaway containers so early into her move. She snorted at her little joke. No. Most people wouldn't expect that either. Using two forefingers, she zoomed in and out, checking out the settlements to the West. She knew she had jumped to conclusions yesterday about her safety here, but she did need to explore the area, canvas her surroundings. It was essential to remain vigilant. Not just for her future, but for her past.

Madeline pulled up her notes app. This was where she kept her lists. Password protected, digital and on her person at all times. If her phone was ever lost or stolen, she could access it using any computer and wipe her details. This was necessary, it was silly to leave any personal information written on paper, for anyone to see, to be lost out of a handbag or sucked up a vacuum. Even just a shopping list could tell even the most useless criminals vital information about their intended victim. And she did not intend to ever be a victim again.

Her eyes settled upon the name. Great Molton. The counterpart to Little Molton, she presumed. It would be as good place to start as any. And, as she noted, around a twenty-seven-minute walk away down the hill. Perfect.

She changed quickly into suitable clothing, leggings and a t-shirt. She called Timmy, and he lost his footing in his scramble to get out on his walk. He wouldn't stop wiggling and another battle with his harness ensued. Eventually, she looped her hands through the leg holes and as he danced around on his back legs, front paws in the air, she slipped it up over and up to his shoulders easily. Clipping the harness together she marvelled at the new technique, slipping her Converse on and checked the time. 09:12. She slid her phone into her convenient pocket on the thigh of her leggings and unlocked the door.

45

Madeline would explore further routes, but today was about finding the village in the first place. She had studied the map and theorised that if she took the footpath left and cut across the field, she could pick up another footpath which would take her all the way to Great Molton. It wasn't clear if this was the fastest route, but that would come. She had time.

They walked the leisurely seven minutes to the end of her road, and Madeline checked the time again. 09:19. Perfect. They strolled up past the cottages and through the housing estate, squeezing around the infuriating Volvo. Finally, they left the construction behind them and the landscape opened up.

They took the path left that ran back along the bungalows. At the fork, she took the left again. A wooded area appeared in front of them and Madeline saw her hunch was correct. The hint of a path ran through from the field into the wood beyond. Madeline stalled for a moment, looking up at the trees. Timmy was itching to get in, he'd seen something he wanted to chase. But Madeline suddenly felt hesitant. A memory from long before tried to wiggle free unpleasantly. She smelt the dampness of the dirt and the old wood drying out in the May sun. Without realising before she had set off, she knew she had been here before. It was almost a year to the day. She had seen it on the maps, but she had not thought about it being the same. Or why it had evoked such a strong, emotional reaction. Further down the woods, south of her position, there was a small, unmarked cut-through that led into Robin Close. Her close. Madeline had loved these woods as a child. She had thought nothing of it at the time, as she stalked through in the darkness, but now here it was. She never would have guessed her return here would bring up such a strong response. She sighed, breathing away the sadness and the guilt.

You are a good person.

A good person. She knew she was a good person. She cared, she looked out for people, she was considerate. She did what needed to be done that day. Shaking away the feeling she stepped defiantly into the woods.

Timmy darted away, his lead stopping him short. Squirrels and birds squawked and balked at the disturbance, she could hear the scuttling across the bark. Madeline kept moving. It was pleasant in here, despite an unnatural chill that developed around them. Nature's canopy blocked out much of the sunlight, the few rays that managed to escape its hold beating down upon the earthy soil. Sliding her phone out of her pocket, she remembered, no signal out here. Checked her phone, 09:42. But now she knew where she was, she could knock twenty minutes off that time.

Timings were good. Timings were consistent. Timings kept her safe. This was a skill she had learned at the age of nineteen. She knew exactly where she was and how long it would take to get to her destinations when she kept timings. She could choose to be early, late, or on time, depending on what the situation called for. She had learned from a lot of her past mistakes. In her youth she had been careless, reckless. She had been chaotic. Timing things helped to slow her down, keep her steady. She couldn't always trust her mind, but she could trust the physical evidence these techniques brought her. They were soothing when she got that itch in her brain, keeping her on the right track.

Timmy had returned to his happy trot beside her, satisfied the squirrel threat was dealt with thanks to his little guard. They walked on in silence, the birdsong ringing through the trees around them. The woods were not large, but the path was uneven. She needed to watch her footing carefully to avoid a fall or injury. She effortlessly dodged the hidden tree root she remembered from before. She had caught her foot on it the last time, nearly wrenching her kneecap the other way. She'd been running then, the latest near miss of many injuries. Since then, she'd chosen the preferable option of walking. She always learned from her mistakes.

The woods lined further fields on the other side of their collection. She felt her chest loosen as they walked out into the sunshine, released from the suffocating hold of the thicket. She gazed across the fields, blinking in the sudden brightness. Checking her maps, she confirmed what she was looking at. The houses were small in the distance, sat together in a cluster, a small winding country road through its centre. They took the narrow, foot-trodden country path through the fields and came to the border.

Great Molton.

Phone still devoid of signal, she checked the time, 10:03. She hesitated before adding her time stamp, thumb hovering over the screen. She knew she would not be using that path again, but perhaps it would be a good idea to keep an eye on the alternative routes. Something she had not considered before. She had never needed to, but you never knew if you needed to know something until you needed to know it. It was advisable to add it perhaps, she never knew when she might need that for future. If she ever needed to get away. She added a flag and labelled the route accordingly.

Madeline had been here in Great Molton before but had never been able to explore. Despite the initial guilt flooding from the devilish woods, she began to feel a buzz of excitement in its place as it began to subside and she got further into the village. She couldn't change what had happened back then, she reasoned she could change her actions for the future. It was a new start after all. A chance to do better, be better.

Despite its name, Great Molton was not much greater than its counterpart, but it was gleefully untouched from any gaudy new-build housing estates. The cottages and houses lined the bendy roads, built from the golden limestone, red tiling, and thatched roofs, still held together by the twisting ivy from years past.

Just as it should be.

The cottages were picturesque with their gleaming bricks and winding climbers up the front of the houses. Wysteria, she noted. South-West facing. She stopped and studied one, Timmy catching up to her heel. The Mini Cooper parked in the drive was gleaming, as though it had just been washed and the door was decorated with large pots of bedding plants. Suddenly a spaniel appeared at the window of the sweet cottage, barking madly. Timmy perked his ears but didn't react, too tired for tomfoolery. She allowed him a few minutes break to catch his breath before encouraging him on their stroll.

They left the house and the noisy spaniel behind. Now that the day was edging on through the morning, more of the villagers were up and about. There were no pavements set aside for walkers here, so Madeline would have to stop and pull Timmy up the grassy, weed-laden verges each time a car ambled past. The driver would acknowledge their courtesy with a wave of the hand and Madeline smiled with a gesture of her own. It cost nothing to be polite.

She heard the sound of a large engine coming from behind her and pulled Timmy right up the verge, out of the way of the lorry. As it passed slowly, the wind from its presence whipping around her face, she saw movement. Something. Someone. Behind her. Darting behind a parked car on the side of the road. Her heart rate began to quicken. This was no mere trickery, someone didn't want to be seen. The fear licked at her chest, powering a new bravado in the open, with witnesses all around. Turning on her heel sharply she marched over to the car, Timmy now vigilant and following her lead. She didn't know what she would do out here, but it was safe. There were people everywhere. She had to see who it was. If it was him.

Her footsteps were light, and her speed quick. Timmy picked up his pace, sensing her urgency. Reaching the side of the road, she stormed around the back of the car and her heart stopped. A peacock stalked out impressively, ruffling its regal feathers, unbothered by her sudden appearance. It didn't give her a second look, even as a small growl emitted from under Timmy's chest at her feet.

Madeline blew the air out of her cheeks. She turned, shaking her head and tried to resume her composure. She was hit with another wave of foolishness, burning at her cheeks and laughing at her racing heart. Her reaction would seem strange to anyone watching, but she knew. She knew. This was how it happened before. She would not be this foolish again.

A Range pulled out of a drive ahead, driving a little too fast and hurtled down the road in front of her, making her jump again. She pulled Timmy to the side, watching incredulously as it flew past, far too close. She squinted her eyes as the light gleamed off its polished surface and she stopped. Was it the same one? She couldn't be sure. Imagining the woman's hand, throwing out the rubbish all over another human. No second thought, littering her way through her life, destroying the environment. The second time she'd seen the car, though... Could she be following her? Did she know? She began to shake. Her heart was pounding in her chest, the itch growing in her brain as she watched it drive away up the hill. She was on edge.

Remember your techniques. Calm yourself.

Five things she could see. Cottages. The peacock strutting. Winding road. Silver Range. Number plate, BO55 S8H.

Four things she could hear. The bird song. Wind across the fields. Timmy panting at her feet. The engine of the car, driving away.

Three things she could touch. Timmy's lead. The picket fence next to the verge. Her polyester leggings.

Two things she could smell. The smell of the fields. Someone cooking bacon.

One thing she could taste. Bile.

She swallowed it. Repeated the technique again. The itch settled. She closed her eyes and breathed deeply. It was a close call. She was jumpy. Too jumpy.

You know it's not the same.

It's your mind playing tricks on you.

He can't get you here.

The thought settled her further.

The litterer was simply that, a litterer. It wasn't a nice thing to do, but it wasn't targeted. The woman wouldn't know who she was. She couldn't. If she thought of a yellow car, all she would see were yellow cars. She knew this, it was a trick of her mind. It was good to remain vigilant, but not to be paranoid. She was verging into the paranoia. It was not the same as last time. There was no evidence he was here, no evidence he would have told anyone. It would be all over the news if he had. She had made it difficult to be found. She had covered her tracks. She may not trust her mind, but it was all there in her lists and timings. Evidence.

She could still see the Range climbing the hill up to Little Molton in the distance. It helped to know she was just overthinking. The threat level reduced, other things were now popping into her mind. Plans, preparations, things she needed to do when she got in, busying and batting each other out of the way, each screaming they were more important than the last. Hands still quaking, she pulled out her phone and added annotations to her lists, dispelling the shambles in her head. Breathing cleaner air, her mind now cleared, she checked the time, surprised to see it was 10:20. She'd somehow lost half an hour in her frenzy. Timmy was tired and she had a new to-do list as long as her arm for when she got back to the bungalow. It would be a good time to turn back.

But as they walked back past the parked car, she couldn't resist another cursory glance around the back of it. Just in case.

*

Timmy slept soundly the rest of the day, curled back up into his bed, just a few inches too small for his little body, but it allowed Madeline to crack straight on with her moving list when they got in. She got started on the living area. Ivy had been house-proud, but the bungalow had remained untouched since she had passed. Dust was collecting in every nook and cranny and the carpet needed a good hoover. When the movers had moved the boxes in from Penny's house she'd noticed they had trudged a thin layer of dried dirt into the fibres. It irked her a little. It was a bit disrespectful to do that in someone else's home. Madeline always made sure to remove her shoes whenever she was in someone's house. It was the polite thing to do. But she supposed she could forgive them. They would have been focussed on carrying boxes. It may have been quite difficult to balance them with slipping one's boot off. She gave them a pass.

Ivy had left her old sofa and TV behind and Madeline was pleased to find it was still set up to receive Freeview. She turned it off and unplugged it whilst she was cleaning and put it back in its place once the thick layer of dust had been vacuumed away. She was tired at the end of the day, but she stood back and admired her work. The décor might be dated, but it was spotless. The door to Ivy's room was ajar. Her eye avoided looking at the lonely bedframe for too long.

Timmy had woken, ready for his dinner. She let him out to relieve himself and he inhaled the kibble the minute she placed the bowl underneath him. She smiled at him, watching him contently lick his lips and curl himself back up in his bed. It bothered her a little she didn't know how old he was. He wasn't a puppy, but he still had a lot of life in him. He loved nothing more than a sleep but still loved his Zoomies when he woke up with energy to expend. She might place him at about five years old. She knew she could find out if she really wanted to, but she decided it didn't matter. Not really. He was safe, happy, and healthy with her. She was glad she was able to give him a home, all the love and walks he could dream of. His previous owner was awful, a disgrace of a human being who never deserved him. She knew she would be able to give him the life of a dog's dream.

Madeline busied herself with the last bits of cleaning for the day and exhausted, fell into the spare bed. Ivy's face still came to her mind as she closed her eyes, but it was less intense now. She sniffed the air, still musty and close around her, making a mental note to tackle the spare room tomorrow. She should face it and move into the main bedroom at some point, but not tonight. She needed a good night's rest tonight. She sighed and turned over, the lumpy mattress pushing its springs into her side.

It was going to be a long night.

I love watching you sleep. It's my favourite thing to do. You never notice, either. Sometimes I move your stuff around, just to see if you will. You never do. Didn't your mother ever teach to be careful? You can't trust anyone, you know.

Watching you now… You're exciting me. You turn me on so much. Just seeing you now, you give me such a thrill. It's taking everything within me now to keep control over myself. The way you breathe, the way you sigh, so peaceful. I need that in my life.

I need you, my love.

There's been too many before you that made me angry. I don't like to be angry, my love. One of the last ones, she made me so angry. The moment I saw her, I knew she would be trouble. And I was right. She made me feel like shit. She treated me as though I was nothing. A low life. Not even worth the second glance.

She was nothing like you. You make me feel so special.

I made sure I humiliated her. She made me feel I was invisible to her. I made damn sure she saw me. I opened those eyes of hers for sure. She soon saw the error of her ways, she'll never do that again.

You should have seen her shudder as I ran my tongue up her cheek. She shook so beautifully, my body on top of hers, it felt like we were dancing together. Maybe we could go dancing one day, my love? Would you like that? I see those hips of yours. I bet you're a natural dancer, aren't you?

But like I said. She made me angry. I don't like to be angry. I slit her from breast to breast. I was slow. Careful. The knife sliced into her like butter, parting that beautiful skin and opening the red sea within. I was like Moses. I enjoyed that. I wanted to do it again. So I

55

did, slower this time. Savouring each precious droplet and groan from her protesting body. I ran the blade down her stomach. Oh, I was so gentle, but she wasn't rude to me then. She was full of shit, as I suspected. I wanted this one on display. I wanted everyone to see the bitch that she was. I left her laying there, legs open wide.

Then I slit that cunt.

4

Madeline

The rest of Madeline's week off was incredibly productive. And, reassuringly, she had no more strange incidents which settled her mind a little. She was able to rationalise any further nasty little thoughts that tried to torture her mind and worry her. It was all in her head. No one was coming for her. She was safe.

Madeline spent her mornings exploring new walks when the sun was cool and the rest of her days organising the bungalow, finding new homes for her sparse belongings, cleaning, tidying, and sorting. She didn't have the heart to throw any of Ivy's things out yet, but one problem at a time. She made more to-do lists, more plans, tested out the timings of her new schedules. She screwed her nose up in disgust as she stared hard at the baby-blue walls, eyes travelling over the scuffs and the grimy stains, the ghosts of activity from the years past. She added *paint samples* to her DIY list.

Monday was spent cleaning and de-moulding the bathroom. Using an old toothbrush and a mixture of vinegar and baking soda, Madeline got stuck into scrubbing into the grime of the grout, an old trick she had learned for removing even the most stubborn of stains. It was hard going, the smell was vile, but worth the stiff fingers and blistered nostrils when the cracked tiles came up sparkling. The toilet required a bottle of strong bleach and strong labour of a brush to remove the stains from the bowl. The toilet seat was beyond saving, so she ordered a new one at the local DIY store, same day click-and-collect and she whilst there, she spotted a new, dotted shower curtain and treated herself to a new, wider shower head. Fixing the seat to the porcelain bowl, she added the final touches; a fake trailing ivy plant next to the sink and a new scented reed diffuser on the windowsill. At the end of the day, sweaty and stinking of bleach, she looked around and smiled. The old porcelain shone and the lingering smell of old mould was replaced by sandalwood and rose. It could almost be a new bathroom. Checking the time, seven hours and thirteen minutes, better than she had expected. That night she washed her hair in her new, spotless shower for the first time, Ivy's old neglect and filth washing away down the plug hole with the suds of her shampoo.

Madeline checked her other lists, scrolling down her phone with a single finger. Biting her tongue between her lips she crossed *dog walker* off Timmy's. She had spent hours the day before scouring the local online community boards and Facebook pages for a walker she could trust. She couldn't trust wholly, no. Those days were long gone. But settling on a nice-looking woman from another local village, this was as close as it got. The woman's services had several good reviews on the local neighbourhood Facebook group and Madeline arranged an initial meet-and-greet before hiring her. In that first meeting Madeline found her to be rather quiet and aloof, bordering on rude, but the woman's eyes had lit up when she was introduced to Timmy. She immediately dropped to her knees, fussing and cooing as she produced a bag of treats from her pocket. Timmy, delighted, bounced around her on his hind legs, his little pink tongue sneaking little licks down the side of her face. She had laughed, nuzzling her head into him. She ignored Madeline completely. Madeline took this as a good sign. Anyone that trusts animals more than people was a tick in her book. And less chat meant less questions. That was how she preferred it.

Madeline had driven out to the village where she lived for their meeting, a little place called Barnbrooke. After the meet with the walker concluded, she decided to explore a little further. Timmy was more than happy with the plan. She could hear his happy little pant at her feet as he trotted alongside her, she didn't need to check to know he was on her heel.

Barnbrooke was a strange place. Rather than being clustered in one area, houses and cottages were spread far apart, dotted around the fields. Many were quite run-down, not very well looked after. Unlike Great Molton, the bricks here were dirty, years of grime holding the crumbling cement together. There didn't seem to be many keen gardeners out this way. Plenty of shrubs, trees, and hedges but a distinct lack of colour in comparison to the bedding plants that adorned the cottages in the Molton's. Madeline walked past a derelict building and narrowed her eyes to read the old inscription on the brickwork. *Barnbrooke Primary School.* She raised her eyebrows in surprise. It was clear it hadn't been used for some time. The old school was fenced off with large, ugly metal gates, held together by clunky rusting chains. Old signs hung off the wire sadly, their messages of warning peeled and unreadable. She could see a small, one-man digger sitting in what she guessed used to be the playground. There was now a hole in the centre of the concrete field, exposing the dirt underneath the aged asphalt and there were well-established weeds growing through the cracks. There was no one about, no sign of anyone doing any work, the rust and dirt upon the digger indicating nothing had been attempted for weeks. Madeline stared at the scene for a moment, before encouraging Timmy on. They left the ghostly shell of the school behind.

A large farmhouse came into view. Old, probably grade-listed building. It stood proudly out amongst the neglect, impressive limestone bricks and dark tiled roof. The owner had tirelessly restored the brickwork to its former glory. Windows had been replaced, new doors that still had plastic wrappings over their fixings and there was a collection of sandbags on its drive. Madeline looked up at it in awe, standing proudly on its own enveloped by tall trees and neat meadows. Further down the road, the architecture changed again; now she had been transported back to the Tudor era, thatched roofs upon a line of cottages, brickwork white-washed, held up and together through the centuries by the darkened contrasting beams. Away, across through the fields she saw a dip in the land, a mirage snaking across the valley as hills stretched behind her.

After only thirty-three minutes, they reached the car again. Madeline added her time stamps and clipped Timmy into the passenger side before returning home. She pottered a little around the bungalow and after a good feed, Weetabix for her and kibble for him, they cuddled up on the sofa together. They both slept well that night.

Madeline had taken Timmy into Lunnemouth for a walk by the river on the Wednesday morning. She discovered a car park conveniently adjacent and together they had spent a couple of hours exploring their surroundings. Lunnemouth was a market town, settled upon the river Lunne. The river ran through the town that bore its name, slicing it in two and exited out across the country. Madeline didn't have time to explore the centre with all of its shopping areas before the heat crept in, but it was nice to explore its outskirts. The river appeared to be more of a stream in Madeline's eyes, but she had laughed to watch the young children paddle on its cobbled shores. There was such an innocence in their faces as they splashed in the shallow water, their parents watching them closely. She sighed. She wondered what her life might have looked like had she grown up here. Would her mother have taken her to play in the water like this? Would she have been cautious, watching over her precious daughter, flinching every time she went under the water? Or slipped on a wet stone? Would she have worried about the risk of drowning to her child? She doubted it highly. No, nothing would have changed. It didn't matter. Her childhood made her who she was. Little Red. And she would still be running, she was sure of it. Always running.

Now, it was the last day of her leave, a lazy Sunday. The warm May days were showing no signs of relenting as June approached so she had waited indoors for the heat to die down a little before venturing out. Her pale skin would redden in minutes without cream in this sun and even if she applied some, the sweat would slide it straight off. The rest of the week had been spent exploring the footpaths around the village. She enjoyed getting out into the fields the most, and she was itching to get going. Timmy appeared less bothered, more content to snooze after his week of adventure. But she knew once the air cooled a little, he would perk up. Finally, four o'clock rolled around. The sun would now be abating and she could get out.

Reacting to her swift movement, Timmy sprang out of bed anticipating the walk. He was more compliant in getting his harness on now, yielding quickly before the battle would begin. Madeline had set regular reminders on her phone to let him out in the days, he was more comfortable, more trusting.

They strolled their usual path down out and down Robin Close, past the limestone cottages and through the housing estate. The path was Volvo-free today. Madeline glanced over to the house, with its red door. She thought she saw movement in the window, making her jump a little, before she rationalised the concern. So what if he was looking out. She had become too wary. The man was allowed to look out of his own window.

Madeline and Timmy settled into the rest of their walk, soon out and across the luscious fields. Madeline took the path to the left again and followed it. Timmy, now familiar with this route, sniffed and cocked his legs at all his favourite spots. Madeline tutted to herself as she steered him away from a pile of drying dog waste in the middle of the path. She made a mental note of its location on the walk and noted the time. 16:32.

They walked for an hour that afternoon, out across the countryside. When Madeline turned back she could just make out the back of her bungalow in the distance. She knew now this path ran all the way along the back of her fence, and on the return journey she added another flag and a time stamp. 17:22.

The sun had barely started to dip as they made their way back across the fields and into the village. Timmy was famished when they got in, hassling her for his dinner before she had removed her Converse. Another dinner inhaled before the bowl touched the floor. She made herself a microwave meal, nothing fancy, pasta with cheese and pepperoni.

Both fed, walked and watered, they cuddled up on Ivy's old sofa and settled in for a night of TV. Madeline reflected on the week's productivity, feeling a flutter of anticipation for her first day tomorrow. This week was just an induction, she was told. She couldn't wait to get onto the stroke unit properly. There was something about helping people, vulnerable and in need, it drove her. She had always been drawn to doing the right thing, studying to become a nurse had fit so well with her, she couldn't imagine doing anything else. She had thrived in her studies. She had never thought of herself as an academic, but once she began her course, she found the passion took over and led the way. It was never about the money for her, never about greed, she was fortunate enough to be in a position to protect the vulnerable, why should that be about money? Doing the right thing was often thankless. There were too many out there wanting accolades, rewards, ready and eager to take advantage of any system or person that could be of benefit to themselves. As a rule, she didn't listen to the news anymore, too many awful people doing awful things she was powerless to stop, but she had heard the whisperings of strike action from her colleagues across the country on her limited social media. The mere idea of striking to her was nonsensical, greedy, and selfish. She would play no part in it.

Eventually, the sun dipped in the sky and before Madeline knew it, her phone was telling her it was 22:18. Letting Timmy out for one last wee before bed, she locked up carefully and climbed into her own.

Madeline was sleeping in the master now, in her own bedding and sheets. But the room still felt like Ivy's. The aged furniture still decorated with lace doilies and dainty china ornaments, discoloured potpourri in glass bowls and wafts of lavender and pine floating in the air. She felt the hair on the back of her neck prickle as the thought of Ivy came to mind. It made her feel uneasy being here in this bed, but she knew she had to start exposing herself to it, hoping she would feel at home here soon.

Madeline set her radio up on Ivy's old bedside table. Classic FM. The only thing that helped her to sleep when she found her mind was itchy. At night, it played smooth classics, the presenters' words dripped off the tongue like honey and even the adverts were spoken in gentle, soothing tones. She liked Classic FM. It helped her to wind down, take stock of the day, clear her mind, cool that itch when she knew it would be a long night. Changing into her pyjamas, she climbed into bed and wiggled in between the sheets. A plume of her own smell hit her nostrils as she pulled the cover to her face. It was a strange scent mixed with Ivy's lingering fragrance, comforting and jarring all at once. Madeline closed her eyes, focussing on the feeling of her toes being enveloped by the soft down, ignoring the persistent image of Ivy behind her lids and eventually finally found herself drifting off.

It was dark. She flung her eyes open. With a start, she shot up in bed. Her heart was pounding, her head thick with sleep. Panic set in, the sickness swirling in her stomach, her skin awash with a cold sheen of sweat. For a moment, she wasn't sure what had happened. Her body and her mind were on alert. Something *had* happened. As her senses came around, her thoughts catching up, she searched for what had jolted her from her slumber so suddenly. With a pang of realisation, she threw off the covers and scrambled to the bedside table. In horror, she reached over to the radio, turning up the volume.

The newscaster was reading the news reports at midnight.

She listened, terror taking over her body, freezing her in position.

No.

No. This can't be happening again.

'*Police have confirmed the body discovered in Great Molton near the town of Lunnemouth is that of thirty-four-year-old Pheobe Larter. They have not released any further details as of yet but they have confirmed they are treating the death as suspicious…*'

Her heart thundered in her eardrums, drowning out the news report. It was a coincidence. It had to be. Great Molton. Near Lunnemouth. Near her. No. *No.* What if it was him, what if he had followed her? But what if it wasn't?

Madeline felt sick. She snapped the plug out of the radio, silencing the newscaster. No longer sleepy or ready for bed, she got up, pacing. Trying to placate her racing mind, trying to stem her panic. Telling herself it will be okay.

It is not the same as before.

But what if it is? The thought nagged at her, firing up the terror within. The strange incident from earlier that week popped back in. That day in the garden. She thought she had seen something then, too. It had been a cat, she knew that. But what if she was wrong? What if it was happening again? In Great Molton. The peacock. No, it was just a peacock.

But the evidence was there. The news had been reported. The body had been found. Thirty-four-year-old Pheobe Larter. The news did not lie. She scrambled through the drawer, fumbling to find her phone. Sleep was long forgotten, adrenaline fuelling her wakefulness. She hurriedly unlocked her phone and pulled up her notes.

Think. Think.

She searched her notes wildly. The timings didn't lie. If he had been there, if it was him, if he had found her…

Don't panic.

It could be a coincidence. The news reporter did not report anything else, other than that a body had been found. They had said police were treating the death as suspicious. Suspicious simply meant not natural. They could be working to the theory she took her life. Perhaps a domestic incident. Isolated. A tragic accident. There was no proof whatsoever that could link her. There was nothing to say it was him.

But no matter how she tried to rationalise, tried to reason, tried to ground herself, her mind would not stop.

Oh god. It's happening again.

Him

It's interesting how she spends so much time indoors, he thought. Must be that skin of hers. She is delicate, like a rose, and though her hair burns like the fires of hell, she would burn to a crisp in the direct sunlight. Like a vampire. The comparison made him chuckle. Accurate. Blood-sucking monster that she is. She took everything from him. If he had any more to take, he was sure she would have taken that too, before spitting and laughing at the shell of his corpse. The thought riled him, he felt the anger pulse within and the veins in his beck threatened to burst. He worked hard to calm himself again.

Be patient. Her time will come.

He had taken to his regular spot at the end of the garden, watching as she mooched around the bungalow. He'd learned his lesson. No closer. Not while she was in the kitchen. He glanced at the time. She'd be getting ready to go for a walk soon. She was becoming a creature of habit. Getting into a routine. He knew it would change slightly when she went back to work. But he was pleasantly surprised.

She was making this very easy for him. He would have thought she would have known better by now. She liked to think she could outsmart him, run, hide herself away. Pretend she was normal, had no secrets. It was impressive, in a way. He watched from his safe distance as she moved away from the kitchen and into the hallway. He checked the time on his phone.

His cue. He knew where she would be going.

He waited. And waited. His patience paid off. He heard the scuffling of Converse and the tip-taps of the Scottie's paws in the dirt. They were taking the path on the other side of the fence. Just as he anticipated. He risked a peek over the fence. Confirmed. A smile crept across his features.

She was becoming predictable.

He moved quickly. Time was of the essence. Predictably predictable, she would be back in around thirty minutes. Forty if he was lucky. Watching was good, it gave invaluable information, but he needed to get closer. He needed to get in.

He darted down the garden around the bungalow. He started at the side where the garden wrapped into old patio slabs, broken and decayed. Two windows here. Old. He peered in the first. A large room within. He could see a wrought iron bedframe and abandoned mattress. Not slept in. The window frame was old, wooden. No sign of rot. He moved to the next. Smaller window. Looking into a smaller room. Single bed inside. A-ha. This one has bedding on it. He smirked. She was sleeping in the spare room. That was interesting. This looked neat, but lived in. This room was the one. He studied the frame here. Old, too, but more splintered. He looked closer, using a pen he pushed into the exposed wood. It sank in. He smiled. Rot. He gave the frame a wiggle and heard the rattle of the loose glass. Easy as that. He chuckled to himself.

She was serving herself up on a plate for him.

He left the window for now. Today was for casing. There

may be better entries. He moved around the bungalow.

Just the one window at the back, facing into the garden. This was the same kitchen window he'd been watching for a while. He inspected it closely. It was new. New*er*, anyway. PVC, rubber edging, and efficient double glazing. Likely changed when the kitchen was extended. Standing back, he could see the subtle change in the colour of the brickwork down to the old, rotten wooden frames. Twenty years old he might've guessed the extension to be. Two windows at the left side. One at the back. Back door leading to the garden. He studied the door closely. Older. Didn't fit with the age of the new work. Likely moved across from the original build. Single lock. He noted the manufacturer in his handheld notepad.

He felt the flicker of anticipation. He'd anticipated a harder job, but he now had at least two points of entry. He only had to wait. Watch. Observe. Be patient. He could get in and out undetected now. He simply needed to wait for the perfect opportunity.

Her predictability would be her undoing, and he would have her at last. People might get hurt along the way, but it was a necessity. Their pain was nothing in comparison to the years of torture he'd had to endure at her hands. He heard the sound of the front door slam. His cue to go. He had to get everything ready for her, but he would be returning. Ducking low, he scrambled out of the garden and flipped himself back over the fence.

5

Madeline

Madeline's first induction day had gone well considering how exhausted she was. She had been up most of the night, panicking, planning, making lists. It hadn't done much to quieten her mind. But in the end, the adrenaline wore away and she had collapsed on the sofa for a few hours of snatched sleep before her alarm woke her.

In the light of day, though, it was as though a switch had flipped in her brain. In the day, when the world was lit and all shadows could be dispelled, she felt calmer. People were murdered every day. There was no proof of history repeating itself. It was likely a coincidence. And if it wasn't? There was nothing she could do about it now other than be more aware. Be more vigilant. Be strict with preparations and time any potential escape routes if she went out. She needed to maintain normalcy, she couldn't let this stop her from living her life. If it was happening again, no amount of worrying would change that. She just needed to be careful. History didn't need to repeat itself this time. She would make sure of that.

The plan settled her.

Despite her frantic and mostly sleepless night, Madeline managed to get around in good time and still arrived at the hospital early. They had emailed her with directions to the matron's office for her first day, and she had been given her timetable for the week upon her arrival. Excitedly, she studied it. Monday was filled to the brim with a series of introductory welcome talks, ID badge issuing, uniform measuring. The rest of the week appeared to be less crammed, but no less important. The official trust-wide induction was tomorrow. The remainder of the week was various introductions to the clinical systems and inductions onto the ward. She would pick up her new uniform from the seamstress on Friday.

The welcome talk was led by her new matron, who seemed in a hurry to get it over and done with, never making eye contact. Madeline was one of four new starters. All registered nurses. Two were due to start on the medical wards and another on a maternity ward. The matron made no secret of the fact their presence there was an annoyance and had busied away before anyone could ask any questions. The others were scheduled for their uniform fittings next, and so Madeline gladly peeled away from their company for her badge issuing. She had never been a fan of small talk. But she got lost badly on her way to find the right building, arriving over thirty-minutes late. The man had waved away her apologies, but it didn't sit right with Madeline at all. She timed the walk on the way back from the building to the main hospital. Six minutes. That is all it should have taken. How annoying.

She skipped her assigned lunch slot so she could be back

on time for her uniform fitting. The seamstress was chatty and, unlike the matron, appeared to have all the time in the world. She asked her idle questions about why she was here, previous experience, friends, family, favourite foods, the lot. Madeline answered them truthfully, but vaguely, and was relieved to see the seamstress was so distracted by taking measurements that they weren't listening to her in the first place. Finally, the end of the day rolled around and grateful, Madeline made her way out of the hospital. It wasn't a long day, not by any means. But the endless new information she had absorbed coupled with the terrible night had left her feeling drained. And in need of a release. Her brain was on fire.

She wasn't set up on the systems yet, and it irked her she had to pay for parking. She scowled as the young parking attendant in the lobby gave her the bad news. Madeline was a bit annoyed her new matron hadn't thought to mention this before, as she reluctantly keyed in her number plate and paid the all-day charge. Staff could set up a parking scheme for the rest of the year once they were on the system she was told, but that wouldn't happen until Wednesday, at least. She recalled the residential streets nearby she passed that morning. That would help tomorrow. It wasn't ideal. She knew residents near a hospital would often be quite put out by staff and patient's parking, potentially blocking their drives, clogging their streets. But she would be considerate. She would make sure her parking never inconvenienced them. Anyway, it was only for a few days. It wouldn't kill them.

It was 17:05. It felt strange to be clocking out at this time. But she reasoned she should embrace it before the long slog of the 12-hour shifts began next week. Lunnemouth General Hospital was positioned on the outskirts of Lunnemouth. Madeline knew little about the town itself, other than it had a river, a market every Sunday, and a lot of history. She had timed the drive to work this morning. It wouldn't be too much longer to the town centre, she suspected. With the thought, she added it as a task onto her list.

Madeline made her way out of the hospital entrance, stepping out into the warm May afternoon. June was only days away now and the sun had warmed the earth nicely. She smiled, in spite of everything that was going on.

It will all be okay.

The sun has a funny way of lifting the spirits, for sure. She strolled out leisurely and into the car park. Staff, patients, and visitors alike were milling about. Some were loading their loved ones into cars, balancing wheelchairs, sticks, and crutches. Others were fretting over their sick children, panic etched across their faces. Staff finished for the day were scurrying quickly back to their vehicles, bikes, and scooters. Some were just pulling in, parking up and readying themselves for their night shifts.

The sound of angrily crunching gravel made her stop in her tracks. Madeline halted just in time as a silver Volvo hurtled in front of her, missing her by a foot. Chaotically, it drove straight into an empty bay to her left, its old brakes squealing, wheels locked and stones spraying everywhere. She glanced at the number plate and narrowed her eyes.

The driver stepped out, no less chaotically and no less frantically. He flapped as his keys danced from hand to hand, as if they had suddenly burned iron hot. Without meaning to, her irritation melted away and she found herself smiling as she watched, her heart skipping a beat.

The man was dressed in the same smart trousers he had been wearing the first time she had seen him. He had a different shirt on today, and thankfully had no papers to battle with in addition to his burning keys. His blue lanyard swung around his neck as he fell out of the driver's side. Now, she could see the subtle hint of white logo upon it. *NHS.* She blew air through her nose, amused.

Always in such a hurry.

He glanced up and caught her eye. They locked onto hers. This time, she didn't feel caught off guard, expecting the exchange. She smiled awkwardly, and he returned it with a toothy one of his own. Curiously, she felt herself blushing. She looked away, feeling a little embarrassed at her sudden lack of composure. But she had liked the way he smiled at her. She left him standing gawkily, grin spread across his face. She didn't look back as she continued across the car park, trying to find her KA. But she could feel his eyes still on her as she left him behind.

The encounter gave her a warm, fuzzy feeling which stayed with her the entire commute back home. It didn't even recede when she was cut up on the main roundabout on the outskirts of the town. The woman didn't appear to notice she had done it, just waved a hand as she drove straight in front of her. Madeline had huffed, mildly irritated at the stupidity but it was busy. It was the middle of rush hour, so Madeline turned her concentration to the remaining traffic. Battling her way through, patience paid off and traffic eased as she drove out of town and onto the main road to the village. She saw the

74

offending car up ahead, and it turned off towards one of the villages. Madeline breathed. She was grateful the car was off the road now, she could relax a bit, in the knowledge the woman could not be the cause of any further incidents. She hoped the woman would realise how foolish she had been. She imagined her getting home, sitting with her family, her dog maybe, reflecting on her actions and making the decision to check both ways the next time she drove. She pictured the conversation she would have with her, giving her the chance to apologise, how she would say it would never happen again. Madeline doubted very much this would be the scene. In fact, she was confident the woman hadn't even given it a second thought.

Timmy was ecstatic to see her when she got in the door, ricocheting around her legs enthusiastically, and presenting her with her own shoes. She petted him, and immediately put him outside. She leant on the doorframe, observing him. He cocked his leg, two seconds, four seconds, then five, six, up to nine and then finally, stopped. Eleven seconds. She furrowed her brow. The dog walker should have come at lunchtime. That was an extraordinarily long wee if he had been let out at lunch. She shook her head. Perhaps she did come and he didn't feel comfortable to do his business wherever she took him for a walk. It was very possible. Madeline would keep an eye on it.

The sun was nice in the evening, and she considered the idea of a gin and tonic in the garden. She quickly quashed that idea. Alcohol did not pass her lips now. Alcohol made people do stupid things. It made her miss details, made her sloppy. Memories of her past threatened to surface and she batted them away. No, she had learned her lesson.

Every mistake is a lesson to be learned.

She always learned from her mistakes. Just as the protagonists did in her favourite Grimm's tales, mistakes made her stronger. Smarter. Safer. She settled on the idea of an orange juice and lemonade instead. One slice of orange. Five ice cubes. And a straw. A glass straw. She didn't like the idea of contributing to the landfill that was currently injuring turtles in an ocean far away.

Madeline took her drink and made her way down to the end of the small garden. She had changed into shorts and a vest and removed her socks. The soles of her feet against the cooling grass felt nice. Timmy darted out between her legs, chasing butterflies and insects around the garden happily. She stood in a moment of bliss, burrowing her toes into the blades, enjoying the sensation with the cold glass in her palm. Sipping the drink, revitalising her perfectly and for the first time, in a long time, she felt good.

Ivy had done a good job out here. Madeline settled herself onto the wooden bench and looked out across the garden. It was picturesque. Timmy was still bounding around the lawn, busy investigating the various shrubs and plants, guarding his territory from the winged invaders. She smiled to herself, watching him warmly. She had always wanted a little dog, since she was small. When she lived with Penny, she had never liked them. Too dirty, hairy, and smelly she had said. And since qualifying as a nurse, Madeline had never felt it was fair leaving a puppy whilst she worked her long shifts. But Timmy had come to her around two years ago, fully grown, in need of a new home. And he had chosen her. She felt like the luckiest girl in the world.

Her eyes fell upon the garden bed to her left as she sipped and her pleasant demeanour shattered. There. Behind the boxwood. Unmistakeable. This time it wasn't in her head. She fell off the bench and scurried over on her hands and knees to get a closer look. She heard the tumbler thud onto the grass, the straw rattle, glass on glass. It fizzed as the orange liquid was dispelled over the ground and ice cubes scattered. She crawled in horror to the garden bed, as time seemed to stand still. There it was. A footprint. Large. The whirls and grooves of a heavy soled boot, imprinted and pushed into the soft soil. Clearly visibly in the mud of the bedded bushes in her garden. And it was fresh.

Her worst fears had been confirmed.

Her past had followed her here.

And he'd been watching her.

There's a candle over there. Didn't you know, naked flames are incredibly dangerous?

That happened once before. Silly girl. She left her candle burning when she went to sleep. Burned the block of flats to its shell. Multiple casualties that night. So many families destroyed in an instant. So many lives lost. She should feel the guilt for those, it was all her fault after all.

She slept so peacefully. A bit like you.

I didn't think twice about that one. It was her own fault. She had the matches, the candle was there. Sure, it didn't have a flame in it then, but it could have. It could have naturally tipped onto her bed, set the sheets alight where she slept. It was her fault, her own undoing. A family of four below, old boy on the ground floor. She should feel guilty too.

It would be so easy to do that again. I could, you know. That wasn't my first time. I nearly made a mistake on the first one, but I was young. Stupid. She burned whilst she slept. I wanted this one awake. I needed to see the terror in her eyes, needed her to know what she had done.

The thought had crossed my mind. But watching you now, I just can't bring myself to do it. I need to hear you breathe, the way that chest of yours takes in each glorious gulp of air. I wish you would take me in, too. In and out of that warm, moist mouth of yours. It's the only thing that stops me every time. Do you know you have such a hold over me? No, of course you don't. You have no idea. But you're starting to get the idea now.

You think you're so mysterious. You keep your secrets, you think no one else knows, but I do. I know who you are. I see you, my love. I see every part of you that you work so hard to keep hidden. And I know why you're here.

6

Madeline

Madeline went into overdrive following her discovery in the garden. She stepped up her security, taking a last-minute day of leave from her induction week and had a brand-new alarm and camera system installed. She had been vague with work, telling them only that she had an emergency. She wasn't lying. The old alarm Ivy had was so antiquated the old woman hadn't realised it had degraded out of good use years ago. The new cameras linked to an app that pinged directly to Madeline's phone. She tested it out. Set the notifications to alert her to any movement. All images were automatically saved and uploaded, she could playback an entire day if she wanted. They were fully remote, she could turn them on and off from wherever she was, the guy told her. A helpful feature she supposed. But they would be remaining firmly on. She called out a locksmith, too, same day, and had all the locks changed. Just in case. She had heard it was sensible to get the locks changed when moving house, anyway. Madeline worried briefly what the neighbours might think. It was quickly dismissed. If the neighbours were watching, they wouldn't suspect anything was amiss. Madeline was simply a normal woman, looking for a bit of extra protection in the home she had moved into alone.

She began compiling more lists and she was diligent with her timings everywhere. She checked and triple-checked. Twenty-three minutes to drive to work, twenty-six on the way back. Fourteen to walk to the field at the back. And seven to the end of her road. Seven minutes to have a shower, three to urinate.

She knew it was him, the moment she saw the footprint. She was a fool thinking she could outrun her past completely. She knew this day would come. But not this soon. How had he found her so fast?

She needed to be more careful, more observant. Don't trust anyone. Her sleep was littered with nightmares again, screams and the flash of a past she hoped she had left behind. She tried desperately to carry on, but wherever she went she couldn't help but look over her shoulder.

She paced around the house, checking all windows and exits. The new security system pinged, indicating it was now online. She pulled up the video on her phone, breathing a small sigh of relief. One at the back, one at the front. From their positions, she could see all around the bungalow wherever she was. There was still that small hope she was wrong, it wasn't him. But who else could it be?

She considered her options. Everything within her bones was screaming *run, run again*. But if he found her once, he could do it again. Wherever she went, he would follow. She couldn't run away again so soon. The only other option was to fight. Fight for her freedom with everything she had. She had to be efficient. Outsmart him. He nearly won once before. She couldn't let that happen again. But she needed time. She grabbed her phone, her thumbs tapping ferociously as she made more lists, more plans. She knew what she needed to do. But she needed to be clever. Work out how. The plans were coming, but she couldn't get them in order.

Madeline went back into work and resumed her induction on the Wednesday. Despite her grumble, she grudgingly parked in the visitor's car park and accepted the inevitable charge. She hadn't had time to suss out the timings to and from the residential area, and with her mind so chaotic and itchy she couldn't trust it would be safe. Luckily, no one asked her about her emergency the day before. In fact, she wasn't convinced anyone had noticed the new girl hadn't shown for her second day. She was mostly left to her own devices and made her way to the IT department to set herself up on the systems as scheduled. The clinical system was one she had used before and so all she required was a quick refresher on the basics and verification of her ID. Once the clinical systems were verified, she turned her attention to the staff system. She set herself up quickly and sorted out her parking permit as a priority. It would take a few hours for the permit to go through she was told, and she was a little annoyed at the extortionate fee she would be faced with later. But she had no other option. She had to grin and bear it.

She was shown around the ward after that by her new band seven, a kind, slightly plump nurse with a deep tan and peroxide blonde hair. Shelly took the time to explain the lunch times, ward rounds, medication rounds, and visiting hours. As they were a stroke ward, they tended to have patients with longer stays than the other wards she'd worked on before. Unlike other medical wards, their focus was acute admission and rehabilitation, with the average patient staying for around six weeks in their recovery. Madeline was excited for the new challenge, it would be a good distraction. Shelly showed her where the medication trolleys were kept, the surplus cupboards, and the sluice at the end of the ward and then directed her to the staff room. Madeline would have a locker to keep her things in when she was on shift. It was recommended she change into her uniform upon her arrival to the ward, and out again before she left for the day.

'But to be honest with you,' Shelly giggled, 'we tend to just chuck our jackets over the top and get going.' Madeline smiled and nodded politely. Another nurse, likely a band five, a couple of physiotherapists, and a care assistant were in there, seemingly on a break. They all waved hello as she entered, briefly introducing themselves. She forgot their names instantly.

Madeline wasn't due to pick up her uniform until the end of the week, and her shifts didn't start until the Monday, but she thanked Shelly for her time. It was nice to go into her first shift with full confidence in the role, despite her wavering assurance in her personal life. She got an unexpected call from the seamstress on the Thursday, however, telling her it was all ready. The seamstress might be chatty, but apparently it did not hinder her efficiency. The matron had shrugged dismissively when Madeline had approached her to let her know she was finished with her induction schedule a day early. As she wasn't rota'd onto any shifts, she was told she was free to go and make the most of her extra day off for the weekend.

The rest of her weekend was spent in a haze of anxiety. Work had been a good diversion from her problems, but she couldn't delay. Time was pushing on and she could not quieten her mind. The itch had grown, but she did not dare to leave the house without a proper plan yet. Even just a walk around the village could be detrimental in this state. She was unfocussed. A stumble in the wrong direction, a sign missed, following her emotions, it was too much of a risk. He could be anywhere; he could be watching the house right now. She had confined herself to these four walls for her own protection, until she could get her mind straight.

Madeline looked around the living area. The weekend had done nothing but fuel the fire in her head. The idea of work the next day now filled her with unimaginable dread. The pretence of being normal whilst her mind was threatening to break her with no way to scratch the fire in her brain, it was too much. She glanced at her new uniform, ironed ready and hung off the door handle to the bedroom. She swallowed the lump in her throat.

Remember why you are here.

You have to keep going.

Those innocent people need you.

I am Madeline Hamilton. I am a good person.

The new camera system was a comfort. The app pushed a notification through every time it detected movement. And, as long as she stayed in tonight, nothing could happen. She could relax a little. Just for tonight at least. She put her phone away for a bit. After floating around the bungalow aimlessly for a while, she decided on a book.

She thumbed through one of Ivy's old, haggard crime novels, the protagonist an innocent woman, a mysterious past, a murder, a guy obsessively stalking her every move, she was running, running from something in her past... Madeline snapped the book shut. Not the best reading material, all things considered. Timmy gave her a disgruntled look as she turned the TV on instead, the noise disturbing him from his quiet snooze on the sofa. She flicked through the channels frantically, finally settling on an American comedy. One of her favourites. Episodes were being shown back-to-back for a couple of hours at least and so with a deep breath she relaxed back into sofa.

Madeline must have nodded off at some point, as when she opened her eyes next the show had finished. She didn't mind the snatched doze, though. She wasn't sleeping well in Ivy's bed for some reason, and she needed rest. She had work to get through tomorrow and had to be on her best form, in case he was lurking in her shadows. The yawn came widely, stretching her mouth to the brim and bringing a tear to her eye. She was so tired. She checked her phone, relieved to see there were no notifications from the new camera system. 20:59. Acceptable bedtime. Just as she was thinking about getting up and letting Timmy out for his last wee the news came on.

The thundering drums of the introduction titles pummelled at her chest as the news reporter read the headlines dramatically.

'Tonight.'

Madeline ignored the woman and stood from the sofa, calling Timmy. He rose lazily from his sleeping position, taking his time to patter through to the kitchen. He waited by the door patiently, as she brought up the app on her phone. She swiped her finger across the image on the screen, remotely twisting the camera around for a full view of the garden. All clear. Satisfied, she unlocked the door and released Timmy out into the back. He was barely through before she'd shut it and turned the key again. Just in case. The news reporter was still reading her headlines.

'*The King's visit at a primary school in South Foggen.*' South Foggen. She'd seen signs for the town on the way to work. She made a mental note to explore there when this blew over.

'*And bird watching in the region. We speak to Tony Burns...*' She chuckled as she watched Timmy on the small screen in her hand. He was following his terrier instincts, sniffing out a hedgehog underneath the hydrangeas. He sat, watching it intently, unwilling to give up his guard. It stayed still, unmoved. He didn't relent his position. Both as stubborn as the other.

'*But first. Firefighters have been at the scene of a fire at a block of flats in Lunnemouth today. Officers were called to the flats shortly before five AM this morning. They believe the fire was started some time in the night...*' Madeline looked up from her phone, listening. Lunnemouth. This must be local news.

'*Four people have been confirmed dead and two are in critical condition. Police have not confirmed the presence of any suspicious circumstances but are urging any witnesses or anyone with further information to come forward.*' Madeline tutted sadly. Four people confirmed dead and another two critical. Terrible, terrible shame, so many innocent lives lost. She heard a scrap at the door, Timmy had apparently forsaken his guard of the hedgehog and was alerting her that he was ready to be let in.

Swiftly opening the door, Timmy skipped in and she snapped the door shut. She locked it behind and gave a final look at the camera. Nothing. She breathed out a little. She was safe for the night at least.

She knew it was going to be tough trying to sleep tonight, so she didn't bother with the bed. A few hours of tossing and turning to give up and return to the spare room didn't appeal to her. Instead, she dragged her bedding out onto Ivy's sofa and switched the TV off in the middle of 'Tony the bird watchers' piece. Timmy had curled himself up on his bed in the corner of the room, she could already hear his small snore. She expected he would be joining her on the sofa before the night was over. After cleaning her teeth and putting her pyjamas on, she settled into the covers as best she could, praying she wouldn't wake with a stiff neck.

When morning came, Madeline's prayers were answered. As well as her neck being pain-free, she had miraculously slept well and woke feeling well rested. She had no nightmares and hadn't stirred at all. She sat up on the sofa, yawning as her phone's alarm tinkered on the coffee table beside her. She was surprised to see Timmy still on his bed in the corner of the room. She had been certain she was going to wake to find him curled up with her, nestled in the covers, perhaps outstretched at her feet. He lifted his head as she rose. The bed and its stained mattress glinted at her from beyond the bedroom door as she stepped around the sofa. She sighed, staring through the slit. Perhaps it was the room. She hadn't thought to make the connection before, but of course, it was in there that it happened. Memories like that stayed in the body and the subconscious.

Timmy was up now and scrapping at the back door. A quick check of the garden told her it was safe, and she let him out. It was early, five thirty AM. She was due to start work at the hospital at seven. Dog walker was due at lunchtime. She checked her maps. Traffic was looking good. No overnight roadworks. She smiled. Everything was just as she had planned. Maybe it would be a good day.

Reflection on thought was a powerful tool she had in her arsenal. When she allowed her mind the space to contemplate without the panic, she could think clearly. She would note the thoughts into to-do lists, evidence lists against the intrusive thoughts. Her lists kept her organised and accountable to herself, so her mind was free to be creative. The unexpected sleep had given her clarity on the latest developments, allowing her to join the dots. And now she realised, it was she who had the advantage, not him.

She had spotted him this time. She knew he was there. And he didn't know she was aware of his presence. He was trying to hide himself. He wasn't ready. He couldn't come anywhere near her house without being seen. There was no reason her past needed to come out, and she didn't need to run. In fact, without realising, she had done it once before. It may have been accidental, but she always learned from her mistakes. And her wins. Her past now gave her the edge, it was all there for her to utilise. She just needed to be smart, keep a level head and not lose her cool. And gather as much evidence as she could. This time, it would be him running.

Him

Stupid bitch got cameras. How fucking dare she. Who does she think she is? He let his rage boil to the surface, clenching his jaw as it clobbered at his innards, twisting his stomach and hollering his lungs. He was watching from the small green across the road, disguised as a cold caller. He'd been saving the leaflets for weeks, just in case. He knew they would come in handy.

He'd watched as the fat, sweating bloke with the ridiculously large van installed the infernal things at the front of her house. He fumed as he watched him take his tools around the gate to the back, presumably to do the same there. It was a last-minute decision to take the watch along the road today and now he felt glad for that change. He was sure he would have been caught if he'd stayed in the hedge at the back. Not by the sweating mess, but by the camera itself. The only silver lining in all of this. Fate had given him a hand today.

The bloke took forever with his drilling and banging around. He had looped the close four times, the neighbours would start to get suspicious. There were only so many times he could pretend to be leafleting. But on each trip past her door, his wrath settled itself eerily into a level plane. Now he had time to think, he was calming down a little. Her sudden paranoia complicated things a bit, but not massively. He'd read somewhere those kind of cameras were quite easy to hack. All you needed was an app and a password. And he still had access to the bungalow whenever he wanted. He could get into the camera and erase it before she even knew. A quick Google search confirmed his theory. It was so easy to get into, that there was a dedicated WikiHow page. He smiled.

In fact, the idea was dawning on him. She had given him an advantage. He didn't need to crouch and hide like a peasant anymore. He could keep an even closer eye on her. He would know exactly who was going in and out. What a stupid bitch. She didn't realise, but she'd inadvertently given him the perfect gift. And the best was yet to come.

7

Madeline

Madeline was thriving back in the thick of it, her epiphany giving her a new sense of power, a control over her mind, leaving her free to attend to other tasks. It had been a busy morning. She got herself stuck into the ward rounds, toileting, MDT's, and got to know her patients. Doris was swiftly becoming one of her favourites. She was eighty-eight, small ischemic stroke resulting in apraxia, and currently engaging in rehabilitation to walk independently. Small, wrinkled with wiry white hair meticulously permed into loose coils on her head and a collection of lace-edged crisp white nightgowns, a far cry from her younger days. Doris had been a rocker, her hair was shocking pink back then and she had spent her best years riding on the back of Harley Davidson's as part of a biker gang. She eventually settled down in her thirties and had a family, but that punk attitude had never left her. She had taken a shine to Madeline and, despite the stroke, she was still sassy and outspoken, keen to tell the other nurses how to do their jobs and wind up the neighbours in her bay for her amusement. Her daughter often found herself apologising on behalf of her mother when she visited, as Doris sat unapologetically, eyes sparkling with mischief.

Madeline smiled as she walked up to the cafeteria on her lunch, recalling the chat with her that morning. Doris morphed back into that radical twenty-five-year-old in front of Madeline's eyes as she cheekily divulged the sordid details of her night of passion with two famous rockstars, not too quietly either. Madeline had worked hard stifling her amusement as she caught Maggie in the bed opposite, pale and eyes bulging, unable to tear her eyes away in shock and disgust. *It's a shame the elderly are often overlooked by the younger generation*, she thought as she climbed the stairs. *They have so many stories to tell if anyone cared to listen.*

She chose her seat, far away from anyone else, deliberately isolating herself. The lunch rush was over, she had taken hers late. It fit with the job. It was rare she ever got away on time, anyway. But it suited her today. She didn't need the small talk from her new colleagues, the risk of questions, probing. And she needed space to formulate the beginnings of her strategy.

She checked her phone. One new notification from the app. Her heart leapt up into her mouth as she hurriedly clicked the link. The video loaded, and she watched as the dog sitter strolled up the drive and used the spare key to let herself in. Madeline released a breath she hadn't realised she was holding. She forwarded the frame, and there they were. Exiting through the door. Timmy and the walker. Timmy looked excited to be with her, and she felt a pang of jealousy. Catching herself, she shook the feeling. It didn't mean anything, of course Timmy loved her more than the walker. It was her he brought shoes to when she came home, her he greeted in the morning. She was his owner now. His family.

A tray clattered down on the table next to her, jumping her from her thoughts. Scowling, she looked for the source of the noise and widened her eyes. He was clambering into his seat, tall limbs everywhere as he tried to tuck himself under the table. She watched, fascinated as he visibly reddened and his chair legs scraped across the floor. The few people that were in the cafeteria were staring at him now and he bowed his head in embarrassment. His mayhem had sent his food soaring all over the table. He tried quietly to scrape what was left on the plate onto his fork. His back hunched, eyes directed down and away, looking down at his meal, trying to make himself as small as possible. Smiling to herself, she turned her attention back to her phone, swiping and scrolling through her apps.

She scrolled through Facebook and her finger hovered over a local news article. Madeline had made sure to turn her location off when she moved, she shouldn't be receiving these, she was diligent. Her finger hovered over the screen. She resisted the urge to tap and read the headline. And re-read. Then noticed the source. National news. This wasn't local at all. Her location was safe. But she felt the bile rise as her eyes focussed. She swallowed the lump that had grown in her throat. National news. She couldn't avoid it this time. She tapped on the article and read.

Police had found another body. In a small village just outside of Lunnemouth, called Lees. She quickly got her Maps up and keyed the village in. Just to check. Pressed direction. One hour and thirty-minute walk from her front door. Nine-minute drive. She pulled the article back up. The details were vague, police weren't saying a lot. The body was due to be identified, but terrifyingly, they had linked the murder to another. Thirty-four-year-old Pheobe Larter, found in Great Molton.

Madeline felt her eyes sting as the panic stung at her gut. It was too much, happening too quickly. It rushed to her head, sending her dizzying and the cafeteria swum around her. She needed time to prepare. She felt sick, it burned at her stomach and felt her breathing quicken, as though she were having an out of body experience.

Stay calm.

Think.

It is not the same. You are safe.

She took a deep breath in and looked around her. Five things she could see. People, empty tables, small chairs, a pile of trays, warmed food display. Four things she could hear. Light conversation, footsteps, the cling of the till, hum of the food warming trays. Three things she could touch. Hard surface of the table, the starch of her uniform, the coldness of her phone in her grip. Two things she could smell. Disinfectant, a mirage of food smells. One thing she could taste. She ran her tongue around her mouth. Sweet potato and chicken. Her lunch.

The beginnings of the panic ebbed away, her mind reconnected to her body and she looked back at the article. Scouring for the details, any clue. Nothing.

Think.

She needed to stay calm. It had happened, there was nothing she could do about it. If they had linked the murders, then they might make other links too. The plan. It was still workable. She needed to trust in herself. She had to trust the police. She had to trust that they would get to him before he got to her. She forced her lungs to take air in and out gently.

Just keep gathering evidence. It will be okay. He can't get to you this time.

She scanned up and around the cafeteria nervously, the thought not really comforting her. She had her plan, sure. But she couldn't deny it was all too close. And far too quick. Movement in her left periphery caught her attention. He swiftly looked away, bashful. She knew he had been staring at her, and it annoyed her for a moment. But he looked back up, caught her eye. And took her off guard when he smiled. Without meaning to, she returned it. He raised a clumsy hand and waved at her. The gesture looked so silly. They were one table apart. She chuckled in spite of herself, earlier panic ebbed a little, and she gave a small wave back. They said nothing.

Glancing at the time, Madeline noted lunch was over. She sighed. The patients needed her. It wouldn't do anyone any good if she was late. Her plan was in place, she needed to be cautious. Careful. Normal. The norm meant showing up for her job, too. She stood from her table and carried her tray over to the dispensary, dumping her rubbish and uneaten lunch into the bin. Placing the now empty tray carefully on a vacant shelf for collection, she made her way back down the winding corridors to the ward. Her heart was racing and her mind was going over what she had read. Again and again.

Stay calm.

It is not the same as before.

She was nearly at her ward, repeating the mantra in her head, and jumped, when she heard footsteps raining down on her from the corridor behind. Whipping around, arms up, ready for an attack. She stalled.

He was running down the corridor, lanyard and limbs flaying around him. He slowed as he reached her, footsteps now heavy and flat as they hit the floor.

'Hey.' He was out of breath, a flush appearing in his cheeks and down his neck. She lowered her arms, but her fists wouldn't unclench as they stayed stiffly at her side.

'Hey,' she replied, a little uncertainly.

'I'm really sorry, I don't usually do this,' he said breathlessly. He had come to a stop, hands on his hips. Bent over slightly to the right. Probable stitch. 'It's just, I've seen you a couple of times and I… Well, I think you are nice and… I think you are so pretty and I…'

She watched with fascination as he spluttered and stuttered through his tired lungs. Still, she didn't relax her hands.

'I was just wondering… And it's okay if not, I won't be offended. I know this is forward. I've never done anything like this before, but I thought, why not take a chance, you know?' He was babbling. She folded her arms. Time was moving, she would be late back if he didn't finish soon.

'So I did. I chased you down. I know it sounds silly… I just wanted to do something I had never done before, out of my comfort zone…' Impatiently, she resisted the urge to tap her foot but it was enough information for her to understand what he was trying to do.

'Are you asking me out?' she interjected softly. She knew her earlier nerves had stirred up the boldness in her question. Madeline wouldn't usually be this forward. But she was slightly agitated. Fidgety. She didn't have time for this. No matter how toothy his grin. He visibly stiffened and turned red again. She could see he was sweating a little.

'Err... Yes. Well, trying to.' He laughed uncomfortably. She laughed with him, releasing the tension a little. Careful not to laugh too much, just enough. She debated for a moment, studying him. She had thought about dating as a cover, and now the possibility was presenting itself, she mulled over the suitor. He was tall, gangly. She could see a hint of acne scarring scattered across his delicate skin, and the way he moved his body told her he was a late bloomer, as though he had only just grown into his height. His hair, about an inch too long, flapped around his head, framing those high cheekbones and large ears. He didn't quite fill out his frame, and his clothes were just a touch baggy. But as she met his eye, she could see the longing. The deepness in the blue of his eye, drawing her in. Was he a good person? The thought of the Volvo briefly crossed her mind, but there was something. Something in his eyes, in that absurd grin of his that made her want to try something new.

'Yes. I'll go out with you.' He blinked at her. That toothy smile spread across his face.

'You will?'

'Yes.'

'Oh, amazing, thank you. I don't mean thank you, sorry that's rude. I just meant, thank you for...' He trailed off and looked her in the eyes. Her eyes fell to his ID badge. *Freddie. Paediatric doctor.* His eyes followed her gaze. 'My name is Freddie, by the way. I'm sorry, what is your name?'

'Madeline.'

'Madeline. That's so pretty. Okay...' He swayed on his feet, awkwardness returned as he struggled with what to say.

'Would you like my phone number?' she prompted gently.

'Oh! Yes!' He fumbled around in his pockets, producing his phone on the third check. She keyed in her details, and pressed call so he would have hers.

'I have to get back to the ward. Text me details, and we can go for coffee?' she offered. It made him grin widely again. She liked that grin. She liked the fact she could do that to him.

'Yes. Amazing. Perfect.' He stammered, dancing on his feet as he turned away. Madeline smiled, watching him, before turning away herself to finish her shift. It was unexpected, a feeling she had never had before. But she liked it. She reasoned it wouldn't last forever, but it would be a nice, normal thing to try. A little bit of fun. And when all of this was over, perhaps she could finally have a return to some kind of normality. Normal would be nice for a change.

That bitch. She was good practice for you. I think she was one of my favourites. I took my time with her, I got a bit carried away, actually. But she pissed me off. I told you, didn't I, my love? It's not good to get angry. But she was fucking raging. Oblivious to the pain she caused me.

I hit her over the head with her own vase, initially. I hated that fucking vase. Who keeps this kind of shit in their house? It's ridiculous opulence. Her own vanity ended up being her demise in the end. I love a plot twist like that.

I memorised her number plate, you know. Stalked that one for a while. I spent time, toying with her. I told you, sometimes I just like to watch. Do you know the thrill of watching someone when they don't know it? Of course you do.

But she knew what was coming. The minute she laid eyes on me, she knew why I was there. They all do in the end. I dragged her out anyway, I took chunks of her hair out in the process. Her scalp in my hands, disgusting bitch. It got under my fingernails. I tied her to her own kitchen chair using her hideous scarves. More stupid vanity. You know those scarves women wear, the tiny ones? What are they even for? Not a chance they keep your neck warm. Her neck was quite slender now I think of it. I got a bit excited, watching her heart pulse in her neck. I could have wrapped my fingers around it, gently squeezed...

Fuck, thinking of that now does things to me. But, no, I couldn't do that. It was too good for her. She pissed me off even more when she wouldn't wake up after that first crack in her skull. I needed her awake. I needed her to know it was her own doing.

I waited for hours. Eventually my patience paid off. I needed to look her in her eyes. When she opened them, she tried to scream. She tried to beg.

It will never happen again, she said.

It's too fucking late, I said. You're a liar.

I left her there in that chair. She'll never hurt anyone else ever again, my love, I made sure of that.

And I took that ugly fucking vase.

8

Madeline

Madeline was still in her great mood as she made her commute home after the long day. Now aware of the state of the traffic on the main roundabout, she manoeuvred through the chaos, the beeps, and the brake lights expertly, and with no incident. She was starting on nights from tomorrow and was looking forward to a bit of a lie-in in the morning. She'd checked her phone before she got behind the wheel, there were no new notifications. Not from the camera. And she realised, frustratingly, not from Freddie. It stung her a little. It had been three days since he had fumbled over his words and asked her out awkwardly in the corridor. He'd not text at all yet. Maybe it hadn't been what he wanted to ask her, and she had assumed. Maybe she was being keen, overly keen. Maybe he didn't like her after all.

He's probably been working.

Yes, that will be it, he was at work.

Don't be so silly, of course he will text.

You're a good person.

The thought gave her comfort. Of course, it was very unlikely he would text at work. And that was a good thing, she would be more concerned if he was texting whilst working. He had shown how nervous he was just to approach her after all. And if his organisational skills were anything like his parking, she might have to take the lead on arranging this first coffee date. She would give him this pass.

Thought abated, she was able to concentrate on the rest of the drive as she moved out of town and onto the main road that would take her home. It was another gorgeous evening. She passed a jogger on the path, decked out in tight spandex and huffing with each deadened footfall.

Maybe she should start running again, she mused. She had enjoyed it so much, it was one of the only times she had ever felt free. The burn in her legs as she pumped them harder, faster, heel to toe as her feet propelled her forward. The stabs in her lungs as she would draw the breath in, the oxygen feeding her blood. She realised she did miss it. Maybe it would help her now.

No.

It drew too much attention to oneself. Look at how instantly her eyes were drawn to the jogger's movement, the clothing, the huffing and puffing and the spandex. She didn't want to become known as 'the girl that runs' around the village. Plus, her walks kept her fit enough, she knew she was able to run if she needed to. Her mind, playing tricks on her again, trying to make her think she needed to change something, go off her plans.

It will be fine.

It is not the same as last time.

Traffic slowed down the road and she applied the brakes gently. It was moving, but it crawled along now, she was in a queue. Seven miles per hour. She strained her neck, trying to see what was happening ahead. She checked the time, a little irked at the delay. Delays were not part of the plan. They messed up her timings, played with her schedules. Braking, slowing, speeding up again. This was a bit frustrating. Suddenly, she saw a car veer onto the other side of the road, and whip back in. Another followed, same movement. Overtaking.

Slowly, the queue moved up and she saw a glimpse of the cyclist. Taking advantage of a gap on the other side of the road, three more cars overtook. They sped away, glad for their freedom. She moved up, and the car in front, a Golf GTI, overtook at speed. It was just her following the cyclist now. She shook her head in disbelief. No helmet, no lights, in the middle of the road. White outlines flashed in her periphery to the left, the unmistakable lines of a cycle path on the raised pavement next to the road. *Why do they do this*, she thought, *there's a cycle path right there*. It's there for his safety. What would his family, his loved ones say when he never came home because of his silly mistakes?

She tried to shake that thought off, telling herself it wasn't her worry but the itch began gnawing behind her skull. She tried to fight it off, she needed to concentrate on what she was doing. She gripped the steering wheel tighter as the pressure radiated behind her eyes. The cyclist indicated he was turning left and she supressed a groan, before reluctantly switching her own indicator left. He slowed and took the turn widely. A car approaching the junction at the turn off swerved to miss him. Madeline slowed down and took the turning carefully. This was a narrow road now, unless he pulled over, she would have no way to pass him. He pushed his legs hard, she could see the muscles straining against the skin in his calves, but he stayed cycling in the middle of the road. She could not pass.

They wove further and further down the windy country roads. He, still not moving to the side, appeared not to notice her following behind. There were not many houses out here, fields of yellow, browns, and green surrounded them as far as she could see. She saw a white string blowing in the wind from near his neck. Earphones. Of course, he couldn't hear her. She pulsed her grip on the wheel, trying to curb her irritation and followed along at what she deemed to be a safe distance.

There was now a small queue of traffic behind her, all fellow drivers just trying to get home after a long day. She did not dare to get closer, wondering not for the last time, if he was aware of the annoyance he was causing. She could hear someone sounding their horn from a few cars back. The cyclist didn't move over. There was nothing she could do now but follow.

She was now holding the wheel so tight her knuckles were white. She had the beginnings of a headache from the concentration. Just as she thought she couldn't hold it any longer, by some version of a miracle, the cyclist turned off sharply across to the right and up the drive of another limestone cottage, sat alone out in the fields. She checked the time on her dashboard; 18:23. She breathed a sigh of relief and pressed her foot on the accelerator.

Let's get home.

Home to safety.

It was 18:36 when she pulled into the drive. Longest journey home yet. This annoyed her. The sun was still warm in the sky, though, and her headache was passing. She knew Timmy had already had a walk today, but she was sure he would fancy another. She was in the mood for a little stroll, a stress relief and there was more of the village to explore.

When she stepped into the bungalow, the hallway was dark. Direct contrast to the light outside. The sun's rays didn't reach that far into the bungalow. She couldn't hear the sound of a pitter patter, no scuffling from Timmy, no greeting at the door. But that wasn't what made her freeze.

A dark stain. Spread across the hallway floor. And splattered up the walls.

Madeline looked on in horror at the scene. The headache from the drive returned violently, throwing stars across her vision. Secrets from her past threatened to spill over into the present. One foot in the past, the other in the now, stuck in a limbo between the two. Shaking, she hurriedly flicked on the light switch. The ceiling light flooded the hallway. She could see little paw prints coming from the smear. Cautiously, she stepped closer to the stains, fearing the worst. It was brown, sticky...

Blood.

Wait.

Dog poo?

No...

She risked a sniff. Mud.

She furrowed her brow, trying to put the pieces together. Her mind returned to her, the fear and panic subsiding.

I am Madeline Hamilton. I am a good person.

Catching her breath, her heart slowed, the stars left and her vision cleared. Why was mud all over her hallway? Was this his way of scaring her? Threatening her? She didn't understand. The door to the living room was closed, and she stepped carefully over the mess. Quietly, slowly, she pulled down on the handle, opening the door slowly and peered through.

Timmy's head shot up from his bed. Her hand flew to her mouth as he raced over to him. He was no longer black. He was brown. Caked. Head to toe. In mud.

Madeline squealed and jumped backwards, as Timmy excitedly bounced up her legs, thinking it was a game.

'No! Timmy, down!' she cried. Her trousers were now coated in the now dry mud. She looked around her living room in shock. It was everywhere. It was clear Timmy had had some kind of Zoomies since she had been gone, and he had spread it all over the carpet, the sofa, and his bed. She stood frozen, looking on at the place in a stupor. Timmy was now sat, tongue out, his little black eyes watching her adoringly, tail wagging happily under his little bottom. She was stunned. Was this someone's idea of a joke?

Her eyes fell to the floor, and she saw Timmy's discarded harness and lead. They looked as though they had been submerged in sludge. Abandoned on the floor.

What happened?

Nausea swirling in her stomach, she pulled out her phone, accessing the files from the day. She didn't know what she was looking for, but she knew someone had been here. He didn't find the mud by himself and Madeline certainly hadn't left him this way. Scouring the images, frantically she found the same video from earlier. Watching closely, she watched as the dog walker exited with little Timmy. The jealousy reared its head again, watching how he danced around her. She suppressed the feeling quickly, it wasn't important right now, clicking on the other time stamps. A bird flying across the camera. The postman, delivering junk mail. And then...

How could she do this?

I am a good person.

I don't deserve this.

Timmy was still pawing at her, and she realised he was probably asking to go outside. She picked him up, lest he spread the dirt anywhere else and carried him out to the back garden. She shut then locked the back door and surveyed the mess in her home. Wondering where to start. The image of the video played back in her mind. How could she? What kind of professional returns someone's dog in that state, and leaves them in the house to wreak havoc?

Her gaze settled on the mud. It was thick, sludgy, set into clumps. It wasn't dusty, it didn't brush away. Where had it come from? It hadn't rained for weeks. Unless Timmy had gone through a lake, or a river. She hadn't thought to look for these. She quickly pulled out her phone, heart racing. Brought up Maps. Searching. There. She zoomed in with her fingers. Small lake. She looked at the small compass in the corner. Northeast. Just past the field if she took the footpath to the right from the new housing estate. She exhaled sharply, frustrated with herself. A giant body of water like that shouldn't be so overlooked. It was another sign. She was slipping. She needed to hold it together, always have her eyes open, be aware of her surroundings. It was a huge detail to miss. If she had missed this, what else had she missed? The thought didn't bear thinking about, but she knew she had to. She added a notation to her list. The plan hadn't changed. But now, she would be more conscientious than before. Double check. Triple check. It would save her life.

Her mind turned back to the dog walker. There was no point in moaning about the state of the place now. Damage had been done. It needed to be sorted. She made a mental note to ask the dog walker about it the next time she saw her. She would be polite, bring it up gently. But she would let her know it just wasn't acceptable. She had never had a dog walker before. Perhaps they needed to be paid more to rinse the dogs down after a walk. Like a dog groomer. She liked to give people the benefit of the doubt, give them a chance to explain themselves, she was sure she wouldn't have done it deliberately. Madeline wasn't a bad person, she certainly didn't deserve to have her house ruined like that. But the walker might think it was a cheek to expect her to wash off her dog. She probably wasn't a bad person, either. But she decided she would mention it anyway. It would be good to know for the future. It was a small comfort to her hysterical thoughts, only made more frantic by the itch still hovering in her skin.

Madeline's phone pinged in her hand, making her jump again. She blinked at the notification. And smiled.

Freddie had finally asked her out to coffee.

Him

He sat in his car, feet on his up on the dashboard, flicking through the images. His socks were dirty, peppered with sand, dirt, and blood from the blisters his old boots had given him, splitting and bursting, only for the fresh scabs to be ripped off the moment he put them back on. He should probably return to his dingy little room at the local Travelodge at some point, change his clothes, freshen up. His hoodie was beginning to smell, it could do with a good wash, his boots were missing a shoelace, and his underwear... well. Less said about that the better. But he was elated, transfixed by the progress he'd made, despite her pathetic attempts to thwart him. She may have changed the locks on the doors, but she had been surprisingly lax with the windows. The little one in the spare room was now missing a hinge, it had taken nothing for him to wiggle it free whenever she was not home. Easier access once he had popped the glass the first time. Stupid bitch. She thought she was so clever.

She was at work. Due to go onto nights tomorrow. He knew this. He knew her schedule now, the copy of her rota hastily scribbled in his notepad. She was predictable. He had plenty of time.

He'd taken great pleasure going through her things. It took everything within his willpower to not thumb through her underwear drawer. Thongs, bra's, knickers, socks. All folded neatly, arranged according to colour. He mustn't touch them. Not yet anyway. She wasn't to know he was here this soon. Things weren't in place yet. Just a bit longer.

He was nearly caught out by that fucking dog walker of hers. Thankfully, he'd heard the key in the lock and swiftly closed the door to the bedroom. Holding his breath, he heard the dog bundle in. He would still call it Sooty. The dog knew he was there. He hid, hardly daring to breathe as Sooty scrapped and threw himself up the bedroom door, desperately trying to get to him. Luck was in the air that day. The walker paid no attention to the excitable animal and left him to it. Thank god for ignorance. When the coast was clear, he had opened the door, fussed the dog a little, and triumphed at the mess he had left before returning to his business.

Your pet's name is not a secure password, by the way. And neither is your birthday.

It took him all of two minutes to get into her Wi-Fi and hack into the security app. He now had full access to everything, cameras included. He took a slug of his slightly warmed beer and tucked it clumsily back into the cup holder, wiggling his tired feet. He pulled up the images and watched closely. So far that day, he had been caught twice on that damn camera, but he deleted it before they uploaded. He left the first time and couldn't resist going back later that day. Just to see if she was there. No such luck. Caught again, but he didn't worry. He flicked through, delete. Delete. Delete. Delete. Delete. Shit.

He had gone too fast. He was in autopilot. He couldn't be sure, but looking at the time stamp, he knew. Frantically, he tried to recover the video, but it was gone. He cursed himself.

He had been too quick, too careless. He double-checked again. The timing was wrong. He couldn't be sure who it was, but he knew it wasn't him. And if it wasn't him, he had a very good idea of who it was.

Men are just as bad as women, you know? Maybe even worse in some respects. I see so many out there, chests puffed, swagger in their walk, giving me the look. You know the one. They think they can take me on, they all do. They see themselves as the alpha, the protector – pah! They have no idea who I am, what I am capable of. They are no match for me. Those big egos get in their way. That's the weakness, my love.

He wasn't my first, but I wanted to do him slightly differently. Make him pay. He was a tall man, actually. Very strong, I knew he kept himself fit. I made sure I did my research on this one.

I hated him. I despised him for what he did. I wanted to make him suffer by his own hand. I'd stolen a chain from the garage on the first visit. I was planning on keeping it, but in the end, I thought it was a twist of irony. You know how I love a touch of irony, my love.

I made sure he was asleep. I watched him for hours, just like I am watching you now. I'm a patient person. I slipped it gently around his neck. Made a tourniquet. One, two, three twists. Then, he woke up. But by then, it was too late.

I wouldn't be here, I wouldn't be doing this if it wasn't for you my love. Do you know that? His death is on your hands, you know. It's all your fault if we look at it properly. The amount of stress you've caused me by your actions. Your actions are the one to blame. Why couldn't you just leave me alone? Why did you have to wheedle your way into my life like this?

It's all your fault.

You are the one to blame.

9

Madeline

Madeline woke late in the day, but she was refreshed. She had taken to sleeping on the sofa, for the foreseeable. She knew she had to move back into the main bedroom at some point, but she couldn't face it at the moment. She had added it to her 'to-do' list and left it for another day.

Timmy fed, she settled back on the sofa with her bowl of Weetabix and switched the TV on. Timmy had already snuggled down contentedly amongst the covers next to her. A creature of habit, she usually saved the Weetabix as a treat. She needed the boost today.

She had a few hours before her first night shift, but she was keen to get out for a walk before she left. The discovery of the lake had unnerved her a little. She thought she had explored all the village had to offer, investigated all footpaths and access, she prided herself on being aware. It was a major oversight on her part, and she could have kicked herself. And after the news of the last few days, she needed to be more vigilant.

The afternoon news bulletins came on. She hated the news, it was rarely cheery and did no good for her mind. She swallowed the initial anxiety that leapt up, lapping at her throat and burning her chest. The urge surged and she almost reacted, almost gave into its demands. But she knew she couldn't. If there was any other news, she couldn't avoid it any longer. She needed to be in the know, despite how much it kicked off the near uncontrollable fear within. The titles thundered and the anchor introduced herself before diving into the headlines.

Another body found. Police had reason to believe they were linked. They were appealing for information and witnesses. And the two in critical condition from the flat block fire had now died. It made for grim watching. But Tony the bird watcher was back, promoting the song of the Nightingale in the summer. It did little to lighten her mood as her Weetabix congealed in her bowl and the panic simmered underneath the surface. It was quick, terrifying, and the police were giving little away. The panic twisted, tempting out that itch in her brain, and she felt her hands shaking as she gripped the bowl, just a little too tightly.

Madeline had doubts about her planned adventure this morning. It seemed silly on one hand, to take such risks. But, on the other, she knew it was needed. And it was speculation in her mind. Yes, some elements were repeating, but she had the upper hand now. Aside from the footprint in the garden bed, she had no further evidence he was hanging around. There had been nothing on the cameras as of yet. It could be possible there was simply a series of murdered bodies being discovered in quick succession, although unlikely, but this time she wouldn't fall into a false sense of security, relax her guard. She looked across at Timmy's sleeping body. He needed a walk before she left for her shift. He was depending on her. She would be safe as long as she stuck to her planned route. Kept to time. And it was light, the sun was still up. Everyone would see her walking her dog. Witnesses.

She shook off the anxiety and got dressed in the face of it. Within ten minutes, she and Timmy were ready and stepping out of the door but the worry still lingered, Madeline was jumpy. She started when her neighbour called a hello from their front garden. She waved back, politely, but couldn't hide the crack in her voice calling back a hasty '*hello!*' Sensing movement across the road, she turned, eyes wide, ears alert. She searched the small green on the other side, hypervigilant. Nothing.

You need to calm down.

You are a good person.

Stick to the route. Stick to the timings. Then you are safe.

She repeated the mantra in her head, pulling out her phone and checking the time. 15:10. She took off down the path, Timmy's claw tapping the concrete gently as he trotted beside her. It was earlier than she would have liked to be out in the sun, but she needed to go. She felt a bead of sweat developing on her upper lip, and underneath her cap along her scalp. The cream on her face started to drip, stinging at her eyes, she couldn't tell if it was hot or whether it was the reaction of her body. A breeze blew down the road cooling her nicely, and she hoped the footpath would be shady.

Madeline and Timmy passed through the cottages and the housing estate. The Volvo was not there to block her path today. Madeline smiled. She knew the driver was at work, in the middle of his shift as a junior doctor on rotation on one of the medical wards. They had arranged their first coffee date for the weekend, when he had the day off and she could meet before her night shift. She found herself surprisingly excited at the prospect as she passed his house and glanced at his red door. It relieved the anxiety she had felt in leaving the bungalow earlier.

It will be okay.

She reached the cut-through, and the start of the footpath. 15:24. Right on time. Right on schedule. Instead of turning left, she turned right and set a timer. Down the footpath and towards where she anticipated the lake to be.

More houses backed along the fields on this side, and she made a note of more cut-throughs from here. One. Two. Three. All into various housing estates. She frowned, as she and Timmy dodged more dog poo on the path like an unwelcome gift. She surmised this must be a busier footpath. Looking at the cluster of houses to her right, close together and in a big estate, she could see it was likely. Periodically, she made another time stamp on her Maps. 15:47. Four minutes.

It wasn't long before the landscape dipped into a valley, and it took her breath away. The hidden stretch of water glittered, the offending lake winking at her, a pale blue in the afternoon sun. Timmy started to pull on his lead, his eyes bright, eager to get to it, he knew where he was. She followed his excitable lead down the little track that wound around the lake.

Timmy was pulling quite vigorously in his harness, clearly desperate to reach the water, but Madeline pulled him back firmly. The dog walker may have let him dive in, but she did not have time to clean him up before she left today. He could wait another day for that excitement. The lake itself was beautiful, greens and blues intermingling with each other as ducks swam lazily and insects rebounded on its surface. It was not large, she could see across the other side fairly easily, but there were several benches set up on the far side, looking across the valley. She made a mental note to check if this was a good angling spot. She could see another collection of houses out in the distance, huddled together. She couldn't be sure, but she thought the architecture might be Tudor. Lots of white, against black thatched roofs. Certainly not in keeping with Little Molton's aesthetic. But not well kept. She checked the position of the sun with a tilt of her head. Glancing at her Maps quickly again, she confirmed her theory. Not Little Molton, but Barnbrooke. Where the dog walker lived. Thirty-three minutes to get around in total, leisurely pace, a strange village of neglect and beauty in equal measure. She paused for a moment, biting the inside of her mouth and gazing across the fields to the ancient homes, deep in thought before turning away, leaving them behind to follow the lake path.

Madeline found she liked being out here. She could see for miles around. Being in closed in spaces made her jumpy, on edge and she didn't like that feeling. Too many places for people to hide, watch her from afar. But out here, she was free. Reaching the other side of the lake and adding another time stamp. 15:51. She sighed. Twenty-seven minutes to get here. The timer was due to go off in three minutes. She knew she should turn back. It wouldn't do to be late for work. Tardiness was tolerated for some, but patients relied on her for their care, they needed her. She tugged on Timmy's lead and felt the dog reluctantly comply for the walk home.

Making their way back down her cut-through and into the new build housing estate, she saw movement out of the corner of her eye that flipped her heart. This time, she wasn't mistaken. It was no trick of the light. The sun was dipping, casting its nasty shadows across the ugly, soulless concrete structures and birds were flying overhead. But she was sure of what she had seen. A dark figure. Darting behind one of the houses. Her mouth turned dry and she stood still. Timmy was content to have a rest and sit on her feet. His tail was wagging and his tongue out. But he was looking in the same direction. Fixed on the source of the movement.

It wasn't in her head. He was following her. Closely. Following her every move. Her eyes darted around the estate. It was fairly quiet, a few people milling about. She saw another figure walking their dog in the distance. She tried to swallow, her tongue sticking to the roof of her mouth. She had tried to reason with herself, but she could not explain it away or avoid it any longer.

Her past was threatening to reveal itself.

Him

He was pissed off. Really pissed off. He thought he had her schedule down. Predictable. That's what he had said to himself. She was predictably predictable. He was pleased. He had almost gloated at how easy she was making it for him.

Who did she think she was, taking the right instead of the left? Didn't she know how much work she was now causing him?

She turned suddenly, and he darted behind a wheelie bin. Frozen. In his haste his hood slipped away, the string currently acting as a makeshift shoelace in his boot. Shit. That was close. She caught him off guard yet again. He hadn't expected to come upon her like this, she wasn't meant to be this way. It was him who was meant to hold the element of surprise, not her. It wasn't fair.

None of this was fair.

She should be the one who lost everything. She should be the one with the tattered life. She should be cowering from him, she should be the one sleeping in her car, unable to sleep, unable to think about anything else...

He risked a peek. She had turned back down the road, making her way home no doubt. Another time, he might have been tempted to wait for the notification on the security app, telling him she had arrived. But after this, no. She couldn't be trusted.

He needed to be clever. He would soon have her, but he mustn't take his eyes off the prize. Back to tried and tested methods. The old-fashioned way. Double down. He couldn't rely on the cameras. He couldn't rely on her. He would ensure he stalked every move, every journey, every action she took. She was sure to slip up someday. And then, finally. After all this time, he would have her.

10

Madeline

Doris passed away. Madeline was utterly heartbroken. It happened in the night, on Madeline's final shift before her rest days. She had stayed with the old woman, holding her hand as she slipped peacefully away. Memories of Ivy resurfaced and the guilt rose again, pricking at the inside of her skull. She should have been there to hold her hand, just like this. Of course, it wasn't the same, she knew that, but she also knew it was a comfort to those passing. To be connected to another as they move to the other side. Since Ivy passed, Madeline had always been sure to do this, it was a new rule she made for herself.

Madeline had driven home in a slight daze from the hospital. 06:07. It was early, even for the early risers and commuters and she had sailed through the roundabout, not seeing another driver until she turned into Robin Close. She had a to-do list as long as her arm, but upon entering the bungalow and letting Timmy out for his business, she knew she needed sleep before she could even think about starting anything. Sleep was important, she could get away with around five hours in order to function properly but she slept majority of the day, waking at 15:02.

When she woke, she cracked on with her lists. She finally got hold of the dog walker, after multiple attempts over the past week. The walker picked up on the third ring on the sixth attempt and Madeline had barely mentioned the abominable mud before she immediately apologised, promising Madeline it wouldn't happen again. Madeline was pleasantly surprised. The woman was extraordinarily honest, telling her she simply hadn't thought it would create such a mess to leave Timmy like that. Madeline couldn't see how she would ever think it was acceptable to leave someone else's dog in that state, but decided to give her the benefit of doubt, another chance. She booked in her walks for the next week.

Madeline took care to ensure she did not avoid the news that night. She needed to be aware, be in the know. The risk of seeing monstrous human behaviour was far outweighed by the risk to herself, from him. She thought she had lost him in Luton but undoubtedly he had been insatiable in his pursuit. The thought sickened her as the realisation sunk in; he would follow her to the ends of the Earth until he got what he wanted. Whatever sick, perverted ideas he had in store for her would only have grown maliciously in the past two years, she shuddered to think how he could destroy her life. And he could. It worried her, how quickly he had picked up her trail again and seeing him there, so blatant, out in the open, she knew he was following her closely. The idea of running, packing everything and starting fresh, briefly crossed her mind again, appeasing her anxiety, keeping her head in the sand. It was tempting, but it was beginning to dawn on her that this is what had got her here in the first place. It was no longer an option.

She had to catch him at his game. And she knew in order to do that, she needed to change tact completely. And that meant instead of ignoring the news reports and bulletins, she needed to study them intensely for any clues. She would have to deal with hearing the atrocities, she had to stay ahead of him, until the police finally got hold of him.

The wait for the six o'clock news was torturous. She tried to distract herself with other menial tasks on her list; laundry, hoover the house, clean the bathroom. Set timers, 16:03 for half an hour, no. Maybe twenty minutes?

I need a release.

No. No, it isn't safe. Stay in, be in the know. Back to her lists, try again. Set a timer for seventeen minutes this time. The footprint. Dust the coffee table. Her scream, his face swimming in her mind.

He was there, he was there that night.

No. Concentrate. Dusting... His face, across the bar, she had known it was him. Timer blaring. He was there, he was with her. He wanted revenge.

He's coming for you.

Quick hoover under the sofa, this hadn't been done for a while, she noted. Searching around the living room. No sight of the hoover, where had she put it? There it is, she picked up the duster. Staring at it. Was this what she wanted? Dusting, she was dusting...

You know what he wants. He must not get it.

Her timer was screaming at her from her phone, screeching its alarm and refusing to be ignored any longer, the tone sending shards through her head. She silenced it, blinking at the time. 17:37. An hour and half had somehow passed and Madeline found herself holding a toilet brush and a dirty t-shirt with no idea how she had got into the kitchen. Timmy watched interestedly from his spot on the sofa. She looked around, suddenly back in the room, her body returning to her splintered mind. Giving up with the idea of a distraction, it was pointless, she discarded the random items and sat next to Timmy on the cushion. Waiting. Giving into her mind, allowing the rampant thoughts to take hold.

She had been so young. Foolish. The mistakes she had made followed her here. Wasn't everyone allowed to make mistakes? If only hers weren't so costly. And here he was again. Trying to dredge it all up. For his sick, twisted idea of vengeance. Her mistakes were repeating themselves, she had missed too many signs. What if it was too late?

Stick to the plan.

She pulled up her lists. Evidence. It was all there in front of her. Evidence didn't lie. Evidence allowed the hold over her chest to relax a little, she found she could breathe. Her mind returned to her.

I am Madeline Hamilton. I am a good person.

She held fast to that thought. She knew she was a good person, despite what secrets her past may hold. She knew it was just a thought, just a tidbit that was thrown out in the media. It didn't mean anything about her. He would claim she wasn't, that it was all her fault, she did a terrible thing. No, she knew she was a good person. She needed to stop doubting herself. It would work, it had to. The stakes were too high if she failed.

Keep going. Just keep going.

Her head shot up, eyes locked to the screen as she heard the sensationalist drums and the dramatic titles of the six o'clock news. The news. This was what she'd been waiting for. Stay in the know, stay ahead of him. She felt the adrenaline, the urge to avoid palpable, it's icy fingers closing their grip on her, pulling, pulling....

No. You can do this. Be strong.

She needed to do this, she needed to watch for every detail. It was part of the plan. Shuffling to the edge of the sofa, hands together. The newscaster, young and beautiful, reeled off the headlines and her heart sank.

Report of another murder.

She waited for the newsreader to finish barking out the bulletins. Her leg rattled uncontrollably, trying to hold her knee, squeezing it. The action only served to worsen the shake, she felt the ripples throughout her body. The titles rolled once more, strange moving graphics interlinking with each other before the journalist was shown back in shot. Serious expression upon her face. Madeline didn't have to wait long before she was put out of her misery.

'Police were called today to an address in Eastrepps following the discovery of a deceased male. We can report the man has been named as Gary Mackintosh. Katie Kerber is on the scene, Katie, what can you tell us about this latest development?'

'Hi, Annie. Yes, police were called to the address in Eastrepps following the discovery of a male body within the property in the early hours of this morning. Police have confirmed the body has now been identified as Iraq-war veteran, forty-four-year-old, Gary Mackintosh.'

Madeline shook her head in disbelief, her eyes watering.

The report made her feel sick. She fought the urge to look away. *Keep watching.*

'We understand the police are treating the death as suspicious and have linked this murder to several other murders in the local area. Police have revealed they reason to suspect his case may be linked to the deaths of thirty-four-year-old Pheobe Larter and forty-two-year-old Maggie Hightown.'

Madeline felt the nausea rising, burning in her chest. All linked. It was absolutely terrifying. The anxiety gripped her chest. Crushed her stomach. Run. It's too close. Time is running out.

No. Don't avoid. You need to know.

She swallowed the nausea, blinking away the fear. Forcing her mind to listen.

'We understand earlier this evening, police arrested a man on suspicion of the murders and the suspect has been apprehended in custody. No further details have been provided to the public at this time.'

'Thank you, Katie. Commuters can expect further travel delay this evening as...'

Madeline heard no more, sitting bolt upright on the sofa. Relief surged like ice over her mind and body, releasing the hold that gripped her like tightened chains. Those two words. Suspect apprehended. Suspect. Apprehended. They arrested someone. A man, they said. This was it.

Finally, she breathed deeply, feeling the tension melt away from her shoulders and her stomach. Her lungs felt full of life.

She didn't need to run anymore. It hadn't been in vain. Evidence doesn't lie.

They got him. They finally got him.

In these moments, here with you, I think about the others. Three years ago I got Kristen. Christ, she was delicious. Well, I called her Kristen, after that Kristen Stewart. You know her? She's an actress. She was in those vampire movies the kids loved. Look at you. Of course you know those films. Were you Team Edward or Team Jacob? Well, Kristen had the same doe-eyes and faux innocence. But she cheated, she lied, she broke his heart. She was fake, phony, just like her. In the end, they all show who they really are.

Oh god, I'm getting excited thinking about it now.

It's taking everything within me to control myself, you know? You have no idea. But I have to. I have to control myself. Like I said, you're special. I need you.

But I'll tell you. Kristen fought like hell, she really did. I had planned to use the knife but seeing that spark in her eyes just lit something in me. She knew what she had done, and she tried to fight me. She tried to argue. She knew why I was there, the minute she clocked eyes on me. She remembered me from before. She got a good punch in, I'll admit, I had to wear sunglasses for a week from the shiner. That's when I learned to keep watch, make sure they would be sound asleep. No nasty surprises. She wasn't really asleep, she startled me, actually. I don't think she ever fell asleep properly, probably all the alcohol she had in her system.

She got a lucky shot in. She almost got away. But her luck ran out.

I sliced and diced that cunt. I licked the blood off the blade, ladled it over my tongue and pushed it between the gaps in my teeth. Tasted like sweet revenge. I told you, she was delicious.

11

Madeline

The dog walker had been increasingly unreliable. Madeline had returned home from shift one too many times to a distressed Scottie, dancing and squirming around near the back door of the kitchen. It would barely be unlocked before he would race outside to relieve himself. She counted. Ten, eleven, twelve, thirteen. Fifteen seconds. Eighteen the next day. Sixteen the day after. Madeline hadn't seen any evidence of her arriving on the camera for a few days and she hadn't replied to Madeline's texts or calls. The final straw came when she arrived home to a large puddle on the kitchen floor and Timmy cowering in the corner. She sighed, fussing him gently, keen to communicate it wasn't his fault but inwardly, she was seething. Her irritation rose, stinging and gnawing, colouring her innards red. After the mud incident she had given the walker so many chances, she'd heard her array of excuses and apologies but this was it. She had to go.

Madeline walked Timmy herself, calm and comforted in her decision to get rid of her. She was a decisive person, uncertainty didn't sit well with her but when there was a clear line, a right and wrong, a yes or no, she was secure. They took their new favourite route right at the footpath from the housing estate and around the lake, gazing across at Barnbrooke as it came into view from afar. The small Tudor houses like little islands amongst a sea of green in the distance, enticing her in with their perilous siren call. She checked her phone. Twenty-seven minutes. Breathing a sigh of relief. Consistent. She could rely on that being an accurate time flag. She released Timmy from his leash, reflexively giggling like a schoolgirl as he bounded with glee into the clear water. It was that moment of clarity, as his small body hit the water, that she knew she was safe in the knowledge she was making the right decision. She didn't like to do it, and it would create more work and stress for her but she knew she couldn't let Timmy suffer anymore at the walker's hands. She felt the itch in her mind soothe, honey dripping over the creases in her brain, caressing each fold and ridge, quietening the angry firing of her synapses as she breathed in the clean, fresh air. She chuckled, arms folded and transfixed by Timmy's innocent joy, leaping in and out of the waters waves, chasing the ducks and insects that flew past his nose, enjoying his unbridled freedom.

Madeline breathed freely now, too, she allowed her shoulders to rest and her lungs to fill. She had felt much lighter in the days following the news the police had *him* in custody. She looked over her shoulder, watched her step and kept up to date on the news yes, but she was more free with her time. Less tense. Reduced schedules. Free to take her walks, engage in her own little form of therapy, without worry, stress. Fear. She could take advantage of her liberty, be less controlled. She didn't check her camera app half as much, there was no need for gathering any more evidence. She had even signed up to volunteer her cleaning services at the local community centre, another way for her to give back, do the right thing. She still kept an eye on her time stamps, but that was just a helpful skill. It was good to be aware of how far she was from home, it kept her to time. And today, she needed to be back on time. It was another date with Freddie.

Since he arranged their initial coffee date a few weeks ago, they had met for a further two. Dating was new for her. In her previous lives it was too much of a risk, she couldn't afford for anyone to get too close. She had made the mistake of trusting another with her body, her soul, long ago, and the mere idea of history repeating itself was too much to bear. Besides, she didn't need anyone else, she never had. She was more than content in her own company. But she found Freddie had flung himself into her life, all teeth and limbs, igniting a spark deep within she never thought possible.

The first date was impromptu, snatched even, hastily grabbed after running into one another on shift and carried out over the over-priced coffee in the cafeteria. The next was organised, but no less casual. Another coffee. Out of uniform, arranged, in Lunnemouth. Between her shifts and the constant stress and anxiety of being watched, Madeline hadn't had a chance to go back and explore Lunnemouth since the trip to the river. But with dating being so novel, it gave her a new anxiety she hadn't felt before. It felt like butterflies, fluttering over the uncertainty and biting in her brain. Confusing, exciting. Dangerous. And where there is risk, she knew better than to leave it all to chance. She needed to explore, take her time, and so she planned it in and prepared herself.

The town took her breath away. It was around sixteen minutes' drive to Lunnemouth town centre. Madeline had arrived early the first time, parking in the public short stay. It was a busy town, touristy. Lots of people coming and going, all ages, genders, with a range of purposes. Just as she liked it. She was just one of many. For all the locals knew, she was a tourist, too. She had spent time walking around, adding more flags and time stamps to Maps. It was a medieval town, once upon a time. Much of the old architecture and old cathedral ruins were still standing proudly, at the side of the roads, in the parks and green spaces, all moulded now into the modern scene. As she walked the delicate gothic structures melted away into Victorian brick houses, narrow and tall. Then Georgian opulence, with large windows and decorative doors. Owners and renters had capitalised on the beauty by planting climbing shrubs that snaked in bloom up the walls. Small bay and olive trees framed the doors and hanging flowered baskets added a pop of magic for the butterflies of summer. Part of an old medieval wall had been built on sometime in the 1920's and was now part of the town's gin distilleries gift shop. As she walked, the town transformed again into a modern shopping centre, with ugly aluminium, panelled structures and bright brickwork. She read the plaque, *Milton Building Services*. She knitted her eyebrows. Casting her mind around the familiarity. Milton. She knew the name. Suddenly it came to her. Milton's flag was all over the new housing estate in Little Molton. She raised her brows, slightly impressed with how far their reach was in the area. Must be local, she mused. She had strolled out of the shopping complex and the construction changed back to the Victorian buildings. Coming upon the coffee shop on her walk and added a time to that, too. When she returned the next day, she was in control.

It was their third date today. Same coffee place, but this time they were getting food, too. Having scouted the area, Madeline was confident she could arrive on time. Her time. She took her time in choosing her outfit, blue jeans and a white top with puffed sleeves. The addition of food to a beverage signified the increase in the trajectory of their dates, she knew she had to make more of an effort. After taking Timmy out earlier, he would be content to lay in the cool living area and sleep whilst she was out. She was in such a pleasant mood she had even put music on to get ready. Jigging her body around the bungalow in something akin to a dance, she brushed mascara on her lashes and slicked a line of gloss on her lips. Permitting herself to enjoy herself once more.

Madeline pulled into the car park, glanced at the time. 12:43. She took the tried and tested route down to the café, twelve minutes. Pulled the large glass door to the café. The large clock behind the counter was analogue, not accurate enough, so she checked her phone. 12:55. Right on time. She turned, searching the tables to find them a seat. She stopped, her heart leaping in her throat. Her eyes fell upon him.

He was early. Waiting for her. She felt the flutter of panic, before calming herself. Panic turned into a mild irritation. She liked to be the first to arrive, to take time to settle in, clear her mind. But he was ready and waiting. He noticed her instantly, and his face lit up with that toothy grin as he clumsily waved her over. Despite her initial frustration, she could not help but feel warm inside, the sting of annoyance that she was so accustomed to now evolved. It was nice to have someone care for her, be pleased to see her. It had been so long.

Madeline made her way across the café, and he stood awkwardly to pull her chair for her. She supressed a chuckle as he tried to help her pull it underneath her, the gentlemanly thing to do, but succeeding to be less than helpful. She waved him away, seated herself and he sat sheepishly.

'It's so good to see you. How have you been?' Freddie blushed a little, the tinge in his face giving his teeth an even whiter appearance. Madeline gripped her phone, resisting the urge to put her phone on the table. That would be rude.

'I've been good, actually, really good.' She answered honestly, sliding it into her back pocket instead. 'How have you been?'

'Can't complain, really. I've been looking forward to seeing you again.'

'Me too.'

They were interrupted by a surly, young waitress who had come to take their order. She could not have been more than seventeen, her eyebrows painted across her face and false lashes that created a breeze whenever she blinked. She was short, there were no pleasantries exchanged as she barked at them for their orders. It made Madeline feel uncomfortable in her skin. She fought hard to respond as she should, tight lipped and on edge, squeezing her hands together on her lap. Freddie seemed oblivious. After they had given their coffee and sandwich orders, and she had grunted at them in response, Freddie turned to her again.

'How has work been going?'

'Busy. But I love it,' Madeline replied, picking at the skin on her fingers underneath the table. Small talk unsettled her, but she was learning to trust to herself again. She had prepared for it, there was no need to be so cautious now. 'We've had a few more admissions even since my last shift, the last time I was on there was seven.'

'Seven, wow. I bet that did keep you busy. Must be the summer heat.'

'Yeah, it must be.' Madeline watched the sulky waitress yawn from behind the counter carelessly clattering saucers and cups onto a tray. She shook her mind away, trying to concentrate on the conversation flow.

'How has your work been? Have you been busy?' she offered. He nodded.

'Super busy. I think that's the way of things now.' He sighed. 'There's talks of strikes, have you heard?'

'Yeah, my union contacted me last week about it,' she replied. 'It's going to be a big one isn't it?'

'Yeah, real big. Not just juniors and nurses either. AHP too, I've heard.'

'Wow. That is huge.' Madeline looked at him and sighed. 'I couldn't go on strike, though. I don't think it's right.'

'It's not right. But sometimes these things have to happen for us to get what we actually deserve.'

Madeline digested this information. She did not want to upset him, but at the same time, she couldn't abandon her principles. She had a strong moral code.

'But, if it means it comes at a cost of patient care, that doesn't feel like it's the right thing?' she argued gently.

133

Testing the waters.

'Patients will still be looked after, though, emergency cover has to be provided I'm sure. But we need to take a stand. The government isn't taking us seriously.' There was a small vein, beginning to bulge and pulsate in his neck. She watched it slide under his skin as he spoke, the muscles protruding deliciously. Gone was the blundering, stuttering fool, and in his place sat a man with passion. Dare she say, a fire. But fire that could be dangerous.

'I guess that means you would go on strike then, if it came to that?'

'Yeah.' He stared thoughtfully at the table for a moment. 'Yeah, I think I would. If the latest negotiations fail, of course.' She hung her head. Her finger was beginning to bleed.

'Right. Okay.'

'You wouldn't?'

'No,' she replied bluntly. 'I get what you're saying, we need to be paid more, of course. But I just think of the cost that could come to those poor patients. Treatment delayed, suffering in pain, not able to see someone. People put their trust in us to help them. Actions have consequences, you know?'

'Yeah...' he trailed off, as the waitress announced her arrival via a clattering of crockery. She slid the tray onto the table and emptied the contents, placing them in front of them wordlessly. They sat in silence. She finished dispensing and left them to it.

'So, how come you moved here?'

The question. The one she had been dreading. Suddenly the hunger that had come at the sight of her brie and cranberry toastie turned into bile in her stomach.

Don't panic. You know what to say.

I am Madeline Hamilton.

Good person.

He was blinking at her, innocently, not knowing the turmoil his question had brought to her. She could not lie, it was not within her to do that. But she knew she could never tell the truth. Since she had agreed to these dates, she knew this question was a possibility. She needed to calm herself. She had prepared for this. And it wasn't lying to just not tell the entire truth.

'I had a really difficult time where I used to live. Something happened, and I was painted out to be someone I'm not,' she said quietly, avoiding his eye. Freddie had stopped eating, staring intently at her. But as she looked back she saw the concern etched over his expression, in the lines around his blue eyes, the line of his mouth. He was listening. He cared. 'I don't want to talk about it, but I needed to get away. Start fresh.' On tenterhooks, she waited for her statement to land, fingers crossed under the table.

'I get that completely. People can be complete dicks.' Her eyes lit up as he returned his attention to his sandwich. He said it so flippantly, so firmly. He meant it. Perhaps she had misjudged him.

'Yeah. Yeah, they can be.'

'So, what do you think of Lunnemouth?' He had moved the subject along naturally, and she felt herself relaxing as they eased into effortless chat. The bile subsided and she enjoyed the first bite of the warm toastie. The brie and cranberry melted in her mouth and the thick, white sliced bread was toasted to divine perfection. She chewed and swallowed.

The conversation flowed easily between them as they drank their coffees and ate their lunch. They laughed, chattered and Madeline even forgot the earlier question that had set her heart on edge.

They split the bill. Madeline insisted on paying her half and he had reluctantly obliged. Madeline joined the small queue to the counter. The queue moved quickly, each customer paying dutifully, the line moving up. Her turn to pay, the waitress printed her bill silently, before throwing it across the counter and thrusting the card machine under her nose. Madeline blinked at the rudeness but said nothing, checking the receipt. She narrowed her eyes.

'Excuse me?'

The waitress only looked at her, eyebrows raised.

'Sorry. I think this may be wrong.' Madeline was careful to be courteous, keen to avoid a heated debate. Any kind of confrontation in public would be awful. 'I think I have been charged twice for my cappuccino?'

The waitress held her hand out for the receipt, furrowing her slug brows as she snatched it away and studied it. Madeline was a little annoyed. How much did it cost to be polite. She was tempted not to leave a tip. Then changed her mind. Just because this one was rude, should not affect the other staff here. Then to her astonishment, the waitress' face folded, and she burst into tears.

'I'm so sorry,' she blubbed, 'I'm not usually like this. My boyfriend broke up with me this morning and I feel horrendous. I just want to go home, and cry, but no one else could cover. And I've been making mistakes like this all day.' The waitress was sobbing loudly in front of her, make up streaming down her neck. Madeline stood still, in shock at the outburst. Other customers were turning in their seats to see what the commotion was. In any other circumstances, Madeline would have despised the attention. But despite it all, she felt sorry for her. She understood that feeling well. Her first break up, she was probably not much younger than this waitress, she remembered the pain well.

'It's okay,' she told her comfortingly. 'It's just a mistake. Easily done. You're young, mistakes will be made. At work and romantically.' The waitress snorted, a grin across her orange tearstained face. The tears had clumped her false lashes and they looked like spikes now coming out of her eyes. It wasn't attractive. She had been insolent their entire meal. But Madeline could see she was a good person. Just a good person, trying to get through a bad day.

'You should take a break,' she offered kindly. The waitress nodded tearfully. An older staff member, presumably a manager, was hovering just behind. She nodded in agreement at Madeline's suggestion. She led the waitress away from the till and handed her a tissue. The waitress took it and stopped, addressing Madeline once more.

'Thank you. For your kindness. I needed that today.' She allowed her manager to take her into the back room. Madeline smiled to herself.

'That was really nice,' Freddie whispered to her from behind. Madeline shrugged dismissively.

'It's nothing,' she said airily. They both paid, their payments taken by a different waitress and Madeline left a tip.

Bigger than the one she had planned, but she thought it was justified.

Freddie walked her out and held the door for her. They stepped onto the pavement and turned to each other to say goodbye.

'Well...' His awkwardness was back. 'It was nice to see you again, Madeline.'

'It was nice to see you, too. I had a really nice time.' Madeline was honest. She found, with great surprise, she had really enjoyed herself. He hovered on his feet, looking around uncomfortably.

'Would it be okay...' he mumbled. 'I mean could I... Could I give you a kiss?' He blushed bright red this time. She noticed how it mottled his neck. She smiled. It was forward, but she was surprised to feel that she also wanted it.

'Of course,' she said shyly. He smiled, and placed a gentle palm on her cheek, drawing her in. The heat rose up her face as she felt their lips connect and the urge to close her eyes pulled at her. She didn't give in, not just yet. His were soft, slightly moist at the joins but it felt nice. When they pulled away, they both stood bashful, like a pair of lovestruck teens.

'Well, I'll see you soon?' Madeline asked timidly. He grinned again. That toothy grin.

'Yeah, I'd really like that.' He gestured behind him with his thumb. 'I'm this way.'

'I'm going this way,' she replied, gesturing in the opposite direction.

'Right, well. I'll see you later. Enjoy the rest of your day.'

'You, too.' Madeline turned away and began the route back to the car. She was pleased she put three hours on the parking ticket. She could take the stroll more comfortably. She felt Freddie's eyes on her as she walked away and smiled to herself. She could not resist turning back, but when she did, she could not see him. She stopped, puzzled, searching for him in the crowd of tourists taking the same path. Then she felt it again. The hair on the back of her neck. Like she was being watched. She glanced around. She thought she saw a shadow, but as she blinked, the figure turned into a young food delivery driver, exiting a restaurant and making for his bike. She turned her back, dismissing the feeling.

She was overly paranoid, and it would take a while to shake that feeling, she knew. But she could rest easy now, knowing that she could ignore it. The police had him. They got him. There was nothing to worry about.

Him

She had started dating now. Same guy as before, she must like this one. Second time they've gone here. He doubted he knew what an evil, soul sucking monster she was, though. She would ruin this one's life too, he had no doubt about it. But there she sat, the picture of innocence as she laughed along politely with his jokes. She wore white today, part of the façade. She might be fooling him and everyone else, but she didn't fool him. Not one bit.

The thought crossed his mind. He should put the guy out of his misery really. Before it was too late. He knew her charms. He knew how you could get sucked into those doe-eyes, fall for that sweet demeanour, become captivated by that fiery mane on her head. She knew how to use it, too, with the subtlest of movements. A finger curled around a strand. The slightest shake of the head, so it cascaded down her back and caught the light. But no, that won't do. Patience is a virtue, isn't that what they say? The fool would find out sooner or later.

He sat in the café across the street. His blood rising to his skin furiously, watching them enjoy their coffees whilst his own turned to ash and fire in his stomach.

Her again. It was her doing. She was doing this to him. The reason his coffee was burnt. £3.60 it cost him for the sick pleasure she had bestowed upon him. She would pay for this. For everything she had done to him.

He sipped, pursuing with the bitter liquid and watched as they exited the coffee shop, grinning like a pair of virgins. He shook his head angrily. Seeing her again in the flesh, it did something to him. Something animalistic. He had been a normal bloke before she had forced her way into his life with that fucking enraging beautiful mop of flame on her fucking head. They kissed. He watched as their lips touched, and they stayed in that embrace. And all the while, the anger forged itself into an untenable rage.

Fuck her. How dare she ever think she could be happy. Fucking bitch. She had skipped out, left without a second thought. Left him to pick up the pieces of his life without ever looking back. She didn't fucking care. She didn't give a shit about who she hurt. She didn't deserve to be happy. And he was going to make damn well sure she never was again.

He presented a challenge. As I said, I usually prefer them asleep, but this one woke up. And he fought. Christ, I was black and blue by the end of our exchange. But in the end, I won. I wanted it more. He should have fought for his life harder if it meant anything to him.

I did it because of you. You have as much blame in this as me. You forced my hand. As I look at you now, my love, I know this is true. I needed to do it. You wouldn't leave things alone. Really, if we look at it properly, it's your fault. Your meddling, your actions. Don't think I don't remember, because I do. Oh, I do, my love.

Fuck me. You turn me on. You sexy cunt.

12

Madeline

Work had been relentless and Madeline was grateful when her rest days rolled around again. She had been enjoying further flirting with Freddie over text, and they had arranged their next date. This time, a proper date.

Madeline was nervous, the prospect of an evening meal out made the dates seem suddenly more serious. She wasn't ready for serious, that she knew. But now her past was safely behind her, the truth tucked away and the police had him in custody, she supposed she could start learning how to be ready for something more. Something she might see a future in. Something normal.

She had liked the kiss they shared at the café. Gentle, soft, and caring. He might be clumsy, unsure of himself and terrible at parking, but he did treat her nicely. She found herself, embarrassingly, checking her phone more often than usual. She had started to get giddy when it pinged. A flashing image of that toothy grin of his in her mind's eye. She liked this feeling and sighed. Perhaps it was time for a change.

The feeling put her in the mood for a walk. The breeze had cooled over the last few days despite the sun's heat, but it made for a more comfortable temperature. Changing into shorts and a t-shirt, she slipped her phone into her pocket and called out to Timmy. She got the harness on quicker now, learning to slip it over before he could start jumping on his hind legs. Madeline unlocked the front door and stepped out. She smiled, as she heard the *ping* in her pocket. She didn't check it, for the first time. The camera was incredibly responsive, catching her movement. She felt the release within her, knowing she did not need this system any longer. But, although it was no longer necessary, she still found it a surprising comfort for day-to-day living.

It had pained her a little to have had to get rid of the dog walker, it wasn't a nice encounter in the end but it was necessary. Madeline was keeping an eye out for other walkers in the area but was certainly not going by Facebook community reviews any longer. As a short-term solution, she had introduced herself to her elderly neighbour on the left. Joan had known Ivy well having lived in the neighbouring bungalow for more than thirty years and was more than happy to let Timmy out when Madeline was at work. She couldn't walk very well anymore, but she offered to sit over with him, keep him company for a bit.

'It would be good company for me, too.' she told her. Joan was a widow. She'd always had dogs and had lost her own little Westie only the year before. 'He left a gaping hole in my heart he did.'

Madeline decided she was trustworthy enough and gave her a key. But she had learned from her mistakes, and you could never be too careful. She decided to keep the cameras.

They set off on their stroll. She didn't check her

timestamps. She was now confident in this route. Seven minutes to the end of the road. There were no elderly's out tending their front gardens, it was too early in the day. They still felt the heat. Out to the cottages. Ten minutes. Out to her cut-through. Fourteen. She checked her phone and smiled. Clockwork.

She felt the pull to take her right and followed the urge, avoiding the dog poo on the dirt path. Madeline had learned it was always left in a similar place, and she anticipated its presence. Timmy trotted along happily, nose in the air and tail alert. She had to see the lake. She wanted to see the way the sun danced off its surface. The ripples that would be created from the cooling breeze. The dragonflies and insects that would bounce off it. The magic on the surface and the secrets it held underneath.

When they arrived Madeline allowed the sight of it to flood her senses. It tickled and glinted, as nature enjoyed its beauty, its mysteries, its allure. If she squinted, she could pretend the ducks were elegant swans. Swan Lake. She chuckled to herself, deep in her imagination. Six of them. Six little swans swimming on the lake. A good omen. Madeline was in such a good mood, she might even let Timmy in it today. Maybe. Her nerves tingled, a mixture of serenity and relief. She had never allowed herself to feel the ease, and now she was breathing it all in. They looped around the lake twice and, on the second leg, Madeline let Timmy off his lead. The moment he was freed, he made a beeline and launched himself into the water. Ducks scattered as Madeline laughed, enjoying the sense of pure joy that could come from something so simple. She let him paddle around to his hearts content, before calling him back. Happy and soaked, he obeyed. She made a mental note to live like Timmy. Enoy the simple things.

Eventually, Madeline and Timmy dragged themselves away and trudged back to the bungalow. As the day was cooling, she passed other walkers with their dogs, on the way to enjoy their time at the lake. They exchanged British pleasantries as they passed.

Madeline changed her mind as they made their way back. She wasn't ready to head back just yet. Her earlier revelations and newfound safety had given her a new bravery she hadn't experienced since before she found that footprint in her garden bed. Instead of turning right into Robin Close, she carried on down the road. Down to the other side of Little Molton.

The houses here were built in the fifties and sixties. Not as pretty as the limestone but certainly nicer than the new bricks of the Milton new builds. They were new once, but they were built with quality, with logic in mind and had stood the test of time. Here, she could see many families had made their homes, small front gardens, littered with toys, slides, and small bikes. She could hear children laughing heartily somewhere behind the houses, no doubt enjoying the lighter hours that summer offered. All had decent sized drives, she noted, leaving the road, and the pavement, blessedly free. She checked the time, added a time stamp. 13:43. The footpath veered away from the main road and she followed it into the small streets. More houses lined on both sides. Timmy was flagging a bit now. She could hear the sound of his claws tip-tapping on the concrete just behind her heel and slowed her pace.

She spotted what she thought looked like a cut-through up ahead. Next to it, a grey streetlight with a crude notice tied onto it. It flapped in the breeze, drumming in the air. A little annoying, but Madeline was in such a good mood that she passed it without care.

Her hunch was correct, it was a cut-through. Her heart racing, the excitement for exploration kindled once more, she inadvertently quickened her step, before remembering little Timmy behind. She slowed. The cut-through brought them out into another street. Madeline took out her phone, pulled up Maps and added a time stamp. She studied the map for a moment, figuring out where she was. According to this, she was not far from the footpath to the lake again. She recalled the other cut-throughs to houses she had seen on her first trip down to the lake. She presumed those houses were where she stood now. They had done a loop. It would be helpful to find where those cut-throughs are on this side though, and so she continued on.

They passed more streetlights, and Madeline noted every one of them had a letter tied to its post. Glancing at them as they passed, she realised they were all the same. She had assumed they were planning notices, a missing cat perhaps. But after passing the fifth, she caught a glance of a woman's face. Her curiosity won over and she stopped to get a closer look. The notice was tied clumsily to the post by a piece of string fed through the middle, dogeared and ripped in places and she needed to hold it open in the breeze to read its contents.

MISSING.
Have you seen Irene Joseph?
Irene hasn't been seen or heard from in four days and her family are incredibly worried about her. If you have seen anyone that looks like her, or have any information as to her whereabouts, please contact
Dani Joseph.

Dani's phone number was listed, and Madeline's heart sank. How terrible for that family. Dani must be a sister, mother maybe. How awful. Her eyes fell on the picture underneath.

Irene. She hadn't made the connection. The dog walker's name was Irene. But the girl in the picture was unrecognisable to the Irene she had met. The woman smiling at her from the photo had long, luscious black silky locks, plump cheeks and radiant brown skin. Her smile looked as though it could light any room she entered. She shook her head. The Irene she had met had short curls, hair balding in places on her scarred scalp. Her cheeks were sallow and her skin was sickly. The Irene she met did not have a smile that lit up a room, rather one that shrunk away under any attention. But the eyes. The eyes... Unmistakable. It was Irene.

Madeline felt the hairs prickle on the back of her neck and she glanced over her shoulder. She tried to ignore the feeling. She was safe. She knew this. It wasn't the same. Just because there were "missing" posters, it didn't mean anything. She cast her mind over the last week, she could count at least five instances in which Irene hadn't shown for Timmy. Studying the tattered paper, she wondered when these flyers had been placed up. A few days at the very least, she might guess. A cold shiver ran up her spine, setting bumps along her skin and her thoughts racing. As her eyes darted around her, her mind played tricks on her again, trying to tell her a figure had darted behind a wheelie bin. Then another, diving into the cut-through. Footsteps raining down behind her. Curtains twitching in the windows around her. She shook her head. Illusion dispelled.

No. It was just a coincidence. It would not be the same. She stared at the flyer a little longer. Missing did not mean dead. Missing meant missing. This thought eased her a little. The lead pulled and she turned to see that Timmy had laid himself wearily on the pavement next to her. She smiled sadly, figuring they should go back. There were always other days for exploration. She tugged on the lead gently, encouraging Timmy to his feet and turned back the way they came.

The journey felt longer on the way back, but Madeline knew to trust to her time stamps. The timing was no different than on the way out. Finally, they trapsed up their close and the bungalow came into view. Timmy perked up a little and raced up the drive to the door. Her phone pinged again. She unlocked the front door and let them both in.

Timmy immediately took himself to bed, leaving Madeleine to stand in the living room in the quiet with only her thoughts. The itch was there and there was a flutter of fear under the surface. She allowed it. It would take time for her to adjust. She needed to go easier on herself. She gazed through to the main bedroom. The door was still ajar, and she could see the abandoned bed within, mattress still stained and sheetless. She sighed. She couldn't sleep on the sofa forever.

And it had been a long time after all. Perhaps now she was sure her past had been left firmly in her past, that time was now. She pulled out her phone again and added notes to her DIY list for redecorating Ivy's room. She was ready for new beginnings.

She felt the prickle on the back of her neck. She deftly ignored it. She was safe. It was not happening again. Time had proved that.

Just because there were "missing" posters, it didn't mean anything.

She was too easy. I was lenient with this one, actually, it's a testament to who I am as a person. She had a substance abuse problem. She made it so simple. She almost did it to herself. All I needed to do is lure her out. Flirt a little. Flatter her, tell her what she wanted and give her what she craved. We kissed. I stripped her down. I was tender, careful and gentle. She was already moaning with pleasure before I even touched her. She wanted me. Not in the way you do, my love, but it was nice she was so forward. I wanted her, too.

She loved it when I pinched her nipple, and I nibbled her neck. Like a little rabbit on a carrot. She dangled that carrot so deliciously, I took great pleasure in the snack and I opened her up, taking my time with her wrapper. I shoved my fingers inside of her. Oh, how she screamed. That scream, I tell you my love, I will take that to heaven with me.

She liked it rough. My type of woman, that.

I could have stayed and played with her all night. She nearly had me wrapped around her little finger. Imagine. She almost replaced you.

But in the end, she knew what she had done. She knew she deserved to be punished. I wrapped my hands around her throat. Not too hard, just enough. She lost consciousness pretty quickly actually. That's what substances do to you. But she took away my enjoyment. I wasn't ready. Don't ever do that, my love. I'll be so upset with you. But it made her stupid, foolish enough to trust me.

Anyway, I dragged her out. She was limp and it pissed me off. I had hoped for a longer session. You must understand, my love, it had been so long since the last one. I needed my release. I was angry. I hit her. Then I hit her again. And again. The useless cunt just laid there. Like a dead fish. She was no fun at all. So I put her back where she belonged.

13

Madeline

Paint samples littered the blue walls in delicate stripes. Madeline had stopped at the DIY store on her way home from her shift and gathered as many as she could. She wanted a neutral colour, neutral provides a sense of calm she reasoned. There had been too much colour in her life, too much attention. Neutral was good. It would be a quick, easy job. So she thought.

She was surprised when she saw there were hundreds of shades of neutral. Did she want a walnut taupe? A cotton breeze? A desert white? An elephant beige? She didn't have a clue. She stood, dumbfounded as she took in the rows upon rows of paint tins in front of her. It seemed unnecessary to have so many shades, but as she studied them further, she could see they were all different. Some had hints of brown, others a yellow tone. Some were more grey and others beige. She shook her head in disbelief. She checked the time; 18:37. The store would be closing soon. She knew the young staff were probably watching her from afar, silently willing her to make her choice and go so they could close the tills for the day. In a panic, she took twenty-two testers. She hadn't brought a basket, she hadn't thought she would need one, so she juggled them in her arms as she hastened to the till. The testers jangling in their new carrier bag, she walked at a more leisured pace to her car, and continued her journey home.

The trip had made her later than she had hoped to be. But after Timmy had been let out for his business and fed, she set to the task of painting them on the wall in lines. As she stood and studied each of the strips, she realised she was no closer to a decision than she was in the store. The minute they hit the wall they appeared to change colour. She glanced down at the pink carpet. Perhaps it was the pink, subtly influencing her decision. That would need to be changed, too. As she glanced over the floor, the echoes of old stains could be seen engrained into the fibres, painting a picture of the place's grubby history. She had always liked the idea of a laminate floor. Much easier to clean than carpet. She pulled out her phone, googling for laminate ideas. Balking at the price, she tutted and decided maybe a vinyl roll would be better. Wood effect, nothing fancy. She scrolled, exasperated. Samples upon samples of vinyl floor, wood effect. Did she want a herringbone effect, plank effect, oak effect, or wood grain? Did she want underlay? And what about beading? Her head spun and she quickly locked her phone and threw it onto the sofa. She needed to make a new list. But it could wait for another day. She would focus on the wall for now. The bedroom and the offending bed remained untouched and avoided.

Madeline found it difficult to concentrate at work the next day. Her head was still full of samples and neutrals. She saw them swimming in front of the elderly patient who was trying to tell her, for the fourth time, the dosage of statins he should be on. She made a mental note to start her new list in her break. Lists were good, they kept things ordered.

But as she was helping another patient with their toileting needs, she realised what else was playing on her mind. It was a bit intrusive, the grin that kept popping into her mind at the most inconvenient times, all pearly teeth, running through her mind like Alice down the rabbit hole. But it felt nice. It wasn't the usual hypervigilance. It was a nervous apprehension. Tonight was her first dinner date with Freddie.

They had arranged to meet at the local pub. The food was good, he said, and they would be supporting their local so Madeline agreed. But she couldn't deny she was anxious. More uneasy than she should be. She tried beating it to the back of her mind as she helped the patient back into bed, but the thoughts kept coming.

What should I wear?

What if he asks me more questions?

What if things get serious?

Will he kiss me again?

What if he finds out?

She tolerated it for the best part of an hour. There was nothing for it. She needed to prepare. She feigned a migraine and cut out of work early. She didn't like to do this, to be so dishonest, but it was necessary. Anyway, she reasoned, she hadn't lied outright, she did have the beginnings of a headache coming, but she hadn't had a migraine since she was a teenager. If anyone happened to see her in the pub tonight, she would simply say she had taken her sumatriptan in time and caught it early. Migraines were an incredible personal experience she knew, and she was unlikely to be questioned on further symptoms. It wasn't ideal, but she couldn't be good all the time.

She arrived home at 15:56. Timmy greeted her with more enthusiasm at her unexpected arrival. Joan from next door had gone just before three that day according to the camera, so she knew he hadn't been left long before she came home. As Timmy curled up next to her, she set about with her preparations.

Lists. Sub-lists. To-do lists. Helpful things to say. The perfect outfit. Everything in place, nothing out of the ordinary to arouse suspicion. By the time she looked back at the time it was 17:22. It had flown, but Madeline did feel better, her mind now organised and everything filed where it needed to be.

She was going to wear her black jeans with a bottle green bodysuit. The green would offset her hair perfectly. She would pair them with her Converse, suitably dressing down the outfit enough for a local pub, but ensuring she still looked as though she had made the effort for their date. It no longer mattered what questions he would ask, she was ready. She didn't need to tell him anything more than the bare bones. She was here for a fresh start, living in Ivy's bungalow and she never spoke to her mother. Her entire truth was secure, far behind her and now he was away behind bars, there was no need for it to come out.

They were scheduled to meet at 19:30. Two hours away. Plenty of time. She fed Timmy and walked him quickly. She didn't go as far as the fields today, preferring to make use of the small cut-throughs and the pavements around the sixties-build houses. The posters, sad and weathered, still flapped from their tired positions on the streetlights.

Home, Timmy fed and sorted, Madeline supposed she should get ready. 18:54. She showered quickly, 19:01. She pulled the body suit on and slipped on her jeans. 19:05. She ran a brush through her auburn locks and locked up for the night. 19:12. Slipping on her Converse, she did one final check of her bag. Keys, gloss, phone. She unlocked the door, stepped out and heard the phone ping. Knowing it was the camera but checked anyway. 19:15. Perfect.

Madeline strolled down the close. It was a nice evening, the sun still lighting the world. The elderly gardeners would have gone in by now for their tea, but the songbirds still sang their sweet tunes. Tony the bird watcher popped into her head. She could see why he loved it so much. It was peaceful.

The Old Ram was only a nine-minute walk from her door. It was just past the cluster of sixties houses. She had found this to be a consistent time in her adventures around the area, a time she could trust. She should arrive and be seated at 19:25. Five minutes early. She figured this was the appropriate amount of time. Not too early, so that she would be hanging around for a while, but not late. She relaxed into the stroll and the pub came into view.

The Old Ram was old, living up to its name, a classic English countryside pub with its limestone bricks and an old, tiled roof. There were benches outside, umbrellas in the middle where many patrons were enjoying an evening pint in the sunshine. It had a large pub garden, partitioned for more seating, a grass area and a children's playground. It was a nice evening, but all tables were occupied. She knew Freddie had booked their table so she made her way indoors.

It was busy inside, too, but surprisingly cool. Tables were

dotted around, the décor a perfect mix of modern country style, in keeping with the Ram's history. The walls were a calming deep shade of navy blue, the bar and its features a rich warm wood. Brass wall lights lit the corners of the room and complimented the brass features of the bar area beautifully. The lighting was cosy, light enough so she could see clearly, but not too bright that it took anything from the atmosphere. All in all, a pleasant pub, Madeline thought.

She was about to make her way to the bar to record their arrival when she spotted him seated by himself at a table. He hadn't noticed her this time, busy scrolling on his phone but his presence shocked her again. She wasn't used to this. She liked to be the first one to arrive. Swallowing her irritancies, she made her way to the table for two, the empty seat waiting for her.

He jumped at her appearance and scrambled up to pull out her chair. In his haste, his hip caught the side of the table, sending the cutlery tinkling across the surface. She supressed a giggle as other patrons glanced their way at the commotion. Red-faced again, he offered her the seat and she took it. He seated himself awkwardly and she saw his nose was sweating a little.

'Sorry, I didn't see you come in.'

'That's okay. How are you?'

'I'm good! Thank you. How are you?'

'Yes, I'm well thank you. Absolutely starving.' At her friendliness he visibly relaxed and chuckled.

'Me too. I hope they still have the beef and ale pie, I've been thinking about it all day!' He pushed a menu in front of her. Madeline took it but didn't need to look. She had checked the menu on the Ram's website earlier in her preparations and already knew what she was having. The waitress, older and significantly more friendly than the one at the café, took their drinks orders—a pint for him, orange juice and lemonade for her. She was efficient and took their food orders when she brought their drinks.

They settled into an easy conversation, and Madeline relaxed into her chair. The pub did have the beef and ale pie. He babbled about his work, the young patients, friends of his, funny anecdotes and she listened intently. She answered with tidbits of her own from the ward and contributed at all the right times, and even made a joke here and there. Other patrons came and went, enjoying their own interactions with each other, each voice blending into a fine hum. She found she was enjoying herself. Really enjoying herself. With a pang she realised how stressed she had been, the worry and anxiety had taken over her life preventing her from feeling any form of real enjoyment. It was over now, she could breathe.

The end of the meal came, and he paid. He insisted. Madeline relented just this once. She would get the next one. He looked at her, his eyes gently searching her face. A flicker of anticipation licked at her stomach.

What now?

'Would you, erm, would you like to come to mine for a coffee?' he asked. It was too late for coffee, she knew. Caffeine disrupted your sleep if it was consumed too late. But his eyes were wide. Pleading and terrified. Anticipating her response. She knew they wouldn't be drinking coffee anyway.

'Yes. Yes, that sounds lovely.' She triggered that toothy wide grin. They exited together and walked side by side. She felt his hand reach for hers. Their fingers interlinked. It felt good and she allowed herself to be led, playing her part. The sun had set sometime before, leaving behind billions of stars glinting in a clear velvet sky. They walked on, hand in hand, back up the road and towards the new housing estate. The Volvo was there. Somehow, he had managed to get all four wheels on the pavement this time. He didn't acknowledge it and made to steer them both around it with a gentle hand on her back. It niggled at her a little, but she said nothing.

They arrived at the red door, and he took out his key to let them in. She pulled out her phone. 22:05. It had been a long night. The little symbols at the top glinted. No notifications. Of course. No signal. He opened the door, and like a gentleman, gestured for her to go first.

The hallway came into view as he flicked on the light. They removed their shoes and she followed him through to the living area. He motioned for her to make herself comfortable on the brown Chesterfield and she looked around as he busied himself in the kitchen. She heard the coffee machine start, screaming noisily as it dragged water through its system, and took in her surroundings.

Madeline wasn't surprised to see his house was a bit of a bachelor pad. Stag prints and artsy photos of guitars upon the wall. Two industrial style bookcases messily arranged. A few of the shelves contained books, but the others were dedicated to sound systems, old vinyl records, and cassettes. There was even a rugby ball balanced on top of a collection of rocks. That surprised her. He didn't look like a rugby player, and she usually had a pretty good read on people. Rugby enthusiast, perhaps? More likely. At university no doubt. TV in the corner on another industrial style unit, far too large for the space it was occupying. Cables leaked messily across the floor, connected to the latest gaming system. Controls were littered across the coffee table in front of her, alongside discarded receipts, coins, and retail loyalty cards. Ring stains sat over the surface. Coasters, apparently unused, scattered. Not matching. Looked to be taken from various pubs or bars. Her eyes fell on the Chesterfield and the cosy chair to her right. Discarded items of clothing lay over the arms and backs. She was distracted by his limbs of anarchy as he suddenly raced back in from the kitchen, frantically picking up the laundry items.

'Sorry, sorry,' he said hastily, throwing them over his arms. She heard a washing machine door being flung open as he dashed back into the kitchen, apparently flinging the offending items inside. He reappeared, flustered and a little breathless, and perched on the edge of the Chesterfield next to her, face red and blushed again.

'Sorry, I wasn't expecting, well you know,' he stuttered. 'I didn't like to presume, I didn't have time after work—'

'It's okay, I—'

'I didn't want you to think I was expecting anything, you know. I promise, I'm not one of those guys, I'd never do that to a woman—'

'Freddie, it's—'

'No, I know. I just want to make sure, you know? You know what I mean... I hope you know what I mean...' A finger placed over his lips and the endless babble ceased. Finally. They stopped still, both staring at each other, frozen in the moment. Neither knowing when to move, waiting for the signal of consent. Madeline felt a fluttering deep within. Something she hadn't felt for a long time. Gone was the worry, the uncertainty. Gone was the urge to prepare. Her body was reacting, it knew exactly what to do, how to behave. They mirrored each other's movements and drew each other in.

Him

She hadn't arrived home from her date. Naughty, naughty. It pissed him off. He knew exactly where she would be. She was with him. He'd been checking the cameras periodically from his car. He liked it here in the car park of the pub. Out of the way. Beer on tap. He could relax, stretch his legs out a bit. All that crouching was doing his back in. His legs were on fire. His muscles weren't used to this. But from here, the hideout and safety of his car, he couldn't be sure. He needed to know, he had to know. It was imperative. One little slip up, and everything could be ruined. He sighed angrily. Didn't she know the work she was causing him? He couldn't drive up there, that was far too obvious, he would miss clues. He'd have to walk and leave his fucking car. More fucking crouching.

He'd watched her enter the Ram earlier that evening. She was wearing a green top, it contrasted beautifully and her hair looked even more outstanding. It even appeared to make her eyes sparkle. She looked good. Fucking bitch. She knew exactly what she was doing to him. He hated her so much.

He'd made sure he would be there for when she arrived. Thankfully, the summer sun had brought out everyone in the village and he was able to blend in seamlessly with the locals on the tables outside. She hadn't even looked his way before she entered. She had relaxed a little, he saw, her shoulders were less tight, her jaw unclenched. She clearly thought she was off the hook. That would be a costly mistake.

He'd been there the night the fool had popped in to book the table. It was a happy coincidence, actually. Lady Luck again. He'd heard great things about the pie here and decided to treat himself. He recognised the bumbling idiot the minute he walked in. All limbs and no grace. *"Table for two on Thursday, please. Seven thirty is great, see you then."* He knew exactly who would be joining him for that.

He huffed. Swinging himself out of the car. Starting on the walk to take the watch. He was fucking angry. She was selfish, so selfish. Who the fuck did she think she was.

Not long.

Be patient. He would have her right where he wanted her soon. Just a little longer. He was nearly ready now. He just needed to keep her in sight. The thought calmed him.

He had heard they arrested someone. A bloke. Probably the reason why she had the skip in her step and the confidence to stay the night. Nice try. She would soon learn the truth. They got the wrong man.

14

Madeline

They made love that night. It surprised her at how careful he was. The chaos he created in his day-to-day actions apparently didn't follow him into the bedroom. He was tender, caring, and gentle, taking time to check in with her. They had started on the Chesterfield. Built it up slowly. They explored each other's bodies bit by bit, taking the time to find just the right spot at the right time. They paused on the stairs for a bit before finally finding their way to his bed. Her jeans and Converse were still on the living room floor downstairs somewhere. Her bodysuit was now discarded across his bedroom floorboards, next to her bra and underwear.

Madeline turned over in the duvet and nuzzled into the pillow. Freddie was sound asleep next to her, breathing so softly. She was content just to watch him for the moment, taking it all in. He had fallen asleep pretty much as soon as they had finished. Why do men do that? But she didn't mind. She felt free. She risked a slight stroke down his cheek, and he stirred quietly. She smiled. She loved to watch him sleep, wondering what he was dreaming of. When they had first met, she had thought she would have finished it by now, it surprised her how light he made her feel. How she looked forward to seeing him again. Maybe this could work after all. Perhaps she could learn to trust, open her heart up again.

You need to go.

She knew she needed to go. She needed to get back. She couldn't stay tonight. Timmy would be waiting. She hadn't made the right preparations. But maybe soon. Maybe soon she could stay with him.

Silently, she slid herself out of his warm embrace. The air was chilly as she moved away from the heat of his body and she shivered a little in the dark. She carefully pulled on her underwear and bodysuit, and crept downstairs to find her jeans. The house was quiet as she stole through the night. She got dressed in the dark, not daring to put on any lights or make any sound. He was sleeping so peacefully, there was no need to disturb him. After a fumble through the items discarded on the floor, she found her bag and checked her phone. 00:18. No notifications. Of course, there's no signal here.

She tiptoed down the hallway and quietly pulled the door open, slipping out and heard the muffled noise as the catch confirmed it was shut behind her. The streetlights were still lighting the roads, not due to go off until one o'clock. Quiet as a mouse, she made her way back home.

Madeline loved the night. There was something about being the only one awake that was invigorating. It was a time where she never had to worry about someone watching her, a time in which she didn't need to pretend. She was liberated, free to be herself, she became a different person in the night. She'd never needed much sleep, five hours was enough for her to function well and so she often took her time whenever she was out after dark. The stars glinted at her from miles above, the gentle moonlight providing her with just enough guidance for her path back. The air was cool, it brought out a hint of goosebumps on her arms, but it felt nice on her skin. She allowed her mind to wander, the beginnings of a plan for the next time she might be there with Freddie. There was a lot she needed to think about. The sex itself hadn't complicated things much, but the insinuation of what signified did. He liked her. A lot. And she was finding, the feeling was reciprocated. She arrived back on her doorstep, and pulled out her phone, tapping it to life and glancing at the time. 00:30. Her signal returned and a couple of notifications pinged. She didn't need to read them.

Timmy was happy as ever to see her when she got in. She let him out, fussed him a little before the two cuddled up in the bedding on the sofa. With a sigh, Madeline found herself looking behind them, across to the unused bedroom. The door was still agape. Her eyes fell upon the mattress. She couldn't avoid it any longer. There would be a time he would ask to see her home, she knew she couldn't keep going to his. It just wasn't the done thing. If she wanted things to continue the way they were, she needed to tackle Ivy's old room.

Madeline had her final night of sleeping on the sofa. The next morning after sorting Timmy out, she stood at the bedroom door, gazing at the bed in the stuffy room. She had been surprised at how much Ivy's death would affect her, how difficult it had been to think about clearing out her things. The old drawers were still full of Ivy's clothes, Madeline's own in the battered chest of drawers in the smaller spare room. The bungalow felt more like home with each passing day, but every time she stepped back over the threshold to the room, memories came flooding back.

Ivy had been alone in her bed when she passed. Madeline should have been there for her at the end, embracing her as the light left her body. She felt guilt for it every day. News of Ivy's death had shocked the village, everyone thought she would be one of those women who lived forever. It had been a difficult year. A year. It hadn't occurred to her, it was coming up to the anniversary. A year was enough time to begin the process, she reasoned. Ivy would forgive her, after all. She would want her to feel at home.

Madeline fetched a bin bag and her Marigolds. She began with the drawers, neatly folding up each item and arranging them in piles on the floor. Underwear, stockings, shapewear. Not suitable for reuse, they could go into a textile recycling bin. Tops, trousers, blouses, all organised and stacked into piles ready for charity donation. She cleaned out each drawer as she emptied it. Drawers gleaming and ready for donation, she turned her attention to the wardrobe.

Jackets, coats, pullovers. All arranged into further assorted charity piles. Ivy's scent floated delicately in the air as Madeline took each off their hangers. She shivered a little. It was as though Ivy was there with her, watching.

It's going to charity, it will help someone else.

You're a good person.

She placed the hangers aside, ready for reuse in her own new wardrobe when she got it. Madeline didn't have many clothes and so had little use for a wardrobe, but she did need a place to hang her uniform and a few jackets. The wardrobe emptied, cleaned, she started on the ornaments.

Ivy loved her ornaments, as many her age did. Small birds, of every description. Ceramic, porcelain, delicate and faded on one side where they had been damaged in the sun over time. The little robin seemed to stare at her as she moved around the room. She gathered an empty box from the garage, left over from her own move. She pulled off the label 'crockery', and wrote a new label 'charity – ornaments', sticking it in its place. Carefully bubble wrapping each little bird, she placed them one by one in the box. The robin looked at her longingly as she picked him up from his watch post. She studied him curiously. He was beautiful. He held his beak high, proudly displaying his redbreast, untouched by the sun. The porcelain was strangely cold to the touch, but his body glinted in the light as she moved him between her fingers. If she squinted, she imagined he could spread his delicate wings and take flight from her hand. His small, black eyes watched her as she took him in. He had seen a lot in this room, she had no doubt about that. She remembered him well. She would keep him. A reminder. Madeline polished him up carefully and placed him softly back on the windowsill. He stood alone, but tall in his watch.

Labelling another box as 'charity – clothing, elderly. Size 14', she packed up the neat piles of clothing she had made earlier. The rest, stained, worn and threadbare went into a bin bag, ready for recycling with the hosiery and underwear. It had taken a few hours, but finally, Madeline stepped back and admired her work.

The room already felt fresher, lighter, as if it were forgetting the traumas of its past. But the bed was hovering over her like a bad smell. She sighed. It wasn't suitable for reselling, or even donation. This would have to be dumped. But driving a Ford KA there was no chance she could fit it in her car, even if she could lift it by herself.

Tiredly, she found her phone and pulled up his number. It only rang twice before he answered excitedly.

'Hey!'

'Hey, Freddie. Sorry to call you out of the blue–'

'No, that's okay! It's great to hear from you! I thought I'd upset you, after last night!' *Last night?* Madeline went blank, her mind rattling going over the events of last night. No, she was well rested, she had been here, she hadn't gone out... had she? As the panic began to descend on her, with a pang, she remembered.

'I'm so sorry! I meant to text you when I got in last night, it slipped my mind. I had a great time, but I needed to get back for Timmy. You were sleeping so soundly I didn't want to wake you.'

'Oh, that's okay. That's really good to know, thank you. I was worried I'd upset you or something when I woke up and you'd disappeared!' Madeline felt a little guilty and bit her lip. That wasn't a good thing to do on reflection, run out and leave someone hanging like that.

'Anyway, how are you?' Freddie was chipper, her transgressions forgiven already.

'Yeah, I'm good. Listen, Freddie, sorry but I was actually calling to ask for your help.'

'Oh?'

Within fifteen minutes, the camera app pinged as Freddie pulled his Volvo into her drive. She tried not to wince as it scraped along the side of the hydrangea's, the beautiful bushes shaking violently, discarding its dark green leaves and peppering the drive with small cream petals. She gritted her teeth, plastering on a faux smile, remembering he was here to help. As he stepped into the living area, Timmy danced around excitedly greeting his new friend. Freddie was elated to meet him, laying down on the pink carpet, letting Timmy scramble over his face in joy. She watched the two of them, amused, and left them to it whilst she made them coffee.

She brought the steaming mugs back through to the living area as Freddie sat up. Timmy took the invitation and promptly curled up in his lap. Freddie looked around.

'Nice place you've got here.'

Shit.

She froze. In her haste to get herself organised she hadn't thought this would be the first time he saw the place. A lump in her throat appeared, she thought carefully about her response.

'Thanks. It was my grandmother's.'

'Oh, nice,' he nodded thoughtfully. 'Was?' Madeline narrowed her eyes at him.

'Yes. She passed away about a year ago.' She watched his reaction carefully. His face dropped a little, the tilt of his head conveying sympathy.

'Oh. I'm sorry to hear that,' he said, sincerely. 'I lost my grandmother a few years ago. It doesn't get easier, does it?' Madeline shook her head and lowered her gaze.

'It's a nice space you've got now, though. You're redecorating?' He gestured to the paint stripes on the wall.

'Yeah. I figured it was time.' She placed the mugs down

onto coasters on the coffee table. Cappuccino for her, americano for him.

'Yeah, she wouldn't want you hanging onto the past, I'm sure.' He looked at her kindly. She smiled back, saying nothing. She opened and closed her mouth, willing the conversation to move on. Thankfully, she didn't need to worry. He took charge.

'Right, shall we look at getting the mattress in as our coffees are cooling?' he asked as he tried to stand. Timmy, disgruntled, moved off of his lap reluctantly, allowing him up off the floor. Madeline followed him as he stepped over to inspect the mattress. He stepped into the room, the boxes and bin bags now sitting neatly in the corner.

'Wow.' His eyebrows shot up his head. He looked at Madeline, nervously. 'Sorry. Sorry. I didn't mean to react like that. You weren't kidding when you said it was in a bad way.' Madeline nodded, following his gaze to the large brown stain over the covering. There was no hiding it.

'This was where she died.' Madeline told him quietly. 'I'm sure you know better than anyone, people lose control of their bodily functions when they pass. It can get... quite messy... I just wish... Wish I could have been there at the end...' Freddie gave a small smile and pulled her in for a hug. She burrowed her face into his chest.

'Sorry. It's just not a nice memory...'

'It's okay. You will have done everything you could. Let's get rid of these bad memories, and focus on the happy ones, yeah?'

Madeline rested her head into his chest. Her heart rate quickened.

'Yeah.'

The mattress was heavier than it looked. They both grunted and groaned from the exertion in getting it off the frame and into the living room. Their progress was hampered by a frolicking Timmy around their ankles. However, after a bit of gusto, they managed to squeeze it down the hallway and out of the door, into the boot of Freddie's Volvo. The boot wouldn't close but Freddie tied the lid down with blue rope he found in the garage, temporarily holding it in place and securing the mattress inside. Exhausted, they collapsed onto the sofa to drink their now lukewarm coffees. Timmy wouldn't leave Freddie alone and she felt another pang of envy. She wondered if he loved her as much as he seemed to other people. She shook the notion from her head quickly.

Freddie had taken the lead, booking their slot at the local recycling centre for half an hour's time. Before they left, Madeline grabbed the textile bag and sat with it on her lap uncomfortably. Freddie put his foot to the floor and she was pinned back in the passenger seat as he flung his car violently down the tarmac.

Cast from side to side as he flew around the corners, taking each around ten miles per hour faster than he should have, she felt the nausea swirling in her stomach. She whacked her head on the window as he whipped them around a roundabout, letting out a little *ow*, but he appeared not to notice. Finally, they pulled into the recycling centre and Madeline was granted a break from the hellish rollercoaster ride of death.

They dumped the mattress and the textiles, and Madeline discovered the centre had a large furnishing charity shop. She popped in and booked a collection next day for the clothing, trinkets and ornaments, and the furniture. She took a deep breath before she hesitantly climbed back into the Volvo for another wild ride home.

Freddie didn't stay for long after he dropped her back. He was due to begin a series of night shifts, but they kissed passionately goodbye before he left. It felt nice. She could get used to this feeling.

Her phone *pinged* as the door shut, and she turned the key, locking her and Timmy safely inside. Timmy went back to his position in his bed and she made to start dinner when she heard the *ping* again. Her hand flew to her phone, the notification tone making her heart stop. Maybe it's the postman, she prayed. She pulled up the camera app and froze. Back door camera, image detected. She clicked on it, willing it load, jabbing at her screen. The notification disappeared. Furrowing her brow, she searched the images diligently. Nothing. She raced over to the kitchen window, pulled herself onto the worktop, face to the pane. Scanning across the garden, nothing out of place. Not even a cat. Her heart in her mouth, she lowered herself watching the camera again. Bees and butterflies passed the scene, but nothing of significance.

She closed the app. Perhaps it was a glitch, she reasoned. But as she made her vegetable pastry tart for her tea, she couldn't shake the unease and doubt in her gut.

Him

Things must be getting serious. He was here, in her house. He was surprised she hadn't got rid of him yet. That was her usual. Lull them in with a flick of that hair. Make them trust her. She wouldn't hurt a fly. Butter wouldn't melt. All of that. Then, when her trap was set, brutally destroy their lives and leave without a second thought to the trail of destruction she left behind. He'd learned that the hard way. That clumsy buffoon would, too, eventually. He had known it was him visiting. He'd heard the Volvo coming from miles away, the spluttering of the overworked engine interspersed with the squealing braking of the driver. Christ he was a fucking mess.

He had gone back to his old posting in the back garden. He was pissed at having to do it again but he liked this watch post. It afforded a quick and easy getaway at the back, far away from prying eyes. People always show their true colours when they are at home, where they are most relaxed. When they think they aren't being watched. If he was going to get her, it had to be when she felt most safe. He knew how to avoid the back camera now. It was a good camera, but it still had its black spots and he expertly navigated through them as he drew up underneath the window.

He was so close now. He could feel it. He heard them chattering inside, that moron in there with him. He risked a peek, standing slowly and peering through the pane. The bloke was tall, gangly. He was sure he would have been nice in any other circumstances, but now he needed to go, he was threatening to ruin everything. He would be next. Run for your life you fucking clown. If only he knew the danger he was in.

He stayed, crouched, head just peeking through the glass. Through the kitchen, into the living room, he saw them leave. He heard the slam of two car doors from the other side of the gate and relaxed his position. The wretched squeak of the wheels being spun and the protest of the machinery told him the engine had been started. His muscles ached from the stress position he had been in. He pulled up the app and watched them pull away. He didn't need the camera really. He was sure he could hear that Volvo from the next village along.

Relaxing a little he sat, legs outstretched in front of him, leaning against the wall. Debating.

What did it hurt? She was gone. He would have warning. It was risky. He didn't know how long they would be out. But he had to get in, get closer. Ducking underneath the back camera, he picked the lock to the back door and let himself in. The dog, Sooty he had named it, bounded over to him. Sooty never barked. He patted the dog and got to work.

She had been busy. He saw stripes of paint upon the walls and the larger of the bedrooms was cleared out. He took a moment to look over the labelled boxes and glanced at the curious robin on the windowsill. It didn't look the kind of ornament a young person would have, but what did he know. He hated this kind of crap anyway, they would be straight in for charity if it was down to him. He moved into the spare room. Where he knew her things were.

He had been interrupted previously, but this time, he would have warning. He took his time, extracting each item from its place in her drawers. He studied them closely. Hairs, skin, anything. They were clean. He looked over at the laundry basket in the corner of the room. Bingo.

He delved deeply, his fingers grazing and caressing each of her dirty thongs, bras, worn tops and leggings. He brought his nose to each, inhaling deeply. A mix of discharge and sweat filled his senses. But it wasn't what he was looking for.

He strolled out of the spare room and through to the kitchen. Sooty trotted alongside him happily. Washing machine. He dug through its contents. His fingers sank into the soggy fabric. He pulled it out. Leggings by the looks of this. Damp and caked in mud. Useless. Her dog walking clothes were of no help to him. He stood, irritated. An old vase sat on the side of the worksurface. It was made of some kind of stone, cracked in places. Made to look old. 'Vintage.' He sneered. These pointless fucking vases. He hated this kind of décor. She'd put some fake flowers in it. Fucking pointless, useless clutter. The flowers even looked fake, plastic and fabric fraying at the corners. What was the point in having this shit around. Tacky as fuck. Vulgar and cheap. Just like her. It made him hate her even more.

His phone pinged. The camera. Fuck. He'd been caught up again, too immersed. He hadn't even heard the Volvo. He raced back to the back door, letting himself out and quietly reinstated the lock into its 'locked' position. He heard their muffled voices in the hallway. He froze. And heard the front door slam again. Had they gone? Curious to see what was going on, he ran back over to the window. In his haste, he had forgotten the camera at the back. Fuck.

The app pinged, and he fumbled with his phone desperately as he killed the image. Stooped under the window, he stalled. Her pale face appeared at the window, looking out. It was haunting, seeing her appear like that. That face would haunt him in his dreams. His ever present, waking nightmare. She disappeared back into the house. Without waiting this time, he took the covert path across the garden and flipped himself over the fence.

15

Madeline

It had been a few days since Timmy last had a walk and Madeline felt a little guilty. Since purging the room of Ivy's things, she found a new lease of excitement and had cracked on with the rest of her list. She had gathered more paint samples, more neutrals, and settled on Egyptian Grey in the living area and Hessian Cream in the bedrooms. Arming herself with an arsenal of decorating tools and equipment, she got painting, finding it strangely therapeutic. It was hard and messy work, but she thrived off the exertion. It wasn't the same as her usual release, but it was a different kind of soothing. She focussed on the living area first and was surprised to find how much cleaner the room looked after just one coat. She moved onto to the bedrooms whilst waiting for the living room walls to dry. Whilst one room dried, another was painted. She moved efficiently between the three rooms. Ivy had chosen a particularly nauseating shade of lime green in the bedrooms, and it took three coats before it started to cover. She stood, covered in sweat and paint splatters, surveying her handiwork at the end of the day.

Madeline had taken Ivy's decorative wall plates into the

local charity shop, exchanging them for some cheap, tasteful prints in delicate frames. She stuck with the bird theme, and chose three beautiful artsy watercolours, a swallow, a bluetit, and, of course, a robin. They sat in a row on the wall, the robin in the centre. He was her favourite. She treated herself to a new bedframe and mattress, ordered online and due for delivery next week. It was flatpack, cheaper to order it that way. She would get Freddie's help with the assembly.

She scoured the Facebook reselling pages for a wardrobe and found a pine one that fit the bill. The seller was local and had kindly offered to deliver the wardrobe to her for an extra two quid. It didn't match her drawers, but in her research she had learned it was fairly cheap and easy to do something called 'upcycling'. She sanded them down, bought more paint, and painted them both in a tasteful dove grey. She needed to wait for them both to dry, but they were already looking better. Clean and fresh. Ivy's aroma that had been hanging around the room was now replaced by the soft scent of paint fumes. She took a deep breath and breathed it in. The smell of fresh beginnings.

She had been working on her new bedroom around her shifts. Joan had still been visiting whilst she was at work, but her mobility prevented her from taking Timmy out for a walk. He was bouncing off the walls, and so Madeline decided to put the paint brush down, and head out to the lake.

The minute they stepped out into the hazy sunshine, it was as if they were both in autopilot. Timmy knew where they were going and he took the lead. Her steps quickened as the urge grew. She hadn't realised how much she had missed this walk, but the anticipation of getting there was now guiding her feet.

They passed the cottages, barely acknowledging the gardeners today. That was rude of her, she knew, but she had to get there. The feeling was pulling her in, its rope around her waist, the urgency increasing with every step. They hastened down the cut-through and turned right.

They flew past the other cut-throughs and dodged the familiar pile of dog poo and, finally, the valley began to drop. Madeline's feet hurried in excitement. She held her breath, anticipating the wave of serenity, begging for the clear waters, the sparkle of the sun on its surface, the magic. Her Swan Lake. She could almost smell it. She could practically taste it on her tongue. The valley dropped and finally... She stopped. Her feet wouldn't move. Her heart shattered.

Yellow tape reflected the sun, thrashing in the breeze. She could hear it ripping through the air, slicing the wind into two. It was everywhere. Fixed around the lake edge, the ugly colour destroying the beauty of the water, defiling its wonder. Gone were the ducks, the insects, the area was crawling with white figures, white boilersuits, climbing over and under the offending tape in their hoards. A white tent had been erected on the far side in the distance, the florescent yellow and blue of the vehicles in the surrounding fields. Police. Swarming the lake. Her lake. The serenity she had felt building imploded in her core. Bile rose in her mouth as she took in the scene. Their presence had attracted a crowd up ahead. She could see the footpath had been cordoned off, blocking public access down to the valley.

Heart thumping, she held Timmy's lead close. She treaded slowly in the dirt, cautiously joining the crowd of gawping spectators. She could hear the excitable gossiping of the locals, theorising and speculating. She came to a halt next to a woman.

'What happened?' she asked her softly. The woman turned to her, her eyes lit up from the drama.

'A body was found in the lake this morning. Can you believe it! In our little village!'

'It's sad is what it is, you shouldn't be taking such delight in the suffering of another.' An elderly man tutted at her. The woman rolled her eyes.

'I'm not taking delight, Alfred, the lady asked!'

'Well, tell your face,' Alfred grumbled. Madeline gazed across the lake, feeling sick. A body found.

'Drowning,' the woman said simply. She had crossed her arms and was staring back across the valley. 'I hope it was accidental, in a way. It's a horrible thought, thinking someone could be in such a dark place to do it deliberately, you know?' Madeline nodded. She watched the officers in their suits from afar, specks in the distance as they surveyed the scene. On the path beyond, she saw a pair of tottering figures making their way down to the tape. One was holding a camera. News had picked up on it already. They were quick out here, it seemed.

The woman was still imparting her idle conjecture on her, but she couldn't concentrate. Not being able to bear looking at the scene any longer, Madeline turned away. She felt on edge. Sick. It wasn't just the body being found, she hadn't realised how itchy her mind had become. She had needed to see the lake. Timmy was as unbothered as ever and continued to sniff and trot along happily. They climbed back up the footpath, and Madeline could see another walker up ahead. She was with a chocolate labrador, off its lead. The lab squatted, doing its business. To her surprise, she watched as the woman waited for it and proceeded to carry on her route. The woman looked up, noticing Madeline watching her and stalled in her tracks. Madeline narrowed her eyes curiously at the reaction, silently daring her. She and Timmy continued on their way. A flit of panic passed over the woman's face and she glanced back at the fresh dog waste, sitting on the path. Sheepishly, the woman rolled her eyes and huffed, pulling out a small black bag. She picked up the waste, glancing at Madeline as they continued towards them. Madeline dodged the same pile they had walked past on the way, and the woman looked at her guiltily, before tossing her hair back and calling her dog. The lab bounded off ahead, and the women passed one another. Madeline said nothing, allowing her face to do the talking as the woman retorted with a scowl of her own. Trying to appease her guilt no doubt. Caught in the act. She knew what she had done.

Madeline was disappointed not to have got to the lake, but she needed to get rid of her nervous energy. A body. A body had been found. The woman's words replayed endlessly in her head, stirring up the nausea from her gut. They carried on past the cut-through and made their way to the path that ran past the back of the bungalows instead. She gazed across the fields. It wasn't the allure of the lake, but it just about did the job. She closed her eyes and inhaled the scent for a moment. They came upon the fences that ran at the back of her row, and suddenly, Timmy started. He chased off to the fence and started scrapping at it wildly.

'Timmy!' Madeline called angrily. She pulled on his lead,

but he hauled at it more, jumping and scratching at the wood. Madeline looked around. What would other walkers think, what would the owners of the property think of her dog going at their fence like that? She finally got Timmy away and realised she recognised it was her fence.

She stopped, scrutinising the panels. Maybe he knew it was home. Or perhaps, it was the cat. Yes, that was it, it would be that cat, winding him up again. It must be somewhere in the garden, taking advantage of the lack of Scottie guard. She breathed away the tension, but the walk had not blown away her unease from the lake. She suddenly had the feeling she should go home. She looked at the fence for a moment. It was tempting just to shimmy over. She looked down at Timmy. No, it was dangerous. She could get over, no problem, but she would never get him over safely. With a sigh, she turned and walked the twenty-four minutes to her front door instead.

Being here now, with that little dog beside you reminds me of her, too. She had a dog as well, you know. Vile, horrible creature. And the dog, too.

She had potential, I saw it. But her arrogance ended up beating out any hope of forgiveness. I gave her the chance, and she chose not to take it. I'm usually a dog person. But it was dangerous. That fucking dog went for me in the end. I guess it was trying to defend her, in its own stupid way. I felt the crunch of its skull when it impaled itself on my blade. It shook the bones in my hand in a way I've never felt before. I quite enjoyed that. I stabbed it, right in between the eyes as it launched itself at me. I saw the terror in hers. I ripped the knife out and slashed at it again. Funnily enough, it didn't make another sound, but fuck me. She did. She screamed. And screamed. And I lapped it up, I bathed in it.

I hogtied this one and did the same to her. Right between the eyes. The terror never left her, and I pleasured myself right there on her body.

Just goes to show, my love. I'm a reasonable person. But never piss me off. You will regret it. They all do.

16

Madeline

The report of the body in the lake hit the local news that night. Madeline watched gloomily as the journalist dutifully gave his report to the camera, her lake glittering in the background. Sadly, the woman had drowned, they reported. Her family were interviewed. She had been identified as thirty-six-year-old Irene Joseph. The image of the sad, dogeared notices on the streetlights flitted through Madeline's mind. *MISSING.* And now found. Apparently, she was an addict, and her family had spent many heartbreaking years watching her abuse her body with an array of substances. She was known to take off on binges, get herself caught up in trouble. But this time, the trouble had come to her. Drugs and alcohol were found in her system, but her cause of death was drowning. The corner ruled accidental death. Madeline sighed. She looked at Timmy, sleeping soundly on the sofa next to her. No wonder Irene had been so unreliable, she couldn't rely on herself to get clean. It was no life. What a sad end.

The camera switched back to the studio. There had been no further updates on the suspect in custody, and no more bodies discovered in the area. Even Tony the bird watcher had not made an appearance, and Madeline felt a pang of disappointment. She'd been enjoying his updates. The local anchor ran through their bulletins; a councillor resigned after allegations of sexual misconduct, a fundraiser for repairs to a church, the inspiring journey of a young boy with Leukaemia. And an in depth look at the predicted effects of the impending strikes on Lunnemouth General.

Those strikes. The talk of definite strike action was growing as union negotiations with governments were breaking down. The government was refusing to budge, and so unions were ramping up the pressure. Madeline had received several emails from her union, encouraging her to *"take a stand"*. She had deleted them all without reading any further. She knew Freddie was prepared to strike if needed, but it didn't sit right with her. She kept thinking of those patients, the ones who relied on them so much for their care. She didn't go into the NHS for the money. She did it for love of the job, for the care of those around her. They were playing with lives in a twisted way.

After a few days, the cordons around the lake were cleared away and access was reopened. Madeline and Timmy were free to take one of their favourite walks again. However, for Madeline, it was tainted. The heavy boots of the officers had trodden mud on the smooth dirt track around the water. The once gentle, sloping banks at the lake edge were churned from the depths of their investigations. The clear water that had been so pleasant before was muddied and clouded, contaminated with filth. Youths hung around, chortling and joking about the ghost of the lake, leaving their empty beer cans trampled into the edge. Girls squealed as their boyfriends pushed them in laughing, pretending to see the tragic ghoul rising from the depths. Locals had now made this their preferred route, desperate to be a part of the drama to distract from their menial lives. There was constant gossip and theories to be overheard from every generation around the path. Madeline just shook her head and walked on.

It pleased Madeline to note that the footpath at the back of the sixties houses had remained clear from any dog foul, however. She wasn't sure whether it was a coincidence, whether the woman was truly the culprit but after a few trips, she confirmed no new waste was being left. She smiled to herself. Her unexpected exchange with the walker of the lab had worked, it seemed. Residents were now free to stride out confidently, without constantly looking down at their feet for fear of stepping on a smelly brown land mine.

Her new bed arrived, and like the gentleman he was, Freddie came over to help her assemble it. It went surprisingly well, considering. She felt she could have put it together quicker by herself in the end, but it was cute to watch him concentrate on the instructions. She played her part, allowing him to exercise a lesser-used part of his DNA; the testosterone-fuelled DIY fix-it genes that rear in any man presented with flatpack. His tongue poked through his lips as he matched the bolts and nuts up to the diagram meticulously, laboriously screwing everything in by hand. They consummated the new bed hungrily and they laid there together afterwards in each other's arms. Timmy poked his head through the door and trotted in curiously, before jumping up to join them and nestling himself in the down.

Madeline had smiled and Freddie petted him gently.

Almost like a family.

She could get used to this if she wanted. It was a nice feeling, this touch of normality. Now her past was far behind her, she found herself wistfully dreaming of her future. She imagined her and Freddie, taking Timmy for long walks at the beach. Moving in together. A ring on her finger. Perhaps a swollen belly, growing their child together. A future like this. Something she had never dreamed of. It had always seemed so out of reach, she had never even thought to dream of it. But finally, she was starting to believe she could.

Good things come to those who wait.

Things weren't quite so rosy in her professional life, though. Work was draining and her matron was no help. They were constantly short-staffed, sometimes dangerously so. Madeline found she frequently missed her breaks in trying to cover just the basics of her role. Nurses were going off sick left right and centre from the constant pressure and the ward's solution was to get cover from bank. Bank staff were okay as a one off, but there was a different nurse each shift now. All of whom needed to be shown around, guided through the clinical systems before disappearing again. Madeline would then have to do the same the next day, the next night, again and again. It made for a chaotic time, with so much turnover and disruption. And when Madeline and her team tried to bring it up with their matron, she mysteriously disappeared.

'Shirking her responsibilities,' Kayla had muttered angrily. Madeline had not made a comment, but privately agreed. The matron may have other wards, but she needed to step up to her duty of care to all, both patients and staff. Madeline had tried to vent her frustrations to Freddie, but when she started to discuss it, he would react in an irritatingly calm manner.

'This is why we are striking, babe,' he stated simply. Madeline bit her lip and turned over in bed. She wasn't expecting him to react with anger, or be as frustrated, but a little more passion, the fire she had seen a glimpse of, that wouldn't go amiss.

But she couldn't deny he was a calming influence on her. He was scatty and disordered, it was true, but now she understood his actions were never deliberate. If he tripped and bumped into someone when they were strolling around Lunnemouth town centre, he would immediately apologise. He hated to be late, she learned this was the reason he was constantly in a rush. This persistent haste had bled through into his driving, she learned. She had even broached the parking situation with him. They had just made love again, in his bed, Timmy downstairs. She told him it bothered him. It wasn't fair on pedestrians to leave a car so far on the pavement like that. She was nimble, but the elderly or a young child having to go on the road to get around, it wasn't safe. But she was shocked when instead of denying, arguing, or justifying his parking, he turned bright red. His eyes misted over and he opened and closed his mouth like a fish. He told her he was mortified. He hadn't realised it was so bad, so unsafe and so noticeable. He said he would change. His response softened her heart and she pulled him into her embrace. She offered to help him with his organisation, it would help stop him being late and rushing around. He agreed. If he was in less of a hurry all the time, he would have more time to concentrate on parking properly. She felt she was a good effect on him, too.

As the days went by, they spent more and more time together. She relaxed more, enjoying the new light feeling in her body. They explored surrounding villages with Timmy and checked out a few of the restaurants in town. Madeline was a creature of habit, but he somehow managed to convince her to try Thai and sushi. She wasn't a fan of the idea of raw fish but was surprised to learn she liked a little spice.

He always lingered in the back of her mind, though. She was still strict with herself to keep an eye on the news throughout all her activities. There had been no further developments, no further bodies found, and so it eased her slightly. But the little niggle of doubt had started to emerge once more. That same feeling. She was missing something. Something potentially costly. It was curious they had not released his name to the public yet. She knew the police usually waited until a suspect was charged. But still. They had him. It wouldn't be long. Surely?

Madeline looked up and around at the pub now, that feeling suddenly making the hair on the back of her neck stand up. Freddie was busy devouring his pie, oblivious to her mind in other places. She scoured around the area. Everyone was busy enjoying their meals, their drinks, their socialising. No one was paying her any attention, and there were no strange shadows that darted away. She stabbed at her chicken in front of her, trying to relax and forget the prickle on her neck.

It is fine.

No one is watching you anymore.

Freddie suddenly looked up and reached for his pint.

'You okay?' he asked, taking a glug. Madeline faked what she hoped was a convincing smile and nodded her head.

'Absolutely fine. Are you?'

'Mhmm.' He had just shovelled in another mouthful of pie. She watched him and turned her attention back to her own dinner. He swallowed noisily.

'What are you thinking about so seriously?' he chuckled. She poked the chicken with her fork. Appetite gone.

'Nothing really.'

'No. It's not nothing. What's going on?'

'Honestly, nothing. Just have a lot on my mind.'

'Oh?' He was gazing at her expectantly. She debated for a moment. She trusted him. She did. But not that much.

'It's nothing major, don't worry.' She made a show of cutting the chicken and stabbing it with her utensils. 'I was thinking about these strikes.' An excuse. It wasn't a lie. It just wasn't the whole truth. A loophole. He put down his cutlery and leaned into her. Showing her he was listening. He cared.

'What about the strikes, babe?'

'You know... The idea just makes me uncomfortable.' The chicken stared at her from her fork. She put it in her mouth and chewed. Moist, garlic, and butter. Hints of basil and parsley. Delicious in other circumstances.

'I know it does.' He reached a hand across the table and she put hers into his palm. He squeezed it reassuringly.

'Do you think they will actually happen?' she blurted. She had not prepared this question. This was something that genuinely concerned her. He shrugged and stroked her hand with his thumb.

'I don't know. It is looking that way, yeah. But you know

you have a choice, don't you? Just because your union is striking, you don't have to.'

'I know. And you have a choice, too. You could choose not to.' She pleaded with her eyebrows, looking deep in his eyes. He sighed and withdrew his hand.

'I could. But it wouldn't solve anything for me. I was only able to afford my house here because my parents gave me the deposit. I studied for six years, at a top university. And I make less than Dave the electrician down the road.' He looked up at her seriously. 'Do you think that's fair?' She considered the point.

'No. I don't think it's fair. But I don't think you getting paid what you deserve should come at the cost of innocent lives. People could die.'

'People won't die, unless they were already going to die,' he retorted sharply. 'I am sorry if that is harsh, Madeline. But it's true. Emergency care won't change. Those that are admitted life threatening conditions are already dancing on the edge of a knife. That is why it is emergency. We fight hard to save them, but even despite us doing everything we can they still slip away. But, if we strike for better pay, better conditions, then we have a chance of retaining the better doctors, encouraging the education of even more. In the long run, the strikes will save lives.' She sat absorbing his words.

'What about those admitted, then? The urgents. They will be affected. If they pass away in the middle of the night and there's skeleton staff. Something could have been done… Someone could be there to hold their hand, ease their passing…' Madeline trailed off, Ivy's face swimming before her eyes once more. He didn't say anything. He just bowed his head and stared at his plate. He remained mute as he picked his knife and fork up and resumed eating. They sat in silence whilst he finished his pie and she prodded at her chicken.

He walked her home later. Timmy was waiting for them, delighted to see his new friend. They watched late night TV together for a bit, and Freddie sat with his arm around her, looking at her longingly. Madeline knew he was asking for an invitation to stay, but she wasn't in the mood. She needed to think. He took the hint and kissed her delicately on the cheek before letting himself out. Timmy chased after him and she heard the door shut. She sighed. Timmy jogged back in, looking at her confused. She heaved herself up and locked the front door. Checked her phone. 22:56.

Despite everything, she pulled up her messages and sent a quick text.

Let me know when you are home.

It was the right thing to do. Out of habit, she pulled up the camera app and did a quick scan of the images. Nothing. Nothing all night. It should have relieved her. She waited for the usual feeling of that great weight to be lifted. But it didn't come. Her shoulders sagged with an unusual heaviness. Her chest felt like a burden pulling on her body, her mind numb. There was no urge for a release, no need for a list. She was surprised to find a tear prickling at her lashes. With a sigh, she recognised the feeling. Sadness. She was sad. It didn't happen very often. It hadn't occurred to her how much she would come to care for Freddie. But she couldn't ignore the facts. She knew she couldn't change people, as much as she could try. Nor could she change her values, who she was, just for a man.

She put Timmy out and got ready for bed. Her phone

pinged.

Home safe. Thank you for a lovely evening.

The back door camera pinged through, and she swiped to ignore it. Timmy was at the back door and she let him in before she took herself to bed.

There's still time. It doesn't have to be this way.

The thought laid heavily on her. The hope he would change. That she wouldn't have to have him out of her life this soon. She didn't want to, she really didn't. She sighed and pulled the sheet. Her mind was torn, pieces splintering. She fell into a broken sleep, full of uncertainty.

Him

She looked happy. It enraged him. He couldn't believe that clown was still sticking around. Not for much longer.

He had been foolish. He'd been searching in all the wrong places. Going through her dirty laundry had given him a sick pleasure, a sadistic power, but it wasn't why he was there. He watched as they left for the evening, hand in hand, strolling down the street. They had no care in the world. She was more relaxed, less vigilant. Perhaps this clown was good for him, after all. Keeping her distracted. He followed at a safe distance, as they made their way down to the local. He followed them in and ordered a drink at the bar. To any onlooker, he was just a normal bloke. They would think he were a local. A tradie, perhaps. Just looking forward to his well-earned pint at the end of a long day. Well, his pint was earned. If he didn't have a trade it didn't matter. He was still working hard.

He sat at the bar, listening to the conversations of other patrons around him. Nothing of note. A few whispers about the murders in the area, theories being flung out. Things had gone quiet, they reckoned the murderer was laying low, waiting for things to blow over, maybe he had moved out of the area, or the police had caught the guy after all. He smirked. If only they knew they were in touching distance of the preparator. Hiding in plain sight. Not laying low as such, rather flaunting themselves in broad daylight. Not running scared, but planning the next. Finishing his pint, he glanced around. They had just received food. Excellent. Plenty of time.

He slipped out of the pub and made his way out through the small passages between the houses to the fields beyond. Out here, he hastened his pace along the footpath, breaking into a sprint, making his way to the fence. He climbed over easily. He was used to this now. He knew to avoid the panel that gave him splinters. Land with knees slightly bent and roll. He crept up to the bungalow, avoiding camera detection and picked the lock. The door swung open.

He stepped inside the garage. Piles of boxes, paint cans and various decorating equipment, garden pots, spades, and tools. Blue rope and packaging. His eyes fell upon the cardboard boxes, unemptied and still sealed with parcel tape. He read the labels. *Uni work. Trophies. Madeline childhood.*

Useless. Her old trophies were of no use to him whatsoever. He was momentarily glad she was so anal, everything was labelled in here. It did make his work easier.

He stalked around the garage. Searching for... He didn't know what. He would know something when he saw it. Anything. Anything that gave him information. He didn't want any nasty surprises.

He stopped. There. Peeking out of the opened box balanced on the shelf. A clump of blonde hair. His heart racing, he found a stool and hurriedly moved it under the shelf. He leapt up, and slowly, shaking, reached his fingers up. He shuddered as his fingertips grazed the mane. He wrapped his fingers around the strands. Closing his eyes. He imagined her now, her face as he wound his hand tighter. Closed his grip. Opened his eyes. Pulled it out. Gently does it. Resisting at first, before easing into the movement. Easy now. The wig fell free. It dangled in his tightened fist and he brought it to his nose. Inhaling. He breathed her in, all of her. He could smell her scalp. The smell of her shampoo that lingered within. It was her. He recalled the moment he had laid eyes on her in this wig. He knew it was her instantly. He would know who she was no matter how she tried to disguise herself. She hadn't seen him. She thought she could hide herself from him, she thought she was so clever. All it takes is a blonde wig and she's invisible? He wasn't that stupid. He held it to his chest, savouring the moment.

He checked the time. He was sure they would only just be finishing their meal by now, but he had been caught so many times before he didn't want to risk it. Not when he was so close now. Backing quietly out of the garage, he relocked the door. He darted back through the garden and over the fence to the footpath.

I love watching you, my love. It gives me such a pleasure you would never understand. Look at you. Those come-hither cheekbones, that luscious hair, your smooth skin. Don't get me started on that body of yours. God, you are quite sexy, did you know that? Of course you do.

I remember the first time I saw you, all those years ago. Remember? We were at school, then. That was a long time ago now, but it's funny, to me you don't look any different. You broke my heart when you went off with that other guy, did you know that? I don't know if you cared, but you care now.

It was fate. Fate that brought you back into my life. I knew, I knew you were the one. The minute I saw you. It was three years ago, almost to the day. My ticket to a better life. It's all you, my love.

Christ. Yeah, you are sexy. Even watching you now, you just turn me on. It would be fun. We could be so good together, together forever.

But don't think that will deter me tonight. I know who you are, you see. Who you really are. You thought you could hide, but I know your little secret.

17

Madeline

Madeline felt a twinge of sadness as she checked her phone. Nothing. The tension from their date had left a lot unsaid. She knew they disagreed on the issue, but she had hoped she could change his mind. She wasn't ready to make any decisions.

You can't change everyone.

She sighed. Checked the camera. Nothing. Not even a postman. Joan should be arriving soon for her little date with Timmy. She suspected the old woman might enjoy her visits a lot. She had noticed she had been gradually leaving the house later and arriving earlier. She smiled. Timmy had that effect on people. He was such a happy little dog. Always pleased to see someone. It was one of the reasons she had chosen to rescue him. He was a good boy.

Roman came into the break room in a rush of dramatic sighs and stomping feet. She locked her phone and zipped it back into her bag.

'Hey, love.'

'Hi, Roman. How are you doing?'

'Knackered, babes. Absolutely knackered.' He threw

himself onto the chair and exhaled dramatically, stretching his chunky legs out in front of him. 'You okay, babes?'

'Yeah. Yeah, I'm fine.' Madeline pushed her bag back into her locker and shut it. 'Just gearing up to go back.'

'You don't have to leave just because I've come in, you know. The ward will be fine for another thirty minutes. Juniors are doing the rounds, anyway.'

'I know. But I've had half an hour so...'

'Up to you, hun. But don't stress it. We've all missed breaks, you're owed some extra time.' Roman slipped off his sensible shoes, groaning. 'I don't even have the energy to get my salad out.'

'Where is it?'

'In the fridge. No don't, I'm just being lazy.' Madeline had already found Roman's lunch in the small staff fridge behind her and produced it. He grinned cheekily as she passed it to him.

'Thanks, love. That's kind of you.'

'It's no problem. You need a break, too.'

'Mmm. Ain't that the truth,' he said and lowered his voice. 'Have you heard about Martha?' Martha. Who was Martha? The face popped to mind. The matron. Madeline furrowed her brow.

'No. What about Martha?'

'She had a full-blown breakdown on the Clarkson ward the other day.' Roman raised his eyebrows titillatingly. It worked. Madeline was hooked in.

'What?'

'Yep. Full on, hysterical crying, screaming breakdown. Shelly was telling me one of the consultants mentioned something to her about spending three hours trying to track down a nurse on the ward, and she just folded!'

'Wow...'

'I know!' Roman was giddy as he divulged his gossip. 'I bet she's off now. Off sick or something. Stress, anxiety, or depression. You don't just melt down like that without something serious going on, do you?'

'No, I guess you don't.'

'Maybe it's a marriage breakdown or something,' Roman continued. He was determined to engage her in this conversation. It wasn't her style. And she wasn't in the mood to pretend.

'Maybe.'

'Or could be she's hit menopause or something. Hormones, they can really affect you, you know? Couple that with everything that's going on here, well,' he threw his hands up. 'I'd have a menty B, too!' He cackled and Madeline laughed obligingly along. Her laugh didn't quite reach her face. The news troubled her. Martha going off had complicated things a little. She had been counting on her to be a support for the upcoming strikes.

'Anyway, I'd better get back.' Madeline saw Roman's face fall a little as she made her excuses. 'It was nice catching up.'

'Don't work too hard, babes, see you in a bit.'

The rest of her shift passed in a blur. She felt a little bad for Martha, but maybe it was a good thing she was off if she was struggling badly. The strikes wouldn't help if they went ahead, either. The strikes. Her mind drifted again to Freddie. There was still hope for him, but it was clear she would have to wait and see.

You know what you need to do. He needs to go.

Madeline shook the thought. It was early days. She still had time to change his mind. She started her medication rounds, whilst the young care assistant was taking blood pressures. There were televisions in each of the bays on the walls. Usually they were tuned into the radio, but Keith in bed five had insisted on watching BBC One. Apparently he watched it all day, every day at home. Since his stroke, he had lost the use of the left side of his body and required a hoist transfer out to a neuro-chair. But his mind was sharp. If anyone, staff, patient, or family, dared to touch the remote they were instantly reprimanded. She heard the familiar titles of BBC News behind her as she was dispensing tramadol for Ian in bed one.

'Welcome to BBC News at one o'clock. This lunchtime...' Madeline ignored the anchor, moving on to bed two. She had been keeping up with her local news channel as a necessity, but as a whole she didn't like the news. Too many stories about too many terrible people doing too many terrible things. It was always the same. She didn't need to know about all of the horrendous events across the nation, it wasn't any good for her.

She readied a bag of antibiotics for the rarely conscious David. He had barely woken since he arrived but had aspirated on his own saliva and developed a chest infection. An infection for a patient like this could be life threatening, so a good care plan was needed. He was receiving antibiotics and regular chest physiotherapy to keep his lungs clear. As she strung up the bag, she tutted as she noticed he was lying flat. Terrible for a chest. She scowled. Probably that assistant.

She had done his toileting earlier and no doubt left him flat. She grabbed the bed controls and moved him into an upright position, making a mental note to prompt her about this in future.

'Police in the town of Lunnemouth have released a statement this lunchtime, advising the suspect who was arrested in connection with several suspicious deaths in the area has been released on bail. Thirty-four-year-old Pheobe Larter was found in her home...' Madeline whipped around, eyes glued to the screen. A photo of Pheobe Larter flashed onto the screen as the BBC anchor reviewed the details of her case. Another image, forty-two-year-old Maggie Hightown. Gary Mackintosh's face replaced hers. And finally, the latest body identified as fifty-two-year-old Petr Milton, prominent local businessman.

Madeline's vision blurred and she lost her hearing, a maddening white noise in place of any discernible sounds. It filled her head and felt the pressure on the inside of her scalp, pushing out painfully. She could see the anchor's mouth still moving with her report but could not understand any of what she was saying. She turned away in a daze, trying to focus on David's drip. She was grateful he was unconscious. She pretended to check the bag.

Think.

Think.

They released him. They released him on bail. Madeline was panicked, she could feel herself drifting away. Somewhere, in the back of her mind her survival instinct kicked in.

Five things she could see: sheets, IV line, crisp white pillow, red emergency alarm, and poor David. Four things she could hear: the beep of the infusion, David's rattled breaths, the hum of people outside the bay, and her own heart with the TV. Three things she could touch: the cold plastic of the bag, the tube in his arm, the keys around her lanyard. Two things she could smell: disinfectant, urine. One thing she could taste: bile.

She repeated the grounding, finally bringing her mind down and her hearing returned. She was back in the room, but unable to think properly, there were too many distractions. She took twice as long as she usually would to complete her medication round. It took all of her energy to put an act of pretence on and engage in small talk with Keith as she gave him his morphine ready for his physiotherapy that afternoon.

She avoided Roman where she could, pretending to busy herself or darting into the toilet any time she suspected he was making a beeline for her. She could do without his unhelpful chattering at a time like this.

Madeline remained in such a state of high alert as she drove home for the night. The clouds that had covered the sky for most of the day were starting to break, but she was too restless to enjoy how it changed the landscape around her. She held fast to the steering wheel, willing herself to think.

Think!

She pulled into Robin Close and drove slowly. Carefully. Twenty miles per hour. She drove slowly up to the bungalow and watched a young woman walking a flat faced dog along the pavement. It stopped and cocked his leg, relieving itself on the small gate at the front of her garden, the owner allowing it. It was disrespectful, not helping her mind, her panic. She slowed the car. Applied the brakes. Stopped. She waited, tapping her fingers feigning patience for them to pass.

Hold it together.

She indicated to let them know she was waiting for them before she pulled into the drive, clenching her jaw, holding on for dear life. The girl and her dog ambled away and she turned in. Killing the engine she sat.

Now she could think. She could think clearly now.

Remember.

Mistakes are there to be learned from. Plan in place.

What do we know?

She needed to continue. He had been released on bail. Bail meant they hadn't found him innocent, he was out pending further investigation. They couldn't hold him as they didn't have enough evidence. Madeline released the breath she was holding. She knew he would be coming straight for her now. But it didn't matter, as long as she kept her wits about her. Evidence. That was the key. She mustn't take her eyes off the ball.

It wasn't over.

She thought she held a secret, too. She thought she was so mysterious. All over social media, cryptic captions, wistful poses. She thought she was a model.

I remember the first time I saw her, though. She was beautiful, I'll give her that. But a model? Not a chance. When I crept into her room that night and saw her sleeping so peacefully, I didn't want to do it. She wasn't a patch on you, my love, but she came close. Her beautiful curls were laying so carelessly across that silk pillow, and her breasts rose and fell, hypnotising me where I stood. I stayed there and I watched her for a while. Those eyes captivated me and I knew she would be trouble. It was as if they knew who I was, what was going through my mind, what I was there for. She was wielding those breasts, they were pleading with me. Cheeky minx. It almost worked. Almost. But she had to go. She knew the rules.

I brought my favourite knife along, but as I looked at her, I knew I wanted something more personal. I needed to see those eyes one last time.

She was one of those girls that loved pillows. You know the sort. The ones that take twenty minutes every morning meticulously rearranging the millions of decorative pillows for no functional reason whatsoever. Never understood it.

I used the smallest one, little with pom poms over it. I gave it a function. She was laying on her back, those beautiful breasts just visible underneath the thin sheet. It gave me such a thrill as I mounted her carefully. She barely stirred, gave a tantalising little groan at the movement, oh God, I nearly lost control there and then. I don't know how I regained my composure but I had to remember. I

204

was there to get the job done.

Those eyes, those beautiful eyes. They snapped open the minute I placed the pillow over her nose and mouth and applied the pressure. She tried to struggle, sure, but I had her pinned. There never would have been a competition had she managed to fight anyway, but you can't be too careful. I squeezed the life out of her. I was slow, I wanted to savour the moment. Those breasts, god they heaved as she struggled to breathe and I was so aroused it took everything within me to slow myself down. But I did it, and finally those beautiful eyes stood still.

I took my time with her body, bringing myself to ecstasy.

It was all practice. This has all been practice for you. I had to get it right.

18

Madeline

Madeline checked her cameras every thirty minutes. On her rest days she walked Timmy and added more time stamps to her Maps, allowing her release to guide her, prevent the itch from erupting. She had shortened her sleep to four hours, it was just manageable, but even when she crawled into bed she found herself unable to relax like she usually would. She was becoming frantic, she could feel it, but she couldn't stop herself. She kept up appearances with Freddie, though, never letting him suspect anything was different. The tensions from the strikes were forgotten, he appeared to forgive easily. She didn't question it. Wasn't ready to think about that yet. One problem at a time. She asked about his day, invited him out on her turn, she laughed in the right places. He would stay over at hers occasionally and more often she would bring Timmy to his. They took turns to cook for one another or pay for dates and she ensured she stayed in regular text contact. Too long in between each reply, he would suspect something. Too eager with her replies, he would think something was wrong. She was never on her phone much around him, she only checked it when he had left the room and rarely had signal on it anyway. She had to keep pretending.

She had thought about it. It popped up often, the indecision. Freddie had complicated matters, it was undeniable. Her past was harder to disguise when someone got close, but every time she thought she had made her decision she couldn't help but feel drawn back to him. She had become hesitant. She knew what she needed to do, but she couldn't bring herself to do it. Just a little longer. She wanted to keep him just a bit longer.

Her mind turned to *him* instead. He was the one getting in the way. He was the one threatening to ruin it all. Evidence. Evidence was what the police needed to take him in. She couldn't afford for him to slip away again. She added to her lists, keeping her mind ordered. It helped to keep her calm. Focus on the end goal. She knew it was coming but this time she wouldn't be caught unprepared. She had learned so much from the mistakes of her past. Sloppiness, carelessness, impulsiveness. They were all part of her, parts she had worked so hard to keep hidden. Threatening to resurface as her world crumbled around her. It was taxing keeping up the pretence, keeping up with the techniques. It took up so much of her energy in the day and she no longer slept properly, up all hours in the night. It was a malicious cocktail. Now, she battled trying to bury those traits deep down, back where they belonged.

Stay patient.

If he was out, he was watching her. More relentlessly than before, she could be sure of this. Keeping up appearances now wasn't just important for keeping Freddie off any suspicions, but for protecting herself.

She continued with her decorating, never truly deciding on a paint colour from the swatches for the kitchen. She just picked the nearest tester from her selection and bought two cans. She painted when she could, no longer enjoying the exertion. It had been a coping mechanism, a distraction from the constant itch in her brain and the relentless threat. But now it felt like a prison of her own. She was caged.

Not long now.

You'll be free again soon.

Her rest days had rolled around too fast again. She had signed herself up for extra shifts at work. She figured that amongst the tensions of the incoming strikes it would seem to be the normal thing to do. The right thing to do. At least it sat well with her. It gave her only one day off and even on that day she found herself angsty. She thought about heading to a flooring specialist place, having a look at samples. But she couldn't bring herself to do it.

You won't be around to enjoy it.

No. She mustn't think that way. They would get him. She had to put her trust in the police, it was out of her hands. She was pulled from her thoughts by a hearty sigh to her left. Freddie sat next to her on the sofa, elbow on the arm, head in his hand. She studied his face. He looked tired, she noticed. More tired than usual. His frown lines were deeper and there were discernible bags under his eyes. His hair looked more unkempt than she thought possible. There were visible tangles in the strands. He seemed to sleep well when she was with him, perhaps he was being kept up by an inner dilemma, too.

We all have our secrets we want to bury.

The TV blared as the drums rolled and dramatic graphics danced across the screen. Time for the news. Madeline stiffened and braced herself. Freddie didn't move, but she noticed he threw a curious look her way. She ignored the glance, eyes fixed on the screen. Desperate for any updates.

'Tonight. Police are still searching for evidence in a series of murders committed in the Lunnemouth area following the release of a suspect on bail.'

Freddie reached for the remote next to her, startling her out of her posture. He threw his hands up.

'Sorry! Sorry. I was just going to change the channel.'

'Oh, erm… okay. I mean…' Madeline stuttered out of her trance. Freddie stared back at her blankly. He blinked. The bulletins thundered on.

'And the latest on the strikes as unions inch closer to industrial action.' Freddie narrowed his eyes, still gazing at her.

'What, you want to watch it?'

'Erm, no. No, it's okay,' Madeline stammered. She shifted her body, sitting on her hands. The itch grew, like a thousand tiny insects scuttling in her brain.

He's coming.

Need to be prepared.

Get rid of him. He's complicating everything.

'Okay, good. There's a really good series that's just started.' Freddie picked up the remote, flicking through the channels. Madeline watched on stiffly.

Act normal. Breathe. Five things. Five things.

Freddie hadn't noticed her changed demeanour, chattering away about this new TV show he had heard about. Madeline felt her eye twitch from the tension, battling the fire

209

under her skull. She needed the news. She needed to know if they were any closer to catching him. Desperately, she tried to recall her grounding, unable to concentrate as Freddie jabbered on. Five things she could smell, no wait. Five she can taste, touch. No. That's wrong. Murders. There was blood everywhere. He's coming. He's coming to get me...

'Madeline!' Freddie's voice tore across her mind, bringing her back to the room. She realised her jaw was clenched, her eyes wide and her body stiff as a board. She was sat on her hands. They were starting to tingle. He searched her worriedly.

'Madeline, what the hell is the matter with you?'

'Nothing. Nothing at all.' Her mouth was dry. She didn't like to lie. But she had no other choice. It made little difference, she could see he wasn't the slightest convinced. He was boring holes through her.

'It's clearly something. Look at you. What's going on?' He glanced between her and the TV. 'Is it because I changed the channel?'

'I...' Madeline opened and closed her mouth. Her mind whirling. What did she need to say? The truth? A Lie? She needed time. She had no preparations. She couldn't remember her plan. Where was she? What was her name? Her heart raced against her chest and she started to perspire.

Five things. Five things...

'It's the strikes, isn't it?' Freddie cut across. She glanced up. He was staring at her sadly. Strikes. Mind cleared. Those strikes. She breathed a little sigh of relief. Grateful for the out. Strikes. Yes. Yes, they upset her so much, she remembered now. Not a lie, but withholding the entire truth.

I am home. I am Madeline Hamilton. I am a good person.

'Yes.' She mumbled meekly and hung her head. Freddie sighed angrily, and pushed himself back into the sofa. Madeline sat, still on her hands, heart still racing. Her hands were now numb. But she was back in the room.

'Look. They're happening, Madeline, whether you like it or not.' He was watching the TV. Not looking at her. She risked moving her hands from underneath her. Flexed her fingers, bringing the blood back. His tone irked her a little. She'd thought it was passion. But now, it sounded condescending.

'I just don't agree with them,' she answered him honestly.

'So don't strike if you don't agree with them!'

'I know... I know.' Madeline felt the tear form in her eye as she looked up at Freddie. He was still staring through the TV, lips pursed. He hadn't noticed. A flutter in her stomach made her pause and reflect. Could she do it? There was always something left unsaid, anytime the subject came up. No, no more avoiding. She needed to know.

'Freddie. I have to ask...' She trailed off. She realised she was scared. Terrified to ask the question. He remained silent.

'Freddie. Are you striking?' She could feel the blood pumping in her ears, dreading the response. She watched as Freddie took a large breath in and exhaled.

'I think I am, yes.' *Think.* It gave her a flutter of hope.

'You *think* you are?'

'Yes, Madeline. You have your principles, I have mine. I have to do what I think is right. I haven't made any decisions yet. But yes, I am swaying to strike.' His words stabbed her in the heart.

211

'But Freddie, how can you...'

'Madeline, I don't want to talk about it anymore.'

'But we have to...'

'No, we don't. Why does it matter to you if I strike, anyway?'

'Because. It's about right and wrong. There's always a right and wrong.'

'In this case, there is no right or wrong, Madeline. No matter what, strikes or not, people are going to suffer. As it stands, staff retention is a huge issue. Pay hasn't risen with inflation. Nobody wants to work in the NHS anymore. There aren't enough doctors to treat the sick. So people are already dying, they're already suffering. Striking is the only way to show the government this is serious. Yes, it means short term, there are less staff. But it's short term pain, for long term gain. This isn't a black and white issue.'

'No. No, this is clear. We shouldn't be striking.' Madeline shook her head. She would not abandon her principles. She was a good person. She needed to hear he was sorry, that he saw it too. She wasn't ready to have him out of her life. He needed to see. Freddie sighed and shook his head. He reached spindly fingers to his face and rubbed his eyes.

'I can't keep going over this with you, Madeline.' He looked at her sadly. She felt the tears coming fast. They were trickling down her cheeks. She realised how much this conversation was hurting her. She felt broken, like her heart had been shattered. With another stab, she realised he was breaking her heart. She bit her lip. She knew what needed to be done, he had to go but she couldn't do it. He was hurting her too much now. She was too upset, she couldn't bring herself to say anything.

Freddie reached forward, attempting to comfort her and she reactively flinched away. He sat frozen, his arm outstretched, watching her helplessly.

'Maybe I should go?' he offered glumly. Madeline nodded. She couldn't look him in the eye. Freddie stood from the sofa, stooped. She wondered for a moment if he might say something.

Tell me you made a mistake.

'Night, Madeline,' he mumbled. He turned glumly. She didn't look up. She heard the pad of his feet against the hardwood in the hallway. The sound of shoes being slipped on. The door creaking open and closing shut. The *ping* of her phone. The notification from the camera. The TV murmured away in the background and she turned it off. Sitting in the silence. The tears came freely this time. For the first time, she didn't know what to do.

Madeline spent another night laying in bed, sleep broken, but this time she didn't get up. She didn't use any of her coping mechanisms. Even the threat of being found was numbed. She just allowed herself to feel sad. It was a new sensation. She had never been an indecisive person before. Black and white. Right and wrong. Yes and no. Freddie had entered her life and disordered her mind with his chaotic shades of grey. She rose groggily the next morning and immediately took out her phone, pulling up her lists. Lists were good. Lists helped with decisions. Making a few more notes she deliberated, sighed and pulled up her DIY list. She spent the rest of the day tackling the last bits of decorating.

Skirting boards touched up and looking fresh she finally stopped. She did feel a little better. Mind a little clearer at the least. She looked down at Timmy and felt the pull. She needed it. Madeline took his harness out and Timmy scattered around the living area. The battle of the excitable Zoomies and the harness began.

Timmy eventually clipped in and lead on, she released him out of the door and followed. Her phone pinged. Camera. Time check. 14:17. He darted down the path from her door and cocked his leg at the gate. Madeline didn't wait. Timmy caught up with her as they made their way down the driveway, she could hear the pattering of his claws on the tar mac. Despite the torrid nature of it, she felt the pull to see the lake. It calmed her, even with its newfound fame. She needed to breathe, to relax. It had been a few weeks, she hoped its morbid novelty for the locals had worn off by now. They reached the end of the road. 14:23. Past the cottages, front gardens an explosion of colour and scent. The gardeners had been working hard. Up to the new housing estate. His Volvo was there. Parked on the road. The path was free. The cars wheels were all in line, two inches from the raised kerb. She stopped.

Parked with care. She felt a tug at her heart. He was a good man, perhaps she had been too hasty. He had changed. She could still convince him. Couldn't she? She glanced to the right, over to the red door. She thought she saw movement at the window again. From the living room.

This is why you don't get caught up.

She was torn in two. Paralysed by her indecision. This

thought was right. This is why she kept herself at a distance, never get too close. She had been a fool to think there was hope for a future right now. Too reckless. Too confident that *he* was gone and would leave her be. But the Volvo. He could change. He had changed. Sudden movement caught her eye, as the red door swung open. A figure, blurred, all limbs and chaos as it raced over. He stopped in front of her.

'Madeline! I was hoping to catch you.'

'Oh? Why didn't you text then?'

'You seemed so upset after our date last night, I didn't think it was right to text. I know you like to walk past here, so I've been watching. Waiting for you.' Warmth flooded her chest, despite her inner conflict. He'd been waiting for her. Madeline smiled.

'No, you're probably right. I don't know if I would have replied.' She sighed and looked down at her feet. She was telling the truth. Freddie grabbed her by the shoulders and looked deep in her eyes.

'Madeline,' he breathed. 'Madeline, I'm so sorry. But please don't let one little disagreement affect what we have. I really think we might have something special here, don't we?' He looked longingly at her. She thought about it. Special. The word certainly fit with how she had been feeling. Torn, indecisive. Unlike her. Special, indeed.

'Yeah. I think we do.' It was true.

'Let's not throw it away,' he begged. She looked up at him seriously. It was now or never.

'Would you at least be willing to reconsider your decision on the strikes?'

'Well, there's no guarantee they'll happen anyway, and I

hadn't even made a decision in the first place—'

'Freddie!' Madeline snapped. She pleaded with her eyebrows. 'Please?' He looked between her eyes.

'Fine. Yes, I will reconsider.' She breathed a sigh of relief. The grey in her mind broke, shades of black and white free to shine through the clouds. Decision had been made.

'Thank you.'

'I can see it means a lot to you.'

'It does.'

'Okay.'

'Do you want to come with us, we're just starting on a walk?' Madeline offered, not really meaning it. She still needed the lake and would have preferred to go alone. But it was the polite thing to do. Freddie shook his head.

'No, I've got bits to sort before tomorrow. But I'll see you soon, yeah?'

'Yeah, that would be great.' Madeline grinned, relieved, and he matched it with his toothy one. Oh, how she loved that grin.

'Nice. I'll text you.' He kissed her on the lips and turned away back into the house. Timmy was scrapping on his lead to get to him, desperate for his own attention, but Freddie didn't turn back. Madeline checked the time. 14:33. Her timings were a little out now, but it didn't matter. They could recover. She resumed her path, a slight bounce in her step.

They reached the cut-through. 14:41. Turned right down the path. They passed other walkers, other dogs on the way. They acknowledged one another politely. Reaching the back of the sixties houses there was still no dog waste left on the path. Madeline smiled, taking immense pleasure in striding out securely. It was freeing. The landscape dipped and she raised her chin, anticipating the dip of the valley with glee. Her phone pinged, but she ignored it. Waiting for the view, the crisp blue sparkling water, putting her under such a spell. Another ping. Nearly there. Why did she leave it so long? *Ping.* The valley dipped. There it was. The scene hit Madeline in all the right places as it washed over like a release. In the centre of the valley the vast stretch of blue that had burrowed into her soul. She took it in, feeling the liberation out here, her breathing quickened. Here. Here it was. The reminder that everything would be okay. Freedom.

Ping.

Madeline suddenly attended to the noise and her hand flung to her phone. Timmy was happily investigating the scents around him as she stared in horror at the screen.

Four notifications of activity from the camera. Three at the front, one at the back. She clicked on them fretfully, bile rising. The app opened. First image, postman delivering mail, not stopping. Second, a cold caller, cap on obstructing his face, tutting angrily as he waited for the door to be answered and shoving a leaflet roughly through the letterbox. Third, a delivery driver, dropping what appeared to be a bouquet of flowers. A smile teased at the corner of her mouth. She was looking forward to putting them in a vase when she got home. She had the perfect one. She made a mental note to text Freddie and thank him for the gift. She was glad she hadn't made any hasty decisions. He was a good one after all. The fourth. The garden. She tapped. And tapped again. It would not load. She checked the images, nothing. She glanced at the time at the top of her screen. 15:01. Furrowing her brow, she clicked through the images. She pulled up the sliding scale and with precision, pulled across the rolling image that had been recorded in the day. Frame by frame, she watched, shifting it only with the gentlest movement of her thumb. 14:50. 14:51. 14:52. Her eyes were blurring from the concentration, and Timmy was getting impatient to move now. 14:53. 14:54. 14:55. 14:59. She blinked. Rolling her thumb over the sliding scale again. 14:55. 14:59. It was no trick, it was no app glitch. Timings didn't lie. They kept her safe. Her eyes watered as the realisation sunk in.

It was gone.

Someone was deleting them.

*

The discovery could have rattled her. It could have sent her into a spiral of panic. But it didn't. It was uncertainty that troubled her. The time stamps don't lie. They were evidence. Evidence of a tampering. It brought her a wave of clarity. Seeing it with her own eyes, it was definitive. He was back. But he didn't want her to see him. That meant he was running scared, he wasn't ready for whatever horrible plan he had in place for her. Not ready to reveal himself just yet. She took Timmy around the lake as planned and was pleased to see it was returning to its normal state. The lake had its desired calming effect. The youths were gone and the paths were drying up in the consistent sunshine of the July heat. The banks were settling down and returning the waters to their glassy shores.

They took the second lap around the lake. There were a

few other people milling about and enjoying the sunshine. She knew she had to portray the image of normality. Smile politely. Acknowledge and greet one another. If he, or anyone else, was watching her, she would be more obvious if she suddenly changed the path she was on or anything about her routine. She studied a few of their faces underneath her sunglasses, none appeared to be paying her any mind. But she knew better than anyone that appearances were deceiving. She kept half an eye as they moved past. Finally, they looped around and Madeline walked the cautious journey back. Like Goldilocks, she was careful not to walk too fast or too slow. Just right.

They climbed the hill and got back to the cut-through. Madeline felt her body physically tense as they emerged back into the housing estate. The bricks of the pavement were warm, she could feel them through her Converse. Residents busied themselves, in and out of their cars. Children running in from school. The Volvo was gone, she hadn't thought to ask Freddie what bits he had to do. They walked back into the cottage area and turned right, up her close. Robin Close. She worked hard now. She felt beads of sweat appearing on her forehead, her nose and her cheeks. She didn't know if they came from the heat in the day or the apprehension. Could be both, she supposed. She tightened her moist grip on Timmy's lead, pulling him in a little closer. Ensured she said a courteous hello to the neighbours. It was still a little warm for their gardening, but they pottered in the shaded areas. She rounded the corner, her bungalow coming into view. Up the drive, onto her little path. The flowers from Freddie were there waiting on the doorstep. A reminder that the tampering she had seen was real. She had seen them be delivered. She saw the gap. Timings didn't lie. She picked them up, gritting her teeth and shakily slotted her keys into the front door lock. Turned the key.

Timmy bounded in and she followed, still holding the bunch. The door shut and locked behind her, it plunged the hallway into a darkness. Breathing deeply, she moved into the living room. It was lighter in here. The paint tray and brushes were drying on the stool where she had left them earlier that day. She was struck by a strange scent, the mixture of drying paint and overpowering pollen. Timmy settled himself on the sofa and she walked through into the kitchen, placing the flowers on the worktop for now. She had the perfect vase for them. It was cracked in places, but she could put an old plastic bottle inside to hold the water. But she had to check first. She moved to the back door, cautiously turning the key. *Click.* She swung it open, and stepped outside.

Insects buzzed lazily, skipping around each other. Birds sang their sweet song. The grass was luscious, cool, the sun still warm as it cast its shadows across the lawn. She could smell the sweet aromas from the shrubs, the hint of manure from a neighbouring field. Someone had cut their grass. Madeline felt the *ping* from her phone in her back pocket. She knew what the notification was. She searched closely, eyes trained around the garden. She studied each bed, each pile of dirt, examined each bush. Nothing. Nothing disturbed. No footprints. She narrowed her eyes. It meant nothing. She knew he had been here. Her eyes rested on the fence at the back of the garden. It wouldn't take much to shimmy over. Not for her. Certainly not for a six-foot man with a grudge against her. She marched to the end and on her toes, peered over. She pulled herself up gently. The footpath, extending left and right, running down the back of the bungalows. Empty. She strained her ears. Nothing. No rustles, no sound of breathing. She lowered herself from the panel slowly, Timmy behind watching her. He cocked his head, his little black eyes staring curiously. She hurried him to her side and hastened back into the kitchen. Swung the door to. Locked. She leant against the door for a moment, biting her lip. She wasn't sure what she had been expecting, him to be there, waiting for her perhaps? What would she have done had she caught him, anyway? In hindsight, it was a relief to have found nothing. It was safer. Her eyes fell onto the vase on the worktop, remembering Freddie's gesture. It was rude to ignore it.

Madeline removed the fake flowers from the vase. She opened the kitchen cupboard and stood on her toes, fingers outstretched to grab the plastic container from the top shelf. The tips of her fingers curled over the edge, and she pulled it gently out. The plastic squeaked as she pushed it inside. She filled the makeshift vase carefully with water and rested it on the counter. It wasn't the prettiest of vases, but she loved it all the same. It meant something to her. It was special.

She moved to the bunch of flowers to begin arrangement and stopped. There. It was blatant. She cursed herself for not noticing it before. The smell was different in here. As she lifted her nose, she detected a hint of patchouli, sandalwood. The smell of a man's cologne. She shook her head in disbelief, how had she not noticed this before? She turned and looked at the paint drying on the walls. She had always just assumed. It blended so well with Ivy's old scent she had never thought to question it. Now the work she had put in had ridden those aromas, it was pronounced.

He had been in the house. He was here. The camera notification. She unlocked the back door again and switched the torch function on her phone. Carefully, she opened the door and stepped around to the other side. Bending her knees she stooped slowly. Eye level with the lock. Lighting it with her torch, she studied. There, the slightest notches on the new mechanism. He hadn't just been hiding in the garden. He had been picking the lock.

The fear surged, taking over her body. She swore violently and kicked out at the door. It swung on its hinges and bounced off the wall. The bang startled the blue tits on the bird feeder and they swarmed away, their songs ruffled and alarmed.

Stupid, stupid girl.

How could she be so witless? She looked up at the camera, still blinking at her. She had no idea how long he had been breaking in for, but he must have been watching her, waiting for her to leave before he made his move. She needed to think.

The police would not be able to do anything without hard evidence. She couldn't bottle the scent and rely on the notches in the lock. They could be caused by anything. They would argue they had been there long before. That she put the key in too roughly. No. She needed something else. She bit her lip, feeling her teeth break the skin. A droplet of blood oozed out onto her tongue. Calming herself she stepped back into the kitchen. She locked the door and put the key back in her pocket. Her eyes fell upon the flowers in the kitchen. The flowers. Such a wonderful thought amongst the turmoil. She supposed she should quickly text Freddie and thank him. That was polite. Despite everything, she needed to appear normal. At now, of all times, when she was so close, she didn't want him to suspect anything.

She sent off a hurried message and paced in the kitchen. *Ping.* She read his response.

I'm sorry, Madeline, I don't know what you're talking about?

She furrowed her brow. He was scatty, he probably sent them a few days ago and forgot. She fired off her reply.

The flowers you sent. They arrived today, they are beautiful. She watched as the messaged delivered. Read instantly. Then the bubble indicated he was typing.

I didn't send you any flowers, they must be from someone else maybe? Very nice of them, though!

She read. Re-read. Darting over to the bouquet, she dug through the precious stems. The heads flew from their stalks from the ferocity, shedding their petals sulkily and raining pollen over the worksurface. Her hands closed around something hard and flat. Shaking, she produced the card. She read it, sweat now dripping between her widening eyes, studying the bouquet properly for the first time. White, large flat petals of white and pink decorated the floor, dusted in a rich yellow pollen. Lilies.

Her hand shook as she held the printed card. On the front, its typed text.

In loving memory of a life well lived.

She read, and re-read the handwritten scrawl inside.

I'm coming for you, Little Red.

I took your T-Shirt the first time I watched you. It was like this that night. Just me and you. You were so peaceful, did you know you sleep like a child? All curled up in the middle of your bed, it's quite cute, actually. Almost makes me think twice.

I got it home and breathed in your scent. Oh! It was delightful, it sent me to sleep. I slept well that night. I curled up with it, in the middle of my bed like a baby. I don't know what it is about you, there is something that draws me to you every time. Like I said, you're different. You're like my personal drug. I need my fix. And when I get that hit, fuck me, I always want more.

The second time, I took your underwear. I had so much fun with it that night. It kept me going for a week. I didn't need to come back for a while, it satisfied me in ways you could never understand.

I did two in one night before. I was insatiable, I couldn't get enough. I would have had three, but the second one, eurgh, the cunt fought me. Why do they always have to fight, my love? Don't they understand, it's for their own good? I took great pleasure in making her please me first. I was so riled from the first you see, she didn't quite do it for me. She shut down, shut up. She was no fun at all. But the second, oh, she thought she could have me. She batted those lashes at me, teased me. I forced her down there. I bet she enjoyed it. I tell you, when she saw her little games weren't going to work on me, she didn't enjoy it, then. I needed something from her, something she couldn't give me. But you can.

The thing is, my love, I need you. I need you more than you know. And now, you need me.

19

Madeline

She had to stay focused. She had beefed up her security even further, hiring an expert to override the camera's feed to the app for a constant stream to her phone. She added deadbolts to the back door. She made lists, kept to her timings. That was where she felt most safe. There was nothing more she could do now than to trust in law enforcement. Oh, the irony.

Madeline tried to stay in her bungalow but staring at the four walls only served to drive her crazier. Her mind spun, the constant thoughts.

My time is up.

It's over.

She knew she needed to get out for her own sanity. She needed an outlet. He had shown he could get in at any time, it wouldn't be long before he found a new way in. But she didn't feel safe going out for a walk. Not yet. She needed to create a proper routine. Normal routine. She pulled up her Maps. Checked her time stamps. Created her routes. The burn in her brain settled and she breathed out a sigh of relief. She would be safe with these. She had tried so hard to blend into the background. She studied others, studied how they behaved, what they said. She worked so hard to appear normal. Not too much, not too little. Always just right.

Another body had been found and identified. Twenty-one-year-old Maisie Sanders. This was no longer small local news, the murders had garnered national attention. Criminologists appeared on special programmes, psychoanalysing the perpetrator.

'A made psychopath. Likely abuse or head injury as a child, due to the sporadic MO. Likely to be acting alone, however, it is possible they have had help, due to the lack of witnesses. They'll be experienced in burglaries, police should be looking at the records of anyone arrested for forced entry into properties. Time between each murder is suggesting the killer is becoming frenzied as the days pass. This suggests they know they are close to being caught...'

Madeline rolled her eyes and shut the TV off. It was interesting, some parts of their analysis could be right but really, they didn't have the first clue of what was really going on. News outlets from around the country had now taken to hanging around Lunnemouth, accosting residents and demanding to know how they felt about the murders.

'Scared.'

'Terrified.'

'I don't want to leave my house.'

'You don't expect this kind of thing to happen in your home town.'

Even Freddie had got caught up in the hysteria. He wasn't one to watch the news, but he brought the murders up very casually in between hastily shovelled mouthfuls of chicken tray bake on her sofa.

'Crazy, isn't it?' he asked, his voice muffled as he chewed.

She swallowed and nodded, the bile rising. He noticed her concerned expression. He reached a hand across her lap as they sat side by side. He gave her knee a squeeze.

'Don't worry. I'm sure it won't happen to you. These things are sensationalised because they're so rare.' Madeline said nothing but nodded again. She could feel his gaze penetrating the side of her face.

'I can stay with you, if you like? Keep you safe? Until this all blows over?' He'd tried to keep his voice steady, casual, but betrayed by the intense look in his eyes. Madeline smiled at him. Right now, that seemed the worst idea. It was hard enough to keep up her pretence for these dates, let alone being around him all the time. She sighed inwardly, wondering, not for the first time, why she had allowed herself to get attached. She could never trust him with the truth. But she liked having him around. That horrible indecision rose again.

'Thank you, I'm sure you're right. It has nothing to do with me. I'll be okay, but thank you.' She lied. It didn't sit right with her, but the lie came easy. Apparently accepting of her response, he answered by shoving more food into his mouth. Her food remained untouched. The dry chicken sat unappealingly amongst a sea of sweaty pepper and tomatoes, oil swimming on the plate.

He'd invited himself over for a dinner date at hers and she had to make a hasty trip to the supermarket. She was tempted to say no, but this would raise his suspicions. She debated again, but she wasn't ready to have him out of her life yet either. His impromptu insistence on coming over, however, had put her under immense pressure. The cupboards were bare. Her food delivery wasn't due for another two days and she couldn't bring it forwards. She had theorised that a supermarket in town would be better than a local shop. Local shops meant local gossips. Local gossip was aflame with conspiracy about who the killer was.

'That Bernard next to me, I've always had such a bad feeling from him. The way he stares from his window when I leave the house, honestly, it's creepy.'

'What about Jimmy, though? His eyes are too close together to be innocent.'

'Don't be silly. That stuff was debunked years ago! But look at Shaun, that goth guy who lives next to the Ram! Always decked out in black leather and those awful boots. And the long hair! He looks like he eats bats, I wouldn't put it past him. Now *he* looks like exactly the kind of person that would get their jollies from gutting another person!'

'That's very true, I heard he was in something called a 'death metal' band, you know. All that angry music, screaming about people dying, maybe he was telling us all along!'

Madeline listened to the blazon and biased judgements as she mopped up the floor in the community centre. She had her earphones in, pretending she was listening to music. She had learned people were more likely to leave her alone if they thought she had earphones in. They were also more likely to think she was rude, incapable of doing things without stimulation, socially anxious, perhaps. Whatever they thought, she didn't care. It kept them away.

'Well, have you seen that Michael just upped and left his wife all of a sudden? Pretty suspicious if you ask me. Married for ten years, then gone with no word. Left three kids as well.

If you ask me, he's behind it all.'

Wrong. All wrong.

She knew exactly who it was.

Madeline had driven to one of Lunnemouth's supermarkets instead. She had breathed a sigh of relief upon getting out of her car. She had made it without incident. It was a mistake. News reporters had swarmed the area, thrusting their microphones into people's faces. Relief vanished, she ducked and darted past as the more brash customers took their fifteen minutes of fame. Finally out of their prying eyes and intrusive cameras, Madeline took a basket from the entrance and turned into the store.

It was carnage. People were frantic. She watched as two women had a fight over the last piece of broccoli in the vegetable aisle. A man in his forties pushed his trolley past her, twenty packs of toilet rolls stacked within. The shelves were bare as she wandered through. Madeline narrowed her eyes in confusion. An older shopper was screaming at a young floor assistant.

'You should be putting on more deliveries to help your area! This is completely unacceptable! I demand to speak to your manager!'

Decency had gone out of the window as the locals panicked hysterically. Captivated by the screaming man, she accidentally bumped into a young boy. He scurried away behind her, eyes wide and terrified.

'Don't worry about the rude lady.' She turned in disbelief towards the small voice, seeing his mother embracing him. Her scowl quickly vanished and she visibly recoiled as Madeline faced her. It was clear the woman hadn't meant for her voice to carry but Madeline didn't have the energy to give the rudeness the time of day. It was clear it was an accident. She obviously wasn't about barging innocent children out of the way. The woman said nothing and Madeline turned away.

'Yeah, I'm talking about you.' She heard her mutter under her breath from behind. Just quiet enough that she didn't really want Madeline to hear her. Madeline clenched her jaw. She counted. Breathed. Stemming her heart. Pulled out her list, adding a note and checking. She was able to recall she just needed some chicken and vegetables to make a tray bake. She flew around the aisles, dodging the crazed shoppers, managing to grab a couple of peppers, a can of tinned tomatoes, and some chicken breast from the frozen aisle. She chose the self-service checkout and eventually found the end of the queue as it snaked around the store. She couldn't help but tut a little at the chaos. It was a little illogical. The killer was getting people in their own homes. Stockpiling and racing to get back from a supermarket to batten down the hatches in their own houses was hardly going to save them. Her eyes travelled down the queue, clocking the rude woman and her child a few places ahead. She had watched as the woman looked around and sheepishly whipped her head back as she spotted Madeline behind. Madeline sighed. Quite a ridiculous reaction really, in the grand scheme of things. But people do the funniest things when they are running scared, she knew that well. She was scared, too. And she had reason to be.

Just act normal.

Madeline remembered the woman now, how her face had changed when they locked eyes. Afraid. Fearful. She could relate to that. Freddie finished his meal with a satisfying belch. He patted his stomach.

'Bloody delicious, thank you, babe.' She grimaced and offered her plate.

'You're welcome. Do you want some more?' Her voice was flat.

'Do you not want it?'

'No, I'm not hungry. I ate a big lunch.' She didn't like this. She had to lie again. It didn't sit well with her. But she couldn't let him suspect anything. Things would get better, she knew. Witnesses, evidence. It was a matter of time before the police had enough to charge him and arrested him again. She just had to be patient. And pray they got to him before he got to her.

Freddie insisted on overstaying his welcome and he slept the night. She feigned another migraine and rolled over in bed, rejecting his advances. Another lie. The third that evening. But it was necessary. She wasn't in the mood for making love tonight. She needed to cope in her own ways.

The next morning he got up to make breakfast. She was already awake, having been up for most of the night. He hadn't stirred as she had crept out of bed in the dark hours of early morning. She climbed back in as the sun was rising, and rose with him at 07:23, pretending she had slept as well as he did. She had managed three and a half hours in total.

He was a good cook, but he had a terrible habit of using every pan and utensil she owned so rather than watch as he destroyed her kitchen she stayed in bed, pulling her phone out of her bedside drawer. Waking it up, the notifications pinged as her signal returned. Pulling up the camera app, she scrolled back through the last twelve hours of activity. There was nothing untoward, no sign of *him* at least. All the timings were as they should be. No tampering. Movement detected at 12:04 and at 02:35 but nothing of significance. She deleted the roll.

Freddie called her to breakfast, so she slid out of the warm and moved to the sofa. Her body ached, her muscles sore and swollen and she grimaced as she lowered herself to the cushion. Freddie didn't notice, noisily enjoying his already half-eaten breakfast. She cut into the crispy bacon and runny eggs, the yolk oozing over the plate in her lap. In any other circumstances she might have enjoyed it. But she usually ate porridge, Weetabix as a treat. That was her routine. It kept her safe, stopped her from spiralling, kept on top of her impulses. Not for the first time, the thought ran through her head.

Time for him to go.

Almost immediately, she felt herself arguing. No, I'm not ready. The TV was already on and she startled, the booming music of the titles indicating the eight o'clock news was about to begin. Before she had time to react, Freddie moved quickly beside her, his hand flying to the remote. The channel changed, a children's cartoon in place of the serious newscaster. The characters had no dialogue, they just squeaked at each other, the volume setting her teeth off. Even Timmy tilted his head in time, transfixed by the strange sounds coming from the TV.

'What did you do that for?' The words were out of her mouth before she could think. Her tone sharp. Too sharp. She knew she should've stuck with porridge this morning.

'Oh. I...' Freddie turned bright red, taken aback by her outburst. 'Sorry, I didn't think you'd want to watch it.'

232

She shuffled on the cushion, monitoring her voice, her body language closely. She was sure to be softer this time.

'Why?' A natural question to ask, she was sure.

'You know, the murders and stuff.'

'Why wouldn't I want to watch that?'

'Well, you know. You were so freaked out last night. And you've been so jumpy lately. I just figured it would be the last thing you'd want.' Freddie looked at her intensely. Madeline swallowed.

Quick.

Think.

Act normal.

'I just think it's important to be in the know,' she said carefully. She was sick of lying. But withholding some of the truth was not a lie. 'You were right last night, I don't want to accidentally get myself caught up in any areas that might be dangerous.' Freddie nodded slowly. He smiled sadly at her, and to her surprise he caressed her cheek.

'I understand. No, we don't want you going anywhere that's dangerous. I don't think I could cope with losing you, you know.' He held his hand to her face. One, two, three seconds. Staring deep into her eyes. It began to make her feel uncomfortable.

'But... If you don't think it's a good idea then maybe I shouldn't,' she offered, appeasing. He smiled.

'Maybe we'll just watch something else. Take your mind off it.' He withdrew his hand and flicked through the channels, settling on a re-run of a cooking show. It was so grainy, Madeline wondered if it had been filmed on a potato. Freddie reclined in the sofa, watching the show intently. He put an arm around the back of her shoulders. She sat rigid, her eggs and bacon now cold on her plate. She resisted the urge to check her phone and forced the now-rubbery breakfast down.

Mercifully, he received a call from work requesting urgent cover. Madeline said she would walk with him down to his house as she took Timmy out for his stroll. He had tried to protest a little, but she had argued it was the middle of the day. Nothing bad ever happened in broad daylight with so many others around. He relented.

They kissed goodbye as they reached his house, his Volvo gleaming in the sun. It was parked well again, all four wheels on the road. It had been cleaned, too, she noticed. There wasn't a speck of dirt on it. It was a nice touch. He walked slowly up the driveway and opened his door. He glanced at her one more time before he shut it behind him and she turned away up the cut-through. They reached the footpath. Madeline hesitated. She needed the pull of the lake. But she needed to check her surroundings even more. This time, she took a left and strolled up the track with a happy Timmy.

Out here in the fields, away from the chaos of the locals speculation, the pretence with Freddie, she could finally breathe. A horrible thought popped in.

Enjoy it whilst you can.

She angrily dismissed it. No, he wouldn't win. Not until her dying breath. If that's what it took.

They passed the back of her fence and she stopped. The dirt was untouched, no footprints or anything to reveal it had been disturbed. But she knew that didn't mean much now. They walked on. After twenty-eight minutes, Madeline's alarm went off and she turned back. Timmy was starting to struggle in the July heat and the ginger DNA in her skin wasn't faring that well, either.

Coming to the end of the cut-through in the estate, she saw another walker on their way towards her. He was elderly, she often saw him around. They usually exchanged pleasantries and carried on about their days.

'Mornin'.'

'Good morning.' Madeline nodded politely, as usual.

'So, this is your regular walk, is it?' She stopped still at the man's words. This wasn't part of the plan.

'Sorry?'

'Out down to the lake at the back there. I often see you, all times of day.' He was looking at her kindly. Had he been watching her? No, he hadn't meant to scare her. He didn't mean it.

'Yes. I... err... yes. You know, it helps me wind down. Being out in the country, by the water, you know.' She panicked.

'Oh, lovely. Yeah, I quite like the walk out of the back there. My granddaughter, she often comes and visits. She's living in London now, you see, misses the fresh air...' Unable to concentrate as the man carried on with his story, she felt her reality slipping away around her.

Fool.

How could she not notice she had become too regimented? In her quest for normality amongst the chaos of her past, she had made herself more noticeable. People would pay attention to her visiting the lake, they would pay attention to wherever she went. She was predictable now, easily placed.

It hadn't helped her blend in at all. If he had noticed her down by the lake, who else had? Where else had they seen her? The panic rising within, she was vaguely aware the old man was laughing. She laughed along with him. Correct response. Inwardly, she was planning. She needed to change her routine. No doubt about it.

The man was waving and making to move past her. She politely said goodbye and hastened into the housing estate. She resisted the urge to glance around. Who else would be watching? She stepped out onto the pavement by the road and crossed earlier. It's in the details. Always in the details. What would a normal person do? One that didn't have a target on their back? She had never known such a life. She had always been chased.

A white van drove steadily towards her and a young man in an orange jacket suddenly appeared from the passenger window. She jumped back in shock.

'Oi oi, how are you doing, good looking, can I have a go on your tits?' he called, leering out as the van raced past. She stopped, her heart thumping, looking back at the van in disbelief as she heard his cackle fade away.

Did he just catcall her? Another time, she might have been flattered. She hadn't been catcalled since she was much younger. But today, right now, it only served to send her into an anxious oblivion. She felt a rush of anger fire in her belly. How dare he. He must know how intimidating his actions were, for a young woman alone. That was the purpose of the catcall. He was the one with the power, the one in the van, he knew she could never retort. Him and his ego were free to go about their day. It was unfair. For him to assert his dominance over her without her being able to do a thing about it. Who would do that to anyone? Who would do that to a young woman, alone? Who would think it was okay to take advantage of a young woman's vulnerability at a time like this?

Only a bad person would do that.

She scowled and watched the van drive away up the road. She didn't worry about her reaction in that instance. She was certain any normal person would have the same response. Madeline clenched Timmy's lead close, clinging onto her senses. The bile rose. The man in the orange jacket, large teeth, leering. Her heart battered at her ribs. Shaking. The street ebbed in and out of view.

Bad person.

She felt herself slipping away. Intrusive images shot into her mind. Him. Laughing. Holding the knife to her throat. She could see the spittle around his mouth as he laughed at her. She felt the tear between her legs. The fear in her body as she froze. She could smell the metallic tang of blood. It was everywhere. In her nose, her mouth, her hair. She could feel it sticking to her scalp.

No. No. Please don't hurt me.

She saw their faces. Teeth bared, cackling at her. One by one, leering over her.

Please, stop.

Shut up. You're nothing, you cunt.

Timmy barked, bringing her back. Her mind reeled from the flashback.

Five things. Five things.

She counted them out, slowly and carefully. Five things

she could see: grey tarmac, pavements, green grass of the cottages, a Vauxhall Corsa parked in the drive opposite, the sign for Robin Close. Four things she could hear: birds, cars, children screeching, Timmy panting. Three things she could touch: Timmy's lead, her hand against the denim of her jeans, the outline of her phone in her back pocket. Two things she could smell: fresh cut grass, melting tar from the heat. One thing she could taste: blood. Repeated the grounding again. Bringing herself back to the present.

I am Madeline Hamilton. I am a good person.

Him

The bodies were piling up. How could she carry on? She knew she was responsible, this was her doing. He wouldn't be here, wouldn't be doing this if it wasn't for her. It was all her fault.

The night was cool but he was burning hot as he hurried away from the bungalow, pulling his hood over his head, obscuring his face. Raging. He could have been so different. His life was on a completely different trajectory before she came along. She tried to take his heart at school and succeeded in ripping it to shreds as an adult. They say that time heals all wounds, but no amount of time would ever stem the bleeding from the injuries she inflicted upon him.

He reached the back of the housing estate and slowed his pace, easing into a comfortable stroll. He wondered if she ever had a conscience. Ever thought about what she had done to

him. Did she even think about him? About the others? He doubted it very much. She got to pack up her life, swan away, start afresh. The pain of what she had done to him would torture him forever. His life wasn't worth living until he had her. Until he had destroyed every part of her. He closed his eyes, imagining his fingers closing around her throat. He imagined how that beautiful pale skin would tint pink, then red. Red just like that beautiful hair of hers. Then her eyes would widen in a panic, and finally. Finally, she would see him. She would truly see him. She would try and apologise, sure. Make amends for her actions. But it would be too late. Her delicate eyes would bulge and he would kiss her lips teasingly, sadistically, as she took that last breath.

He shook his head, banishing the image. No. He mustn't get ahead of himself. He wanted more than her death. He was here for her life.

He jumped. Loud bangs, quick succession. The sky lit up over the houses behind him. Fireworks. Fucking fireworks. He hated fireworks. Anyone who let them off when it wasn't bonfire night or New Years was a cunt. They scared dogs, people. They were no good for anyone and they should be banned. He shook the anger from his body.

He thought about the little dog. Sooty. It didn't matter what she called him, he would be Sooty to him. Another thing she stole from him. Sooty should have been his. She stole everything from him. It was time she got a taste of her own medicine. He was going to take everything from her.

But first, he was going to play. He wanted to toy with her, torture her in the way she had tortured him. He was never this person before, never violent, this was her doing.

He stopped on the path, pulled out his phone and looked at the number. Tapping the side of his phone, he thought. She was panicked. She had been stupid enough to forget her phone in the house when she went to work that night. He'd taken to breaking in whenever she wasn't home now. He just wanted to be near her, to remind himself what he was doing this for. Her phone was disappointing. No social media, no photos. A sickening amount of texts and calls to that clown. Freddie was his name, apparently. But now he had her number.

It was so fucking hard to keep cool, to keep going. He wanted nothing more than to end it all now. But there would be no satisfaction in that. That fucking lanky streak of piss who was glued to her side like a barnacle was complicating matters too much. He was close, he could almost touch her. But not yet. He wasn't ready. But it didn't mean he couldn't watch her suffer in the meantime. She was panicked, skittish. Scared. She knew what he was capable of doing. And he was ready to turn up the heat.

Too long had she had the power, all the control. Now she would know what it was like to be the one who was losing everything.

These people put themselves in danger. They have no one to blame but themselves. When someone knows they are about to die, they show you their true colours. It's always the ones you least expect who put up a fight. And the ones you would think would fight are the ones that break down, beg, and start snivelling. They try and appeal to you, they pray, they try and stroke your ego. Pathetic. All of them.

But I like to stretch the game out a little. Those ones who beg. You don't know what it does to me to see that look in their eye when I comply with their silly little sentences.

"We could be together, you know? I know you're misunderstood." That's what they try to tell me. I play along. I tell them what they want to hear. That spark behind their eyes just burns brighter and brighter. And when I extinguish it, I make sure they give that pleasure to me. It's fun to see that fear in their eyes when they realise. Oh sweetie, it's all part of the game.

One wasn't enough, anymore. I needed more. More practice, more rehearsal. Everything had to be perfect for you. It surprised me. They were so different. I do like a fighter, though, it turns me on. I wonder which one you will be, my love? Will you be a lover or a fighter?

20

Madeline

More bodies found and identified. Twenty-six-year-old Cieran Jones and twenty-nine-year-old Megan Fowler. Madeline felt sick. It was too much, too fast. The acid was burning holes through her stomach. Police were coming under fire from locals, protestors, councillors, and journalists alike to catch the perpetrator. The chief inspector held a press conference and was disgustingly elusive on any developments. He had only revealed they were following up on a significant lead and appealing for any witnesses. It was no help, too vague. Madeline found herself glued to the TV as a result, desperate for any updates, any leads, even a hint. She had switched to the twenty-four-hour news channel whenever she was home and had ensured Keith had BBC on whenever she was on shift. She timed her medication rounds in his bay for the breakfast, lunch, and evening news. She thought about it more than once, she was tempted to run. To escape. But it wouldn't make a difference. He would still find her. It would happen all over again. She had to trust in the evidence she was gathering.

The strikes followed as the next huge national story. They

were inching closer to industrial action by the day and it unnerved her even further. She felt like a kettle at its boiling point. One small knock and she might explode. Freddie had remained quiet on the subject. But he had promised to reconsider his decision to strike, and he'd kept to his word. A good one, that one.

Just like you.

Her release, her coping mechanisms, they weren't enough anymore to stem the panic. She switched up her walks, returning to the routes in the surrounding villages, ensuring she never became too regimented or walked the same route twice. She still had her favourites, the ones which helped to quieten that itch, but she kept to her time stamps and waved politely at other walkers and neighbours. It wasn't lost on her how many kept their head down and hurried along, however. She had not seen any further activity on the cameras or in the bungalow, but she knew it meant nothing. It was clear now he would do whatever it took for his revenge. It didn't matter what she had done was right, he would never see it that way. He was never going to give up, not as long as he had his freedom. She just needed to be clever, outsmart him at every turn and remain vigilant.

Keep gathering that evidence.

She pulled out her phone as Timmy bounded ahead in the woods of South Foggen. She liked it here. It was cool amongst the trees. The woods were old, the air was close and thick, the eyes of the trees boring down upon them. The sun's rays couldn't warm the Earth as much under their gentle cover. But in stark contrast to the woodland at the back of Robin Close, she felt safe. The woods were protected, busy enough so there were witnesses to her walking there, just in case, but not so busy that it overwhelmed her. She was cautious, but here she was calm and in control, reminded of who she was and what she was capable of. She pulled out her phone, periodically checking her apps. Time. 14:33. Maps. Walking south. Flagged. Camera. No activity. Her finger hovered over the Messages app. She locked the phone and put it in her pocket.

Madeline had barely heard from Freddie since he had been called away from their date. The one he had insisted on, and she had reluctantly cooked for. She was frustrated. He brought out such indecision in her. It was alien and she didn't like it. On one hand, she didn't mind the space he was giving her now. It allowed her room to breathe, make plans, add to her lists and she didn't have to pretend she didn't know she was being stalked, that her life was in danger, that she was playing the part. But, on the other... He had been so insistent on staying with her, protecting her, and now. Nothing. Absolutely nothing. She didn't know if she wanted him to stick around, or if she wanted him gone. When she had said yes to a date she had been confident it would only be a few dates before she got rid of him. A bit of fun and moving on. But she couldn't deny he had got under her skin, she found herself wondering about him, checking to see if he'd read her text, worrying about when the next time would be she would see him. It was infuriating.

She didn't like it. It made her want to pull away. To her ruin, she realised she had started to see a future, them together, and now he was playing with her heart.

This is what you get for trusting people. I warned you.

She shook her head.

Give it time, the decision will come. You don't have to decide anything now.

Her phone pinged in her back pocket and she whipped it out. Notification. Text message. It was as though he could hear the war raging in her head.

Fancy dinner later? The Old Ram?

She smiled. Her fingers flew across the screen tapping out her reply.

Sounds great!

Time check. 14:36. They were starting to loop back towards the carpark on the woodland path. The trees began to thin and the sun's rays streamed through the gaps. Timmy was starting to slow, and she looked out across the fields through the sparse trunks to the collection of dwellings in the distance. The fields were gold, the golden barley dancing in the gentle breeze, framing the small community. The village was small, the inhabitants concentrated along either side of the main road. There were no housing estates, no closes or off-streets there. South Foggen... she racked her brain, picturing each face. Megan Fowler. That's who it was. Her body found in the house just over there. She could pick it out, terraced, third from the middle. She sighed, turning her head away sadly. Time was running out.

They made it back to the car and she opened the passenger side door. Timmy jumped in and she clipped him secure. Another ping. She pulled out the phone, shutting the door and walking to the driver's side.

7 ok?

Glued to her screen, she opened the driver's door and bent

to slide inside.

Sounds perfect. She watched the message send. Delivered. And immediately read. She smiled and shut the door. Keys in the ignition, she started the car and the engine roared to life. She put the KA in reverse, and began to back out slowly, checking all mirrors. A horn blasted somewhere behind and she slammed on the brakes, the force propelling her and Timmy brutally forward. Her head smarted and her neck jarred as it came to a forceful rest upon the headrest. The Jeep, horn blaring angrily, hurtled behind her, barely visible from the dust cloud enveloping the scene. She heard the wheels screaming wildly as it came to a rough stop, sending debris smattering into her paintwork. Madeline, both hands on the wheel and horrified, watched as the driver's door flew open and a tall, reddening man leapt out. He marched around the wagon, red-faced and angry, storming in her direction. Her hands still on the steering wheel, she couldn't do anything as she watched in shock. Frozen still, her body not daring to move. He was roaring at her, at the top of his lungs. A vein threatened to pop in his neck. He banged furiously on her window, slamming his palms into the glass. She jumped in time with each smash. Timmy cried, his ears back, cowering away. Madeline released the wheel and held her hands up as if to apologise, but the man was still berserk, screaming obscenities and ripping out his throat. He gestured aggressively to her, then back to the Jeep and launched a booted foot at her car. She jumped again at the thud as it connected with something on the driver's side. The door? The wheel maybe? She didn't have time to think about that, she was focussed on the man. The build of his body, the height of his frame. The short, cropped, greying of his hair. His face. Brown eyes, leathered skin. She caught the words.

'Stupid woman! Learn to drive!' before finally, he relented, huffing and puffing back into his wagon. The Jeep hobbled on its wheel axis as he hurled himself back in the driver's seat and slammed the door. She felt it, the rush as her body and mind tried to disconnect, trying to pull her down into the darkness. She looked at the numberplate, trying to calm her racing mind, bring herself back.

AR73 KEV.

AR73 KEV.

She recited it over and over again. The Jeep's wheels spun as he pushed the car harshly away.

AR73 KEV.

AR73 KEV.

AR73 KEV.

Eventually, her heart rate slowed enough, and she released the breath she was holding.

Five things she could see: Wheel, dashboard, trees, field, houses.

Four things she could hear: Birds singing outside. The woosh of the occasional car on the road behind. The hum of her engine. Timmy, licking his paw for comfort.

Three things she could touch: The leather of the steering wheel. The smooth, hard gearstick. Timmy's soft fur.

Two things she could smell: Woodland. Petrol.

One thing she could taste: Bile. Slowly dissipating.

She was back in the car. She glanced in her mirrors, once twice. A third check, before she moved the gearstick into reverse and pulled back again. More slowly this time. Far enough back, she put the car into first and lifted the clutch, slowly applying pressure to the accelerator. Everything in step, everything in order. Pulling away slowly, the car rocked as the wheels drove over the uneven ground, and she reached the main road. She checked both ways, just in case. All clear. She turned left and pulled out into the main road.

And now, she could think. Madeline knew everyone was agitated, on edge at the moment, but she couldn't help but think the reaction of that man was completely uncalled for. It upset her a little. He had tried to make her feel she was the bad driver, the bad person. She had checked her mirrors dutifully, and it was her slow speed which prevented any collision. Her sensibility. He had been driving far too fast, far too carelessly in a parking area, she knew it was his fault. It had rattled her, but she reasoned with herself. She couldn't imagine any gentleman being so aggressive at a woman like that. Because of his mistakes, too. What a terrible, terrible person.

Her journey home was gratefully uneventful and she pulled into her drive. Killing the engine, she sat in the car for a minute, processing what had just happened. Timmy watched her expectantly. She pulled out her phone. There was the expected notification from the camera, catching her drive in. She blinked. Another notification from twenty-one minutes ago. She wondered why she hadn't heard it, before realising it probably pinged through when the man was screaming at her.

She opened it. Another text from Freddie.

Slight change of plans. Any chance we could do 8?

She sighed. It was a good job she hadn't made any plans or preparations yet. It would have annoyed her to have him change the timings if she had. She tapped out her reply that it was okay and locked her phone.

Reaching over, she unclipped Timmy and he bounded happily from the car, trotting up the path. He sat on the doorstep, waiting to be let in. She locked the car and followed him up the path, slotting the key into the lock.

Another ping. She rolled her eyes, anticipating another change of plans from Freddie. She clicked on the message and her eyes widened.

Not from Freddie. But an unknown number.

Once upon a time, there was a young girl called Little Red. You've probably heard the story. Her skin as white as snow, her hair as red as the apple she devoured. But in this story, the poison of the apple spread from the rot of her core. Prince Charming won't be able to save her. She will rot alone.

Consider this your kiss, Sleeping Beauty. Wake up. Tick tock. Your time is up, bitch.

*

Miraculously, she arrived at the Old Ram at five to eight. The message had sent her into a spin. How the hell had he got her number? It was a trick, a way to freak her out, get inside her head. She hated to admit, it had worked.

She relied on her timings, her lists, frantically adding notes, reminders, and alarms, desperately trying to claw back some kind of normality. Step by step.

15:45. Make food. Chicken. Leftovers in fridge.

16:00. Let Timmy out.

16:30. Clean up kitchen. Set timer for one hour.

17:30. Wash hair. 17:44. Dry hair. 17:54. Check camera.

18:00. Another reminder, time to feed Timmy. Evening news on.

18:05. Headlines absorbed, in the know. Checked lists, made a plan for tonight.

18:15. Checked camera. Nothing of note. Garden and drive were clear. No visits from the postman today.

18:20. Timmy asking to go out again, she let him out. She did a sweep of the garden. Nothing but birds singing and the shrubbery basking in the sun.

18:30. Check the plan. Any further preparations she would need? She added them to the lists.

19:00. Get ready. Jeans and a black top. Quick check of the weather. The temperature was due to drop a couple of degrees, better to take a jacket.

19:30. Let Timmy out one last time for the night. Locked up the house. Ready for 19:45.

She walked the nine minutes down to The Ram. She strained a smile against her will, ensuring she greeted each of the neighbours as she passed. One foot in front of the other, heel to toe, a second each. She was agitated, it took every inch of her to maintain her pleasantries. Her thought strayed to *him*. That was her motivation. She wouldn't run again. It was his turn now.

She was disappointed to see she was the first to arrive. It irked her. Freddie always arrived first, she had adjusted. She needed the distraction. She sat at their usual table and looked around, fidgeting her leg. The plump barmaid took her drink order, orange juice and lemonade. She sat straight in the chair, her brow beginning to sweat. The tables around her were

filling up, the next dinner rush. She checked the time. 20:00. Looked around her some more. There were too many people. Too many witnesses, too many noticing her. She felt exposed. A few gave her curious glances. The waitress brought her drink. She sipped it slowly. 20:05. She counted the sips, slowing herself down. Time crawled to 20:10. Where was he?

She tapped her nail on the side of the glass. This was not part of the plan. He was meant to be here. Quarter past eight now. It was so unlike him to be late. She had been counting on him to be here. She needed him to be here. She caught the barmaid staring at her sadly from behind the bar. Probably thinking she had been stood up. This was not good.

She resisted the urge to get out her phone again, mentally trying to create a new plan. How long should she stay for? It must be at least twenty past, now. She had nearly finished her drink. The barmaid tiptoed over, asking if she would like to order food.

'I can come back if you like?' she offered, smiling at her sympathetically.

'Yes, please. He'll be here shortly.' Her voice cracked in the reply. Madeline was stiff, she knew that. She needed to act normal, keep up the pretence. Her leg began to twitch and she bit her lip. Straightened her back. 20:23.

Freddie finally sidled into the pub at 20:34, glancing around and spotting her. She stood quickly with such relief her chair flew back further than she expected. But, instead of the wide grin and overexcitable greeting she was accustomed to, he went straight to the bar, not looking her way. She stood, awkwardly as he muttered a quick order and finally made to meet her, none too enthusiastically. It was a pale kiss he left

251

on her cheek, before seating himself quietly. Madeline stood, puzzled. He hadn't offered to push her chair in today.

She furrowed her brow and sat back in her seat wordlessly. He picked up the menu on the table and studied it. She watched him curiously. He hadn't said a word to her, his attention focussed on the menu in front of him. The barmaid brought his pint over and he thanked her abruptly. Taking a sip, he finally looked up at Madeline.

'You okay?' his voice was flat. She raised her eyebrows in surprise. He offered no other questions, no explanations.

'Yeah... are you?' she asked uncertainly.

'Yeah. What are you having, then?' She didn't answer, narrowing her eyes. He took another swig of beer. If he had noticed her surprise he was doing a good job of pretending he hadn't.

'Soup. I think. Then the macaroni cheese.' She spoke slowly, carefully, keenly watching his body language.

'Nice. I think I'll do the stew.'

'Okay.' No pie today, then. She knitted her fingers together and squeezed her palms tightly in her lap. He placed the menu down and looked across the bar searching for the waitress. Madeline sat back in her seat, dumbfounded. He was calm, cold she might say. No flailing of those gangly limbs, no idle chit-chat. His face looked tired, irritated perhaps. She caught the subtle flinch when a fellow patron roared with laughter a few tables away. As he turned his head, she noticed faint, three red raised lines down the side of his face. He didn't say anything to her. She broke the silence.

'So. Where have you been?' she prompted gently.

'Hmm?'

'You're a bit late...'

'Sorry. I got caught up with something.' He was blunt and offered no further explanation. Madeline nodded slowly, her eyes travelling over his shirt. It was clean, crisp. But she noticed a sprinkling of dried mud dusted underneath. The waitress took the hint he was giving and came to take their orders. He adjusted his clothing gently, as though he were taking a great pain in moving. Madeline watched on, the feeling of uncertainty prickling through her body. He was hiding something.

'What have you done to your face?' Madeline asked nervously when orders were taken and the waitress had gone.

'Nothing.'

'What do you mean, nothing. There's marks on your face?'

'Oh. Possibly the dog.'

'Dog?'

'Yeah. A dog slipped its lead earlier. I was helping the woman to catch it and it scratched at me.' There was little emotion in his voice, but she noticed he couldn't quite meet her eye.

'Oh.' Madeline looked down at her empty glass. Condensation was dripping down the sides. 'What woman?'

'Just a woman.'

'Who was she?'

'I don't know, Madeline. A woman. A woman who lost her dog.' He sighed, exasperated. His tone was short, biting. Madeline felt the unease rising. She bit the inside of her mouth, the pain reminding her who she was, where she was. He'd never been this way with her before. Rather than looking uncomfortable in his own skin, for the first time, he looked settled in it. Their meals arrived and he tucked in. He didn't eat as fast as usual, slowly chewing each mouthful with his face screwed in concentration, avoiding her eye. She spooned her soup and sipped it carefully. Finally, she couldn't take it any longer.

'Why are you so quiet?'

'I'm just tired, Madeline.'

'You've been busy?' She heard the irritation in the second sigh.

'Yes. I have been busy.'

'What have you been up to?'

'Just stuff. Sorting bits. Work.'

'That's very vague.'

'I don't know what to tell you.'

The starters finished, they were cleared away. The mains arrived. She stabbed at the gooey pasta, her own irritation now rising. It was hard work, and now she couldn't stop the suspicion rising. She tried to lighten the mood, tell him a few anecdotes from her day. Still, he didn't meet her eye.

'You're not being very good company tonight,' she said, finally. She heard him sigh as he rested his fork on the side of the plate.

'Sorry. I'm just tired.'

'Why are you so tired?'

'Because I am!' he snapped. 'I'm just tired, Madeline.'

'Why did you ask me to dinner, then?' she snapped back. 'You invited me here.' His eyes flashed, she couldn't catch the look. Then his face fell, the fatigue replacing whatever was there before, finally looking at her. He reached a hand across the table, palm outstretched. She pursed her lips and placed her hand in his. He squeezed it.

'You're right. I did invite you here. I'm sorry.'

'That's okay.'

'I'm sorry for being grumpy.'

'I forgive you.' They smiled. He withdrew his hand and cut at his stew.

'If it's okay, I'm not going to be too late tonight.' Her heart fell a little.

'Oh. Okay.'

'It's just, I need to get back. I've got some more bits to do.' There it was again. The old trick she used. Be vague on details, don't give too much away, the truth is in there enough so it isn't a lie...

'Bits?'

'Yeah.'

'Work stuff?'

'No.'

'Then what?'

'Jesus, Madeline, will you drop it? Just bits, okay? I don't need to tell you everything.' He clattered his cutlery loudly on the plate. Madeline baulked at the outburst.

'No, I guess you don't,' she replied sadly. They finished their meal in silence and he paid. She let him without fuss. One final peck on the cheek and he turned on his heel, leaving her without a second look back. She sank back into her chair and leaned her head in her hands on the table. It was around quarter to ten. She sat quietly, amongst her thoughts for another hour. Another patron took pity on her and sent another drink her way. She drank it. Contemplating.

This had not gone the way she had hoped. She was

expecting to go back to his, fall asleep in his arms. She could sneak out from there. Timmy was at home. Her plans, carefully made, ruined. She felt stupid. Embarrassed. He was hiding something. And he had made her look like a fool. It rolled around to quarter to eleven and many of the locals thinned out. She knew she couldn't sit here any longer. She would have to go home.

Big man, aren't you? That's what I said to him. Big man, treating a woman like that. Billy big bollocks. Let's see how big those bollocks are.

I would never have spoken to you in that way, my love. Never. Despite all my flaws, it's something I pride myself on. Never lose my temper, never snap. It doesn't do to lose your composure like that. No matter how angry I get.

I am here, to protect you, my love. You need protecting. You think you have it all figured out. But you don't have the first hint of a clue. You try so hard to hide those secrets. You really thought you had, I know you did. You thought you could just come here, do what you needed to, and it would all go away. It doesn't work that way, my love. Actions have consequences.

His actions were abhorrent, though. I strung him up and took him for a ride. He lost consciousness after only a few minutes. It was fun, watching his head bounce around like that. I thought it might fly off.

He was long gone by that point, but I was curious, though. I had to see. I used a fishing wire, and gently split them open. Turns out his bollocks weren't that big after all.

21

Madeline

Madeline had barely slept since she crawled into bed and she woke groggily after a hectic night. Freddie's coldness at dinner had affected her more than she cared to admit and she certainly hadn't planned on waking up alone. She tried to have a lay in, catch up on sleep but Timmy had other ideas. She rose in protest, let him out and fed him, as the little master requested. He, content and satisfied, settled back down for his morning doze, but now Madeline was too awake to try and sleep any further.

She heaved down on the sofa, her heart as heavy as her bowl of porridge. She didn't fancy breakfast at all, but she knew she had to keep some kind of structure. Some semblance of normality, routine. Things were on the verge of spiralling dangerously out of control, off plan, and she forced herself through her morning routine. Turning on the TV shakily, the morning breakfast news programme was already in full swing.

The coverage of the murders was round the clock now. She listened tiredly, using her will alone to concentrate. Thankfully, there were no major updates, and the small details remained the same, the reports just reviewing what they knew. The images cycled of the victims and now graphics of maps had been created, showing the locations of each of the crimes and their proximity to one another in the area. Footage from the Chief Superintendent's press conference was replayed. The same reporter was still stationed in Lunnemouth, different colour blouse each day. Interview clips of the same locals were shown. And the bulletins moved on.

Madeline knew she was in the minority, but these murders were the last thing on her mind. Her past was threatening to emerge any day now unless she could get a handle on it. He'd been in the house. He'd had access to her camera. He had her number. God knows what else he had. Police were not putting the clues together as fast as she needed. Of course the murders wouldn't stop. He was relentless. She had no idea what he would have told police to get himself out on bail, what deals he made. It didn't bear thinking of. And now she had Freddie to worry about.

She wracked her brain, for any clues on what she might have done for him to ice her out. She was polite, she responded to his messages on time. She made sure she accepted his dates, despite everything she had going on. She had helped him organise his house, his life. She had always ensured to engage him in excellent conversation. She made sure she had enough of her own things to do, to not appear too available and yet not so much she was distant or appeared disinterested. Of course, she was a little jumpy at the news, but who wasn't? There was a serial murder spree, it would look strange if she was settled. He had taken it upon himself to distract her from it all, and she had let him. She was, to all intents and purposes, normal.

Her phone pinged. Stretching her body across the sofa, it lit up as she brought it to her face. Her eyes widened and her heart fluttered. She shot up as she tapped the notification.

Morning, babe. I hope you slept well?

Re-reading the message, she frowned at the resurgence of the pet name. *Babe.* She hesitated, debating on the best response. She couldn't say what was really going through her mind.

I slept like a baby. And you?

Send. Delivered. Read instantly. The bubble popped up. Typing.

Yeah thank you! I miss you.

She stared at the three little words. Was he joking? Before she had time to analyse, it pinged again. Another text, underneath it.

Are you working today?

She stalled slightly before tapping out her reply.

No, are you?

The reply came swiftly.

Do you fancy a day date in Lunnemouth today? Thinking we can go back to our café. Share some cake and stuff?

She paused, her thumbs hovering over the keyboard. Distracted momentarily by the TV in front of her. The local news segment now. Reporter was interviewing a farmer in Settersford, on the other side of Lunnemouth, whose fields had been churned up by joyriders overnight. The images of the ruined crops, thick mud and tire tracks were being shown, the farmer pointing for the cameras. She felt bile rising, not knowing how to handle this. How to handle any of this. He was acting ordinary, completely normal. Looking at her phone screen she bit her lip. Freddie was acting like nothing happened, like he did nothing wrong. She cast her mind back. Was it her? Had she imagined the exchange? No. She was certain. The barmaid had looked at her pityingly. The patrons had sent her drinks in unity. She had written it down. He was late. No eye contact. Illusive. It was here, on her notes app. So, why was he being nice again? She took a deep breath. And typed.

Sure. Sounds great. What time?

Send. Delivered. Read. Typing. Then blank. Nothing. She stared at the little screen, waiting for the reply. A minute passed.

?

She sent. Delivered. Instantly read. Two minutes passed. Her heart began to thud.

???

Same again. She tried to sit back, watch the news but by now an hour had passed and they were repeating the same bulletins as before. No updates. Images cycled, locations shown. Footage from the police conference and another pointless insert from the reporter in Lunnemouth. And the bulletins moved on.

Why did he have such a hold over her, how was it he could have her hanging on like this. He was meant to be a casual thing, a cover. A chance at normality. He had infiltrated her life, buried himself under her skin and nuzzled into her heart. She yearned, her heart skipped at his thought, she looked forward to seeing him. He even had her questioning her decisions. She was not an indecisive person like this. She may not always trust her mind, but she had always trusted her gut. The intrusion came bitingly.

You ignored your gut. I told you not to get close.

She had got close. She trusted. And she shouldn't have. She had almost taken her eye off the ball, got herself caught up in the fantasy. She got up and stretched, padding to the bathroom. Her phone pinged. Despite her attempt to keep aloof, unbothered, she practically leapt onto the sofa to reach it, checking the notifications. Text. *He wants to see me, he is going to apologise.* She opened it with glee in the anticipation. Her eyes misted over. Her breathing quickened and her hearing clouded.

Nice 'date' last night. Silly bitch. I hope he was worth it.

She flung her phone instinctively as though it had burst into flames in her hand. It clattered against her newly painted wall, leaving an ugly scuff down the fresh paintwork. Timmy, disturbed, raised his head and huffed at her before tucking his chin back into his legs and closing his eyes. She barely registered any of it, panic flooding her senses.

He had been there. Last night. He had been there and she hadn't seen him. He was right. Silly didn't begin to cover it. How could she be so stupid, so careless…

It was Freddie. If she hadn't been so caught up in worrying about him, wondering why he'd been so weird, so secretive. She would have kept her wits about her, she would have noticed him there. Watching her. *Watching her.* She screamed. She screamed until her throat bled and voice was hoarse. She screamed as her fists took chunks of her hair from her scalp and her muscles turned to ice. She screamed until she could no longer stand, feeling her knees finally give way and her body sunk into the piled carpet. Timmy pulled back his ears and watched her from his bed.

That was it. She couldn't afford any more mistakes or she would lose everything. He was obviously content to taunt her, play with her before moving in for the kill. She thought she had time. But time was limited. Time was up when he decided, that was clear. She needed to move things along. And fast. She strode across the living room floor and scooped up her phone. There was another text notification but she ignored it. If it was Freddie, it didn't matter. She would worry about him later.

Madeline wrung every bit of use out of her techniques, desperately and frantically trying to claw back any trace of control she fooled herself she had. This time, it didn't calm her, no matter how hard she tried. She paced around the living area, glued to her screen. She walked into the back of sofa and pranged her shins on the coffee table, barely flinching. She needed to get out. And she knew exactly where she needed to go.

She dressed in a hurry and snatched up Timmy's harness. It was just before 9 AM, and he was excited for the impromptu stroll. She knew people would see, he might be watching her, but it didn't matter. The lake was calling her. She needed to see it again. She needed the reminder, who she was, what she could do.

I am Madeline Hamilton.

She made to turn the TV off, when she noticed the news feature had changed. A crowd, chanting, holding signs and banners outside a building. Timmy bounced around her legs as she watched the scene. The building looked familiar. She read the signs. *Fair pay now. Fair pay for junior doctors.* The strikes. In her frenzy, she hadn't noticed. Negotiations had failed.

The camera panned across the crowd, and she tutted, shaking her head. Now, the patients would suffer. Her phone pinged again and she glanced at the screen. Another text. Remembering the text from earlier, she opened the notifications. They were both from Freddie.

How about 12?

Sent at ten past seven earlier that morning. She scrolled to the second. Sent thirty seconds ago.

Actually, can we make that later? About 4? Somethings come up.

She rolled her eyes and they caught the image on the TV. Her heart dropped. Her phone slipped out of her hands. There he was. Standing at the front of the crowd. Megaphone in hand. He'd gone on strike.

*

The lake did little to placate her mood. If Freddie hadn't done enough to hurt her already, this was the final nail in the coffin. He had lied to her. She hadn't replied to him, instead locking her phone and heading out with Timmy. They walked round the lake five times. The sun moved over in the sky above, tinging her pale skin pink. She felt the burn, the scald, the fire. On her skin and in her heart. But she couldn't delay it any longer.

The signs were all there, they had been dancing in front of

her for a long time. She had chosen not to see it, willed it to be different. The feeling in her gut had been right all along. She finally came to her decision as she knew she would. He had to go. Her heart broke upon the realisation of the implications. She would be alone, again. But she didn't have a choice. She could have perhaps forgiven the outburst, the blowing of the hot and cold. But she couldn't forgive him for this. He had lied. And his actions were now having serious consequences for every patient in the area.

She had eventually come home when Timmy started to tire and immediately signed up for further shifts on the ward. She finally replied to him at five to four.

Sorry. Can't do today. Maybe tomorrow night?

Yeah sounds great. Old Ram? 8pm?

Sure.

She sighed deeply. It was a full circle moment. Their first dinner date there and their last. She would never be one to have this kind of conversation over the phone but she wasn't ready to do it today. She needed to prepare, to look him in the eyes. She would hear his side of the story. He might apologise. He might even beg. *"Please don't do this."* She knew those words would try stall her, they would cast a niggle of doubt in her mind. He might fight her, it might get violent. But it didn't matter now. Her decision was made. Her gut was finally leading the way.

Madeline popped over to Joan's, asking if she would nip over about 9 PM to let Timmy out. Joan's face lit up at the request.

'Oh, it would be my pleasure!' she exclaimed.

'Thanks, Joan. I really appreciate it. Sorry for the short

notice, I'm now on shift tonight. Emergency cover.' Joan's eyes widened knowingly.

'Oh...' She looked searchingly at Madeline. 'You're not on those strikes, then?'

'No. No it doesn't sit right with me.'

'No. Well, you have to do what you think is best. You're a good girl, Madeline.'

'Thanks, Joan. And thank you again. Timmy will be excited to see you.'

'Any time, my dear. Any time.'

An hour later, Madeline was on her way into work. The roads were busy, and traffic built up further as she neared the hospital. She pulled into the car park and reversed into an empty bay. 17:23. Right on time. As she exited the car, she heard the noises of the protest carrying on the wind. She walked deftly past the crowd of juniors and nurses, in front of news cameras that were stationed around the striking staff. She avoided the eyes of the crowd. She felt the hair on the back of her neck prickle, eyes watching her as she walked in through the main entrance, but she didn't look back. Let them watch. She needed them to see she was there.

She arrived on the ward and headed straight for the staff room. She checked her phone, one last time and turned it off. She wouldn't need it overnight. Zipping her bag she closed the locker.

'Oh my god! Babes!' Roman made her jump as he came hurrying in.

'Jeez, Roman.'

'Sorry, sorry,' he hissed, a cheeky grin over his face, not sorry at all. She smiled. She liked Roman, despite all the dramatics.

'Babes. You are not going to believe this. She's gone AWOL!'

'AWOL? Who has?' Madeline scrunched her face, searching her mind for context.

'Martha!'

'Martha?' Madeline was thoroughly confused. Then, with a start, she remembered. 'Hold on, what do you mean, she's gone AWOL?'

'She's gone! Absolutely AWOL!' Roman's eyes were lit up and a huge grin on his face. 'Can you believe it!'

'What does that mean exactly? She's gone off the rails?'

'No, babes! She's gone! Taken off somewhere!' Roman threw his hands up. 'Like full blown *Gone Girl*. Disappeared! It was meant to be her last day of sick a week ago, but she never came back! Managers tried calling texting, nothing!'

'I mean, is it possible she's just on strike?' Madeline questioned, processing the news. Roman did have a flare for the theatrics after all. 'She might just be out there?'

'No, babes,' Roman said seriously. 'Not a chance. Our Shelly is quite close with her. She popped over. Door was unlocked, house bare, no car. She's taken everything and bolted.'

Madeline's mouth dropped open. 'Oh my god. Is she okay?'

'I'm going to guess no, babes.' Roman raised his eyebrows and folded his arms. 'She hasn't been okay for a while, has she? I reckon she couldn't take it anymore, just ran away. I mean, what fully grown adult even does that? So childish. What adult do you know that just runs away from their problems?' Roman tutted, shaking his head. He turned back out of the door. 'Anyway, I had to catch you and let you know. I'm off home now. Bye, Hun, have a good shift!'

Roman's parting words rang in her ears. He had a point. What full grown adult does run away? It wasn't a solution, it never was. She had learned that the hard way. Martha could run as much as she liked but her problems would always catch up with her. She needed to face them head on. Just as Madeline was doing now.

Him

He had kept a few paces behind. She had become so distracted since getting with her new fella. She didn't even look over her shoulder when she went out now. He'd watched her through the darkness, oh how she enjoyed herself, he could hear her laughter ringing through the night. Took a couple of videos, a photo here and there. She didn't even notice when he accidentally left the flash on. That's when he decided to step things up. He was enjoying toying with her. The flowers were a particularly nice touch, he thought. Followed up with the texts, it was gold. He was proud of himself for that one.

He sat in the dark now. Waiting for her. She should be home any minute, he'd seen the strikes on the news. There they were, all protesting outside Lunnemouth General. And there she was. She walked straight past the camera, stupid girl. Right in full view.

Gotcha.

That man had made her so self-absorbed, she was dropping the ball. She used to be so careful, so cautious to not be seen, and so meticulous he had begun to worry he would never get her unawares. And finally, his net was closing in. It would soon be over. He would have his revenge.

The stars were glinting in the sky as he sat, crouched on the pavement. Watching. Waiting. He could feel it. Tonight was the night. Finally.

A car's headlights lit the road as it turned around the corner and he shrunk further into the shadows. He watched as it came into view. No, the headlights were too high. It wasn't her. The Tiguan passed him slowly and pulled quietly into a neighbouring drive. A couple got out of the car, mumbling quietly to one another. He watched as the woman opened the passenger side door and pulled out a sleeping toddler. It didn't stir as she held him close, his head lolloping over her shoulder. The man kissed them both gently on the head. Wistfully, he sighed.

It could have been him, having a life like that. He should have the nice house, the stable job, the child. The partner to settle down and grow old with. The family van that would become the sports car once he hit his mid-life crisis. It was a life snatched away so cruelly by that fucking bitch. She had broken him with a swift, simple action, and he had lost it all. He felt the anger broiling, sweat beginning to pool under his hoodie as he watched, seething with jealousy. The man unlocked their door, flooding the driveway with light. The woman was lit in full view as she carried her precious cargo in, their hallway light left on for their arrival home. Or to deter burglars. He shook his head. A constant light like that only served to alert people outside no one was home. She disappeared inside, leaving the man to gather the things in from the car. Suddenly he heard a bark in the night and the man cried out.

It happened so fast. The dog raced towards where he was crouched, tongue out and tail wagging. The man bolted after him, his voice booming commands at the animal.

'No, Clifford! Come here now!'

The dog was nearly on him. In horror, he realised it had spotted him and was making a beeline to his location. *Shit.* Adrenaline took over and he bolted from his hiding place, pumping his legs as fast as they could carry him. The patter of the dog's paws rained just behind, enjoying the hunt, and as his foot slipped in his boot he prayed the bodged hoodie string holding it together would endure. The man was close, gaining on them both. He had spotted him and was now roaring as he made chase.

'Oi! You! Stop!'

He didn't relent. He knew the routes now, all the cut-throughs and alleys. He darted this way and that, expertly dodging the fat dog, who was easing off. The cries of the man were getting fainter as he left them behind, now into the close of houses behind the Ram. He leapt easily over the fence and scurried over to the children's play area. Throwing himself up the wooden steps of the climbing apparatus he launched himself into the small wood playhouse at the top of the slide. Flinging his body down, he laid still. Belly to the wood. His heart was beating in his ears. He dared not breathe. He strained to listen. He could hear a scuffling coming from the other side of the fence. The man was hissing.

'Where'd he go, boy?' More sniffing. He held his breath. He heard them move away, and finally give up the chase. He gently released the breath he was holding, slowing aware of the ache in his muscles. A stitch was developing under his left ribcage and his legs were burning. But he stayed put. He wasn't sure how long he had laid there before he dared to move. He risked a peek out of the small window in the little house. No one around.

He slid out, as quietly as he could. His feet touched the grass, and he took off on a fast stride. He needed somewhere to lay low, he couldn't go back to his car until he was sure the coast was clear. The locals were on high alert. Word would get around about this fast. They would be searching for him. He walked up past the Ram and quickly crossed the road, finally taking rest in a ditch the other side.

He leant back against the verge and closed his eyes.

Fuck!

He had her. He fucking had her. That fucking dog. Ruined everything. He knew he should have waited inside, but fuck, he just wanted the pleasure of catching her completely unawares before she had time to suspect anything. He knew it was dramatic, but he just wanted her to taste that terror. She fucking deserved it.

His own arrogance, his quest for revenge had clouded his judgement. He'd made such a stupid mistake. Keep it basic. Get it done. Next time he wouldn't be fancy about it.

After a few hours, he checked his phone. It had been quiet for some time, deeming it safe enough to head back to his car.

As he emerged from the ditch and crossed the road again, back towards the Ram he froze.

It pierced the air from afar, ripping through the silence of the night. Muffled, somewhere over the back of the Ram.

A woman's scream.

22

Madeline

Madeline sat at their usual table, sipping her orange juice and lemonade. She resisted the urge to check her phone. She knew he was late. No point in checking it again. She ran her fingers over the condensation on the glass, her fingertips created little trails over the surface, like snails trails. It was a warm July night. Even inside the Ram it felt unusually humid. She put her phone on the table, face up. Half an hour passed, and she saw the barmaid watching her out of the corner of her eye. She finished her drink. She pushed the screen to life. One hour.

Madeline signalled the barmaid and ordered another orange and lemonade. She brought it over with a kindly smile and asked if she wanted any food. Madeline shook her head.

'No, thank you. He should be here shortly. We'll order together.' The barmaid nodded, acknowledging her request and left her. Madeline checked the time. 21:17. She wondered how long she should wait for. What was the appropriate amount of time? She was acutely aware of the patrons at the bar, glancing across at her lonely figure. She sipped her drink and looked around. Other couples sitting around her, gazing into each other's eyes, sharing bits of their food, clinking their glasses. She felt a pang. The loss of a dream. That could have been her future once. But the decision had been made. There was no turning back. Her eyes fell back on the empty chair opposite her. She finished the second drink. 21:52. She felt a rumble in her stomach. This was enough time. She made to stand and caught the eye of the barmaid. The barmaid smiled reassuringly and Madeline made her way dejectedly to the bar to pay. A couple of men were leaning on the bar, drinking their pints.

'Don't worry about it, love.' She waved away Madeline's bank card. Madeline stalled.

'Sorry?'

'They're on the house, love.' She lowered her voice and leaned across the polished wood. 'Don't let it worry you. He's obviously not worth it.' Madeline lowered her eyes. She felt a tear spring under her eyelid, but didn't let it fall.

'He's a prick, love. Don't stress it. You're way too good for him.' The man closest to her added with a gulp of ale. He smiled kindly, the lines in his face deepening. She couldn't help but smile back.

'Thank you,' she said quietly.

'You don't have to go, you know,' the man offered the stool in front of him. 'You can stay for a drink with us if you fancy.'

'Oh. No, that's okay. I'm just going to go home, have something to eat, I think, and go to bed.'

'You can order something here, if you like,' the barmaid interjected. 'Kitchen will close soon but I'm sure Gus wouldn't mind whipping up some chips for you, if you want?'

Madeline's stomach growled in response. She did like the chips here. 'I mean, that would be lovely. If it's not too much trouble?'

'No trouble at all.' The barmaid busied away and the man closest to her extended a tanned, leathered hand.

'Name's Graham.' She shook it bashfully. He stepped back from the bar, and his friend behind peered around, smiling warmly.

'Richard.' He presented his hand, and she shook his too as she introduced herself. Richard's hand almost swallowed hers.

'Lucy has been keeping an eye on you, you know,' Graham said. Madeline's heart flipped.

'Oh?'

'Yeah, especially with everything that has been going on around here.' Graham gestured with a dirty thumb behind him. Richard nodded in agreement.

'You can't be too careful,' Richard added, eyebrows raised. Madeline nodded.

'It's a scary time,' she agreed. Lucy bustled back in from the door behind the bar, a bowl and a condiment basket in her hands. She placed the fat, crispy chips and condiments in front of Madeline. Madeline's stomach gurgled. She shimmied herself onto the seat, helped herself to a good squirt of ketchup and ate gladly. She hadn't realised quite how hungry she was. Lucy hung back with the two men and Madeline, and they casually chatted, occasionally leaving her post to serve another customer before returning to their conversation.

Graham was a local tradesman, recently divorced with

grown up children. He and his wife had them young. They had quickly realised they had long fell out of love with one another but they had stayed in their loveless marriage for the sake of the kids. When the youngest had eventually flown the nest, they parted ways amicably.

Richard had been Graham's best friend since they were at school. He was happily married, with a son still in high school. Lucy has worked at the Ram since she was sixteen, starting out as a part-time waitress on a weekend and never left. She was around ten years younger than the two of them, but in the same class as Richard's brother at school. Madeline smiled, asking all the right questions and listening intently. She ensured the attention never remained on her for too long and gave vague answers to their questions about her before batting another question back. They didn't notice, all three were more than content to talk about themselves and their own gossip from the village. It was interesting, the sense of community around here. It seemed no one ever really left. Very unlike the big city where she had come from. People didn't care who you were there, they didn't care if you left and never came back. Unless they were hellbent on revenge.

Time rolled on and the bar area thinned out. Only one couple remained on their table in the restaurant area. They didn't seem to notice. In their own little world, they were gazing lovingly into each other's eyes and whispering sweet nothings to each other. Lucy called last orders, and Madeline checked the time. 22:55.

The couple stood reluctantly from their table, seemingly unable to tear themselves away from the other. Madeline sighed and yawned.

'I suppose I had better be going,' she announced. 'Thank you for the lovely evening, guys. It turned out to be much better than I thought it would be.' Richard and Graham smiled at her, settling their tabs with Lucy.

'You're more than welcome, sweetheart. It's been nice to meet you,' Graham replied. He watched her curiously for a second. 'How are you getting home?'

'I'm walking. I only live down the road.' Madeline slid off the bar stool and threw her bag over her shoulders. Richard and Graham glanced at each other. Lucy mirrored their expression.

'You can't walk alone.' Madeline looked up. They were all looking at her with worried expressions upon their face.

'Honestly. I'll be fine.' Richard shook his head.

'No. We'll take you home.'

'Don't want a young woman walking home by herself late at night, especially at a time like this,' Graham added. The couple had reached the bar and Lucy moved to them to settle their bill.

Madeline waved her hand dismissively. 'Well, it might be out of your way. I'm up on Robin Close. Plus, I'm sure it will be fine.'

'No. Not taking no for an answer. Not risking it. Not when this crazed psychopath is on the loose.' Graham was firm. Madeline opened her mouth, and the man from the couple cut across the bar.

'We're in Robin Close, we'll walk you home.'

'Oh, okay. Thank you,' Madeline stuttered, studying them. The man tapped his phone to the card machine. The beep indicated payment had been received. The woman looked at

Madeline, then between Graham and Richard and raised her brow.

'Jake nearly caught him the other night, you know, Graham. He's been hanging around in the village.' All eyes were now on the couple. Madeline's eyes widened. Graham's arm was poised, cash still in hand as he was passing it to Lucy.

'Yeah. Got back from the police station earlier today.' Jake puffed out his chest and placed a protective arm around his partner. His wedding band glinted on his left hand. Not partner. Wife. 'Clifford spotted him. Hiding in the shadows up the close. Good job he did, he went straight for him, I'd never have seen him myself. I thought he was just being a pain in the arse at first, you know what cockapoos are like.' Jake rolled his eyes. His wife giggled at their shared joke. Madeline didn't get it. She had no clue what cockapoos were like.

'We chased him all the way down the road, into the village. Bloke had his hood up, dark clothing. I couldn't see who it was, but definitely looked like a bloke from his body shape, you know? Broad shoulders, tall. I lost him at the back there.' Jake gestured over his shoulder at the back of the pub. Madeline's heart was beginning to race.

'You nearly caught him? What did the police say?' she asked breathlessly.

'Nothing, just thanked me for my statement,' Jake shrugged. 'He's fucking lucky I didn't get a hand on him. Fucking creep. I'd have killed him myself.'

'Violence for violence is never the answer,' Richard interjected. Graham raised his eyebrows.

278

'I wonder if it's the same bloke...' Graham trailed off looking at Lucy. They exchanged knowing glances.

'What bloke?' the woman asked, eyes gleaming.

'There's been a lot of sightings of some guy in a dark hoodie hanging around the village lately,' Lucy said slowly. 'I hear all the chat, working here. Gerry caught him at the back of his fields once. Said he'd been seeing him down there a lot but he couldn't get to him before he'd disappeared. A few others have mentioned this weird guy, always in a hoodie in this heat. It's far too hot for a hoodie in the middle of day at the moment, you know, it makes people wonder what you're up to. Apparently, though, he's been hanging around for a few months now.'

'What's he been doing?' Madeline asked anxiously.

'So far, nothing. Just hanging around. But that's the creepy part. Darting behind bins and hedges when he thinks no one can see him. And no one can get close enough to ask him, he quickly vanishes.'

'Few months. Isn't that how long these here murders have been going on for?' the woman quizzed. Richard nodded.

'Yeah, something like that.'

'But people have died all over the area here, Millie. Not just in Little Molton.' Jake gave his wife a squeeze as he refuted her theory.

'He could be travelling. Or maybe he's not alone. Or, maybe he wants one in every village.' Millie paused in thought. 'There hasn't been one in Little Molton, yet, has there? Just Great Molton, I think.'

'Not this time, no,' Jake conceded. Madeline shot around and stared at him.

'What do you mean, *this time*?' she blurted.

'Yeah, it must be coming up to about a year ago, actually. Wasn't a series, but an old lady was brutally murdered in her home, here in the village. Police never caught him,' Jake said casually. Millie looked up adoringly at her husband.

'There you go, then. He's casing the area maybe. They always say these psychopaths like to go back to the scene of their crimes, don't they?' Her tone was gentle, soothing, despite the topic. It was very nonchalant, as though she was giving her opinion on the weather.

'You watch far too much true crime, Millie, my love.' Jake laughed teasingly at his wife. She heard a few other chuckles but Madeline's mind whirled out of the pub. The bile rose and she felt sick. Suddenly, the idea of the close-knit community felt like a cage.

'No need to worry, Madeline. We'll make sure we get you home safe, I promise.' Jake's voice swam into her head. He was smiling kindly, noticing her sudden fear. Madeline gave what she hoped was a smile of assuredness to Jake. He was tall, muscular. He did look strong. And fit. But she doubted she would feel any safer with him walking her home. Jake couldn't even catch him with the dog to help.

The patrons bade each other goodnight, and Madeline followed a pace behind Jake and Millie. They had only been living in their bungalow in Robin Close for about eight months, but Jake had grown up in the village. He had met Millie at university and they married soon after they graduated. They had bought a flat in Lunnemouth town centre, but when their boy, Archie, came along unexpectedly, they needed to upsize. Fate dealt its hand, the bungalow came up for sale, and Jake felt the pull back to his childhood village. In return, Madeline divulged her rehearsed background of how she came to be here, and thankfully they reached her door before they could enquire on why she moved out of the big city.

Her phone pinged, and she pulled it out of her pocket, glancing at the camera notification. Jake and Millie saw her into the door, and insisted they would wait for her to lock it behind her. Leaning against the now-locked door in the hallway, she took out her phone to access the camera feed. She watched them amble back down the drive and up the road out of sight. Sighing, she let herself into the living room. Timmy was excited to see her home, and this time she sat on the floor with him. Just as Freddie had done. She fussed him for a bit and went back to her phone. 23:22. Her finger hovered over the messaging app, in two minds. Indecision again. All because of him. She decided it was the best thing to do. She knew she needed to. Finally, she tapped on his name and wrote out a message.

What happened to you tonight?

She watched as it delivered. No read receipt came.

She sat on the floor staring at her phone until the screen timed out and the phone locked itself. It was done. There was no going back now. And in the end, people show you who they really are.

Secrets. Funny things, aren't they? We keep them because we think they could harm us if they get out. But the fact is, my love, you keeping your secret is what is going to harm you the most.

I won't harm you, don't worry. Not yet, anyway. I need you.

Fuck, just watching you now. Do you have any idea what you do to me? I bet you never stopped to think of the hold you have over me. In a way, you could argue you are making me do this. I've been waiting for you for so long. It's been so painful. I've been sneaking in, every night I can, just to watch you sleep. It's taken all of my strength never to touch you, only to watch.

He had a secret, you know? He thought it would never come out. And in the end, his secret harmed him. He had to go. I debated, but he was too close. You might not see it now, but you will. You'll see what I mean. He was pathetic really. I would've bullied him if we were in school. If he'd been bullied more, you never know, he might've lived. Might've had some fight about him. But that's the way things go sometimes.

But I needed the practice. I needed everything to be perfect before you came to me, my love. You deserve nothing less. I know how you love your fairytales, my love, just as much as me. And I deserve the perfect fairytale ending. The prince will save the princess in ways he never knew he could.

23

Madeline

The strikes were in full force, with more staff having joined. Madeline had been called in to cover on more than one occasion. The striking crowds and lecherous news crews were still swamping the hospitals general and emergency entrances. The ward was also busy, admissions had increased in the summer heat and the staffing level was skeletal. Madeline was relieved to see Roman was still at work, they passed like ships in the night at handover. They would give each other snatched pep talks and he would squeeze her shoulder reassuringly as one took over from the other. It was nice. She felt a little solidarity amongst the unease.

Martha had still not made an appearance, and management were chaotic. Alongside the strikes, sickness was at an all-time high. Madeline would often find herself being called in for cover with ten minutes notice, which irked her no end. It interfered with her plans. She had heard nothing from Freddie, as she knew she wouldn't. It hurt more than she had expected. She lamented, watching Timmy bounce around her feet enjoying his walk. He was always so happy, so content, it made her smile. At least he would never hurt her.

Madeline felt her phone vibrating in her back pocket and slid it out. It was the hospital. Again. She answered the call from work and grudgingly told them she would be in as soon as she could. Hanging up, she tutted. How was she meant to make preparations like this? She finished her walk early, luckily today she was not far from home. Time check. 17:42. She would be late to get there, but unfortunately that was the way it went sometimes. They couldn't expect her completely on time calling so late. She was doing them a favour. Madeline and Timmy strolled back home, knocking on Joan's on the way who was once more delighted to look after Timmy and offered to have him for a sleepover if she wanted. This was a pleasant surprise and suited Madeline immensely. It would mean she didn't need to worry about getting back in the morning, and Joan said she would feed him his breakfast, too. Seven minutes later, Madeline had showered and changed, Timmy and his belongings were dropped off, and she was in her KA driving out of Robin Close.

Summer was truly in swing, the beginning of August, and it seemed everyone was in the summer mood. The long sunlit days and the heat had put the locals in great spirits, despite the threat of a killer and multiple murders lingering over them. Children squealed excitedly as they played on their bikes, their anxious parents watching over them like hawks. Teenagers lounged around in short shorts and vests, smoking and drinking what looked suspiciously like WKD. Everyone seemed jovial, determined not to be beaten by fear or terror. It made her smile. She would like to stay here when all of this was over, despite everything that had happened. Perhaps she could have a fresh start, after all. Be one of them. Finally belong somewhere. No more running.

She was pulled from her thoughts and slammed on the brakes as a car swung out of the Old Ram's carpark, missing her by inches. The Mercedes veered over onto the other side of the road before pulling back in, in front of Madeline's KA. It's left wheels hit the verge, scuffing dried grass and dirt up its side. Despite the speed it left the car park it was now driving at twenty-one miles per hour. The driver made no effort to say sorry, or apparently even acknowledge the accident he nearly caused. She followed, leaving a large gap between them and watched as, again, he swung out across the white lines and an oncoming van blared its horn. The Mercedes swerved back, just in time, slowing down to fifteen miles per hour. Madeline looked on from behind, dumbfounded. It was all over the road. It slowed down and sped back up. The Ram's pub garden was crammed when she had passed, pub garden season in full swing. She narrowed her eyes at the dangerous driver in front.

Drink driving kills.

She groaned and gripped the steering wheel tightly, feeling the adrenaline rising. Concentrate. Breathe. She focussed hard on the car in front. Black detailed, Mercedes-Benz, driving at twenty-five now, apply the brakes, keep a safe distance, A-Class, back up to thirty-two, speed up a little, remain watchful, LA74 DGR, brake lights, new tyres, veering to the left, overcompensation to the right, black detailed, Mercedes Benz, A-Class, more braking, apply the brakes, keep a safe distance.

Without indication, the Mercedes suddenly swung down a

small country lane on a left turn. She applied her brakes again. She had kept a safe distance and finally the road ahead was clear. Madeline released the grip on her wheel and the breath she had been holding, taking the KA steadily up to forty-miles-per-hour and continued her journey on the main road into town.

The staff car park was bare, unsurprisingly. It took her no time to get parked. She tutted at the striking crowds as she passed, glaring at one member who held a sign, *protect our values, protect our patients.* How this was ever protecting patients she couldn't fathom. She stemmed then swallowed her irritation and threw herself into the work in a bid to get through the night.

The advantage to the skeletal staff is that during her long shifts, she did not have time to dwell on what was happening outside. Her conversation with the locals the other night had stirred up new nerves. Jake had mentioned a murder the year before, unsolved. Could it be the same one? She hadn't dared ask the question, hadn't wanted to poke or prod, but with the news of the hooded man who had been stalking around the village being the gossip, she had breathed a sigh of relief. Jake had gone to the police, given them a statement. They would now be putting two and two together. Soon, it would be over. And she would never have to worry about this again.

Madeline busied herself with ward rounds, medications, toileting and patient safety, all the while ensuring she was by Keith's bay to listen for the news. She finally took her break, an hour later than she should have. This was dinner. She was meant to have one hour, but she already knew even half of that would be pushing it. There was an extremely sick woman admitted to bay A, and David in bay D had taken a turn for the worse over the last twenty-four hours. Just because the others were content to just let him die, didn't mean she would contribute to that. She would not have that on her conscience. Twenty minutes, that is all she would allow herself. She turned her phone on and checked the time. 01:37. The ham sandwich she had made earlier had warmed unpleasantly in her locker, and she tried not to cringe as she shovelled it down her throat. She had hoped to get out in her break, she needed a release from the itch in her mind, but this turn of events had meant she wouldn't get that tonight. She felt the flicker of agitation and pulled up her list. More notes added, new plan made for tomorrow. The agitation subsided. She felt the beginnings of indigestion as she chewed on the sweaty sandwich. Hovering over the messaging app, she opened it. She didn't want to, but she knew she had to. Typed slowly. Send.

Are you okay?

She watched, as the receipt indicated delivery. She stared at it for a moment. With a delicate finger she scrolled up checking the one from last night. Delivered. No read receipts on either of them. No surprise there.

She placed her phone beside her and finished her disappointing sandwich. Brushing the crumbs off her chest, she made herself a quick coffee. She had fifteen minutes to drink it before she would get back.

Freddie played on her mind, wondering how many messages to send him. She reflected back, wondering where it had all gone wrong. She should have known better than to trust him. She had imagined them having a future at one

287

point, she had lowered her guard, let him in. *That's where it went wrong*, she thought. The coffee was steaming, it smelt bitter. Burnt from the boiling water. She sighed. It would have to do. She would look forward to a nice cappuccino from her machine tomorrow. She sat back down on the old sofa in the staff room. Thinking.

She knew she had made the right decision in the end. It had taken a long time to get there, and there was part of her which regretted even contemplating any kind of future together after everything that happened. Hindsight was a wonderful thing, though, and Madeline learned from her mistakes. Her mind had led the way, she knew better than to allow that in any circumstance. And at least she had had the decency to want a conversation with him, talk to him. She was the good person in this situation, not him. He was the bad person.

She would wait until the end of her shift and send another text. She missed this part of her nature. She had become too indecisive when it came to Freddie. It was nice to get back to herself in a way. Madeline left the inadequate coffee mug half full. She was so used to timings by now, she knew she was coming up to her twenty minutes but checked the time anyway. Bang on. She smiled, zipping her phone back into her bag and shutting it in her locker.

The ward was eerily quiet at night. Peaceful. She had always liked the night, there was something about being the only person awake in the world, in her own company, free to be herself. She had never minded being alone. Screw Freddie for making her think there was ever a better alternative, she knew better than that now. Strolling down the ward silently, into bay A, she completed the observations on the poorly woman and tiptoed out.

The patients were all sleeping soundly. She could hear the gentle snores, the muffling, the pleasant dreams of sleep from each bay. She reached bay D, and leaned on the door looking in at the still figures in their beds. It was comforting to watch them sleep so serenely. Keith had been complaining of pain all day according to his notes, but after Madeline had dispensed his much-needed morphine, he was finally able to get some rest.

Madeline moved quietly into the bay, her shoes not making a noise upon the lino floor. She stole around, smiling softly. Even David looked as though he was simply asleep. He could almost be dreaming, resting in a pleasant slumber after a hard day's work. She caught a movement through the window at the end of the bay and blinked. The bay was dark, the night lights only providing just enough light for her to move around. The blinds were open and the light was reflecting in the glass pane a little. For a moment, she doubted her eyes. The ward was on the ground floor, facing out to the car park, it was possible it was a trick of the light. Then again. No mistake. Movement. A dark figure, hurried under the lamppost lighting the car park. She darted to the window and pulled herself up against the wall, away from view. Her breathing quickened as she stood still, palms on the wall behind.

He was here now, too? Why couldn't he just give her a break. That was a stalker, though, she supposed. Stalkers in their nature, will do anything to follow you. They will follow you everywhere. They stalk. She focussed her mind and relaxed against the wall. Thinking. The peace of the night gave her space to contemplate. It was where she thrived.

He couldn't do anything whilst she was here anyway. He couldn't get onto the ward. It was double locked, identity key card access on both doors and an intercom system she had to answer. And she would not be letting him in. She could relax there at least. Breathing deeply, she peeled herself away from the wall. She stood herself in the middle of the window, looking out. She couldn't see anyone else, but she knew he was there. Watching. But that's all he could do. Watch her.

Let him watch.

Madeline was grateful she realised, in the most ironic way, for the strikes. She paced back through the bay doing her visual checks on the sleeping patients, her fingertips grazing the ends of their beds. Their selfishness had inadvertently shortened her break, stopped her going out there tonight. He would have been sure to catch her if she had. And he wouldn't have much hope of catching her by the time her shift ended. The car park would be busy again, protestors and staff alike returning to their posts.

She was safe.

She padded out of the bay and slipped into bay C, silently checking on the patients. A machine bleeped in the corner and she crept over to the bed. Air bubble in the IV. As she rectified it, she wondered if he was still watching. What was he expecting to see? She hoped the police hurried up already. They must have tons of evidence by now, she reasoned. The villagers had seen him. Jake down the road had even reported him. What on earth were they waiting for? The air bubble out, the machine reset, it ceased its alarm.

She debated for a moment. She could go to the police.

No.

You know why you can't do that.

No, she knew she couldn't. It was tempting, it would speed up the process for sure. But it would also cast a horrible spotlight upon her, too. She would be linked. It was too dangerous, too risky. She had to trust in their work. The evidence was there when they needed it from her. They would get him.

She snuck out of the bay, and into the next. One of the patients had fallen to the side in his sleep. Right sided muscle weakness, no strength to pull himself up. She supported him back to lie straight, plumped up the supportive pillows on either side and sat him back up in the bed. He hadn't stirred through the whole repositioning. She smiled, looking around her. Watching the patients sleep, so innocent. Their lives in her hands. She was a good nurse.

She had wanted to be a nurse for as long as she could remember, she'd always been fascinated by the human body. She was naturally very good at her job; her personality was a good fit. She was organised, hard-working, level-headed in a crisis, able to think on her feet. She was curious, she cared strongly about innocent lives, doing the right thing. She had a strong moral compass. It showed she was a good person. But she knew that hadn't always been the case.

There had been a time where she had been off the rails. Impulsive, careless. Selfish. Made stupid decisions and many, many mistakes. She didn't care back then. When those mistakes bit her back and her freedom was threatened, she changed. She strived to do the right thing, use her skills for good.

The calming silence was brutally ripped open by an alarm. Madeline jumped, processing the alarm quickly in her mind. Fire. Intruder. No. Emergency alarm. It was the emergency buzzer.

Without hesitation she fled into the corridor and towards the flashing light above bay A's door. She hurtled in, to find two panicked young care assistants frantically pummelling at the woman's chest. The buzzer was wailing. Patients rudely awakened, were sitting up in their beds in a daze. She strode to the wall and pushed on the buzzer, ceasing its racket, and realised who it was.

'No!' Madeline screeched. She fought the care assistant nearest to her, wrenching him off the patient, his face pale and terrified. He paid Madeline no mind, his focus on the patient in front of him. She threw him off violently, he almost toppled with the ferocity.

'No! No! Stop!' She scratched and clawed across the bed, desperately attempting to stop the other assistant from thumping her palms into the delicate ribcage. The assistant leapt back, looking at her with a horrified expression on their face. Madeline whipped around and turned to the patient, eyes searching her widely. The poorly woman was now Cheyne-stoking, gasping, the rattling and wheezing as she choked on her own airway. Her eyes were blank and glassy. Madeline held the care assistant back as they watched her chest jerk up and down violently. Finally, she fell still. Her eyes glazed over. Madeline glared at the two assistants in rage.

'She has a DNR,' she spat. They gawked at her, silently in

shock. Too angry to speak to either of them, she marched out of the bay to call a doctor to declare death, leaving them rooted to their spots. She stormed over to the nurse's station, throwing the phone receiver to her ear.

Madeline was furious. The woman, so poorly, so ready to die. She was deserving of a peaceful end. Innocent, she had put her life and death in the hands of people she should have been able to trust. They had let her down in the worst way possible. That woman just died. And she had suffered, too. Suffered in one of the most unimaginably painful ways.

The old lady was relatively quick, in the grand scheme of things. One of the quickest I've ever done. It was as though the minute she saw me she gave in. It was like she knew. She knew it was her time. Accepted her fate.

One. Two. Three. It was over in a flash as my knife sank in and out of her doughy abdomen, slicing through her delicate nightgown like it was nothing. She made a mess, too. Shit, piss, and blood, fucking everywhere. I usually enjoy the thrill of it all, but it was over so quickly it took all of my satisfaction. I'll never forgive her for that.

The bedroom looked like an abattoir, the irony was she was a vegetarian. Imagine. The juxtaposition of that. Even now it makes me chuckle.

But she taught me a valuable lesson. I carry that one with me, so many things wrong there. I was never that quick again. Took my time. It doesn't do to be reckless.

24

Madeline

Madeline reported the two young assistants that night. Gross incompetence. Basic patient care. She was so angry at their negligence; she would make sure she never had to work with them again. She didn't want either of them anywhere near another patient as long as she could help it. Her anger had pumped her body full of adrenaline, and she worked on autopilot for the next three hours until her shift ended. They had approached her sheepishly several times, trying to make their apologies. She had deftly ignored them.

No. This time, apologies, excuses. They would not stand. It was unforgivable. A glare in their direction and they backed away. They had their chance. Soon as she could get rid of them she would. They would never step foot in this hospital again, she would be sure of that.

Roman had pranced in at 05:55, giving her a little wave as he skipped past the nurses station to the break room. Despite her anger she felt a little relieved at his arrival and was silently impressed at his time-keeping. Many other nurses and assistants arrived dead on 6 o'clock, precisely when their shift started. They didn't think about the time it would take to remove their jackets and place their belongings in their lockers. Eating into precious time they should be looking after others.

Madeline was still at the nurse's station, typing up her last few notes when two hands slammed on the station in front of her. Startled, brows raised she looked up to Roman. His face was alight, practically dancing on the spot.

'Babes. Oh my god.'

'Hi, Roman.' She knew it was pointless asking him what was up, he was going to tell her no matter what she said.

'Babes. She's been found!'

'Who?' The thought crossed her mind. 'Martha?'

'Yes!'

'Thank god for that. I need to take something to her—'

'No, babes. No.' Roman rudely cut her off, his expression serious.

'Why? Is she not coming to work?'

'She isn't coming back to Earth, Hun. She's dead.' Madeline's mouth dropped out and his words hung.

'Dead?' Her voice cracked. Roman raised his eyebrows and nodded theatrically.

'Yep. Dead. Shelly just text me. They found her at her parents. Both parents dead from stab wounds in their beds. And she was hanging from the stair banister.' Madeline's hand shot to her mouth.

'Jesus...'

'I know!' Roman stared at her. She glanced back at him, a little annoyed. She wasn't sure, but he seemed to be revelling a little in this tragedy. Enjoying the gossip a bit too much.

'Did she... Like... did she...?'

'Do it to herself? Yeah. That's what police think, Shelly says. Murder-suicide.' He leant over the station and lowered his voice. 'Apparently both of her parents had dementia. She's been trying to care for them, sell the house, get them into a home, you know? I told you she would crack under the pressure, didn't I? Just didn't know she'd crack like that!' He played with his lanyard, and flung it over his shoulder, suddenly looking her up and down.

'Anyway. Isn't it time you went home?' He raised a sharp, defined eyebrow and glanced at the clock behind her. She sighed tiredly.

'Yeah, I know. I'm just finishing up my notes. Had an incident in the night, CPR given to A6.'

Roman's eyebrows shot up his forehead. 'A6? The same A6 that was here yesterday?!'

'Yep. Same patient. She's gone now.' Madeline replied grimly.

'Shit... What idiot was responsible for that?'

'Two of them. The bank assistants.'

'Carly and Justin?'

'Probably. I don't know their names. But they won't be back, that's for sure.'

'No.' Roman looked at her sadly. 'Well, shit...'

'Can't help but think, if it wasn't for these strikes...'

'Babes. Stop. You can't think like that. These things happen.' Madeline said nothing but pursed her lips. He watched her awkwardly, leaning on the station. Eventually he stood and tapped gently on the surface.

'Should we do a quick handover? Then you can get off

home. Think you need a good rest.'

Madeline completed handover fairly fast. Now David was the only critically ill patient there wasn't too much to go through. She stepped out from the cool hospital lobby, the early morning sun hitting her legs and heating her up. It was going to be a warm day. The first of the protestors had started to filter in and set up and she stopped. She threw daggers at them, the look alone enough for them to recoil. This was their fault. There should have been another nurse on with her. Trained nurse. Who knew what notes to read. Someone to monitor that side of the ward. She couldn't move, the anger immeasurable as it rose up her body. Eventually, she pulled herself away.

When Madeline got into her car, slamming the door, she didn't turn the engine on. She needed to think, calm down before she started driving. Driving like that was not safe, she couldn't trust herself. There was no chance she would be able to sleep when she got home, she needed a stress relief. She doubted Joan would be awake at this time and didn't fancy small talk to get Timmy for a stroll around the lake. She needed something strong, a reminder. A good long walk at one of her favourite places. She pulled up her maps and checked an old timestamp. At this time, traffic hadn't started to build yet. One hour and forty-five minutes away. It was a long drive after a long night. But she needed it. She turned on the engine and pulled out of the car park.

She arrived in Rockbridge at 08:30 exactly. The drive had calmed her somewhat as she returned to the town where she grew up, but she was tense from the concentration. Rage worked just as well as coffee as a stimulant, however, and she barely felt the near twenty-four hours she had been awake. She checked her phone. No notifications from the camera. Nothing from Freddie. As she knew there wouldn't be. She fired off another quick message and put her phone in her pocket. She paid for her parking from the antiquated machine. There was no need, traffic enforcers stopped coming out here years ago, but it was the right thing to do. She placed the small ticket on her dashboard and set off around the park.

Rockbridge wasn't a big town, it didn't need to be. Twenty minutes away from the big city, it had no need for large shopping centres, supermarkets, and restaurants. It had been abandoned as the city suburbs swelled, swallowing up its resources and leaving behind an empty shell. Those who could afford to, moved into the city leaving those less fortunate behind. It had become a dive before she was born. But in the years since she left, it had become more derelict than she imagined possible. She saw graffiti sprawled over the old buildings that once held local grocers, pharmacies, café's, their shutters now doomed to remained closed forever. The offie survived though, she noticed. Of course it did. It was one of the only ways to cope for many around here. Despite its sad little standing, she had fond memories of that place.

She had flirted shamelessly with the owner's son, flashing her breasts in exchange for free vodka. Eventually, he had asked her out. They would date, although she wasn't sure she would call it 'dating' now. The dates in question tended to take place on the rocks under the bridge where the town got its name. He was sweet and caring at the start and she practically lived with him. Her mother never cared, too drugged out of her mind to even recall she had a daughter. She would cut classes at school, not that she bothered to hide the fact she was sneaking out. She could walk straight past the teachers and staff smoking their fags outside the office, none would ever be concerned enough to stop her. He would pick her up from school in his modified Saxo, sweep her hair gently back and trail his finger gently up her leg when she climbed in. He liked her thighs, so she folded the top of her skirt over and over, shortening it just as he requested. He treated her to bags of greasy chips and stolen sweets from his dad's shop and puffs on hastily rolled joints. When he kissed her, he was tender and gentle. He was sweet.

But soon, things changed. Their once-cute, albeit pitiful 'dates' over shared chips descended into weeklong benders where hard drugs, cheap booze, and frenzied sex were the theme. He got his and she got nothing but bruises and friction burns along her back, pain masked by the concoction of substances pumping through her veins. Then, she was introduced to his 'friends'. It stayed that way, until his demands had got too much and she finally had the courage to do the right thing. He had been her first. The first time should be special, and it was. Despite all of it. But after another night of being raped so violently by all four men that she lay broken and bleeding, something in her snapped. That was the trigger. That was when she decided. She never bothered to say goodbye to her mother. She got on the bus with nothing but a small bag of her belongings, blood-stained skirt and travelled for three hours. Finally, in the safety of a refuge, she met her school's psychologist for the first time, and throughout her therapy sessions she was introduced to a different world where the good guys do win. Realising that same power was within her, she worked hard for a new life, to ensure the bad people never won again. And she promised herself she would never make the same mistakes. Never again would she trust another person. No more would she be a victim. And she would remember who she was.

She paused on the path and gazed across the park at the grey block of flats on the other side. The window on the ground floor was smashed and the buildings were coated in grime. It had barely changed since she was here all those years ago. She was young, only thirteen in that bedsit with four predators. He had been so nice to begin with and it was a shame he was swept up into that life. There was a time that she felt guilty. She had told herself she should have been there, by his side. Maybe things would have been different for him, she could have changed him. But now she knew he was responsible. He had no one to blame but himself. He was eighteen. He was an adult. He should have known better. He deserved what he had coming.

There were no memorials that she knew of. His dad had disowned him a few weeks prior to his brutal murder and in the aftermath, he sold the offie and moved out of the town. She had sat in a state of shock as saw the articles shared all over social media. It was a blood bath, apparently. Like a horror movie, they said. Police theorised it was gang-related, a violent dispute over drugs gone wrong and closed the case. She heard nothing more. She felt nothing for those monsters, and no longer felt any guilt for his fate. But sometimes she still thought of the innocent, sweet boy she once knew.

She liked to come here. Not for those memories, no. She battled those every day, pushed them under where they belonged. They would always be with her, she didn't need to be back here for that. But, standing in front of that building again she was reminded of the promises she had made that day, and the mistakes she had vowed to learn from. It kept her on the right path when she felt she was straying, keeping accountable to no one but herself.

You are a good person. You didn't deserve that.

Noone did. She kept the flats in view as she walked the laps around the park. Children on their bikes were starting to come out and there was a strong smell of weed around them. Old cars drove past with loud music booming, the bass rattling into her bones, and rusty exhausts kicking up fumes into the air. She walked. Her legs began to ache, and her body began to bow. She felt the fatigue creeping into her face as the lack of sleep finally caught up to her. After lap ten, she changed course and headed back to the car. She darted in quickly, locking the doors behind her. Gone was the anger, the rage, the impulsivity. In its place was the clear, calmed mind of the woman with a plan she was now.

I am Madeline Hamilton.

I am a good person.

She needed a nap before driving the now two hours fifteen minutes back, but it wasn't a good idea to sleep here. She recalled a service station about five miles away on the motorway. She put the keys into the ignition and her little KA roared to life. She pulled out of the car park slowly, and headed for the service station, leaving her past behind.

Him

Finally. There'd been bumps in the road, near misses left right and centre but finally. This was it. He had her right where he wanted her. It had taken so long, but he could almost feel his reward now. He watched the police, streaming in and out of the red door like little black ants. It was an ugly scene, with yellow tape and their vehicles blocking the road. He watched as a bus tried to squeeze past the carelessly parked patrol car abandoned on the pavement, passengers ogling with their faces pressed grotesquely against the dirty glass. Trying to catch a glimpse of the drama.

He didn't need to hide today. No need for darting behind bins, stalking the shadows. They were all out. The locals had congregated around the road as soon as news had spread. Like vultures. He hid in plain sight. It had been a real shame that that man had to get caught up in her actions. He lost his life and it was all her fault. He'd been watching them for so long, he could see he was a decent bloke, after all. But it was too late now.

It was time.

He turned away, walking comfortably up Robin Close. Remembering. He had seen her, that final day of the trial. She tried to sneak in, she crept in at the back. It was clear she didn't want to be seen, she was wearing that crude blonde wig, a pathetic attempt at a disguise. A small strand of copper hair had given her away, though. He'd seen her straight away from where he sat. Her eyes, he would always remember her eyes. They'd captivated him from the moment he met her at school. And that's when he knew for sure. He'd had his suspicions, he always had. But her presence that day confirmed it. It was her.

The victim's statements are always the last part of any trial, and he had seethed as they had stood to read them out, one by one. He couldn't hear a word of what they were saying, his eyes fixed upon her. She disappeared after that. But it was too late. That was the day he had started to watch her. He'd chased her for the best part of two years, out of the city and to places she thought she could hide. And he wasn't letting her go this time.

He had been patient, he had stood by, watching and waiting all this time. But finally. Everything was ready. Now, it was time to reveal himself.

25

Madeline

Madeline had finally rolled into the bungalow at 11:46, tired but revitalised, finding Timmy had already been dropped back. There was a note left on the coffee table.

I thought you might want to come into him when you got home. He's had his breakfast. I hope you had a good night. J x

She smiled at Joan's kindness, and beckoning him through to the main bedroom they slept for the majority of the day. Madeline was ravenous when she rose, the growling of her stomach waking her insistently, and she woozily checked the time. 17:47. She hadn't slept this well for a long time. Too many thoughts and urges had been gnawing away at her, torturing her to the point that she had to get up for a release, worrying each time could be her last. Her excursions this morning had finally put her right, put the doubts to bed. Reminded her exactly who she was. And what she was doing this all for. The risk, the running, the hiding. It would all be worth it. He would be damned, she vindicated.

Nearly there, just keep going.

Timmy stretched and rolled onto his belly, nestling himself into the duvet, clear he had no intention of getting up.

She chuckled and forced the reluctant dog outside. He did his business—twelve seconds today—and trotted straight back in for another hard-earned rest on the sofa. She switched on the TV and checked the time again. 17:56. Four minutes to wait. She stuck a microwave meal in on high for three minutes. Another minute to rest. Perfect timing. She was spooning the steaming pasta into a bowl when she heard the dramatic drums announcing the programme was due to start. She ambled into the living room and sat herself comfortably on the sofa.

'Tonight, at six o'clock. Unions meet with government to discuss the ongoing pay dispute. A drought warning issued by the Met Office following the record-breaking July temperatures. And meet the bear who has become best friends with a penguin.' Madeline snorted into her rubbery pasta.

'But, first. There have been significant developments in the investigation of a series of murders around Lunnemouth, police say...'

Madeline shot up. Pasta cast aside. Tapped the remote. Volume up to 15. This was what she had been waiting for. Timmy lifted his head and sniffed the air. She didn't notice.

'Police released the statement earlier today. BBC News correspondent Aria Patel is outside Lunnemouth police station now. Aria, what can you tell us?'

Madeline fought hard with her mind, concentrating on every detail as the image switched to the young journalist standing outside the large sign. **Lunnemouth Constabulary.**

'Thank you, Fiona. Police released a statement earlier today confirming there had been further developments in the investigation into the series of murders that have occurred in and around the

small town of Lunnemouth. They have advised they now have
sufficient evidence to suggest these crimes may have been committed
by the same perpetrator and are asking all residents to remain
vigilant. Police did caution, however, that they cannot rule out any
other leads at this point in time. But they strongly suspect these
cases are indeed linked, and are the crimes of a single, serial
perpetrator.'

Madeline sat with her hands to her face, unable to believe
what she was hearing. The pressure building inside her body
burst, with unwavering ecstasy that flooded her veins. Finally.
Finally. They were finally putting the pieces together.
Frustratingly, they hadn't released what these developments
were. But she knew it was deliberate. Holding key details
back about the crime and the evidence they had gathered
could be vital in interviewing any suspect. She felt the weight
on her lift, her freedom so close.

So close now. Be patient.

She remembered the elation and false sense of hope she
had felt before when he was arrested the first time and calmed
herself. Not getting too far ahead, not allowing her guard to
slip completely. But, it was another step closer.

She picked up her phone and pulled up her messages
again. All sent, none delivered. Just like she knew they would
be.

Can you please get back to me?

Where are you?

This is really unfair, Freddie. I don't deserve to be ghosted
like this.

Freddie where are you?

Freddie, I'm starting to worry now. Your messages aren't

delivering?

Freddie, please call me back.

Or text me.

Freddie this isn't funny. Please can you just get back to me?

I've been called into work, just in case you pop over.

Freddie, I can't do this. You're breaking my heart.

Freddie. Please.

She typed out one, final message. She studied it closely. It had to be perfect. Re-reading, once, twice, three then four times and pressed send.

Okay. Fine. I get you don't want to hear from me anymore. I wish you all the happiness in life I really do. You won't hear from me any longer. Take care of yourself, Freddie xx

A bulletin flashed up on the news in front of her. Breaking news. Madeline watched curiously, her phone still balanced in her hand.

'*We interrupt the story on Benny the bear to bring you some breaking news. Lunnemouth police have just announced they have found a further two bodies at separate addresses in the surrounding areas. The bodies have not yet been identified and the circumstances around their deaths have not been released. Police have not yet confirmed whether they are connected to the series of murders that are being investigated, but they have advised a statement will be issued in due course.'*

Madeline remained composed. Collected. Another two found. She did the numbers, counting up in her head. It was only a matter of time now.

Her pleasant aura was disrupted with a banging at the

front door. Frowning, she pulled out her phone and saw the notification. She obviously missed it when she was glued to the news. She pulled up the image.

Two figures, male and female. Both wearing smart black trousers. The male was wearing a tie, the female in a blouse. She studied the image curiously and recoiled again as the knock, sharper and louder, rang through the bungalow. Timmy was up, dancing around, whimpering. She rolled her eyes, sat back on the sofa and ignored it. Cold callers, more than likely. She had seen a few of the down this area, she usually watched them on the camera as they walked away. But these were persistent. A ring of her doorbell now. It echoed through the walls, unnaturally loud and pinged through another notification on her phone. Realising the callers were not giving up easily, Madeline groaned and stood from the sofa. She didn't like to make a habit of answering the door, but whoever it was knew she was in. Another loud rap on the knocker as she reached the hallway. She pursed her lips. This was getting a bit rude now, she still had enough poise to be polite but they were beginning to get on her nerves. She would stick with being firm, but civil. I'm not interested, thank you, that's what she would say. She thought about heading to the local DIY store and getting one of those signs for the door; *no cold callers*. She could do that tomorrow, it would take ten minutes.

Pulling the door open she rearranged her face into a smile, not wide, but small enough to appear friendly. The figures from the camera stared back at her, mirroring her expression. Just as she opened her mouth to speak, the man cut across.

'Madeline Hamilton?' Mouth agape, she baulked. How

did they know her name?

'I'm DS Chandra, and this is DC Mulley. We're from Lunnemouth Constabulary.' The bile rose. This wasn't part of the plan. She glanced down the street at the black BMW parked inconspicuously on the side of the road. With a flash of annoyance, she noticed it had been parked up the pavement.

'Are you Madeline?' She stared at the car for a moment, watching as an old man shuffled past on the path. She could hear the scuffing of his belt down the side of the bodywork. Realising they were still waiting for her, she pulled her attention back as he freed himself from the other side.

'Yes. Hi. Sorry. That's me, yes. What can I help you with?' she answered, clutching the door. Drawing on her calmed demeanour, acting the part. All the while wondering, trying not to get too excited, show too much emotion. What did the police want with her? Was it him?

'Could we come inside?' *No. No you can't*, she wanted to say. But she couldn't. Madeline gritted her teeth and stepped back by way of an answer. She didn't want to, but it was the right thing to do. The detectives wiped their shoes on the mat but didn't remove them. She clenched her jaw even tighter and showed them down the hallway into the living area.

Timmy was hopping on his back legs, elated at the unexpected visitors. DS Chandra flinched a little and took a small step back, but DC Mulley immediately dropped to her knees and stroked him behind the ears, a wide grin spreading across her cheeks. Madeline hovered, straightening her spine.

'Um. Would you like a drink or anything?' It was polite to offer guests a drink. Even if they are coppers. Thankfully, both declined the offer. They stood uncomfortably in the living room, the TV still blaring. Madeline hastily grabbed the remote and silenced the news as DC Chandra took charge.

'Miss Hamilton, perhaps you would like to sit down?' He was motioning a hand to her own sofa. It wasn't an invitation, it was an instruction. Confused, she stepped over slowly, and carefully sank into the cushions. DC Mulley had stopped her attention of Timmy, and asked if she could sit next to Madeline. Madeline nodded as the petite woman perched herself on the edge of the cushion, balancing herself uncomfortably. DS Chandra remained standing. Neither of them spoke. Madeline was unable to take the tension any longer.

'Sorry. What is going on?' She caught the glance shared between DS Chandra and DC Mulley. It was quick, but it was there. Her heart rate quickened.

'Miss Hamilton, I understand you are romantically involved with Freddie Warner.' DS Chandra stated. It wasn't a question. Freddie's face shot to mind, her heart began to thump.

'I... er... Yes,' she stuttered. She knew she couldn't lie. 'I was.'

'Was?' They picked up on it. Of course they did.

'Well... He stood me up. We were meant to have a date the other night. But he never showed.' Madeline looked up at him, blinking slowly. She drew her eyebrows together. DC Chandra had pulled a small notebook from his pocket and was flicking though the pages.

'When was this?' he asked gently. Madeline thought hard and bit her lip.

'Last Thursday night.' She watched anxiously as DC Chandra took some notes and sighed. His face fell, and he placed his notebook back in his pocket. Adjusting his trousers, he bent his knees and sat on the balls of his feet. It was impressive balance.

'Miss Hamilton, have you heard from him since he stood you up?' She shook her head, furrowing her brow. Parting her lips slightly.

'No, I've been texting him, he hasn't replied, though.'

'Miss Hamilton, I'm really sorry to have to tell you this…' Blood rushed to her head and her world spun as the reason for their visit was revealed. The officers faded in and out as her world came crashing down around her. Her mind panicked and spiralling, and her body frozen. She was vaguely aware of a hand placed kindly on her knee, but her hearing had gone. All she could discern were two words.

Freddie.

Murdered.

The police were here. They were here in her home, telling her Freddie's body had been found in the night, murdered in his sleep. It was too close, too much. The bile rose to her mouth and coated her tongue. She knew she needed to come back, to think. Keep her mind clear. Say something. She needed to say something.

'He's dead?' Her voice cracked, barely above a whisper. DC Chandra nodded slowly.

'We're so sorry.'

A hot mug was placed into her hands. It helped ground her, bring her back to the room. She focussed on it. Plain white. With a large M. Recently acquired. She stared at the M, remembering where she was when she had seen it. She studied the shape, the curves and the colours. She liked this mug.

You have done nothing wrong. You are a good person.

It helped. She allowed a tear to fall. It dripped sadly down her cheek, she could feel it edging closer to her neck. It was cold against the warmth of her skin. She vaguely heard DC Mulley encouraging her drink and she complied. Tea. With a spoonful of sugar. The same trick she had used many times before to comfort traumatised relatives. For the shock.

Shock. That's what it was. Seeing them at the door, their uniforms. Even the well-rehearsed way in which they sat to bring her the news. The same expressions on their face. There had been no time to prepare for this. How could she have known they would have been here? Memories tried to resurface, old guilt rising with bile. Of course, she knew these were not the same officers as before, but the similarities were there.

They had done the same that day. She had happened to be staying at Penny's. They knocked on the door, faces sombre and grim. They sat them down on the sofa. Made them tea. She had sat, just the same as she was now, anxiously awaiting the reason for their visit. And they delivered the news of Ivy's brutal murder in the night. They never caught the perpetrator, Jake was right. Her family couldn't even have a funeral for her. They had a memorial instead. And the minute Penny could, she turned her back on her again and flew off to the big city. Ivy's face swum to her mind. She had died alone. She should have been there to hold her hand. It was the right thing to do. It was suffocating her, it was all too close.

313

Madeline felt movement from her left. DC Mulley had sat back down.

'Take all the time you need,' she said kindly. 'This must be a huge shock for you.' Madeline said nothing in reply but nodded. She sipped at the sickly-sweet tea and stared hard at the floor.

'Madeline, I know this is hard for you. But we need you to come with us to the station when you're ready.' Madeline found DC Chandra's face.

'The… The station?' she stuttered.

'You were one of the last people to see Mr Warner alive,' DC Chandra explained softly. 'We just need to take your statement.' One of the last to see him alive, the words, their implications hit her in the chest.

'S…S…Statement?'

'It's nothing to worry about. You're not being arrested, Miss Hamilton.' Madeline's eyes shot to meet his. Arrested. One of the last. Murdered. Her mind was clear.

'The news. Police said they had leads. Is his murder linked to the ones that have been happening around here?' DS Chandra looked at DC Mulley, mouth open. Madeline felt the impatience, the injustice of it all rising.

'Is it linked?' she asked firmly. Maybe too firmly.

'Miss Hamilton, we have not made any assumptions at this time. We need to conduct a thorough investigation into the victim's death.'

'You think it's linked, don't you?'

'Miss Hamilton, as I said, we have not made any assumptions. It would be dangerous to jump to such conclusions this early into the investigation.' DC Chandra was

314

stiff, he gave nothing away. Madeline pursed her lips and sat back on the sofa. Deep in thought.

'Miss Hamilton, I appreciate this is a delicate time. But I'm sure you understand, it's a matter of urgency now. We could do with your statement.' He was pushy. Her eyes travelled down his body to his shoes. He was cleanly dressed, smart. The shoes were shined but she could see a hint of dirt along the sole. They had been tramping into the pink carpet, bringing in the summer dust from the dry heat. Her thoughts strayed to the mud. She hoped it hadn't stained.

They were both staring at her, anticipating her response. She knew she had to go. She wouldn't get away with it, she needed to give her statement. But what would the neighbours think? They would see her leaving with them. Would they think she was being arrested? There were no police markings on the car, but it was obvious who they were. The locals noticed everything, she had seen that herself.

'We can take a preliminary statement here today, if it's too much?' DC Mulley offered. 'We would just need you to come into the station as soon as possible for a full statement.' Madeline smiled at DC Mulley through her eyelashes, hearing the irritated exhale under DS Chandra's breath. She liked her, she decided. They weren't giving much away, it was dangerous, heading in there with them but she knew it was important. She wanted more than anything, for them to catch him but she needed time. She swallowed the lump in her throat and nodded slowly.

'Okay.'

The officers took her informal statement, and she agreed to go into the station later that day. She saw them out, another tear rolling down her cheek as she closed the door gently behind them.

Madeline leaned against the closed door and rested her head back. She watched on the camera as they got in the BMW. But they didn't pull away. Not right away. Her heart quickened, before she dismissed the worry. They were probably just debriefing. It can't be a nice job having to give such awful news to loved ones like that. Eventually she heard the sound of an engine, and watched on the slight delay as the car pulled away and down the road.

She padded quietly down the hallway, deep in her own thoughts. Now the initial shock of their visit had subsided, she realised she felt sad. She was truly heartbroken at Freddie's loss. She had really liked him, despite it all. But she realised she didn't have time to wallow in that now. She only had a few hours. A few hours to prepare and prep, get herself together. Or everything would unravel.

Her phone pinged. She knitted her brow and pulled it out of her pocket. A text. She tapped on it hungrily before her eyes widened.

Three little pigs inside a brick house. The pigs can't help you now.

Your time is up, Little Red. What big teeth you have. All the better to eat your grandmother with.

I'll huff and I'll puff.

And I'll blow everything to smithereens.

You silly, silly cunt. How did you ever think you could get away with this? I told you, I've been watching you for a long time. Watching you run, watching you hide. I bet you thought you were so clever, hiding behind your pathetic disguise. You really thought you could outsmart me? Don't forget, I know you, my love.

People tell you a lot about themselves when they don't think they're being watched. They do the craziest things. They think because they are alone, they're not accountable. I know exactly who you are. What do you think I've seen you do when you thought no one was looking? I've been watching you all along. Since the minute I saw you.

You have no idea what I am truly capable of. Do you know how easy it is to fake your own death? I enjoy it. I thrive off it. And looking at you now, that terrified expression in your eyes as you take me in, finally.

Finally, you truly see me.

I see the cogs turning in your mind. I've woken you, truly. It's setting in, isn't it? The truth. Your secret is safe with me.

Jesus Christ. You're turning me on so much. I want you so bad, my love. And I will have you before this night is over.

26

Madeline

Lunnemouth police station was bright and yet dingy, clean yet grimy with an old smell of mould and bleach hanging around. Madeline felt the heat rise in her face as she stalked slowly through the age-stained corridors, the suspicious-looking marks splattered up the wall from which the aromas seemed to originate. The place seemed to became smaller and more grotesque with every step. She felt eyes burning into her back from the man in the waiting area she left behind, as she followed DC Mulley away from the lobby to the interview room.

Memories tried to resurface, the smells, the sounds. She jumped, wide-eyed at DC Mulley who was unperturbed as a maniac cackle rang through her ears. She opened her mouth before realising it was coming from inside her own head.

Keep it together. You are a good person. Remember who you are.

I am Madeline Hamilton. I am a good person.

DC Mulley was chattering lightly about the weather and the horrific sunburn she'd suffered at the weekend and Madeline nodded along politely. She was nervous. But she made no attempt to hide it. The girlfriend of a man who had just been mutilated in his sleep would be nervous. She mentally rehearsed the preparations she had made earlier that morning, and the memories began to ebb in their intensity.

They reached a door, 'Interview Room C'. DC Mulley smiled kindly and held it open for Madeline, gesturing for her to take a seat. DS Chandra was already seated across the table, pen in hand. A camera blinked from the top corner of the room. Positioned for the perfect angle of the three of them in the room.

Madeline took her seat on the hard, plastic chair and took her time to make herself comfortable. It wasn't an easy feat. DC Mulley watched her sadly. DS Chandra didn't betray a hint of emotion. Finally, after crossing and uncrossing her legs, she found it better to sit with the chair tucked right under the table. It sat her hips at the right angle and her back straight, allowing her hands to rest in her lap. She looked up between the two officers in front of her.

'Hi, Madeline. Thank you for coming in,' DS Chandra began. 'I appreciate this might be difficult for you. We would just like to ask you a few questions, then take a statement from you which will be used to support the investigation into the murder of Freddie Warner. Your statement will be recorded and may be used as evidence in a court of law. Do you understand?' Madeline nodded and bit her lip. DS Chandra cleared his throat.

'Okay. Miss Hamilton, can you tell us what your relation was to Mr Warner?' Madeline was prepared.

'We had been dating. We had crossed paths in the village when I first moved here three months ago. We both work at Lunnemouth General Hospital, but on separate wards. He's a doctor, I'm a nurse. He asked me out for coffee initially. And then we carried on dating, until he stood me up about a week ago.' Madeline averted her eyes and stared down at the table. She recalled it all. Her stroking his cheek gently. The rise and fall of his chest as he snored. She would carry them with her forever.

'Take your time, Miss Hamilton.'

'He stood me up at the pub,' Madeline said. 'I messaged him. I thought it was a little rude. Now I know…Well…'

319

'Okay, Miss Hamilton.' DS Chandra glanced at DC Mulley who was taking notes beside him. He looked back across the table and folded his fingers together.

'How was the relationship in the lead up to his death?' Madeline was prepared for this question. She knew it was suspicious. There had been witnesses seeing them squabble in the Ram.

'It was okay, I thought. I won't lie to you, we had bickered a little bit near the end. He was always such a gentleman. He would do little things. Like, always arrive early so I would never be meeting him alone. Pull out my chair for me. Hold the door, that sort of thing.'

DS Chandra nodded along. 'But you said you bickered a bit?'

'Yes. He changed. It was like... Almost like he was irritated by me. He was suddenly short with me, kept cancelling plans and...' Madeline trailed off as a memory popped back in. Flitting across her periphery, something she had forgotten. Seeming insignificant at the time.

'He turned up to one of our dates late. *Very* late. And, when I asked him about it he just said he'd been busy and was tired. But, I don't know, I felt like he was just fobbing me off... I noticed he had these strange scratches over his face... and mud over his neck...' Madeline looked at the officers as they both leaned in slightly.

'I didn't think anything of it, actually.' She was sincere. It hadn't occurred in her preparations to mention it. 'He said he was helping a woman who had lost a dog, or something. Said he caught the dog and it scratched his face up.'

'When was this?' DS Chandra stared. DC Mulley took her notes. Madeline thought hard for a moment.

'A couple of weeks ago.'

'Okay. And he told you he got these scratches from a dog? Helping a woman?'

'Yes.'

'Did he happen to mention who the woman was?'

'No. I did ask, he just said a woman. Then told me to drop it. I did, at the time, because like I said, I didn't think it was a big deal. I was more worried about how off he was being with me at the time. It wasn't very nice.'

'No, I can imagine it wasn't.' DS Chandra narrowed his eyes slightly. 'Did he happen to mention anything else during your time together? Ex's, other women he was seeing, perhaps?'

'No. We didn't really talk about each other's past.'

'Why not?'

Madeline felt the prickle of heat on her neck at the intrusiveness of the questioning. 'Because... I guess we didn't think it was necessary. Maybe, if we'd got a bit more serious we might have moved onto conversations like that. He never asked me about my past, either.'

'What about other women in the present? Was he dating anyone else whilst he was dating you?' DS Chandra was staring into her. Madeline widened her eyes in surprise. She hadn't expected this question.

'No... I don't think so anyway...'

'You don't think so?'

'No...'

'I need you to think very carefully, Miss Hamilton.'

Madeline felt the beginnings of a headache as she screwed up her face. Thinking. Carefully, as DS Chandra had suggested. A woman. He was fixated on a woman, was he insinuating... No it couldn't be.

'I never saw any evidence of a woman at his... and he didn't mention one, either.'

'What about friends?'

'Friends?'

'Yeah, friends. You had been dating for a while, three months? Surely you met some of his friends.'

'Um... No, I didn't. He mentioned a couple of friends, but I

321

never met them.'

'That's a little strange, don't you think? You never met any of his friends in the time you were dating?' The statement threw her. Now she pondered it, it was a little strange. Freddie had never mentioned the idea of meeting friends, she had never thought to request it. It would have been normal to meet friends.

'I... I guess it is a little strange, actually. I'd not thought about that before.' She was quiet. But it was honest. DC Chandra only nodded. Pausing briefly before his next question.

'Okay. Miss Hamilton, what made you move to Lunnemouth?'

Here we go. You can do this. This is what you prepared for. You are a good person.

'I moved here when my grandmother Ivy passed away,' Madeline said stoically, the lines well-rehearsed. 'She hadn't updated her will. But Penny changed it and signed everything over to me.'

'Penny?'

'My mother.'

'Your mother? Why do you call her Penny?'

The heat tickled her skin. Madeline prayed it wouldn't show across her pale complexion. 'She... She hasn't ever really been a mother to me...' She answered truthfully, averting her eyes again. They would be able to see this was difficult for her. 'She was selfish. Never around. She lives in London, I used to stay with her on the occasional visit. But she has a dependency on substances. Alcohol, drugs. I have never been able to call her 'mum'.' DS Chandra nodded, and DC Mulley had paused her notetaking, looking at her with empathetic eyes.

'That must be really difficult for you,' she interjected softly. Madeline nodded, and a tear sprang to her eye. DS Chandra was not biting.

'So, your grandmother passed away, is that correct?' he asked simply. Another nod from Madeline. 'Your grandmother is Ivy

Hamilton, is that correct?' Her nodding again.

'Ivy Hamilton, who was murdered in August last year in her home at the age of seventy-four?' DS Chandra pressed. Madeline nodded slowly. Her heart thumped. She knew this might happen, the police here were diligent.

'That is correct, yes.'

'That must be really difficult for you, living in the same house she was murdered in?'

'Bungalow.'

'Sorry?'

'Bungalow. It's a bungalow.'

'My apologies. It must be difficult living in the bungalow she was murdered in?'

'Yes. It is. It haunts me every day.'

'So, why stay there? Why not sell it, move on?' DS Chandra questioned. Madeline sighed.

'I needed a place to stay,' she said. It was true. 'And I loved Ivy. She was always kind to me, I knew she wouldn't want me to sell it. So I've been trying to make it my own. Baby steps.'

'You've started to redecorate?'

'Yes.'

'Why did you move here? You said you had nowhere else to go?'

'My rental was up for renewal. I knew I couldn't stay with Penny. I slept in my car for a bit. Then I saw the job up at Lunnemouth on the stroke unit and thought it would be good. I've always liked it out here in the countryside.' None of it a lie, just enough of the truth.

'When did you move?'

'Erm...' Madeline thought hard. She hadn't anticipated this. 'Not sure, a few months ago?'

'A few months ago. Can you be more specific?'

'Um, sure. Moving date was...' Madeline pulled her phone out of her pocket. 'Fifteenth of May.'

'You moved out here from Luton, that right?' Madeline froze, trying not to let her shock reveal itself. How did they know that?

'Yes. Yes, that is correct.' Her vocal chords strained, threatening to betray her fear.

'And you were in London before that?'

'Yes.'

'And have you been settling in well?'

'Yes...' Madeline looked at DS Chandra curiously. She couldn't read him at all. He was glaring back at her, dead pan expression on his face.

'What do you think of the countryside? Bit different to the Big Smoke?'

'Very different. But I like it.'

'It's curious, isn't it? You move here, then all of a sudden, a series of gruesome murders start. Including your boyfriend. Do you find that a little curious?' Madeline's throat dried. Everything clicked. Of course, they weren't just collecting her statement.

'It is curious, yes.'

'If we told you, we had reason to suspect the perpetrator may have had links to London, would that shock you?'

'It would...' she observed. 'Am I a suspect here?'

'We're just investigating all lines of enquiry, Miss Hamilton. You're not under arrest. You are free to leave at any time.' DS Chandra was plain. He gave nothing away. Madeline gripped her hands underneath the table.

'Tragedy seems to follow you around, doesn't it, Miss Hamilton?'

'What do you mean?'

'You were the sole survivor of a fire in a block of flats that housed NHS nursing staff in Luton, last year, is that correct?' DS Chandra was boring holes into her. DC Mulley continued to take notes. Madeline opened and closed her mouth. How the hell did they know that.

'Yes. But that doesn't seem very relevant. What does this have to do with Freddie?' DS Chandra shrugged nonchalantly.

'It's just interesting. Ten people died that night. Then your grandmother. Now your boyfriend. Death seems to follow you, is that fair to say?'

'Wait. I am under suspicion, aren't I...'

'We would not be doing a good job if we didn't investigate everything properly.' DS Chandra raised his eyebrows and looked upon her sternly. Madeline felt another tear roll down her cheek.

'No, I suppose you wouldn't.'

'You have to understand. You move into the area, then people start dying. We have to ask questions.' Madeline felt her heart begin to thump behind her rib cage. She felt her breathing trying to quicken.

Just tell them.

Tell them about him.

No. No, she couldn't. If she told them about him, they might find out about *her*. It was too risky. She had to trust they would follow the right trail.

'I understand, I do.' Madeline looked between the officers pleadingly. 'But I promise you, I have not done anything wrong. And I have told you the truth.'

'Okay, Miss Hamilton. We will take your word for now. This is not a formal interview at this stage.' DS Chandra leaned forward over the table. His eyes blazed into hers. Madeline fought the urge to look away.

'But if you do have any information, anything at all, that could be linked to this case you are not telling us, we will find out. It wouldn't do good to lie to us.' DS Chandra raised his eyebrows seriously. Madeline bit her lip. Eyes welling, she shook her head.

'No. I have not lied,' she said. Truthfully. DS Chandra held her gaze for a moment more. He pushed on the table and stood noisily from his chair.

'DC Mulley will take your written statement now, Miss Hamilton. It's been good to see you.' He held out a confident hand, and Madeline took it shakily. DS Chandra swung the interview door open, leaving Madeline with the DC. She began to explain what they needed, how to write the statement and to be as factual as possible. Madeline barely heard her but nodded along. Shaken, her mind was whirling.

It was too close. Even with days, she would never been able to prepare herself for this. It terrified her, how much they knew. How much more did they know? How much were they holding back? She shuddered. If they had found out about Lily, it was game over.

*

Madeline walked out of the police station into the blazing afternoon an hour later. Her car would be a hot box now in the sun. She had tried to walk out as calmly as possible, but her mind was so full, even her five senses technique couldn't bring her back.

Lily. She hadn't thought about Lily in such a long time. She walked away from her long ago. They had buried her under a granite headstone, and she had buried her deep down where she belonged. Her little secret.

Things were teetering on the edge of a knife. Everything was at risk of collapsing around her and she needed, desperately, to claw back control. Unlocking her KA, the heat hit her in the face as she opened the door, attacking her delicate cheeks. She felt the flush of red as the blood rushed to her face. Turning the key in the ignition she wound all the windows down, praying for a reprieve. She couldn't move, sat in the driver's seat, sweat dripping from her scalp, down her neck and her back. Her t-shirt stuck uncomfortably to her body. She wasn't sure if it was the heat or stress. She pulled out her phone, searching for her coping mechanisms when life became chaotic. She pulled up her lists. The welcome wave of calm washed over her, albeit small, but enough.

Lists kept things in line. They kept things organised. Timings didn't lie. She knew she hadn't done anything wrong, despite what the police seemed to believe. It was all here, all evidence. She had to trust the police would arrest the right person soon.

With a sigh, Madeline gave up on any hope of cooling the tin can of a car any further and started the engine. The fan blasted, hot air streaming into her eyes. It wasn't pleasant, she didn't have air conditioning, but it was mildly better than the stagnant heat of before. She kept the windows rolled down as she checked, left and right. She pulled out of the bay and crawled out of the car park, carefully, slowly. Checking her mirrors methodically, mirror, signal, manoeuvre. Reaching the exit, she indicated, checked left and right again and pulled out onto the main road.

Madeline gripped the steering wheel tightly as she followed the building traffic out of town. Timmy would be wondering where she was. She hadn't expected to be this long. She hadn't expected a lot of what happened in there to happen. But, amongst it all, she remembered one key piece of information.

Links to London.

Finally. They were putting it together.

She pulled into the drive twenty-one minutes later and killed the engine. She breathed deeply, before stepping out of the car slowly. Her phone pinged in her pocket. She knew what it was.

Madeline walked up the path and let herself quietly into the bungalow. Neighbours were strolling past behind her, but she kept her head down. She wasn't in the mood to exchange polite greetings. Door shut and locked behind her, she turned to remove her Converse and the waft made her heart stop. It was that same smell. It was stronger than before. Fresh. Sandalwood and patchouli. She looked cautiously down the hallway towards the open door that led into the living room. Timmy was sat, waiting patiently in the open doorframe. He did not move to greet her, but glanced to his left instead. She froze. She knew she had closed the door before she left.

He was here.

He had finally come.

She took a deep breath into her lungs, trying to still her frantic heart. Stepped slowly down the hallway. Her feet barely made a noise on the hardwood floor. Heel to toe. The smell grew, wrapping its tendrils around her nostrils. She reached the doorway to the living area and stepped to the threshold, past the little dog. He didn't stir, he just watched. She turned, slowly and steadily into the living room, with its pink, stained carpet. Her heart in her mouth. But she had never felt so alive. She was free, free to be herself, to do what needed to be done. This had been what she was waiting for. Her eyes searched the room vigilantly before falling upon a figure.

He was standing there. He was waiting.

'Hello.'

'I thought you would never come.'

'I'm here now.'

'I know, I'm so glad. Did you know I've been watching you? I know your little secret, I know who you are. Shall we talk? I'll tell you everything.'

I've been waiting for you.

You think you can stop me? You think you can help? You and your secrets. You are fooling no one, my love, your secrets are out there in the world. One only has to look.

But I'll admit. I couldn't believe it when I heard it on the news the first time. I panicked, you know? I lost sleep that night. That pissed me off, I rarely lose sleep. I always make sure I get enough. This time it was quick though. Far quicker than last time. The way the news picked up on it, I thought for sure I was busted. I thought I would have to leave again. They wouldn't stop either. Round the clock coverage. National news. Theories on the murders. Interviews with the locals. I guess that's how it goes out here in a sleepy village. These things never happen in a place so quiet, that's what they always say. I fucking despise the news. Politicians, paedophiles, shallow celebrities all getting the attention they want. And those news reporters, they give them that attention! Terrible, terrible people. There's too many terrible people in this world, my love, out there doing their terrible things without consequences. Well, actions have consequences. The good guys win, and the bad guys get punished, isn't that how it goes?

I can see, I know. You're not a bad person, not really. But now, your actions will have consequences. If only you had left well alone. If you had just left it, we wouldn't be in this position now. Do you know how much I've been watching you? You like to think you are so innocent, but you are as bad as the rest of them. I see the dirty underwear on the floor, the washing up in the sink, it will wait 'til tomorrow, will it?

Well. One day, tomorrow won't come for you.

But I will. I will always come for you now, my love. When you turned up, I knew. I just knew it would be okay. And now, we are here, in it together. And you're going to help me.

329

27

Him

'You're insane.'

'Maybe. Or maybe I am the only one in this world who does what is right.'

'You'll never get away with this. Not now.'

'Oh, I will. I always do.'

'Why did you do it, Lily? Or is it Madeline? Or Jane. Or Mary. Whatever you're calling yourself these days.'

'For you, it will always be Little Red, my love.'

She smirked back at him, her emerald eyes flashing as he resisted the flinch that lashed his body.

'Okay, *Little Red*.' He felt his voice crack from the pressure, the name like fire on his tongue. 'Why did you do it?'

'Do what?' She blinked at him in surprise. Her little monologue, confessing to all her crimes had stirred up such nausea he thought he might be sick. He wanted his revenge, he wanted justice. But he hadn't gone through all of this, waited all this time, not to get answers now.

'You know what. What did she die for?'

'She?'

'Don't play the innocent, now. Charlotte. What did she die

for?'

'Who the *fuck* is Charlotte?'

'You know who Charlotte is, you fucking cunt!'

Lily laughed viciously and he cursed himself for losing control. Clenching his fists, he looked at her defiantly, raising his chin. She would not beat him this time. 'My sister. Why did you kill her? I saw you there. That final day at her trial. I knew from that moment it was you. You murdered her.'

She curled her lip into a grotesque imitation of a smile, curdling his blood. 'Oh, you clever boy, you. I knew I always liked you. How did you know it was me?'

He swallowed the rock that had appeared in his throat. 'I saw you. I saw you at the trial. You snuck in at the back, wearing that ridiculous wig. But it was that look in your eye... I'd seen it before. All those years ago, at our school, about thirteen years old. You were tiny, skinny as a rake then, but then... boys would find razors in their lunch, acid would fall out of lockers, one kid was stabbed late at night in an alleyway, a girl was poisoned...'

'I bet you remembered me, I gave you the time of your life behind the old trees at the back of that field.' Lily winked at him and put her forefinger in her mouth. She wrapped her red lips around her knuckle, pulling her finger gently through her tongue. Her delicate pale skin glistened, the moisture from her mouth gliding on her skin as she pulled it sensually from her mouth. Watching him. Noticing him watching. Smirking at him. She was devious, enjoying the effect she held over him. He shivered but was unable to tear his eyes away. Finger out, smirk gone, she frowned again. 'Before you pied me. You broke my heart, my love. Anyway. They were bullies. All of

331

them. They got what they deserved. But that means nothing. It was a long time ago. You need to get over that now.' He felt his heart rate rise. She was smiling at him again cooly. Awaiting his next move.

'Then, I remembered I'd seen your face that night. You were there that night. The night she was killed.' He tried desperately to keep his tone steady. Keep her talking.

'Maybe I was, maybe I wasn't.'

'Lily, I'm not playing these games anymore.'

'But haven't you enjoyed our little game over the last few months?' Her eyes sparkled with glee. 'I'll admit, you got me good! Our little game of cat and mouse. Hide and seek. You should have seen me! I was fearful, really panicked. Honestly, you nearly fucking had me. And when the police turned up, fuck, I thought I was a goner, for sure.'

'Lily. I want answers. Why did you kill Charlotte?'

'Charlotte?' Her tone was deliberately provoking. Light, dangerous. Like the delicate blade of a samurai. He said nothing. He just stared at her. He wouldn't rise to it this time. Drawing her out.

'Oh, of course,' Lily replied playfully, realising he would not cave to her psychological game. 'I called her Kristen, you know. I told you, yeah? Yeah, I liked her. She looked so much like that actress, she was quite alluring.'

'Her name was Charlotte. What did she die for?'

'Oh, but she didn't look like a Charlotte, did she?'

'I'm not doing this.'

'She was a cheater, too, she cheated everyone.'

'Stop it. What did she die for?'

'Oh, you're such a bore.' Lily stuck her tongue at him and

rolled her eyes. 'Fine, if you really want to know.' She folded her arms. Her face fell, eyes darkened. 'She hit into my car.' Her words fell on the humid air. Stunned, he blinked at her. Waiting for more.

'What?'

'Stupid bitch. She was so careless. I'd been watching her in the bar that night, you know? Flicking her hair back, laughing too loud, drinking far too much wine. Prosecco by the bottle, Gucci belt, Chanel handbag and that ridiculously large Porsche she couldn't fucking drive. She was a walking cliché. And quite frankly, she shouldn't have been driving, anyway. Drink driving kills, my love. I followed her out, I was going to be friendly, perhaps suggest she cut back on the drink, offer to take her home, have a girl-to-girl chat, you know? But instead I watched as she backed that fucking Porsche of hers all down the side of my car. She never stopped, never even attempted to leave a note, just drove away. She really thought she was better than everyone. It makes my blood boil even thinking of it now.'

'You killed her... Because she dented your car?'

'She deserved it!' Lily screamed suddenly, eyes flashing wildly. 'She drove away! She had no intention whatsoever of leaving any kind of note! She left the car park without even stopping to look! She fucking deserved it.' She spat out the last statement with such venom that her mouth began to froth, like a rabid dog. He was in disbelief, all cool lost, the shock setting in. Tears formed at his eyes and he shook violently.

'She dented your car! My sister died because she dented your fucking car?'

'Well, let's be honest, she had also had a few too many

glasses of wine. She'd have killed someone else if I hadn't stopped her, anyway. So, in a way, it is two things.'

'I can't fucking believe this... This is unbelievable.' He shook his head, the tears stinging his face. His body hung off his frame, like a deflated balloon that had been slashed in two.

'Don't worry, I made sure her dog was well looked after,' Lily cackled, leaning against the wall. She'd stayed by the doorway since she crept in, but she was practically giddy. Sooty licked his leg comfortingly and he felt a fresh rush of tears. The little dog hadn't moved from his side since Lily had walked back in. He had beckoned straight to him. His sister's beloved Scottie, now holed up with this complete psychopath. Charlotte's front door had been wide open when her body was found. They all assumed Sooty had ran away.

His head thumped, taking it all in. It was so trivial. After all this time. She had ruined his life. His father never recovered from Charlotte's murder. He had lost two of the people he cared most about because of her. He had spent the last two years on her tail. He'd lost the love of his life because of this pursuit. His future in tatters, but that was the sacrifice he had made for this. And now, now she was here in front of him... There had to be more. He was ashamed, but it somehow felt like an anti-climax. He hadn't been sure what he was hoping for. Closure, maybe. A reason. A real reason he could rationalise, why Charlotte died, why her life had been stolen, why he had ruined his life.

'The others. What did they die for?' he asked quietly.

'What others?'

'Don't play dumb with me. The others, the ones you've just told me about. You know fucking well who.'

Lily laughed again. Her laugh was joyful, childlike. She looked so angelic, that red mane streaming over her pale shoulders. It made the hair on the back of his neck stand. The devil in disguise.

'Course I do, I'm just enjoying our little exchange. It's fun to watch you, I told you. I like watching you sleep, watching all of your little expressions. You're quite sexy, you know.'

'Lily. Please. I'm begging you. What did they do?'

'They knew what they did.'

'Tell me.'

'You're quite impatient, you know? Aren't you enjoying the sexual tension between us? I know you've been waiting for this moment as much as I have.' She looked at him wildly for a moment. He remained motionless where he stood, too broken to react. When it was clear he wouldn't respond, she sighed huffily and rolled her eyes.

'Fine.' Lily pulled out her phone gleefully. 'Lucky for you, my love, I keep lists. They keep everything in order.' She scrolled on her phone, her movements frantic and jittery, he could hear how her nails connected on the screen. She threw glances at him with a demonic grin on her face. Waiting for a reaction. He stood tall, despite the turmoil that was raging within. She wouldn't get what she wanted from him.

'Right, let's see…' She tutted. 'The bitch with the beautiful eyes, oh, those breasts… I told you about those breasts, didn't I? Christ, so perky, and perfect. Never been so jealous in my life. Anyway, she let her flat-nosed dog piss up my gate. Can you believe that? Terrible person. Maisie, I think they said her name was. So disrespectful. So she had to go. The one I tied up and smashed with her vase? Ugly fucking thing that, useless. I had to put a plastic container inside for your beautiful lilies, thank you for those, by the way. Very clever. Very... intimidating. Anyway. Maggie, her name was, apparently. Heard that on the news. She cut me up, right on the busy roundabout in town. Bitch even had the audacity to turn and stare at me! Can you believe that! She smiled at me, looking straight in my eyes as she did it... I made sure that one was awake. I looked her straight in the eye as I slit her throat. I guess you could say, I cut her up, too!' She laughed to herself as he glanced at the vase in the corner, its cracks visible from its abuse and felt sick to his core.

They were victims of opportunity. All of them. Died for their sins. Whatever 'sins' she decided were punishable. Lily was manic now, she had started to pace, leaving her position of the doorway, her face lit up from the thrill of her atrocities.

'Katie. I wanted to make sure the litterer burned. Karma, that was. Her littering all of those takeaway wrappers, cigarettes, I watched her do that with my own eyes. She hit me as well, fucking rude. Complete selfishness, disregard for anyone. I mean, who even smokes anymore, anyway? It's all about vaping now. I figured, if she was contributing to global warming, burning the planet you know, why couldn't she burn? Punishment fits the crime, as they say. It's a shame there were other casualties caught up as a result of her selfishness, but that's her own fault. That's the way it goes sometimes.' She turned erratically, spinning on her toes, still scrolling through her phone.

'Who else... The cyclist. Gary. Fuck, I hated him. It took everything in me not to ram him off the road there and then. Too many witnesses, though. You know that's not my style. I got my revenge in the end. I used the chain from his own bike. The dog walker, Irene, I gave her multiple chances. She had a substance misuse problem, I told you. I gave the chance to change. But she made too many mistakes. She hurt too many people. I drowned that bitch in the lake. Do you know, I returned there a lot? It was the only one that was never linked, I was particularly proud of that. Going back, it helped me gain clarity, it helps me see it can be done. The world is better without her kind, now.'

He felt his heart sank as she reeled them off, never taking a pause to breathe. The evening sun setting her hair aflame, those long, copper waves cascading around her like hellfire.

'The one I sliced? Phoebe. Pheobe Larter. Fuck I got sick of her face on the news all the time. She was so fucking rude. Nearly took my arm off when she rammed into me. Wasn't even giving any attention to that spaniel of hers. Imagine, imagine if I had been elderly? She could have broken my shoulder! It's just rudeness! But don't worry, my love, that's another one out of the way.'

The sickness was threatening to spill over now. These motives. It was over nothing. All of these innocent people died for nothing. Their only crime was existing in the vicinity of a psychopath. Sooty leaned into him, as though he could sense his need. Lily wasn't paying attention, scrolling through her list and talking to the room.

'Susan Kilbryan. Kept leaving her fucking dog's shit all over the public path. That fucking woman, I could have killed her there and then. Kevin... Who the fuck was Kevin... Oh! Ha ha ha, I remember Kevin. He thought he was so tough and scary. Attacking a woman in her car like that. He loved that fucking Jeep so much, I could see why, to be fair. It drove beautifully across the fields, even with him strapped to the back of it by his neck. Well, you should know, you were there for that one, weren't you, my love? You saw our little 'date'.' He jumped as she laughed hysterically. It was high pitched, in any other setting, he might have said it was the kind of laugh that filled a room. But here, now. It turned him to stone. Worse. She was still going, her finger tapping on her screen wildly.

'This was around the time I got a little frenzied, they all merge into one. I blame you, my love, you had me so stressed. I needed my release, you know? Where are we... Megan, stupid bitch in the supermarket. Thought I was the rude one, the fucking audacity. As if I would deliberately barge into a child. Keiran. The cat caller. Cunt. Won't be intimidating women like that again in a hurry. Oh, aww...' She paused. It could have been a trick of the light, but for a moment he thought her eyes could have misted over, a hint of emotion within. She blinked and it was gone. The monster replaced the glimpse of the human again.

'Poor old Freddie... My Freddie. Yeah, he was a tough one. I'm usually so decisive. But this one, he got under my skin, he did. That fucking grin of his. He's not a patch on you, my love, but he was close. But, one too many times, he did the wrong thing. I forgave the Volvo, the scattiness, the uncleanliness, but lying? That's unacceptable. Those strikes hung over my head too much, you know? Terrible, terrible shame that. Yeah, that was hard. But, I had to do what needed to be done. Never get attached, my love, it doesn't do you any good.' She tutted and continued to scroll.

'Petr, urgh, hideous construction ruining the English countryside. Nobody wants that. Oh! The old lady! Ivy. Yeah, she was a shame, actually. I made mistakes with her but I needed to move, escape the heat. She bled everywhere as well. You know I still can't sleep properly in that room even after I sorted it out? I feel a lot of guilt for that one, as well, actually. Learned a lot there. There's rules, you know? Things you have to do... I freaked out. I ran. She died alone... I should have been there to hold her hand...'

'Good to know you have some kind of a conscience.'

'Fuck off,' Lily whipped around in a fury. 'Fuck you. I am the only one around here with any kind of conscience. These people, they have no morals, no values, no regard to other people!'

'You have no morals, no values. You have no regard for anyone. You're a monster.'

Lily became very still. Her face changed. Gone was the fury and in place of the pale complexion were two black holes glaring at him from the centre of his face. Eerily calm and collected. He could see the horns protruding from her red mane. As though he were looking at the devil herself.

'I am not a monster,' she said quietly. 'I am a good person. My therapist told me so.'

'What nutjob therapist told you that?'

'How dare you. She was the only one who ever understood me. I am a good person, I have a strong moral compass...'

'Your compass is broken, Lily.'

'Incorrect. I do the good deeds for society... I get rid of the bad in the world. Actions have consequences.'

He felt the anger surge within, boiling under his skin. 'I can't wait to see what consequences come to you.' She rolled her eyes, clicking her tongue.

'I don't know what you're so upset about, really. You got your justice in the end, didn't you?'

'You know damn well we didn't get any justice. An innocent man is rotting in prison for a murder you committed!'

'Pah!' The exhale of breath was violent from her small frame. 'Innocent?! Don't make me laugh! He was fucking drug dealer, a low life! Just because he didn't kill your fucking sister didn't mean he wasn't killing others!'

'You should be where he is now. Somewhere worse. Even prison is too good for you.'

'Don't be silly, I am doing the world a favour. I am a good person. Kind of a Robin Hood. I could be Robina Hood! Little Red Robina Hood. Of Robin Close. Ridding us of bad apples and the bad wolves, one at a time. You should be thanking me.'

'Why in the hell should I be thanking you?' he hissed. She stepped closer to him, and he instinctively stepped back. Her eyes were fierce and she was smiling, looking up at him between her eyelashes. Seductively. She bit her lip and twisted a strand of hair around her small, porcelain finger. Dropping her voice, barely above a whisper.

'I know you and your sister fought a lot. I know she wasn't nice to you growing up. She cheated. She lied. And she wasn't very nice to your parents at all. Are you not going to thank me? She's out of the way, now.'

'I loved my sister.'

'I'm sure you thought you did. But it doesn't matter, you'll see it before long. She was the bad guy, not me.' She was close to him now. Too close. He could feel the gentle breeze of her breath. He felt the arousal creeping up his body, telling him to run. To freeze. To fight. To comply. His body couldn't react quick enough as her form appeared to change in front of him. He felt his mouth dry.

'That's not true, Lily.'

'It is true. I know you think it, too. I know your secret. I know that night you'd had a fight with her over her selfishness. She was partying too much, never calling your parents, never visiting your poor Dad in hospital. She had a problem with drinking and partying.'

'How do you...'

'I was there, like I said. I followed her and I found you there. Waiting for her to come home. I watched you both. I like watching you. I've been watching you for a while. You fascinate me. You always have, ever since I met you. You were so good to me. The only man to ever treat me right. I couldn't believe my eyes when I saw you again in the city. You were the only boy to ever turn me down. The one that got away...'

Her eyes turned wistful as she stared across the room, lost in some sick, twisted fantasy she was concocting in her head. Suddenly, she shook her head violently, dispelling the story. 'And when I saw you again that night... I broke in that night, you know? After you left. I thought we could have that conversation. For you. Until she showed her true colours.' Her voice was down to a whisper, its tones silky, smooth like honey. Luring him into her trap. His heart began to palpitate and his palms were sweating.

'It was one fight, Lily,' he said hesitantly.

'Then why didn't you tell the police about that fight when they interviewed you, hmm? Seems like crucial information to me.' She ran a small finger gently over his ear, tenderly tucking a strand of hair away from his face. He was sure she could hear the thundering of his terrified heart.

'I didn't... I didn't think...'

'No, no, my love. You lied to them. They asked you outright, when was your last contact with your sister? And what did you tell them? Be honest, now.'

'I...' His eyes misted over with his recollection of that dreadful night. Hanging his head, remembering how Charlotte had leapt at him, scratching at his face in a drunken rage when he confronted her about her behaviour. She left finger indentations all over his face, her nails had broken his skin. He had left her there in her flat to visit his dying Dad and she had gone out anyway. And later that night, she was murdered. He knew the police would never believe his story.

'I'll finish your sentence for you,' Lily cut in. 'You told them you hadn't seen her for a week. Didn't you?'

Banishing the memories from his mind, he shook his head, swallowing the tears. 'It doesn't matter now. I've got you, and your confession. And I'm going to the police, now.'

'No, you're not, we're having fun. We could...' Lily nodded playfully towards the open bedroom on his left. 'Take this to the bedroom? Finish off where we started all those years ago? Freddie was okay, don't get me wrong. He did the job. But he didn't have the fight you've got in you that really turns me on. What do you say? You can choke me. I'll even let you cut me. I know you want to.' She lifted her eyebrows and licked her lips provocatively. They were ruby red, plump, shimmering from the work of her small pink tongue. He willed his words to leave his mouth. She would not win.

'Lily, I don't like women. I told you that back at school. And if I did, I wouldn't touch you even if you were the last woman alive.'

'Oh, foreplay!' she squealed, dancing on her toes and recoiling away from him with such a start he felt the breath rip from his body. 'Fuck. That's brutal. I love it!' She clapped her hands gleefully, releasing him from her wretched spell and he came to his senses, stepping towards the doorway to the hall to make his escape. She moved so swiftly, in front of him. Blocking his path.

'Where do you think you're going?' She eyed him suspiciously, her tone accusing. He swallowed his grief, his tears, the sickness and looked up at her in her cold dead eyes.

'I'm going to the police.'

'No, you're not.'

'Yes, I am. You're not getting away with it this time. No more innocent people will go down because of your crimes.'

Lily spat at him with laughter, wild-eyed and howling. 'Innocent? Don't be naïve, my love. Drug dealers, alcoholics, burglars the lot of them! Who cares if they went down, they got what they deserved! They all got what they deserved!'

'And this time, so will you.'

'Police will never believe you.'

'I think they will.'

'My love, don't be so foolish.'

'I have proof.'

'Oh, darling! The only reason you have 'proof' as you say,

is because I kept you alive. Think about it. Why do you think I've kept you alive?' He stalled, pondering the question.

'I imagine it's because you knew I would overpower you.'

'Psh. Don't be ridiculous.' Lily pulled a face and dismissed him with a wave. 'You sleep like a baby. You know I do my work at night. I thrive at night, it's the only time I ever get to be me. No, I had plenty of opportunities. But I decided in the end, I need you alive.'

'What do you mean?' He felt his heart skip a heavy beat. She smiled at him derisively.

'Have you not thought to ask why I've been watching you?'

'You're in love with me.'

'Well, yes. But I'm not quite as silly as you think, my love. Have you never wondered why I took your things each visit?'

'Why, then?' he asked, humouring her. He risked another small step closer to the doorway. He knew she was playing for time, but she was so psychotic now he had to play this carefully. The audio recording was still rolling in his phone, carefully stowed away in his pocket and he needed to get it to police.

'I never got much of a childhood, as you know. I know those kids laughed behind my back, I know the rumours that swirled. I heard them all. They didn't know the half of it. I missed out on so much fun normal kids would have, going to the park, having fun, playing games, I love playing games. Cat and mouse. Hide and seek. Dress up and pretend. But it was the fairy stories that stayed with me the most. They taught me so much about life, about your purpose. Have you ever thought about your purpose in life?'

Of course he had, but that glint in her eye was flashing and he daren't say any of these thoughts out loud.

'Well, if you haven't, you should. We all have a purpose in life. And when my therapist showed me those Grimm's fairy stories, I knew I'd found mine.'

'I don't see what this has to do with me...'

'Patience, my love. It's a virtue.' She was walking her fingers up and down the door frame. Lost in her mind, her voice reverting to a child-like state. 'I loved all of the Grimm's stories. Especially Little Red. I felt a certain... kinship with her, should we say.'

'Yes, we all knew that.'

'Lily wasn't good enough anymore. But Little Red... she was fighter. She was everything I knew I could be. Standing up to the big bullies, the bad people.'

'No one bullied you, Lily. It was all in your head.'

'Well, not after Casey Matthews. You remember her? She was in the year below.'

'Yes. I remember.'

'She soon learned. So did everyone else. The big bad wolf got to her, unfortunately. I liked that, by the way. Nice touch.' She nodded at him mischievously. 'If I hadn't been so worried you had more on me, at the time I might've congratulated you for that little message. It had me spooked. I'm proud of you.'

'Thanks,' he mumbled.

'Lessons are there to be learned. Have you ever heard of the six swans? Swan Lake they call it now. That one taught me all actions have consequences, no matter how many years you wait. Little Red taught me to stand up to the bad wolves. Goldilocks taught me the importance of not doing too much,

345

or too little, but getting everything just right. But this time, for you, my love, I took inspiration from Hansel and Gretel,' she said dreamily, widening her eyes. He narrowed his eyes at her, confused.

'The one where the witch eats the children?'

'She does, she does. And as a child I loved that part. But, as an adult, it inspired me.'

He furrowed his brow. She was crazy, she wasn't making sense, going off on her psychotic ramblings. 'You want to eat me?'

'Pah, don't be absurd. Not unless you want me to,' she added, flirtatiously. 'No, my love. Breadcrumbs.' She let her words hang, as they hit him in the chest. He stalled, the panic rising.

'What have you done?' his voice cracked. She smiled, and he cursed himself. With horror it dawned. She had him exactly where she wanted him.

28

Him

Lily hadn't moved from her stance in front of him. All five foot nothing, eight stone dripping wet of the weight on her ghoulish frame leaning on her small hip, her arms folded across her lithe chest. Her skin, clear and soft, with the smattering of dainty freckles over her nose, eyes green as emeralds and the inferno on her scalp ablaze. He had spent so long searching for her longingly, dreaming of this moment, picturing how he would take her down. Countless days, endless nights, he saw in his mind's eye how she would beg, plead at him for her freedom, as it slowly dawned on her, it all was over, she was done. He would delight in revealing how he had followed her, tracking her from place to place, all this time he knew who she was, what she had done. He imagined, with unwavering clarity, how those bright, green eyes would cloud over with fear when she realised how he had executed his perfect plan. She thought she was so clever, her disguises so perfect. He would torture her with everything he knew, slowly revealing the details of how he had followed her and how she had been caught by her victim's brother, no less. He would finally be the one to bring her to justice. He was finally the one with all the power. She would despair, shrivel in front of him like the coward she was. But the woman standing in front of him now did none of those things. Fear fuelled her, where others would cower, she thrived. She was cold, calculated, malicious, and clever. She enjoyed her games, the risk was her reward. His quest for revenge had clouded his judgement, his memories, he had forgotten how evil this adversary was. And he never could have imagined the extent of her malevolence. All this time, he believed he had the upper hand, and now he was realising. Her trap extended way beyond anything he could ever imagine.

Suddenly, she transformed into the girl he remembered. Standing in her oversized uniform, fluttering her eyelashes and twiddling her coppered hair, eyes wide and innocent whilst distilling terror into the hearts of anyone that dared to cross her. The memory of young boy who mysteriously swallowed a razor blade, the whispers behind the headmasters back detailing how it was conveniently hidden in his mashed potato. The girl who fell from the roof one lunch break, wheeled out of the school on a gurney, as Lily slyly joined the back of the watching crowd, twenty minutes later than everyone else. The fire that claimed the teachers car. The same teacher who had given Lily detention earlier that day. The socially anxious girl who accidentally took the wrong jumper home, hospitalised after eating a cake she found in her locker, the popular guy who was jumped after football practice in the alley close by… Nothing could ever be proven, but they all knew the truth.

'Breadcrumbs?' The words forced out of his mouth, sticking to his dried throat.

'Yes, my love. Little breadcrumbs everywhere. You've been following me for a while, haven't you? I know. And where have you been following me to?' Lily smacked her lips, her eyes glittering. She was in her element.

'How did you...' he stuttered before stopping himself. She knew. It didn't matter now, anyway. 'Yes, I followed you. And I followed you to those houses, too. I can place you at the scenes.'

'You've been trying to catch me in the act, oh, I know, don't worry. There's no need to tell me. You never did catch me, though, did you? Shame. But it wasn't for nothing, don't worry, my love. In following me, you've managed to place yourself at every single scene. You've been leaving little breadcrumbs of yourself, my love. You learn from your mistakes when you've been in this game for a while. They will have been found by now, of course, police will already be on your trail. They've already made the links back to London, you know.'

'They won't believe you. Not after I go to them.'

'Oh, but they will. Because you're not the only one who has been playing. I've been gathering evidence, too. Evidence of your movements are now near every crime scene they are investigating.'

'What... How... What have you done?'

'Haven't you been missing a few items of clothing lately? Odd socks, shoe laces?' Her eyes darted to his tired boots, the right still held by the tired hood string from his top. She licked her lips excitedly.

'Didn't you notice you've misplaced a few pages from that little notebook you carry? You should be more careful with what you leave laying around. Handwritten notes about locks, details of each murder, dates, locations. In your own writing, no less. Those will be easily matched. Throw in a dropped receipt from the coffee shop you like to frequent, bills from the Ram, you really like the pie there, don't you?' She laughed cruelly. 'And you have helped me out marvellously by scattering a bit of DNA and evidence yourself. I bet you're wearing the same boots now you wore to stand in the fields when you watched my fun with the Jeep, aren't you? The very same you imprinted into my flower bed, and countless other places you've frequented in the night. You tried to catch me in the act, you only served to add a little of yourself. At every. Single. Scene.'

The world around him spun, he felt himself staggering on his feet as his muscles lost all strength and her devious plan was finally revealed.

'It doesn't matter,' he stuttered, trying to regain his composure. 'You can't prove it. I will tell them, I was following you. I have evidence you were there, too. I took photos of you on my phone.' He jumped as she slapped her thigh theatrically.

'Oh, yes! This is the best part. The phone!' she cackled. 'I saw you that night, at Freddie's. I imagine you were trying to take photos of me, catch me in the act? Aren't you a clever boy. But, oh, hold on.' She reached her finger to her chin dramatically, a great pretence of deep thought. 'Now, my love, I bet you didn't think to set it to airplane mode during this valiant attempt to foil me at any point, did you?'

'No...' What did airplane mode have to do with anything?

'Or turn off your location services?'

'What, why...'

'Now, I'm no expert... But I imagine your phone will have pinged to the nearest signal tower in every location you've been. And your GPS on your phone would have been tracking your every move via those apps you have. And as you've been following me... I would imagine, my love, the police can now see you were in every area where a murder was committed. Now, I was sensible enough not to have my phone on at the scenes. I left mine at home when I snuck out at night. But... You didn't. Can you see the first little flaw in your plan?'

Panicked now, he frantically racked his brain. He only had two clear photos of her, at only two locations. The others were blurry, could be argued to be anyone.

'I'll tell them the truth. I was following you. When I tell them about the other murders, they'll be able to see where you've been, place *you* in every area. And not just here, but all over the country. They will search you, see your name. They'll see, it all links!'

'And who would they search for? Madeline Hamilton? Mary Thomkins? Jane James? It's easy to fake your death, my love. I've lived many, many lives. And you... I imagine you've been giving out your real name all this time? What's the name on the reservation you've made at the local Travelodge?'

He stalled.

'Honestly, my love, it's basic. And, whilst we're at it, change your plates on your fucking car once in a while, do you know how many cameras there are around here? On traffic lights, buildings, even on people's houses now. You've made it so easy for me. I've seen your car everywhere I've been, and now, so will the police. I do my best work on foot. Untraceable, timed to perfection.'

Cars, names. She was right, he could be placed in the area, and not just here. Everywhere he had followed her. He was jumped out of his thoughts as she snapped her hands loudly together. The crack even startled Sooty as it echoed through the room.

'Oh! And I think this is my favourite part, my love.' She stepped to him slowly, eyes gleaming at him. 'We have witnesses. Multiple witnesses. I didn't even plan for this, you walked straight into this one.'

Fuck. *Fuck.* His mind raced at a million miles an hour, trying to process her words.

'A few of my neighbours have said there's been a suspicious man hanging around the village for the last few months. The one down the road saw him darting into his hedge, and the local farmer reckons he saw a strange, hooded figure hopping fences at the back of his fields. And apparently, someone else chased him out of the close! Just outside! Now, I wonder who that could've been...' She threw back her head and laughed. 'They've already gone to the police. It's incredible what you can hear down the local, I'm telling you. I nearly danced when I heard them talking, honestly it was so hard to keep under control you should've seen me!' Her laugh rang shrilly around the room as he stood frozen. He swallowed a lump of fear, unable to speak.

'I told you. I needed you alive, my love. I couldn't ever kill you, not until the time was right.' She lifted an unkind hand and gently stroked his hair. The skin on the back of her fingers was soft. He looked up at her and saw her face had changed. Gone was the torrid glee and the crazed flirtation. In place was a cold, dead expression. The real Lily. Still blocking his path, she brought her hand down from his hair and outstretched her palm in front of him.

'Your phone,' she said simply.

'What?'

'My love. I'm not stupid,' she scoffed, 'I know you've been recording me.'

Fuck. She smirked at him. 'What? Did you really think you could break in here, surprise me, get me on my monologue so you could record me and then hand that into the police?' She laughed. 'I mean, don't get me wrong, it was great to talk about it all. You've no idea how long I've been waiting to tell someone. But it won't go further than this room.'

She stood still, hand unmoved. He studied her in a panic. She was smaller than him by a large sum and she had no weapon. He could easily fight her. She had said it herself, she preferred her victims asleep, his sister had got a good punch in. But there was something in her eye that terrified him. It was animalistic, unhinged. And whilst she was blocking his exit he had no doubt she had the edge. She narrowed her eyes.

'Don't try anything funny,' she snapped, reading his mind. 'Phone. Now.'

His eyes darted around the room desperately, gripped in equal measure by fear and sheer will. Will to win. To bring her to justice. For him. His family. For Charlotte.

'No. I can't.' He wouldn't move. He couldn't let her get away again. He needed to get this to the police.

'Well then, I'll have to come and get it, won't I?' To his

horror, she slowly produced a small penknife from her back jean pocket, the blade catching the light as she flicked it open. Clean as a whistle. Freshly cleaned. The vomit threatened to spill out and he stepped backward. Lily played with her knife and looked at the vase in the corner.

'Now, what will it be, my love? I'll give you the choice. You've been quite cute to watch, I've got quite fond of you. You fancy a bludgeoning with that minging vase, just like ol' Maggie or I can give you a nice slice like your dear, poor, dead sister?'

'Oh. You are generous.' He heard the weakness in his voice, trying to conjure up a boldness, a fight in him. Anything.

'I am, aren't I? You know, not many people see that? Even the latest bloke. Freddie. I thought he was alright, to be fair, but he kept parking that fucking Volvo on the footpath. Do you have any idea how inconsiderate that is?'

'You're insane.'

'And you're pretty. But I'm done with this little game, now.' Standing from the wall, she advanced on him.

'Phone. Now,' she snarled. They both stared at each other for a beat, locked eyes anticipating the others next move.

It happened so fast. He lunged as she flung herself to the left, out of his path. She smashed into the wall and screamed. The artwork on the wall fell with a crash, the glass frame shattering, sending tiny shards scattering over the carpet and tearing the delicate watercolour birds to shreds. He watched, dumbfounded, frozen to the spot by terror and confusion as she continued to scream and hurl herself into the wall.

'No! Stop!' she howled at the top of her lungs. Fear taking

over, his body wouldn't move as she thrust herself towards him and smashed herself into the other wall, missing him by an inch.

'Please! Stop!' she shrieked, tears streaming down her face. In a mixture of alarm and confusion he watched her, wondering what had come over her, wondering if he should help her, when suddenly, she turned to him. The fear was gone, in its place a horrifying smile. She waited. As if in slow motion, she threw her face violently back into the wall. He heard the crunch as her nose shattered in her face, and blood sprayed up the fresh paintwork. Pulling herself away, her nose gushing and her eyes now swollen, she grinned at him demonically. Glued, he watched on panic, transfixed by her show. Never breaking eye contact, she stumbled a few steps in the centre of the room with her fiendish smile. His hands whipped to his face, ready to defend himself from the attack as she threw herself forward and launched herself into the coffee table. The glass smashed into fragments. They glittered as they were cast through the air, caught in the deep orange glow of the setting summer sun. She screamed again, ripping at her vocal cords.

'Stop! You're hurting me!'

Fuck.

With a pang he realised what she was doing, reigniting the adrenaline that was freezing him to his feet. He needed to think fast. Front door? No. That's what she wanted. Right in the view of neighbours. Back door. Over the fence. It was his only shot. He turned, quickly as he could, leaping past her and the broken glass, making the desperate break for freedom. Into the kitchen, he felt a forceful hand land on his shoulder, dragging him back. His vision starred and his head swooned, he felt himself pulled off his feet roughly, falling behind him, the back of his head smacking on the floor. Dazed and winded, he felt her slight frame clamber atop his body, straddled either side of his bruised torso. He heard her wheeze from somewhere above him, his vision blurred and his senses numbed. Something wet, thick, and sticky, dripped on his face, as a thick, gurgle erupted from somewhere above him. She was laughing.

'And where do you think you're going?'

He heard her voice, thick as toffee and through the haze, he saw the flash of light. The penknife. Reflexively, he flung his hands upwards, hitting out and grabbing onto anything he could. He felt the sting as the blade sliced at his open palms, barely registering the pain as his fingers found something soft, long. Hair. He wrapped his fingers around the strands urgently and tightened his grip, pulling down with all of his strength. He heard a scream, he wasn't sure if it was coming from him or her, but he didn't relinquish, yanking and tugging as hard as he could. He felt a strange thumping in his forearm, she was stabbing at him with the small blade. Reaching with his other hand, he tried to find the weapon, the screams the only sense that were guiding him. She was bent over him now, locked in position by his hold on her scalp. Gripping with force he never knew he was capable of, he tossed her head away to his side and heard the merciful *crack* as her skull connected with a hard surface. Rewarded by a small groan she emitted, he felt her body weaken over him. Using his will alone, he wriggled free from her grip, his skin slippery and body weak, stumbling to his feet, his vision still clouded and his ears ringing. Fumbling around he found the door, blessed relief, his hands frantically searched for the handle and pulled.

And pulled. It wouldn't move. He tugged at it again, nothing. He heard a cackle from behind him, realising too late the grave mistake he had made. He turned, slowly, accepting his fate. Lily stood, bloodied and bruised in front of him. Dangling the key in her left hand and raising a kitchen knife with her right. His vision focussing, he took in the outline of the large knife, the blood smear across the knife block on the worksurface above the cupboard he had just smashed her into. One knife now missing. His gaze fell to the coffee machine next to it. State of the art, brand new. Bought for Charlotte for her twenty-seventh birthday. He spent months researching the perfect one, he ensured the colour matched her kitchen, scraping and saving to show her what she meant to him. His little sister.

Lily obstructed his field of view, her face stained red, mouth wide and eyes ablaze. She licked her lips. Blood spread over her teeth, dripping down her chin, pooling in her clavicles. Deeping the crimson in her hair. Inhuman. Vampire. Blood-sucking. The monster she was.

He felt the punch to his gut and the wet, thick liquid seeping out. He lurched again as the knife plunged deep into his abdomen. She pulled herself in close and he felt something smear across his cheek as she brushed her mouth against his face. She gasped into his ear for a moment, breathing rattled and ragged, as though she was fighting for its control.

'I told you I would have you, my love.'

Her voice was the last sound he heard as she wrenched

the knife out of his body in a violent, fluid motion, taking everything he had. Something hot, like liquid gushed from the new wound, soaking his clothing and running down his leg. His vision hazed as he felt a hand rifle through his pocket, lightening as something was pulled out. Finally as his eyes focussed for one last time. Standing in front of him, as she was. Not a monster. Not a devil, or a vampire. He heard a laugh, somewhere in the distance, as his vision blackened.

29

Lily

The neighbours had called the police. Just as she had hoped. Disturbance at thirty-two, Robin Close. Woman heard screaming and noises indicative of a domestic incident. Likely violence. Police dispatch advised to wear stab vests. Perfect. She couldn't have planned it better herself. In fact, she had. She sat in the back of the ambulance, wrapped in one of those foil silver blankets as paramedics fussed over her injuries and stuck a variety of needles into her skin. She barely felt the pricks. She watched intently as police cordoned off the bungalow with more yellow tape.

CRIME SCENE. DO NOT CROSS.

Timmy was in the arms of the old biddy from next door, licking her hands to death as she looked on the scene in horror. Lily suppressed a smile. She'd given the nosy bitch enough entertainment to last her the rest of her miserable life, at least.

The neighbours were out in their droves this evening. Swarming like a plague of locusts, attracted to the bright flashing blue lights, the yellow tape, and the drama. The crowd had spread down the close and across the green. Word really did travel fast in this community. She spotted Lucy and Graham's concerned faces from afar. Surprised they managed to tear themselves away from the bar. She chuckled inwardly. She would love to be a fly on the wall in the Ram tonight. They would be full of it. *Crazed psychopath.* That's what Graham had said. She shook her head. She wasn't a psychopath. She wasn't a terrible person, a monster like those headlines in the London newspapers had painted her out to be. She just did what needed to be done.

The paramedics were peppering her with questions and she was giving vague, one worded answers. They were irritating the fuck out of her. That level of non-response fitted with her presentation anyway. Her face really did hurt, but she was focussed on the front door to the bungalow to pay any real attention to what they were asking. They would think she was traumatised, in shock. Really, she was waiting. She had to be sure.

He had put up a good fight in the end. And she really did meet her match in him.

He was the only boy she couldn't have. The one that got away, she had never forgotten him. After escaping Rockbridge and ending up south in the city, she found herself being picked up by concerned police officers in Watford. They could never verify her identity, and it was then she learned how easy it would be to disappear. She gave her real name then, and was placed into St Peter's Comprehensive by her hastily assigned, overzealous, spotty children's worker. Malnourished, neglected, with pale, freckled skin and fire in her hair, she immediately acquired a target on her back. She knew they were all whispering about her. One girl stole her jumper, the football lot kicked balls at her, the teachers purposively sought to embarrass her, they thought she was stupid. Bullies. All of them. He was the only one of her peers to take pity on her, show her kindness and empathy, and for all of her sins, she fell in love with the older boy. She showed him her love in ways only she knew how, she gave her soul, her body, and her heart to him, only for it to be ripped to shreds by his bitch of a sister. No-one can be turned gay, Lily knew that, but it didn't stop Charlotte. She knew it was her, knew she was to blame. She lied to her face, trying to protest her innocence, but Lily knew better. The girl cheated and lied her way through life and the vile rumour she perpetuated whipped throughout the school like wildfire. They moved away before Lily could take her revenge, but it felt like fate when, three years ago, she saw him again across the blues bar in Fulham. He had barely changed, his cheeky smile and smooth skin, the ability to put even strangers at ease, stirring up that old infatuation from before. She had been lying low after leaving 'Rosie' behind in Croydon, dead in a burnt-out car. It was easy to fake a death. She'd had so many names it was difficult to remember who she was. She had to remind herself regularly. But seeing him there, that night, laughing so gaily with his friends, she was Lily, his Little Red again just for that moment.

She had stalked him for a while, she learned a lot about him. He had moved out to Fulham, but all of his family, including that fucking bitch Charlotte, were still in Watford. He visited them a lot, apparently he was still close to her. Although she could never understand why. Charlotte was still as awful as she had always been. Her parents loved her unconditionally, despite the abhorrent way she treated them. She hadn't lied to him, the night she killed Charlotte she had every intention of talking to her, allowing her the chance to explain herself, apologise for her transgressions. The odd mistake does not make a bad person, good people can still do questionable things, but not Charlotte. She was bad, through and through.

There were many points she had thought he would win. He had her so anxious, so jumpy, she fucking hated it. She trusted in her gut, gathered evidence, made her lists, kept to her timings and her shortcuts away from every kill and, in the end, he was no match at all. He tried. Bless him. He gave her a good scare. But it wasn't a fair fight really, she supposed. She had years of experience on him at this little game. Timings were crucial evidence in a court of law.

She had left him to bleed out, she calculated that she'd punctured just the right spot but she hadn't time to check. She barely had enough time to delete the pathetic audio recording and any incriminating photos before tossing his phone to the side. The minute she heard the sirens on the road outside she needed snap back into her role. She brought the tears to her eyes on cue, a trick she learned at the tender age of fourteen after that girl's parents accused her of poisoning her, and gave herself a quick puncture wound in the leg. In and out. Correct angle. Perfect force. It stung like a bitch. The police smashed their way into the bungalow as she was collapsed next to him on the floor, screaming and crying. All they saw was Madeline, the young innocent, red-headed pale woman, who, after being finally confronted by her stalker, miraculously managed to fight him off and lived to tell her tale.

She had been convincing. She acted out her role. He'd played his part well.

But she had to be sure his part was over.

After what seemed like forever, they appeared. Two of them, in those white boiler suits carrying a stretcher. She strained her neck to see. They twisted around as they walked. Her heart soared within. Large black bag. Zipped. He was in a body bag. Feeling the smile creep across her face, she dipped her head, shielding her reaction from view. She watched as two booted feet entered her field of vision and looked up to see young DC Mulley standing in front of her. The small DC looked concerned as she studied the crusted blood over her face and the welts on her eyes. She saw it in her face, how poor she must look.

Yes, poor little me.

Lily arranged her features, ensuring she looked just the right amount of shock at the events and relief at police presence. *I'm just glad it's over. I can't believe this happened to me.* Playing her role.

'Miss Hamilton?'

'Ye... yes?' she replied meekly. Her voice cracked, accidental, a result of the screaming that had destroyed her vocal chords. But a nice touch. She looked at the officer pleadingly, her heart racing. The officer's face folded into visible empathy for her.

'Miss Hamilton, you may not remember me, my name is DC Mulley,' she said kindly. 'How are you feeling?'

'I remember you, yes. I'm okay... I mean, I'm not. Everything hurts...' Lily stuttered pathetically, her eyes darting behind the officer, as the bag was being loaded into the back of a dark van. DC Mulley clocked her gaze.

'Is he... I mean, is that...' Lily asked quietly. She dropped her eyes again, looking at her feet in a pretence of shyness. DC Mulley smiled at her kindly.

'Yes, Miss Hamilton. He can't hurt you anymore, don't worry.'

'Oh my goodness... I just can't believe it... Why did he do this to me?' She conjured more of her tears, sobbing noisily.

'It's not your fault, sweetheart,' DC Mulley said comfortingly. She glanced behind her and then bobbed down to seat herself next to Lily.

'Who... Who is he?' she stammered. She had to know. How much had they found? DC Mulley took the bait.

'He's not a nice man. Really, not a nice man.'

Lily resisted the urge to roll her eyes as she saw the news reporters clamouring behind the tape. They had battled their way to the front of the crowd with their overbearing cameras and ridiculous microphones. Several residents were already being interviewed around the cordon.

'I just can't believe it.'

'You don't expect this kind of thing to happen in our sleepy little village.'

'Nothing like this ever happens here.'

Always the same. DC Mulley followed her eyes as she watched them set up and cameras rolled.

'It's about to be released to the press, so we thought we should let you know now. It doesn't bear thinking about what could have happened to you today, but you should feel proud of yourself for your courageousness. We managed to recover his car over the other side of the green and found evidence that links him to an address in London. I'm sorry to tell you, but we strongly suspect this man may have been following

364

you for a while, Madeline...'

Her heart skipped a beat, and she raised a shaking hand to her mouth as she opened it into a small 'O'. Widening her eyes just the right amount, portraying the perfect mixture of shock, pain, and surprise. Not too much, not too little. Just right.

'Oh my goodness,' she breathed. 'I never realised... I should have known...'

'There's no way you could have known. You can't blame yourself. Sometimes, these stalkers, they get obsessed.' That was true. Lily studied her. DC Mulley was incredibly kind. She could see she truly cared. It almost made her feel a little bad for playing her. Almost.

'But, why me? Why did he follow me?' It would be a natural question for a victim to ask. But Lily needed to know. What did they know.

'We may never know. It takes only a trigger. He lost his sister a couple of years ago. It's very possible he had a psychotic break and happened to see you at the time. There's no telling how long he may have followed you for, but you mustn't blame yourself.'

'I'll try. I just can't believe how close he came to getting what he wanted...' Now, ain't that the truth.

'You can't think like that. It's over now.'

'I don't know. I don't think I'll sleep well at all tonight. What with this and the murders around here. It's too much.' She dropped her eyes, watching DC Mulley stiffen in her periphery.

'Madeline... This is going to be released to the public shortly. And this won't be easy to hear.' Lily looked up, wide eyed at DC Mulley as the DC took a breath in. 'We have uncovered evidence this is the man we have been looking for. The perpetrator of the horrific crimes that have been in the area. We've found handwritten notes in his car, details of your shift patterns, the manufacturer of door locks. We need to send it off for analysis, but it appears to match evidence found at the scenes of other victims.' *Bingo.* Lily feigned shock and shot her hand to her mouth. Inwardly, she was elated. Never leave a paper trail, even the slightest detail can reveal too much. Lily always ensured to keep hers on her phone. Password protected, digital. Easy to delete.

'It was him? We got him?'

'Yes, Miss Hamilton. You and the locals can sleep safely tonight. We got him.' DC Mulley gave her what she was sure was meant to be a reassuring smile and Lily returned it, resisting the urge to roll her eyes again. Did they fuck. But she was right, the locals were safe. Lily had learned from her mistakes. DC Mulley stood from the ambulance and gave a small nod. The paramedic returned, slapping a blood pressure cuff around her bicep for yet another fucking check on her blood pressure. They were nothing if not diligent. DC Mulley turned away, her hands behind her back. Lily watched her as she strolled slowly away, stepping over the yellow tape into the bungalow. She sighed.

It was just over a year ago, almost to the day, that she had taken Madeline's identity. London was a big city, she'd had many good years there but the net had started to close in. Too many close calls. She took the job at Luton, in a bid to escape. It was more luck, really, when scummy Dwane Myers was fingered for the deaths around Watford.

Lily and Madeline had watched the news that night. They sat side by side on their sofa in their small shared flat in the nurse's accommodation block at Luton hospital. His face flashed up as the judge had given his ruling on his sentence. Life. Madeline had tutted. Life didn't mean life these days. Lily had nodded in agreement.

Lily and Madeline had known one another since nursing school. It had made sense for them to share a flat when they found themselves working together again. Lily was called Mary back then, leaving Rosie behind. He'd turned up suddenly, unexpectedly back in London after Charlotte's trial concluded and Dwane was convicted. She'd had the quick sense to hide herself as he sniffed around her dilapidated bedsit, asking her neighbours questions. He took to hanging around there, trying to follow her, fancying himself as some Miss Marple type. But he was getting too close. She had enjoyed her time at nursing school, it fit well with her values, so when she saw the job posting she quickly dispatched of Rosie, fleeing to Luton as Mary once more. Madeline had just broken up with her boyfriend and took the job in Luton to escape her own past. A chance for a fresh start away from the city for the both of them.

The fire that night claimed the block of flats, also claimed the life of ten others. It was an accident, a candle burning that got out of control. Mary was the only one who walked away. Madeline had tried to escape with Mary, but she hadn't been so lucky. The smoke got her first. Her body burnt to ash. Lily had been heartbroken as she watched the flames engulf her friend. But when she stood amongst the trees, watching the firefighters battle from afar, she remembered her therapist's words as she sat in the refuge when she was just thirteen.

You are a good person, Lily. It wasn't your fault.

Madeline's passing was a shame, but it was her way of giving her friend a real fighting chance at a new beginning. Madeline's mother, Penny, had always been so shit. She was so drunk and coked out of her head she hadn't even realised it was her own daughter she was burying, not the strange girl that accompanied Madeline when she occasionally came to stay. Madeline had worked hard to repair a relationship with her mother, Mary was there to support her during these fractured visits. Everyone remarked on how Lily and Madeline looked so alike that they could be twins, but a mother should know their own child. Lily took the opportunity.

She knew Madeline's grandmother was on her own. She'd met Ivy a few times. It was a year ago today. The fourth of August. She'd crept up the close using the cover of the woodland just beyond the bungalows and broken in through the window in the spare room. Ivy was sound asleep and the porcelain robin had watched the violent scene from his post in the centre of the windowsill. Lily was grieved to have to do it, but she didn't have a choice. For the first time, she couldn't watch as the old woman's life slipped away. She should have held her hand as she passed. A comfort in her dying moments. She had whispered her sorry's in the dark over the last few months, late at night as she lay in Ivy's old room, the guilt too much to bear. She learned from her mistakes, she made sure to hold the hands of every one who died at her hands ever since. It was particularly important for Freddie, she had cared for him after all. It almost made her think twice about her purpose. But it was all for the greater cause. There were too many bad people out there that karma just missed. Penny never visited after Ivy's death. Never called to check in on her. She couldn't have cared less. She just had her lawyers sign the deeds to the bungalow over to her without question, and Lily never contacted her as Madeline again.

She was Madeline now. Scummy Dwane might have gone down for the last spate of murders, case closed, but somehow Charlotte's dumb brother had figured it out. He'd chased her to Luton, she had covered her tracks and he still found her. He knew her, that was her mistake. She was too close. There was no telling who he told, who else knew. It was time for Madeline to disappear. Mary, Jane, Rosie, and Ellie were long gone. Far in her past. She would never be any of them again. Lily would remain her little secret, buried deep within from her first kill at the age of thirteen. He was a sweet boy once, her first, but he got caught up with some terrible people. Lily could have been so different, if only those scumbags hadn't held her down and climbed on top of her, one by one. He'd picked her up from school. He'd driven her there. He'd watched. He'd joined in. He offered her up. They violated her, laughed cruelly as she sobbed in pain and bled from between her legs. They punched her until she was black and blue and burnt her delicate skin with lighters. Lily had her revenge in the end, though. She had waited until they were asleep, induced by the drugs swirling in their systems. None of them had seen the danger until the blade had pierced their throats and ripped their stomachs open. She had lain there in his arms afterwards, savouring the moment as the blood pooled around them on the floor. The bliss from the release was like nothing she had ever experienced. Bad things happen to bad people. Little Red taking down the big bad wolves.

Lily sighed, watching the reporters. It had been a great summer of fun. But summer was nearly over now. Yes. Madeline needed to disappear. But there was no telling who she would be next.

She watched the old biddy scuttle over. Timmy was content, trotting along beside her. Lily smiled. She had become so fond of the little dog. His previous owner was no good. Lily had given him a good life.

'How are you feeling, my dear?' Joan asked wheezily. Lily rearranged her face and looked up at her pathetically.

'I'm holding in there.'

'Oh, I'm sure you are.' Joan tutted and shook her head. 'What a terrible, terrible time of it you've had. You're such a good person, you didn't deserve any of this.'

Lily smiled up at her warmly.

'Remember dear, tough times don't last but tough people do, as they say,' Joan told her, tapping her gently on the shoulder. She nodded meekly.

'What will you do tonight? Do you have somewhere to stay?' Joan enquired. Lily made to answer before stopping short. Ivy's bungalow was the scene of a crime now. She wasn't sure when she would be allowed back in.

'I don't know. I hadn't thought about it,' she answered truthfully. 'I remember seeing a hotel in town, I'll probably stay there a few days.'

'You don't have to stay in a hotel, my dear. You can stay with me, if you want,' Joan offered. Lily opened her mouth, ready to protest, trying to think of a reason. Quite frankly she had been looking forward to a bottle of gin in the Travelodge tonight to celebrate her achievements. She'd already checked in. The room down the hall would have been combed by officers by now, they would have found a plethora of evidence to link to their investigations, but hers offered a delicious view of the scene via the small peephole in the door. Her box of trophies were already there, with a few new additions. A cracked vase, a mug from Milton Housing developments, and a small bubble-wrapped ceramic robin. But she couldn't say that. Thankfully, Joan wasn't finished.

'Although, I suppose staying next to the bungalow where all of this happened is probably the last thing you want, isn't it?' she sighed, gazing at the garish crime scene tape. Lily nodded noiselessly. She bit her lip, trying to hide her delight at the inadvertent excuse.

'Yes. Thank you, Joan, but I think it's just too much for me at the moment...' she trailed off, watching the officers exit and enter the bungalow. The cameras were still on, she could feel the notifications pinging on her phone in her back pocket. She looked up at Joan. Timmy was still gazing up, tail wagging.

'In fact, I think there are too many bad memories here to ever return...' she said. Hoping Joan would catch the bait.

'Oh, of course. No one could ever blame you for that.'

'The only thing is, I won't be able to take Timmy to a hotel...' Line was cast. 'Joan, do you think...'

'Oh, of course, my dear, I would be more than happy to look after Timmy for you. Just until you get back on your feet.' Hook. Line. Sinker. Joan looked down at Timmy and bent in the middle to offer a gnarled hand to his head. He burrowed his head into her wrinkly fuss. She heard the cracks in her spine as she straightened but watched as Timmy's tail wagged again, looking up at her adoringly. She looked between the two of them. Her decision was made. They would be good for one another. She didn't need Timmy in her life anymore, but Joan did. Another good deed done. She *was* a good person.

Acknowledgements

To Dad, Mum, J, and C. Thank you for being my rocks, my biggest supporters through every part of this journey. Thank you for being so proud of me, for backing me at every corner. It's you that I credit with my drive, my determination. The unwavering unconditional love.

To my family, to you all, thank you so much.

For my other half. The love of my life. For 'leaving me be', giving me time to unleash my creativity and let my imagination run wild, for every bit of your support and patience. For encouraging me at every step. Thank you for everything. I love you.

For all of the little ones, I love you so much.

For my friends, for being my biggest cheerleaders. You were the light that I needed when I found myself sucked into the darkness of Madeline's head.

To everyone at SRL Publishing, thank you for taking this chance on me.

SRL Publishing don't just publish books, we also do our best in keeping this world sustainable. In the UK alone, millions of books are destroyed each year, unsold and unread, due to overproduction and a greed for bigger profit margins.

Our business model is inherently sustainable by only printing what we sell. While this means our cost price is much higher, it means we have minimum waste and zero returns. We made a public promise in 2020 to never overprint our books for the sake of profit.

We give back to our planet by calculating the number of trees used for our products so we can then replace them. We also calculate our carbon emissions and support projects which reduce CO_2. These same projects also support the United Nations Sustainable Development Goals.

The way we operate means we knowingly waive our profit margins for the sake of the environment. Every book sold via the SRL website plants at least one tree.

To find out more, please visit
www.srlpublishing.co.uk/responsibility